THE RING OF FIRE

AN EPICUREAN ADVENTURE

BY

MORGAN MILES CRAFT

Palisadian Press
bookmakers

EPICUREAN (EPƏˈKYOŌRĒƏN)

*A PERSON DEVOTED TO SENSUAL ENJOYMENT, ESPECIALLY THAT

DERIVED FROM FINE FOOD AND DRINK.

"THERE IS NO SINCERER LOVE THAN THE LOVE OF FOOD."
- GEORGE BERNARD SHAW

For Nicki —
And all the adventures
that lie ahead —

ISBN: 978-0-578-95716-6 (Paperback)
ISBN: 979-8-201-18077-5 (Digital edition)
Library of Congress Copyright Control Number: 2021914787

Many references to historical events, real people, or real places are used fictitiously. In addition, some names, characters, products, and places are products of the author's imagination.
All images are either by the author, rights purchased, rights granted, or public domain.

Front cover design by Alexander Von Ness, NessGraphica
Printed in the United States of America.
First printing edition 2022.

Palisadian Press
PO Box 124
Cornville, AZ, 86325
www.palisadianpress.com

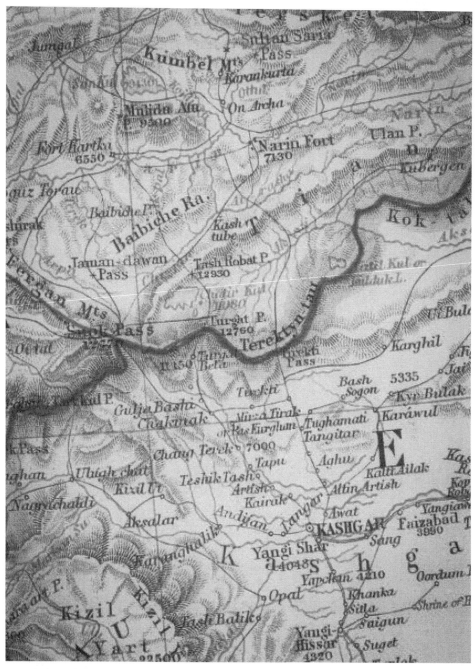

THE TIEN SHAN MOUNTAINS, KASHGAR, TORUGART
PASS, TASH RABAT AND NARYN, KYRGYZSTAN

Acknowledgments

The Ring of Fire represents a journey, both mine and Max Little's. Ten years in its evolution, the story accompanied me through many transitions and passages, more friend than albatross. Along the way, my son Chase Morgan was born, and this tale is for him, someday.

When I had the good fortune to open a Mexican cantina in 1994 in Miami Beach, my amateur hot sauce passion became something else entirely. Mexico trips to Baja, Sonora, and the Yucatan to develop our menu and buy decor introduced me to Mexican hospitality and extraordinary regional cuisines. Everywhere I went, I collected hot sauces and a growing knowledge of the world of chiles and their stories. Bottles of hot sauce from my travels and recipes concocted in our kitchen adorned the walls of Moe's Cantina in South Beach, and Max Little emerged as my alter ego, living a life I could only imagine.

Having no formal training in writing, I applied to a Master's program in creative writing and was summarily denied. Nonetheless, I plugged away, and this is the result, birthed purely from imagination, passion, and exhaustive research.

Undying thanks go to my editor and friend, Dean Lamanna, whose honest and insightful critiques took my manuscript from whimsical pipe dream to readable reality. Alexander Von Ness is a wonderful designer whose cover perfectly embodied the journey. Deep gratitude and respect belong to my wife Nanaiya, who patiently pushed me to complete the work and loves when I read my writing to her. And my mother, whose regular inquiries of "Is it finished yet?" pushed me along through the years.

The chiles and most places I write about are authentic, except the Fire of the Valley and the Eden where it lives. I should mention that any resemblance in the story to persons or entities existing today is purely artistic and probably coincidental.

Sedona, January 2022

Chapters

Laguna Beach, California

The voice on the phone was hollow, crackling from its journey halfway across the globe. It spoke in Russian, but with a heavy accent betraying its tribal origin.

"Find the man they call Little," it said calmly. "He is there in Laguna Beach. If he and Nickolai connect, it could spell trouble for us. You know what you must do."

Through mirrored glasses, he watched the traffic pass on Pacific Coast Highway, gaze following a convertible full of bikini-clad young women heading to the beach. Mist hung in the air from a southerly swell pounding the coastline. The thought of the violent surf terrified him, used as he was to the placid Black Sea lapping the shores at Odesa. In another time, he would have donned his red speedo and cruised the beach to show off his athletic body, battle scars and all. America was a paradise with too many people, he thought, as crystalline sand ground under his feet, and he tasted ocean salt in the breeze. The fact that he now plied his dangerous trade from Osh, in the country farthest from an ocean on earth depressed him. He longed for a margarita. Then his commando training kicked in.

"Yes, boss. I will find him. Josef and I will not fail you," he said. "We are prepared."

He could hear an exhale of smoke on the line and imagined the corpulent man standing on the marble balcony overlooking the Ak Buura River valley. Probably in one of his blue silk robes.

"Our futures may depend on it," his powerful employer said. "And no more mistakes like in Istanbul. He's no good to me in a full-body cast," before the connection clicked off.

He knew that it meant his future, however, and his partner's, the mess they'd created in Turkey still fresh in his mind. "Come on, Josef, stop looking at the girls. We've got a mission to complete."

Tash Rabat Caravanserai

THE VENETIAN

He was a Venetian of many generations, a trader by birth, sent from the eastern outpost of Constantinople in search of silk and jade. For five months, he journeyed across Asia Minor, Persia, and the lands of ruthless Mongol Khans and fierce Arab Sultans, seeking the markets at Kashgar on the western edge of the notorious Taklamakan Desert of China. He exhaled with fatigue, trying to comprehend a journey of three thousand miles through lands few westerners had seen, aside from Marco Polo and a smattering of monks. Ahead, a long line of pack animals filed, winding through amber, grassy hills toward distant, snow-capped mountains which they would need to cross. He listened to the shouts and calls of the drivers, keeping the animals in line and moving forward. Some beasts carried men, while others bore large bushels or locked strongboxes strapped to their backs. Everyone carried a weapon of some sort. They spoke in a language he did not know, exotic, tense, perhaps Khotanese, and he appeared as unfamiliar to them as they to him. Yet, finding safety in numbers, he had paid the levy to the Tajiks in Samarkand and traveled willingly among them, part of a caravan heading east with the late-day sun on their backs. The year was 1511, when the reign of Tamerlane brought Central Asia into Persia's vast empire, and the Czarist and Qing dynasties of Russia and China contested the empire's endless borders.

As the pack train wound through the remote hills five days east of Osh, a lush vale appeared, cut by a white river fed by mountain snows. In the center of the river valley stood a heavily walled complex featuring a central domed structure, round and forty feet tall. The Venetian could see a far-flung encampment of tents and yurts outside the fortified structure, teeming with activity, punctuated by smoky fires, tethered animals, small gardens, and colorful banners marking ethnic groups. A din began to make its way to his ears, the sounds of making camp as men called to one another, laboring, settling in for the night about to come.

The caravan he traveled in consisted of dozens of beasts, along with forty men, dark-skinned and stout Tajiks, with long beards and headgear of leather and fur. They were conspicuously armed with curved scimitars, as they bore valuable goods from Persia, Constantinople, and Venice. The caravan threaded its way through the outer reaches of the encampment, and many eyes fell upon the men and their desirable cargo. Hunger plagued the travelers, having ridden for days through the foothills and river valleys, and the prospect of hot food was a welcome one. Atop smoky fires, meat sizzled, and cauldrons boiled, carrying the scent of cooking across the valley.

Men arrived from the encampment to walk alongside their caravan, shouting and waving their arms. Some pointed to the sacks and crates sitting atop the animals' backs, while others called and gestured towards one or another of the flowing cloth banners that identified their groups. Chinese, with pale skin, silk caps and long ponytails, coming from Kashgar and Xi'an; Hindus from Kashmir and Varanasi, with colorful robes and painted faces; Persians, superb horsemen in colored cloaks, rulers of many lands; fierce Arabs with crescent blades, riding two-humped Bactrian camels; and on oxen, the mountain people of the Central Asian kingdoms, who traveled through Tashkent and Samarkand. There were warlike Mongols, imperious Turks, surly Uzbeks, and tall Slavs from the Urals. Like the Venetian, there was a smattering of adventurous Europeans far from home, sent to satisfy the western demand for silk and pepper.

The Tajiks from his group pointed to the camp, and he heard the words "Tash Rabat." They had arrived at a trading center in the foothills of the Tien Shan mountains, a caravanserai, where many people communed for commerce and rest. The small bazaars dotted the pathways across Asia for a thousand years, following the international trade routes. Other caravans were trickling in on one of three paths in the waning light. From the east, after crossing the passes of the Tien Shan mountains from Kashgar and the vast Taklamakan desert, the Chinese; from the north, across the plains and steppes, Mongols, and Slavs; and from the south and west, Turks, Arabs, Uzbeks, Hindus, Persians, and curious Europeans. They had crossed the scorched Uzbek and Turkmen deserts and steep passes of the Karakoram, Hindu Kush, and the Pamir Mountains, then known as the "roof of the world."

Around the stone structure, an outdoor bazaar thrived, hosting an array of goods traded from all over the globe. The Kyrgyz plains and lush mountain valleys allowed a welcome respite after the deserts and high mountain crossings, both east and west. It created a cacophony of sounds, with the voices of commerce backed by singing, drums, hammering, and animal calls. Row upon row of stalls filled with various products on display took up the area closest to the wall. From the east, with the Chinese, came silk, jade, mirrors, medicinal herbs, tea, gunpowder, and paper. India to the south sent pepper, batik, gems, incense, and nutmeg. From the west came perfume, ivory, furs, colored glassware, metals, chocolate, wine, and the horses so valued by the Chinese.

And food. Each group brought the foods and ingredients common to their lands, and numerous stalls traded comestibles and supplies in the bazaar. The caravanserai represented a vibrant intermarriage of culinary traditions, regional recipes, and native foods. Seeds of every type traded back and forth, and caravans carrying black pepper had to be heavily armed due to its incredible global demand. From the Far East came chicken and pork, rice, soybeans, cucumbers, and ginger. Central Asia sent sheep and cattle, wheat, and breads. The Venetians and Greeks brought squash, chiles, corn, and potatoes, ferried across the Atlantic by the Spanish and Portuguese - lords of the newly discovered western lands between Europe and Asia - far from their origins in Central and South America.

On the camp's outskirts, people tended small patches of colorful fresh produce offered for sale to the merchants and travelers and used in the caravanserai's tent kitchens. The traders had traveled far over perilous roads, and the steaming pots and smoky grills provided a welcome sight. Then, the sweet and unique scent of peppers roasting over the fires found their way to the Venetian's senses, a pleasure he had not experienced since Aleppo three months before. He breathed deeply, taking in the smoky earthiness of the seared fruit, eager for the feel of their hidden heat on his tongue. It was an entirely new olfactory experience for many people in the camp, this piquant spice called both pepper and chile, brought halfway across the globe from the New World.

This was to be the Venetian's last venture on the Silk Road's overland trail, as the new, faster sea routes charted by the Portuguese to Asia were making the land journey obsolete. The caravans would soon slow, the merchants would leave, and the caravanserai would disappear beneath the sands and stand forgotten for five hundred years.

THE KYRGYZ

Nazaat Buntun, breathing hard, stopped to peer up into the misty glade that rose into the foothills. He had been this way many times and knew the mountains well, though the place he sought remained hidden from view in the mists. He and his clansmen guarded the location carefully, as they did not want others to discover the prize they kept hidden in the remote, rocky vales astride the narrow river's plain.

Midday light glanced off the canyon walls, forcing the stout tribesman to shield his eyes as he traced the narrow path snaking over the ridge. A wrong step would mean a treacherous plummet into the chasm below. Another approach below followed the course of a stream that issued from the canyon they called "home of the fire." However, that track soon became impassable in the narrow gorge, mired in brambles and boulders. Only Buntun and his people knew the higher goat trail leading into the secluded canyon beyond, a secret kept for generations. Even now, in 1999, sinister eyes and ears were everywhere and kept secrets could be dangerous in the newly independent Kyrgyzstan.

Reaching the ridge, he scanned the valley behind him for anyone who might have followed, satisfied that he was alone. With the two large baskets hung from either end of a pole balanced across his shoulders, he scrambled down the slope, working hard to maintain his footing. The last stretch to the valley floor required him to maneuver between looming boulders, as the icy river cascaded over and between the big rocks, creating a billowing, cloaking mist navigable only by the few who knew the way.

Nazaat breathed deep as he emerged from the boulders, reaching the secluded, verdant valley. A sea of violet and orange opium poppies grew everywhere, blanketing the valley floor and hillsides, dancing in a light breeze. Intermingling with the poppies, thick shrubbery abloom with tiny purple and white flowers punctuated the hardscrabble landscape along the creek, filling an area barely sixty yards square. Hanging abundantly from the bushes were round fruit the size of hens' eggs, chiles in various stages of ripening; green, yellow, orange, red, purple, and even black. Setting down the pole, he slung one of the baskets over his shoulder and inspected every prized pod before harvesting, handling them gently, checking for firmness and color. He snapped the worthy candidates from their stems as he spoke softly to them, leaving those unripe for another trip.

GASANOV

Nickolai Gasanov walked the open-air market in Osh, Kyrgyzstan's oldest city, inspecting produce that had arrived from the countryside. With a discerning eye and a vindictive reputation, he surveyed the market's bounty: walnuts, almonds, apples, melons, strawberries, plums, grapes, apricots, rice, flour, spices, fresh meats, and peppers. The stalls stretched nearly two miles along the Ak Buura riverbanks in the fertile Fergana Valley of Kyrgyzstan, and the market had been operating like this for two thousand years. The stalls stocked the widest variety of goods and produce found in the country and represented his domain. His imperious inspection rounds took most of the day, and the merchants both feared and mocked him.

At a small stall far off the main thoroughfare, a tribal woman from the countryside displayed a rainbow array of peppers he had not seen before, as he rarely ventured into these side alleys, fearing reprisals from vendors he had harassed.

"Are these yours?" he inquired of the seller.

"Of course they're mine. I am selling them, am I not?" said Adilet Buntun warily.

"Where are they from?" asked Gasanov impatiently. "Did you harvest them?"

"I am not a farmer. They are from Tajikistan, near Karakul," said the woman. "Farmers sold them to us in Gulcha, coming from Tajikistan on the Pamir Highway. I am from the Naryn River valley, here to make money from this overpriced and poorly located stall since one cannot grow much in the Tien Shan foothills."

Gasanov knew instantly she was lying. Tajik farmers occasionally came as far as Osh's market, but never to transport something as perishable as fresh peppers. The journey took many days, across a border, and to allow a crop to spoil would mean ruin to a small farmer. He remained skeptical as he inspected the fruit, digging a fingernail in its side and sensing the pop of fresh skin. He had never seen its kind before. It was fresh and harvested within the last few days, engaging his suspicious mind.

"Give me a kilo, some of every color," he demanded.

MAX

Head back, Adam's apple exposed, Max Little craned for a view of the clouds that had just soaked him to the skin. There were few to be seen, except on the far horizon down toward the Gulf. Late spring storms were fleeting but intense in Louisiana's bayou country as clouds evaporated quickly after emptying themselves randomly, and roads flooded within minutes. The fast-moving deluge had caught him unprepared as he hitchhiked on the southbound side of Route 89, outside Lafayette.

Trees clustered thickly along either side of the roadway, moss hanging from their limbs, creating a surreal tunnel effect. However, they had offered no shelter from the rain as Max stood helpless under them, their broad leaves funneling water in streams down his neck. His boots disappeared into three inches of muddy road ditch, which had begun to seep between his toes. Unfazed, he stuck out an outstretched thumb, expectant as a truck bore down on him. The speeding semi's only response was a bracing bath of muddy runoff.

Max laughed aloud as he stood dripping, absorbing the water and the scenery. Rich, flat farmland stretched out in all directions with no dwellings in sight. He was exactly where he wanted to be, though the mysterious men who had followed him from Laguna Beach had him constantly looking over his shoulder.

Southern Louisiana's Lafayette County is the world capital of chile peppers - the kind used to make hot sauce, among other things. McIlivrain & Ivins, the famous hot sauce makers, had miles of farms and a cavernous bottling plant to the south, on humid Acadian Island. The moist, low land is the perfect environment for numerous chile varieties, the diminutive but fiery *tabasco* chief among them. The ubiquitous chile pepper has, over time, become one with the region's culture. Max had traveled to the bayou to pursue it and learn its secrets.

The sauces and powders made from chile peppers come in many guises across the world. The chiles used can range from sublimely mild to insanely hot: cayenne, guajillo, piquin, habanero, poblano, datil, morita, puya, rocoto, jwala, aji, malagueta, tabiche, scotch bonnet, jalapeno, chipotle (a wood-smoked jalapeno), and serrano, among a host of others. A recently discovered pepper variety in India, the *Bhut Jolokia*, or Ghost Pepper, reportedly tested three times hotter than any on record. Used solo or in combination with other ingredients, the chile pepper represented a $4 billion annual industry in the United States alone.

Max was a traveling gourmand, of a sort. His hot sauce emporium in Laguna Beach, Little's House of Fire, was renowned for stocking the most varied and unique sauces on the West Coast. Most sauce retailers did business at trade shows or via the Web, but not Max. He stayed well ahead of the market by going directly to the source, creating relationships, and outthinking his competition. In the process, he had visited much of the world and become recognized as an authority on the subject. One could say his life was consumed by peppers and spicy food, making Max a fanatical entrepreneur.

There is a small purple pepper, the *Bere-Bere*, grown in Ethiopia, where tribal clans use it to cure meat, and its heat and flavor are so intense it is used as currency. Max spent the better part of a winter there, living with the Amhara people and partaking in their meat-curing rituals. The Bere-Bere pepper bunch tattooed on his arm was a gift from the clan's chief after Max had shown the tribe how to make a sauce from the curing juices. Little's House of Fire went on to sell the meaty, maroon Bere-Bere Hot Sauce under an exclusive license with Ethiopia's Amhara ethnic group.

Max had a masochistic palate and reveled in it. Attached to his belt was a small leather pouch that held a glass vial of potent crushed chocolate habanero chile flakes that he used to liven up boring foods, which he encountered almost everywhere. An epicurean to the core, he relished the sensual pursuit of spicy delicacies across the world and connecting with the colorful, passionate characters who created them.

In Austin, Max had sampled a smoked habanero venison chile so flammable that they made him sign a release before they would serve it. Luckily, the Texas Chili Parlor where the self-immolation occurred sat right on Lake Austin, into which he promptly jumped. While passing through southwest Florida, the vagabonding epicure had chanced upon the high-octane Felda Gator Sauce at a roadside joint in the hamlet of Felda, on swampy Gator Hammock. Over fried alligator, he drenched a concoction that caused his entire body to redden and his feet to swell, rendering him unable to walk. Max had missed the second half of the Super Bowl while sampling the "Hottest of the Hot Buffalo Wings" at the Original Jim's Buffalo Wing House in Buffalo, New York. He could not see the television due to temporary blindness. In Lima, Peru, during a four-hour lunch fiesta at the humble but famous Sonia Cevicheria, he dove into a *tiradito* ceviche laced with rocoto chiles so potent that his hands went numb. Unfazed, he convinced his hosts to feed him the rest of the heaping incendiary bowl.

Hot sauce and salsa had surpassed ketchup as the premier condiments of choice on America's tables by the middle nineties, and the hot sauce boom began. In every state, pepper-crazy entrepreneurs had sprung up, producing small batches of sauce for trade at county fairs, at food shows, on the expanding Internet, and in restaurants. The competition created a growing market for the hottest and most original sauce on the planet. A ridiculous subculture of extreme hot sauces developed, capitalizing on a heat-sensitive trend; Armageddon Hot Sauce, Acid Rain, Dragon Breath, Nuclear Hell, and Belligerent Blaze. They concentrated the fire of the nascent ingredients into a mouth-burning elixir that few could actually ingest. Members of this subculture began to call themselves "Chile-heads" and sometimes "Pepper-heads."

After closing his Laguna Beach espresso bar, Max opted to keep his lease on the small shop fronting Pacific Coast Highway and opened his dream business in 1996, a spicy foods emporium and global hot sauce museum. It succeeded immediately, thanks to his community standing, skill in selecting unique delicacies, and delectable tales of hot sauce adventures. Max, as a result, had become highly regarded and envied among chile-heads worldwide.

The old Ford pickup Max drove from Laguna via Santa Fe had died outside Amarillo, Texas. He left it with a mechanic who shared his affinity for old trucks and stopped just long enough for some Texas barbeque at the Amarillo Armadillo, where the house "Roadkill Red" barbeque sauce laced with fire-smoked chipotle chiles made his nose run like a faucet. With Louisiana pepper country on his brain, Max hitched south to Lafayette with several charismatic folk, like old Milton Bloom, who was distantly connected to the Hunt family of condiment fame and saw the rise of hot sauce as a threat to American commerce and values. Even so, he liked Max. From an electric cooler outfitted in his expansive Cadillac trunk, Milt produced a bottle of "vintage" Hunt's Catsup, circa 1965. Incredibly, it tasted sweet and smoky over Angus burgers at the Cattlemen's Truckstop in Odessa.

"It was a gift from my great aunt instead of Hunt's stock on my eighteenth birthday," Milt explained. "Turns out I am the illegitimate product of a Hunt's factory manager and my gin-loving mother, who'd been excommunicated from the Hunt family. Take a bottle for your little sauce museum, but keep it refrigerated. Stuff'll last forever."

Now Max stood somewhere outside of Brousville, deep in the southwestern Louisiana delta country, wet, carless, and with only a name to go on in his search for answers.

"Old Jones's place is way south, off Route 330," was the vague tip he had gotten from one of his lifts, a farmer in an old El Camino. "But you won't see many people driving that way. He's at the end of the road."

JESUS JONES

Max had heard the name Jesus Jones for the first time in Rehoboth Beach, Delaware, at a joint called Pete's Piquant Pepper Diner. Pete's was a vital outpost in the chile-head universe and boasted the grandest collection of hot sauces on the planet in its retail store. During a stint that saw him down six beers and three dozen oysters dashed with Pete's Absurdly Hot Hot Sauce, he encountered an old-time chile-head from Chicago named Otis Pepper. Otis had grown up in south Chicago's barbecue and blues joints, where his father, Balzac, had been a chef and sax player himself. Jesus Jones was his childhood friend, an accordion player, and blues singer in an ensemble with Otis named the South Side Five. In addition to the regular clubs, they had carved a niche playing the barbecue joints for which Balzac cooked, and it was here Otis and Jesus learned of blues and bourbon and fiery foods.

Walking south along Louisiana Route 89, Max recalled how Otis Pepper got his attention after oyster number seventeen with the promise of a tremendous chile-head tale. After being drafted into the Vietnam War, as Otis told the story, Jesus Jones returned home to Chicago a changed man. Agent Orange had seared his throat and nostrils so badly it rendered him unable to smell. Anything. And his scorched vocal cords left him incapable of singing the blues. Coming back to the South Side Five represented unbearable agony for Jesus, unable to savor the smells of the old joints on 75th Street, their women, and their life-giving grub, or to sing about them. He left the group for good, diving down a rabbit hole of depression.

It turned out Jesus had inherited a piece of land in Louisiana from a half-brother he never knew. He believed he descended from slave folk whose line went all the way to Ghana in Africa, yet it happened that his great-great-grandfather had fled a pre-Civil War plantation and stowed away on a boat to British Honduras, which eventually became Belize in 1960. At the conflict's end, Grafton Jones returned to the States with his Belizean wife and her family, where they homesteaded what most considered unusable land far out on the Mississippi Delta, on territory only recently acquired from France with the Louisiana Purchase. Chile peppers were an ancient staple in British Honduras, and Jones had brought seeds with him to the bayou. The fiery tabasco chiles took spectacularly to the loamy, mineral-rich soil, and the Jones Pepper farms grew and quietly prospered.

Not long after, Harper McIlivrain and Constable Ivins, friends from a decimated Confederate Army unit out of Alabama, came through Lafayette County on their way to find gold in Arizona, or so they thought. Straight from the fields of Civil War pestilence and inedible food, they were offered shelter from a hard rain by the Jones family, who prepared for the men a wondrous stew called *etouffee* in the Cajun language of the region. It was sweetly spicy with fresh tabasco and cayenne peppers, rice, okra, shrimp, and an array of seasonings they had never encountered. To enhance the meal, they poured freely from a crock of red-orange pepper mash that had been preserved in salt and vinegar.

"If only we'd had this brew to dress our battlefield slop, things mightn't have been so bad," McIlivrain remarked, a spicy sweat forming on his brow.

"True," added Ivins. "This sauce could've disguised the horsemeat, too."

So enraptured was the pair by Mrs. Jones's cooking and Grafton Jones' peppery sauce that they decided to stay and make a go of pepper farming. The McIlivrain & Ivins Pepper Company was launched in 1868.

McIlivrain & Ivins now produced 100,000 five-and twelve-ounce bottles of pepper sauce monthly for worldwide distribution. Its product became the eight-hundred-pound gorilla of the hot sauce industry, consuming smaller companies or forcing them out of business. Besides expansive landholdings across southern Louisiana, McIlivrain & Ivins contracted for chiles in Peru, Hungary, and China from thousands of privately owned farms. The sauce was so sought after that former Soviet Premier Nikita Khrushchev famously kept a bottle on hand to spice up his potatoes and vodka.

Jesus Jones hit rock bottom in 1973, living out of his Buick on Chicago's tough south side, anesthetized by bourbon. One frigid January day, he was jarred into consciousness by a loud rapping on the passenger-side window. It was old Odette Washington, who had received a letter at her barbecue joint, Washington's Smoke House on 75th Street, where Jesus had frequently played and dined. "Looks like it come from Looo-easyana," she yelled through the fogged glass, "from someone named Ephraim Jones."

As the McIlivrain & Ivins sauce operation proliferated, it acquired vast delta landholdings from 1868 onward. The Jones property soon was surrounded, accessible only by a one-lane road threading through endless McIlivrain & Ivins acreage. The company had tried for generations to assume the Jones property, 160 acres of rolling, tillable land that was some of the most fertile in the region. The peppers grown by each generation of Joneses were brighter, sweeter, and hotter than any from its giant neighbor's extensive plots. McIlivrain & Ivins settled for buying Jones peppers for use in its sauces, creating a comfortably profitable existence for the smaller farm. McIlivrain & Ivins' agricultural scientists had attempted to study the Jones' land for years, trying to determine why its peppers outshone the rest. Still, the phenomenon of the Jones' peppers remained a regional secret.

By the late 1970s, Ephraim Jones no longer wanted to wake to pepper farming upon reaching the end of his seventh decade. He was the fourth Jones to work the family farm and proud of its legacy. The problem was, his wife had died, taken too young by yellow fever, and they had no children, no one who could inherit the farm. Jones farmed alone for decades, forever missing his wife, never wanting to replace her. Yet he felt his sunset approaching, and he was ready to relax. Based on family history, the last thing Ephraim wanted was McIlivrain & Ivins to acquire the land. The company's lawyers circled like vultures, searching for any legal loophole to gain control of the property. Although Jones was comfortable enough to retire to Austria, where he planned to learn the violin and read until he died, he first needed an heir.

As a youngster working the pepper fields, Ephraim heard the rumors of his married father's interest in a particular alluring Belizean farm worker. Her name was Iris, and she bore her employer an infant boy, who was quietly dispatched to friends in Chicago. The child was never heard from again, and Iris was forced to leave the farm. She had named the boy Jesus hoping that he might someday help enlighten the world's confused and wicked people.

For Ephraim, locating Jesus Jones in Chicago had not been too difficult. The city's south-side black community was tight-knit, and Jesus was familiar about town, even after Agent Orange hastened his decline. Ephraim felt compelled to pursue his only living relative to right his father's wrongs and save the Jones estate from the sharks.

"Ephraim who?" croaked Jesus to Odette from the Buick's backseat.

"Jones!" she barked.

Jesus would never forget the day he read the mysterious letter from Louisiana. He had lived life believing he was an orphan, with a succession of foster homes as his troubled, ever-changing family. Leaving the Buick on Eighth Avenue for good, he rode the Greyhound bus for three days to Lafayette with visions of pepper fields and fortune in his head. He re-read the letter each hour to make sure it was real.

Jesus Jones, if this letter finds you, then wake up and taste (for I heard your nose don't work so well) the chile peppers of good fortune. I am your older half-brother, Ephraim Jones of Lafayette County,

Louisiana, and I have a family matter to discuss with you. Get your ass down to the town of Lafayette by March 3 of this year and meet me at the bus station there. If you are of sound mind and able body, you will now be almost rich. If you're a drunk, loser, or con man, then this is your way to redemption. By the way, your mother was a beauty named Iris, and she was from the islands of Belize.

Jesus admitted that he might have been drunk beyond reasonable expectation and could have been seen as a loser on occasion, but he believed the letter to be his salvation. So off he went, to change his life in a place he'd never seen.

Soaked by beer and stuffed with mollusks in Delaware, Max Little experienced some difficulty following Otis Pepper's meandering tale. The sun had set, and he was abuzz with a high dose of Absurdly Hot Hot Sauce, having accepted a challenge to match Otis spoonful for molten spoonful. Otis was a player in the hot sauce pain game, in which chile-heads around the world meet at spicy food joints to engage in tolerance contests, a meaningless practice to all but those in the know. Except for people with the last name Pepper, hanging out at a place called Pepper's. Max was unsure how Jesus Jones's personal stroke of good fortune would mean anything of value to him.

"Ahh, now you will see, my sauced-up compadre," Otis crooned, continuing the story.

Jesus arrived in downtown Lafayette, smelling musty and smoky from the 78-hour heartland bus journey. As fellow travelers made their way toward idling cars or other buses, he waited. Finally, all that remained in the station parking lot was a lone man on a rusty tractor, smoking a thin cigar and looking skeptically in his direction.

"I see you got my letter. Drunk, loser, or con man?" the man said.

"None of the above, mister," said Jesus, choosing to overlook his recent history. "Only a tired former blues singer with no pipes and a scorched sniffer. But I can taste some, and I do enjoy my bourbon."

They rode south, side by side on the belching, bouncing tractor the fourteen miles to the town of Atchafalaya, in the heart of America's largest swampland. It was another six miles to the McIlivrain & Ivins property entrance from the tiny bayou burg and yet another full mile across their pepper fields to the Jones homestead. Surrounding a clean, white, two-story house were the outbuildings usually associated with farming. There were no animals except for two feisty beagles who seemed to own the place. Rows of ripening red and green pepper bushes fanned out to the horizon.

"Our property stretches for eighty acres in every direction," Ephraim said. "McIlivrain & Ivins land surrounds all of that." Jesus had no idea to whom Ephraim was referring, but he figured they may not be friendly.

The farm sat on a vast underground salt mound rising twenty feet above the amazingly flat delta land, affording a circular view of the region. Humidity gathered visibly in low-lying areas, but the Jones farm was just high enough to enjoy a languid, salty breeze. The place radiated a stillness he had never experienced, and Jesus Jones could feel the air in his hands as Ephraim gestured broadly.

"That direction is the Mississippi Delta and the Gulf of Mexico about twelve miles beyond. The peppers here are the most special to be found anywhere in Louisiana. It's all yours if you want it. If you believe you deserve it." Jesus felt faint and dropped to one knee, only to be licked mercilessly by the beagle twins. "Them, too," Ephraim said.

"And that," concluded Otis Pepper in Delaware, "was how in 1977 Jesus Jones came to be the owner of the sweetest pepper farm in the Louisiana delta. He's a magician with the soil. If you're truly a chile-head, and I'm gathering that you are, then I know you'll want to taste 'em for yourself."

Reliving the chile pepper tale that had brought him to Louisiana caused Max to overlook that he had walked five miles, dried out from the rainstorm, and then gotten soaked all over again with perspiration. And that mysterious, violent men were chasing him. He also didn't immediately notice that an old Ford flatbed was idling in the road as he walked.

"Where ya headed, fella? Or you just out for a soggy stroll?" The syrupy voice belonged to a Creole woman with wavy, sun-streaked hair, green eyes, and strong hands resting over the wheel. She wore a yellow South Louisiana Seed t-shirt and had dirt under nails that were cropped short. *A farmer,* thought Max.

"The Jones Pepper farms," Max said.

The woman's demeanor turned slightly apprehensive. "Jesus Jones? He a friend of yours?"

"Not yet," Max said. "But I want to talk to him."

"Well then, I guess you might as well get in," she said. "I'm headed there myself."

The woman sensed right away that the muddy fellow didn't have nefarious intentions, a thing she was acute at reading. She had a protective side, and Jones was a particular concern, with McIlivrain and Ivins folks slinking about. Max didn't have time to register the shock of the fortuitous encounter and jumped in the passenger door.

Once he was in the vehicle, the woman looked him over. Max was six feet, bronzed by the sun, with a lithe body and an easygoing face sporting a few days' worth of stubble. His boots were caked with mud. Across the man's temple was a nasty cut in the process of healing. He wore frayed jeans and a Bob Marley t-shirt and carried his belongings in a worn canvas duffle bag. *He could use a bath*, she thought, but he smelled manly, maybe a bit salty. The fact that he had been hitchhiking made her wonder how far he had come.

"You don't look like a lawyer or a real estate man," she said. "What would you be wanting from old Jones? You're not from around here, are you?"

"Nope. California," he said. "I own a hot sauce shop in Laguna Beach. I hear Jones is an authority on peppers, and I have some questions about some new types of peppers he may know about. Plus, I hear he has the sweetest and hottest crop of Louisiana tabasco peppers around, and I have a thing for chiles."

He gave her a sideways glance. "My name is Max. And who might you be?"

The woman's eyes flared, but she answered softly, looking out over the flat farmland.

"Oh, just a bayou gal trying to change a confused and wasteful world. Lilah. Lilah DeVillier. I'm a botanist and agronomist working on sustainable organic pepper farming. Too much pesticide from farming flows into the Gulf, killing it off, and Jones happens to be the case study for my doctoral thesis while I teach at the university in Baton Rouge. His soil is incredibly healthy and quite unique. And his peppers are legendary."

Max sensed her note of pride. "Well, isn't this uncanny. Good day for me to be hitchhikin' I guess. And I had no idea there were organic peppers in McIlivrain & Ivins sauces," he said.

"There aren't, except for the product off the Jones farm," she said. "Has been since the mid-1800s. That's why I'm studying it, to find out how it's so different and help Jones do it even better. Plus, maybe save the world in the process. I want to share the findings freely with farmers worldwide."

Max watched her speak and immediately regarded her with a level of interest he reserved for few people. Her research aligned with his own philosophy, and her passion for it was evident. The fortuitous encounter would not fully register until later.

After a meandering trip through bayou farmland, they passed through an open gate, and a quarter-mile later brought the flatbed to a stop in front of the Jones pepper farm. Max slowly stepped out, craning his head in a circle. All around him were the same sweet, ripening red and green peppers Jesus Jones had seen almost thirty years before, thriving in the same humidity, the same salty Gulf breeze.

"It feels like pepper country," he sighed, sensing the heavy air on his skin, familiar, like a prodigal son returning home after years astray.

Lilah nodded, breathing deep and scanning the landscape, feeling the land in her bones. "The very heart and soul of it."

Two barking beagles bounded from the dense rows of vegetation and leaped straight for Max, knocking him to the ground. The dogs, a part of a fiercely loyal canine lineage stretching back to the Civil War, greeted him like an old friend with eager licks and wet-nosed sniffs. Both hounds accepted his ear scratching with abandon.

"Not often they do that," came a raspy voice from the shade of the compost shed. "Usually try to part a man from his throat if they don't know him." White-haired but robust and smiling, Jesus Jones strode toward them.

"Praise Jesus," said Lilah with a laugh.

"And hello to you, little lady," said Jones. He extended a hand to Max to help him stand. "You must be Mr. Little. I got a message you were coming from Chuck DeWindt in Santa Fe. Sure are a long-shot away from La-gooona Beach, Little."

He took note of the wound on Max's head. "Been through a bit to get here, eh?"

Max brushed off the last comment. He felt some of the cool, damp soil slip into his boots as Jesus helped him up. It was an oddly welcome sensation.

"Feels like home to me," said Max as he consumed the moist air, sweet with peppers on the vine. "Must make Chicago seem a long way off as well, Mr. Jones."

"Just Jones'll do, and no more jokes about it, please," said the old man, winking at Lilah. "I've lived with the Jesus thing all my life, so you might as well get used to it, too, if we're gonna be spending any time together. Ain't been back to Chi-town since I left, made my home here ever since. Otis Pepper says you're alright, too. We spoke not long ago, so welcome. Funny, he knew you'd be showing up here at some point."

Jesus led them on a short, informal tour of the farm, partly shaded by ancient, moss-strewn oaks. Distinct borders formed of manicured apple trees separated the fields of different pepper varieties. They lined the access roads, along which Jesus, Max, and Lilah were carried by that same wheezing old tractor that transported the farm's heir here in '73.

"Closer to the barn and house are the oldest fields for tabasco and cayenne, almost 130 years of cultivation," he said above the tractor's growl, his wrinkled hands cranking the vibrating wheel. "Constant care of the soil has kept the fields producing all these years. Farther on are the hybrid strains. With Lilah's nudging, we've recently planted some exotic heirloom varieties from around the world. Even a weird purple one from Ethiopia."

Max, who felt much as though he were visiting old vineyards at the chateau of a first-growth Bordeaux, started at the mention of Ethiopian peppers.

"The Bere-Bere?" he blurted. His attempts at domestic cultivation in Laguna Canyon had been a frustrating failure. Now here he was riding through a solid acre of them hanging purple on the vine, like rediscovered friends.

Lilah turned to Max, amazed. "How could you possibly know such a thing?"

"I'm the first Westerner ever initiated into the Ethiopian Amhara people's 'rite of heat and fire,'" Max said proudly. "Bushmeat is cured by rubbing it with fermented purple Bere-Bere pepper mash and then set in a smokehouse for three days. Tribal elders celebrate the bountiful hunt by exposing themselves to the same process. I spent time with them in Yejju, their village."

Lilah then took a closer look at the necklace of small, intensely purple beads around Max's tanned neck. "Is that where those came from?" she asked.

He took the opportunity to admire the sheen of perspiration on Lilah's collarbone. On it rested a braided silver chain from which a rounded, golden amulet hung, carved with swirls and signs in an unknown script.

"I was given a strung necklace of fresh Bere-Bere peppers to wear throughout the ceremony by the Amhara chieftain. They oozed and dripped hot oils over my body as they cured in the smoke. Excruciating, but chanting with the elders helped me through it. This is what remained after three days in the smokehouse."

"Whatever for?" asked Lilah incredulously.

"Because he feels the pull of the pepper, young lady," said Jones, regarding Max with an understanding stare. "There is magic in it, the heat of the earth, the Ring of Fire."

In chile-head circles, the Ring of Fire was an early-internet linked group of websites peddling super-spicy products and a general obsession with all things hot. Most enthusiasts were outright heat junkies, and many were also members of the International Society of Hot Sauce Aficionados. Yet within a tight subculture of the Ring, there existed a group of hardcore pepper-heads whose motivation in life was to discover new varieties around the world, create hybrids, and capitalize on the new fruit - primarily for bragging rights. Max went much further, hoping to preserve heirloom varieties and experience the cultures that bred them.

Every man has his Shangri-La, and this was Max's, a global epicurean adventure. His passion had led him around the world, usually off the beaten track, to small villages and remote valleys, where he forged relationships and gained the trust of people often wary of outsiders. His shop in Laguna Beach became the repository of these escapades, filled with the stories, images, and ultimately, the tasty products derived from them. Max's niche was the exclusive licensing arrangements he made with the pepper producers he found in far-flung corners of the world.

While on a six-week kibbutz sojourn in the Holy Land to learn low-water farming techniques, Max was fed a salty yellow pepper so clean and smooth it made his ears tingle, to him the sign of a true heirloom variety. Near the Dead Sea in Israel, archeologists had unearthed jars from the sixteenth century containing miraculously preserved ancient pepper seeds not far from the finding of the Dead Sea Scrolls. Israeli scientists extracted the DNA and reproduced the original fruit, a relative of the Peruvian Aji Amarillo. The Dead Sea Yellow became the base for a licensed sauce called Biblical Fire.

In Lijiang, in the province of Sichuan, China, Max was gifted a statuette of Confucius fired from bright-orange local clay. The same earth had been spawning the Golden Emperor pepper for hundreds of years, and the shiny local pottery was glazed with the orange pepper mash, spicy to the touch. Max partnered with the village, and Golden Emperor Pepper Sauce was a big seller at Little's, as were the pepper-orange Confucius statuettes.

Vagabonding in Calabria, in southern Italy, Max once had been served pasta topped by a puree of the local "Devil's Kiss" pepper with anchovies and capers in a sleepy seaside café. It was salty, sweet, and absurdly spicy as he slurped up three bowls of the fiery dish. The Peperone Piccante Calabrese grew in fields across from the café, near the village of Copanello along the Ionian Sea. Max and the café's owner collaborated to make a Devil's Kiss sauce, infused with capers and anchovy. It became a popular go-to condiment for dashing into Bloody Marys.

Over many trips through the desert, Max had crisscrossed the American Southwest. At the Javelina Cantina in Sedona's famous red rocks, he got invited to the Hopi reservation in Northern Arizona to view one of their closed ceremonies after offering a ride to a young Hopi man. Max often made a side trip through the town to load up on the iconic cantina's enchiladas with red hot bird pepper mole sauce, made with chiles off the dusty mesas of the Hopi land. Ben Nuvamsa was to play a Kachina, a Hopi spirit, in the next day's ceremony at his village of Oraibi, on the reservation's ancient First Mesa. Amidst a run of bad luck, his truck had broken down on Highway 89 after delivering chiles to Sedona. In typical Hopi fashion, he was unconcerned about his deadline, believing that something would work out if he were meant to be there.

"You get me there, you can be a VIP at a very special event," he said. He was to portray the Tsil Kachina, the spirit of the chiltepin bird peppers that grew wild on the reservation. "*Tsil* is the Hopi word for chiles, and these are the only wild chiles native to the indigenous lands this far north. They represent our spirit. In a centuries-old tradition, I chase the young runners in a race around our village on Third Mesa and if I catch them, stuff a hot chile in their mouths."

Receiving such an offer was impossible for Max to resist, and the six-hour ceremony up on the Hopi mesas was powerfully symbolic to a chile-head. The Tsil kachina wore a yellow helmet of light cottonwood topped with a crown of bright red chiles and carried a whip of yucca root. The race, where Ben caught only one runner, was followed by hours of ritual dance and singing. After an overnight in the Nuvamsa home, Ben took Max to see his family's patch of domesticated *chiltepins* that they dry-farmed under cover of mesquite trees by a dry riverbed.

The tiny round peppers were concentrated and salty from the dry soil and packed a walloping spicy punch. Max partnered with Ben and the villagers on Third Mesa to produce a bright-red bird chile hot sauce called Hoppin' Hot Hopi Fire Sauce, which directly benefited small farming initiatives on the Hopi reservation. It had a dancing Tsil kachina spirit with its crown of chiles on the label and sold abundantly at the Oraibi village gift shop and Little's House of Fire.

Max gained a reputation as an honest businessman by splitting profits fairly with the hardworking local folk and enhancing the lives of the people he met. Farming cooperatives were established, agronomists Max knew were enlisted for consultation, brands created, and pepper farming flourished. The agriculture institute Max funded with his cut of the Bere-Bere sauce turned out skilled pepper farmers every season in Ethiopia. This altruism allowed Max to find a balance between business, global odysseys, chile freaks, and the world's diverse peoples. The balance worked, though he lived and worked mostly alone.

Hearing his story caused Lilah to view the scruffy Max with curious respect. Training small farmers was something she saw not only as admirable but also vital, mirroring her own efforts. Yet, she didn't feel it was the time to laud the scruffy newcomer just yet.

"I've heard about a group of fanatical chile addicts chasing heat all over the globe," said Lilah, shaking her head, "but I never thought I'd meet one. Amazing."

"In the flesh, ma'am," said Max, grinning. "I was originally a coffee bean freak but was ahead of the trend. When I had to close my espresso shop in '92, I decided to travel. Visiting my old coffee contacts in Costa Rica, I stumbled across a farm where bright red Rican chiles and coffee beans grew side by side. The coffee had a rich spice, and the local pepper sauce was dark like a mocha mole on fire. I'd never experienced anything like it and was instantly hooked. I collaborated with the local growers, and it became Mocha Lava Sauce, my first import. Roasted chile powder-spiced coffee followed. Ethiopia and the Bere-Bere were next, and I decided to bottle and sell the sauces back in Laguna for the U.S. market."

By 1995, Max had rented a commercial kitchen in Laguna Canyon and was experimenting with sauce blends. He enlisted the Mexican labor pool's help from local cantinas that knew a thing or two about hot sauces, and the aroma of roasting peppers and cooking sauces filled the canyon. A warehouse for imported dried peppers and a refrigerated container for fresh products were added to the operation. The Mexicans became his partners, and he employed a full-time food chemist to help him extract and concoct the savory flavors he bottled and sold. In the chile world, he had become well-known, admired by many, envied by others.

Nevertheless, the lasting relationships he established provided Max with a reason to do what he did and love it, even alone. By creating interconnections among people worldwide who had a strong bond with the earth, who loved food and drink, and supporting small farmers and entrepreneurs against the massive industrial machine, Max found his place in the world.

As Jesus piloted the tractor to the farm's highest point and slowed, Max could see not only the entire Jones farm but the surrounding fields of McIlvrain & Ivins as well. Humid mist hugged the ground, though Jones' farm sat strategically situated above everything else, a subtle promontory in the delta's flat land. Max noticed an out-of-place complex of buildings and equipment in the distance, just beyond Jones' property line.

"What's there?" he asked.

"The Acadian Salt Company," said Jones. "We sit on a unique geological feature called a salt dome, which provides our land with better drainage than the flat fields all around. Thanks to luck or foresight, my fruit ain't watery and has more concentrated flavors. Some of these salt domes are thousands of feet deep, and Acadian bought the rights to this one way back. There are caverns and tunnels all over underneath my land. It was the local salt, peppers, and vinegar that made the first pepper sauce, right here."

Parking the tractor under a large shady oak, Jones produced a basket packed with breads, relishes, cured meats, cheeses, fresh peppers, and, of course, pepper sauce. Made in his kitchen, the sauces were in earthen jars that kept them from spoiling.

"I'd planned to lunch with Lilah and talk business, but seeing as how you're here, you're welcome to join us. There's sauces of tabasco, cayenne, habanero, and my Bere-Bere sauce," said Jones.

Max tasted the fresh peppers first: hard, smoky Tabasco; clean, fiery cayenne; sweet, hot habanero; and finally, the familiar earthy burn of the purple Bere-Bere. He sampled them like a sommelier, taking small bites and evaluating their character, turning them in his fingers. He found them meaty and crisp, with unblemished skins and sweet, earthy aromas. Jones had done a remarkable job in their cultivation, Max thought.

Lilah watched in amusement as he hummed while slathering pepper relishes on the bread and savored the pepper-infused cheeses and meats. It was a piquant meal made in heaven for Max as he looked over a sea of Louisiana pepper plants. It pushed his chilling memory of the violent men who pursued him to a distant corner of his mind.

"Where did you get the seeds for the heirloom varieties?" said Max in between bites. "They're not easy to come by, the Bere-Bere."

"Now, that's an interesting question," said Jones. "Still a mystery to me. I'll let Lilah tell you about it. She's the expert on this stuff."

Lilah dabbed at her mouth with a cloth napkin.

"Not long after I came here last year to begin my doctoral research," she said, "unmarked envelopes began arriving at the farm in my name. In them were seeds, origin unknown. I knew they were pepper seeds but had no idea which varieties. My first thought is that the USDA had gotten wind of my research and was sending me seeds to augment my efforts since they'd much rather have a doctoral researcher do the work than their salaried field agronomists."

Lilah had gained notoriety in agricultural circles for her research on pepper varieties and organic farming. Jones had met Lilah's research request for setting aside some plots for growing the seeds, and both were astonished by what sprang forth.

"There were alternating rows of peppers in every shape, color, and size you could imagine," she said. "We sent them to the USDA lab for identification, and while there were some known varieties, others proved more difficult to name."

Resorting to genetic tracking, USDA scientists finally sorted out the unique varieties. Gambian Reds, Italian Cigarettas, Chinese Tien Sins,

Hungarian Blacks, Egyptian Shata Baladis, and purple Ethiopian Bere-Bere.

"Someone had gone to a lot of trouble to assemble a variety of chile seeds from all over the world," she said. "Plus, one that simply couldn't be identified."

"Unidentifiable? Even with genetics?" asked Max. "Was there not at least some indication as to the mystery seeds' origin? A new variety possibly?"

"Yes, eventually, but not the seeds." she continued. "USDA sent the envelopes the seeds came in over to the FBI. They were from Kyrgyzstan, so the seeds must have been sent from there."

Max felt the blood drain from his heart. Hyperventilating, his vision began to go dark as suddenly he grew faint.

"Sorry," he gasped, collapsing beneath the ancient oak. The farm's perfectly arrayed pepper fields became a dark green smear as he blacked out.

Anybody can make pepper sauce. And although the recipe for Tabasco's sauces has been kept secret for over a century, they are essentially this: fresh chile peppers, vinegar, and salt. The chiles are crushed, salt and vinegar are added, and the mixture is pureed, strained, and bottled. Some sauce makers like Tabasco ferment the "mash," or crushed chiles and salt, and age it in oak barrels before adding vinegar and bottling. Some sauces are cooked, and some use reconstituted, dried chiles, while others employ various vegetables, fruits, and spices. Others use fire-roasted chiles, blistered skins adding their unique, smoky flavor. Every culture on earth infuses its own unique ingredients. There are many experts and just as many opinions on how to attain the best sauce.

Chile peppers of the genus *Capsicum*, a member of the Solanaceae or nightshade family, have been cultivated for six thousand years in the Americas, migrating from the Amazon basin worldwide. With the arrival of the Spanish in 1492, they soon found their way into every culture and cuisine on earth, the fastest migration of any food in history. The Inca regarded them so highly that they became one of the four elements of their creation myth, worshiped as a sacred plant. The deity Agar-Uchu, also known as Brother Chili, was one of the four brothers of the Incan pantheon and brother to the first Incan king. The name "chilli" derives from the ancient Aztec dialect of Nahuatl, which called the pepper *chiltepin*. The Incas called them *aji*, the Maya called it *chilli*, and the Spanish confused the entire world by calling it pepper, though they did change *chilli* to *chile*. Columbus originally gave the spicy, bright-red fruit its newer name, *pepper*, because of the hot flavor. He wrongly assumed that he had arrived in the Orient, home of *Piper nigrum*, black pepper.

The idealistic and opportunistic Columbus screwed up on multiple fronts, with long-lasting implications. He named the natives of the Americas *Indians*, believing he had reached India from the east. They called the piquant chiles they encountered *peppers*, hoping to convince his benefactors that he had accomplished his mission to locate pepper and India. Both chile peppers and Indians in the Americas have had to bear the mistake. By the 1500s, peppers from the New World began to be seen in Europe as a cheap substitute for black peppercorn, which was exorbitantly expensive and had to be imported from across the globe in India and Sumatra. The irony was that chile peppers soon replaced black pepper as the most widely traded piquant spice on the planet. Venetian, Spanish, and Portuguese explorers carried them along on their journeys as chiles found their way across the Mediterranean, Africa, the Middle East, and eventually into Asia. It was Greek traders who first called them *chile peppers*, trying to avoid confusion between the pepper fruit and peppercorns. Chiles, chilis, chillis, peppers, chile peppers, or *Capsicum* are all spice masquerading as fruit and only found in the market's vegetable section.

Chiles have also been a powerful equalizer as they spread across the globe and became infused into hundreds of cultures. Other piquant spices like peppercorn were prohibitively expensive through the ages, reserved for the upper classes. The chile pepper fruit could be grown by anyone and brought life to traditionally bland foods, used by both peasants and kings to enhance a meal.

Today, Hungary takes immense pride as the origin of paprika, where it is called "red gold" and is the national spice. The Hungarians say, "One man may yearn for fame, another for wealth, but everyone yearns for a paprika goulash." Sichuan cuisine in China is identified by its pepper-infused fire, and the Chinese culinary concept of *ma la*, or the sensation caused by chile peppers comes from characters meaning "numbing" and "spicy," respectively. It also is the Chinese word for anesthesia. In India, chiles are believed to possess a supernatural element, and a bunch of chiles hung over a doorway wards off the evil eye.

Chiles give the heat to ubiquitous curries and a host of other dishes in India, and the country is now the largest producer of peppers in the world. It is the potent spice in Indonesian sambal, Italian pepperoni, Korean kimchee, and Thai soups that identifies those places' cuisine. Americans have eagerly embraced the chile pepper, which has created its own industry, and pockets of proud fanaticism are found across the country. The city of Santa Fe owes much of its notoriety to chiles, and the entire American Southwest is famous for the fiery foods derived from them. Festivals worldwide celebrate the fruit, which in many places has fueled a "pepper economy."

Humans are the only mammals crazy or lucky enough to eat chiles. Pungent alkaloids, called *capsaicin*, reside in the chiles' veins and placenta, where the seeds attach. These membranes, usually white or yellow in color are the home of the heat. Capsaicin has a unique ability to act upon the pain receptors in the mouth and throat, producing the familiar burning effect. The body, sensing an attack, releases addictive endorphins to combat the threat. And while it cannot actually burn, this potent compound can ignite a response so overwhelming as to render the recipient immobile. Just try taking a shot of concentrated pepper spray in the face, as Max did on a bet in New Orleans. He knew he would survive it, and he enjoyed nine sweaty, blurry-eyed courses of Paul Prudhomme's Cajun cooking after that, paid by the bettor.

From the day Max tasted his first smoky, coffee-infused Rican Red in 1992 Costa Rica, he was hooked. The quest for the fire had consumed his life and become his business, and his world had become populated by people with the same decidedly offbeat passion. It was because of this that he found himself lying under an old oak tree in Lafayette County, Louisiana, where Lilah had revived him with a splash of water to the face.

"Anybody home?" was the first words he heard. She was standing over him with an empty glass as old Jones propped him upright.

"I guess I blacked out," Max groaned.

"I'll say you did," said Jones. "You dropped like a sack of potatoes as soon as Lilah said 'Kyrgyzstan.'"

The first time Kyrgyzstan had fully registered on Max's map had been nine days before his blackout in Louisiana. He was operating the store in Laguna when a tourist in heavily faded jeans, cheap aviator glasses, and a brand-new *Baywatch* t-shirt came through the door. Max had learned to read customers well, and this guy was not in the market for a bottle of hot sauce to take home to wherever he was from.

"Hey," Max said. "What can I do for you?"

"I am Nickolai Gasanov from Kyrgyzstan," the man said in a thick accent as an introduction.

"I understand you are an expert in the world of spicy things. I have information that will make you the most famous person in the Ring of Fire. However, with this information, you must act quickly. There are others who hope to benefit from it."

Up to that point, Max had understood the Ring of Fire only to be the collection of small business entrepreneurs, misfits, and heat junkies he met at spicy foods exhibitions and in the bars of offbeat locales.

"Welcome to Laguna Beach, Mr. Gasanov," he said. He noticed that Gasanov was perspiring as his eyes darted around the store's offerings and over his shoulder. "Can I offer you some iced Costa Rican spiced coffee? You look a little overheated."

"*Jok!* No!" blurted the man. "I am not overheated! I am...earnest!"

Max took a step back, making sure the pepper spray was within reach beneath the counter. "Okay, fella.

Why don't we go out front in the cool beach air so I can hear your story?"

"*Jok!* No!" Gasanov uttered again. "Can we go somewhere... *privat?*"

Little's House of Fire was also Max's home. Above the shop was a one-bedroom apartment facing Pacific Coast Highway with decks in the front and rear. Gasanov was a wiry, agitated man, but he was not a threat to Max in size, so he led him up to the rear deck, which was quiet and shaded by tall eucalyptus trees. Plus, there was Max's bulldog, Clyde, who ruled the house. Clyde was keen at reading Max's emotions, and the dog kept a wary eye on Gasanov as they sat on wooden deck chairs. Max chose the chair under which lay a sizeable hatchet, which he used for splitting firewood.

"You're a long way from home, Mr. Gasanov," said Max.

Gasanov seemed to relax in the secluded setting despite Clyde's exposed lower fang. He sat back, crossed his legs, and lit an unfiltered cigarette.

"Nickolai, please," he said. "People who will soon trust one another use first names."

A long pause ensued during which the only sounds were of crashing waves down at Oak Street Beach and cars passing on the highway. Gasanov exhaled a long ribbon of tobacco smoke and began to speak in clear but heavily accented English.

"I am a vice-minister for the Kyrgyz Ministry of Agriculture in Bishkek, the capital of our country. The Minister of Agriculture is Mr. Azim Isabekov. Recently, I encountered what appears to be a new variety of pepper possibly growing in the foothills of the Tien Shan Mountains. I have been dispatched to bring you there to verify this discovery."

His introduction finished, Gasanov sat back and drew more smoke, looking pleased with himself as he awaited a response.

Several threads of thought ran through Max's mind at the same time. One, he was not trained as a biologist, botanist, paleontologist, or any other designation that would qualify him for such a task. Two, how did these people find him, and why were they here? Three, he knew things were undoubtedly going to get more confusing. Max's response was to scratch the folds of Clyde's neck and stare skeptically at Gasanov, the man from the Kyrgyz Ministry of Agriculture.

Gasanov was compelled by the silence to fill the gap. "You may be wondering why we have chosen you for this task. All I can say is that it will become clear in time. For now, you should feel honored that the government of Kyrgyzstan has decided to bestow this honor upon you."

Kyrgyzstan is a landlocked nation in central Asia, intensely wild, remote, and strikingly beautiful, and much of it is ribbed with high mountains. It had been, until recently, a closed society due to its remoteness and subjugation by outsiders. The seventy-year control of the Soviets had forced a tight reign over the restive province, allowing few people to come out or in until independence in 1991. Some eighty-eight separate mountain ranges make up the country's bones, and its people live an isolated, mountainous existence. Max had read stories of adventurers returning from the pristine Pamir, Ala-Too, and Tien Shan Mountains and a proud, ancient culture that sat at Asia's crossroads.

Three separate land routes of the ancient Silk Road reportedly crisscrossed Kyrgyzstan, with caravans carrying goods from far off Europe and silk from China. The southern Kyrgyz city of Osh was a major trading center on the route, and being an essential stop on the Silk Road, medieval Osh became the beneficiary of the goods and cultures the road ferried. Traders, craftspeople, mercenaries, and farmers interacted, exchanging goods, money, information, and food from across the world.

As Gasanov unfurled this tale, a synapse sparked in Max's brain. The spark fired small gears, creating thoughts, then theories. A simple *What if?* arose, unleashing a torrent of possibilities that Max was unable to contain. What if an undiscovered pepper existed at the ancient crossroads of Asia? What if, at the confluence of cultures, there had been a merging of their foods? Such a discovery would surely get the folks in the Ring of Fire agitated.

"I see your head is already at work, Mr. Max," said Gasanov. "That is good."

Clyde, who had appeared to be snoozing but had kept a single eye trained on Gasanov, perked his head under Max's hand, alert to some new occurrence.

The sound of shattering glass and screams from below was immediately punctuated by alarmed barking from Clyde, who raced into the apartment and down the stairs to the store, the source of the noise. Max immediately followed, and just as he perceived the scent of fuel coming from the lower level, he screamed, "CLYDE! NO!"

The explosion blew both Clyde and Max back up the stairs. Clyde somehow ended atop Max, not moving.

Max lay splayed on his back on the apartment stairs, covered in sauce and glass. His ears rang at a piercing decibel. There was no sign of Gasanov. Max's body had broken Clyde's fall, and now he held the big bulldog's head in his hands, fearful for his best friend's life.

"Yo, Clyde, buddy," he managed with a scratchy voice but didn't try to shake the dog awake. "Yo,

Clyde." Clyde groaned, exhaled, blew snot all over Max's face, then rolled over, asleep.

Relieved, Max got up and ran for the fire extinguisher in the kitchen. He smelled fire down below but knew not what else.

The fuel bomb had been thrown through the shop's front window. It contained more vapor than liquid and had generated more concussion than flame. Only a stack of ceremonial Fijian Cava mats had ignited, and the small fire was quickly dispatched. The front windows had been blown out, and the floor shone slick with the liquid of shattered hot sauce inventory. Intense sauce vapor filled the room, and Max's eyes began to water as he crunched across the shop to the front door, which was no longer there. A crowd had gathered outside, and traffic on Pacific Coast Highway altogether stopped. As Max emerged from the dust and smoke of the store, people gasped. What they mistook for blood was spattered Louisiana Red from off the shelf.

In the crowd of gawkers, he made out the face of Octavio, who owned the Taco Loco just down the road. "You okay, Ese?" he asked Max. "That was one *grande* blast."

"I'm all right," said Max. "Clyde's a little shook up, but he'll be okay. Did you see anything?"

"As soon as I heard the window break, I ran out to see," Octavio said. "All I seen is two guys in red tracksuits running across PCH, and then BOOM!"

"Thanks, amigo," said Max. "I'd better get inside and clean up the mess."

This was a significant event in the small beach community, and the news traveled fast. The Laguna Beach police appeared fifteen minutes later and asked Max why anyone would throw an incendiary device into his store. The detectives, who knew Max well, took him at face value when he said he had no idea why anyone would want him or his store out of operation.

Detective Sanchez looked Max in the eye and said, "This is serious, Max, ATF stuff. And we have no witnesses. So, you're telling me everything there is to know, right?"

Max suggested that the bombers had the wrong address. There was that guy next door making bad home loans to people who couldn't afford them and the investment advisor down the street who was reportedly funneling dough into a Ponzi scheme. Or that it was merely a prank gone awry by some local surf hooligans. The look on Sanchez's face told Max he was not entirely convincing.

"You know as well as I do that this business attracts tourists, not terrorists," Max said in explanation, holding out his hands. "I'm just as perplexed and frustrated as you are."

At which point, he noted aloud that he had been dragging his feet for years regarding installing a video security system. The store's proximity to Pacific Coast Highway made it an easy target for accidents.

Hours later, after he had boarded the windows, cleaned up the mess of sauce and glass, and fancy-footed through further questioning from the police, the public, and the local news, he opened a beer and sat on the deck. He considered why he avoided telling the cops about the men in the tracksuits or about Gasanov, who had fled the scene. They would undoubtedly investigate further, but Max gambled that no leads would connect him to the event. The adventurer in him, he finally accepted, wanted this bizarre and now sinister scenario to play out. Clyde opened one eye and groaned.

"Sorry, buddy," said Max, scratching the folds of the bulldog's neck. It was then he noticed the hastily handwritten note pinned to the eucalyptus tree.

"*Mr. Max,*" the note read. "*Dark forces are at work. I suggest you shutter the shop and escape your town for a while. There is more we need to discuss, of extreme importance. Meet me at the Jemez Hot Springs in New Mexico in three days. Make sure you are not followed. Gasanov.*"

Once in the Spanish conquerors' hands after 1492, chiles spread from the Americas across the globe by several means. The world's spice trade routes had already been established, and peppers followed much the same route as the "big three" foods of Mesoamerica: corn, beans, and squash. Carried by Spanish and Portuguese sailors, they made their way to Europe and across the Mediterranean. From Venice, they reached Constantinople and spread through Persia and Central Asia along the Silk Road, climbing the Tien Shan Mountains of today's Kyrgyzstan into China. After settling in India at Goa and conquering the Sultan of Malacca in Indonesia, the seafaring Portuguese reached

China in 1513 and began establishing trading posts. Chiles spread quickly across China, from both east and west, becoming such an essential part of the culture that in the 1700s, Dutch taxonomist Nikolaus Joseph von Jacquin mistook China as the origin of the plant, based on its ubiquitous presence in the cuisine. The false term *Capsicum chinense* refers to the hottest members of the pepper family that originated in South America: the Amazonian habanero, Caribbean scotch bonnet, African Fatalii, and possibly, the Indian Jolokia.

Other pepper varieties had been identified, with *Capsicum frutescens* (including Tabasco, Thai, Chinese Tien Jiao, and African Birdseye), *Capsicum pubescens* (the ancient Incan Rocoto and Mexican Manzano), the Peruvian *Capsicum baccatum* (Aji Amarillo), and the Mexico-origin *Capsicum annuum* (Cayenne, Jalapeno, New Mexico, and Bell peppers), the most prominent. In the holds of ships, atop medieval caravans, and the bellies of migrating birds, chile peppers conquered the world and took root in every culture.

As he cruised along Interstate 40 east of Kingman, Arizona, Max was processing this information. He had left the store's repair in the hands of the trusted warehouse staff and their friends from Oaxaca before hitting the road in the truck with a stack of seventies cassettes. The Laguna Beach Police had his number, and Max promised to keep them updated if he came across any additional information. Still, he had not divulged the existence of Gasanov, and it occurred to Max that the intrigue of the man's story made him choose to keep it a secret. Whether that was a sensible decision remained to be seen, but his pepper sense had been activated, overpowering rational thought. He had not seen the tracksuit terrorists again, and he liked to think that rather than running from danger, he was ready for a road trip. New Mexico was always a desirable destination for a chile-head, and Max had many friends there. Plus, a bath and some calm in the quiet Jemez Valley might set things right. *Amazing the Kyrgyz man knew about it.* His need to detach was such that he had deliberately left his cellphone on the nightstand, loaded with a new and innocuously vague outgoing message: "Hi, you've reached Max Little of Little's House of Fire. I'm on the road chasing down hot stuff just for you, so please leave a message. Or better yet, send me an email. Keep it hot!"

Max reviewed his conversation with Gasanov and the events that had gotten him to this point, traveling nearly a thousand miles to find a man he had spent fifteen minutes with, after which he, his business, and his dog were nearly blown to pieces. Why would a government employee from a remote central Asian country travel all the way to Laguna to speak to him directly? Why was this particular chile so important, and what did it have to do with him? Gasanov had seemed agitated and must have known he was being followed. He probably knew of the threat his pursuers posed, and Max was going to get the answers he needed.

After an overnight in Flagstaff and an obligatory visit to Diablo Burger on old Route 66 for a habanero chipotle jalapeno buffalo burger, Max headed north up New Mexico Route 4 into the Jemez Valley and the crimson lands of the Jemez Pueblo. Northwest of Albuquerque, the Jemez Mountains rose, exposing the iron red bands of sandstone so familiar to New Mexico and the source of the area's mystical red sand. Past the Jemez Indian pueblo settlement, Jemez Springs is famous for its magma-heated waters, which rise through fissures in the Miocene-era volcanic rock.

Outside, he scooped up a handful of red Jemez sand on the side of the building, which he had made a ritual of throwing into his bathwater when he visited. The 100-year-old public baths comprised Jemez Springs' downtown with the Jemez Mountain Inn and the Laughing Lizard Cantina, and an hour soak would run Max fifteen bucks. Legend touted its high mineral content, medicinal properties, and healing powers, and Max was stiff, tired, and sore from driving and being blown up.

The individual baths afforded some privacy, but Max left the curtain open to see who might be coming and going. Though there appeared to be no one else bathing on this Tuesday afternoon, he wanted the upper hand on Gasanov. Max knew he could take him one-on-one but did not know who else might be around, so his old Pony League baseball bat stood in the corner, within reach. An attendant had led him through the steamy row of baths, and he slipped deep into the nourishing, hot waters of bath number six.

"Were you followed, Mr. Max?" It was Gasanov's thick accent from bath number eight, just over the wall. He had already been there, waiting for Max.

"No, I was not, Gasanov. I've just driven a thousand miles to find out about the bomb that blew up my business and almost killed my dog, so start talking."

"Please, Mr. Max, call me Nickolai." Gasanov implored.

While he did not trust Gasanov, Max was not afraid of him. There was a committed air to the man that Max usually only experienced when in the company of serious chile-heads and Ring of Fire types. Max sensed that Gasanov was into something way over his head and possibly operating outside his authority.

"I had nothing to do with the bombing of your store," Gasanov continued. "That was an act of terrorism. I am not a terrorist."

"You probably aren't capable of being a terrorist," said Max, increasingly agitated, "but I'll bet you know who those men were, and I'll bet they're after you, not me."

"That they are after me means they are now after you," said Gasanov. "I cannot change that. I am sorry."

This was not what Max wanted to hear. He jumped from the bath, grabbed the Louisville Slugger, approached Gasanov with the bat, and raised his voice. "Who are they, and why do they want to harm me? I want answers now!"

"Everything alright in here?" called the attendant through the doorway.

Max stood over Gasanov in his bath, dripping, bat in hand.

"We are fine, sir. Thank you," said Gasanov. The attendant nodded warily and left. "Relax, Mr. Max, and please put on a towel. Let us talk like gentlemen while we bathe."

Max retreated to his tub, and once in the water, felt the adrenaline subside. He took a few deep breaths and decided that clubbing the information out of the Kyrgyz man would not be beneficial. Over the dripping of water from the springs' faucets, Gasanov began to speak.

"The men in the red tracksuits who firebombed your store are members of the Kyrgyz mafia," Gasanov said. "They are most certainly former Soviet Spetznaz commandos in the employ of criminal elements of our society. I have been followed since I departed from Kyrgyzstan over a week ago. They do not want me to conduct my business here in America. My business with you."

"Business with me?" asked Max. "What business with me and why? What business could the Kyrgyzstan Ministry of Agriculture or your mafia possibly have with me?"

A part of Max's mind knew the answer even as he asked the question. Sitting in a steaming tub in New Mexico, talking over a wall to a man he hardly knew, Max began to theorize that Kyrgyzstan's government, its mafia, or perhaps just Gasanov, wanted to capitalize on and develop products from a previously undiscovered variety of pepper.

"Max, Max, Max." Gasanov seemed surprised that Max had not got it yet. "Your spicy foods industry alone generates four billion dollars a year in revenue. That is equal to my nation's entire agricultural output. We have tried to cultivate non-native varieties with little success. Everyone wants 'heirloom' these days. If we have discovered a new chile pepper unique to our terrain, where do you suppose it will be most beneficial to bring it to market? In the markets of Osh in my country? No. In the supermarkets of America, developed by you."

The commercial kitchen in Laguna Canyon had gained a reputation for creating innovative, palatable, and successful spicy food products from around the world. Max and his Mexican partners had become widely known for their efforts in getting products with unique origin stories to market. It had not been hard for Gasanov, the Vice Minister of Agriculture in Kyrgyzstan, to make a few discreet inquiries and locate him. If he thought about it hard enough, it was an understandable unfolding of circumstances. It was getting past the fuel bomb that was problematic.

"While we are a remote country with an agrarian economy, Mr. Max, we are not without our resources," said Gasanov, who seemed to be embarking on a prepared speech. "The Agriculture Ministry has certain...diplomatic measures at our disposal, which allowed us to profile you and determine your worthiness for this project. You have the experience, reputation, connections, and facilities to bring it to fruition. You are not a criminal. You care for your mother in Long Beach. Your father owns a bar in Tacoma, and we know you have not communicated with him since he left your mother. And while we know you do not extensively use drugs, we have chosen to overlook the trips you made to Brazil and Mexico for, shall we say, 'mind-opening, cultural exploration.' This does not concern us."

Max's eyes widened, shocked at hearing details of his life. No one had mentioned his father to him in a long time, and he had pushed the angry thoughts of the man aside for even longer. In 1986, his father had departed for Tacoma, Washington, and never came back. His mother was devastated, and Max had supported her ever since, paying the mortgage on the bungalow in Long Beach to keep a roof over her head. The ayahuasca in Brazil and the peyote in Mexico, he decided to let stay where it was. An enlightening memory, albeit a psychedelic one.

Gasanov continued. "The people of Kyrgyzstan are an immensely proud, hardy, and independent lot, Mr. Max. The Agriculture Ministry is committed to bettering opportunities for our farmers and our country. Again, you should feel proud to have been selected for this potentially lucrative task. The Minister of Agriculture has tasked me with bringing you to our country to explore the issue and develop a successful product line. Believe me when I say that many others would like to exploit this opportunity, starting with the employer of the red-suited bombers. And a host of international corporations, some of which I believe are already on the hunt. But first, we need authentication."

While highly competitive, the fiery foods industry was generally benign. People were not blowing up each other's businesses to get ahead. The introduction of the Kyrgyz mafia and the track-suited commandos threw the whole picture out of alignment.

"And the firebombing henchmen being here in America? How does that play out?" asked Max.

"This is a very involved and complicated issue," said Gasanov. He exhaled wearily through the steam as though the subject dogged him and would not go away.

"As in all Asia and the former Soviet republics, organized crime is entrenched and poses a threat to progress and democratic institutions. Various criminal groups operate in Kyrgyzstan and compete to solidify control over territory, with connections to other groups in neighboring countries to transport contraband, levy tariffs on trade, and terrorize citizens. Under the direction of Ruslan Bakiyev, a particularly aggressive group controls the southern city of Jalalabad and the ancient market city of Osh, with its huge bazaar. It is in this region that rumor of a potentially lucrative cash crop has begun to spread. This is why we must act quickly to identify this plant, register and trademark it, and bring it to market before the criminal gangs."

With that, Gasanov appeared to want to finish the conversation. He rose from his steaming tub, put on a robe, and lit a thin cigarette. "That is all for now," he spoke to Max as he passed. "I will see you at the bar of the Laughing Lizard at seven, where we will get to know each other better. And please, no baseball bat is necessary."

Max had checked into a familiar room at the old Jemez Mountain Inn, overlooking the creek that ran behind it. After a call to check on the shop cleanup's progress and say hello to Clyde through the phone, he dressed and ambled across the street to the Laughing Lizard Saloon, the only bar in town and one with which he was quite familiar.

Apart from a few regular-looking locals sitting at the tables, the only other person at the bar was a wiry man, overdressed in tight Lee jeans, a cheap Indian-blanket shirt, and a gargantuan cowboy hat. The black loafer slip-ons immediately defeated Gasanov's forced attempt at local attire.

"Mr. Max! Welcome!" he said. "How do I look? I purchased some garments at the inn's gift shop."

"You could easily get a job on an American cattle ranch, Gasanov," he said.

"A cowboy! Excellent!" blurted the Kyrgyz man. "I have dreamt of being in New Mexico ever since I saw *Valley of the Sun*, which was shown at a ministry movie night long ago. And now, here we are."

Gasanov, grinning and glassy-eyed, proud of his reference to a 1942 American western, had three full shot glasses of tequila in front of him, set up with salt and lime. He looked as though he had already had a few.

"Drink with me," he said to Max, offering a barstool beside him.

Max settled onto the stool one further away and motioned for a particular bottle of tequila, giving the bartender a wink as he did. The bartender reached for the top shelf and dusted off a square, opaque glass bottle before pouring a long shot into a bucket glass.

"What is this?" Gasanov asked, reaching for the bottle. The label was faded and old.

"That's an extraordinary bottle of San Matias Oro, aged for five years in oak casks," said the bartender. "The heart of the agave cactus is roasted over fire, which creates a smoky, sweet nectar. This particular bottle happens to be forty years old. The owner came across a few cases of rare, vintage tequilas a while back at an auction in Mexico, and we are lucky to have them in our collection."

The bartender also placed a plain, bourbon flask-shaped bottle in front of them. There was no label on it. "Salt and lime work fine for the first few shots, gentlemen, but after that, you may want a drop or two of this in your shot glass to keep you attached to your senses."

Inside was a deep orange liquid with flecks of black and yellow. "It's made by some friends of ours over in Chimayo from *piquin* chiles," said the bartender. "Rumor has it that the deep orange color is actually from the holy red silt of the sacred Santuario de Chimayo."

The bartender produced a basket of hot, freshly fried tortilla chips, glistening from their stay in sizzling oil. Max poured a couple of grams of the orange sauce onto a salty hot chip and slowly savored the bite. He stared at the wall of bottles as he let the mix fill his mouth and work on his taste buds, awakening his senses. Piquin had a lighter, more acidic tone to it than other peppers. Essences of fruit, vinegar, garlic, and black pepper preceded a building fire that cleanly overtook all other elements, filling his head with flavors and responses. He felt a familiar tingling of his ears and a ribbon of sensation shoot down his spine that occurred often in these particular moments. As he swallowed the fiery delight, he ascertained a slightly chalky aftertaste, undoubtedly the sacred Chimayo dust subtly infused into the sauce.

"Nice," was all Max said, exhaling deeply.

Then he drank the tequila in a single, deliberate swallow, savoring it as it flowed over the residual pepper sauce in a wave of fresh, liquid fire. This process was repeated two more times until Max felt his mojo rising and his inner chile-head begin to take over.

"Okay, Nickolai. It is time for you to join the Ring of Fire."

At the mention of his first name, Gasanov's eyes shone eagerly with anticipation.

"What must I do?" he asked breathlessly as if a secret ceremony was about to begin.

"Stick out your tongue," said Max.

The heat in chiles, hidden not so subtly in the capsaicin alkaloids, causes pain receptors in the tongue, throat, gums, and lips to register heat – a false pain, a pepper ruse – which in turn induces the body, thinking it is under attack, to release endorphins. These endorphins, dispatched to alleviate a pain that does not actually exist, are addictive. The hottest of peppers have been termed "psychotropic" in their ability to induce a mind-altering state. Chile-heads can be called endorphin junkies looking for a high. However, Max existed on a different plain, reveling in the fruit's source, what the French call *terroir*. The heat, the perceived discomfort, was a necessary step on the way to discovery, the journey beyond immediate sensation toward *knowing* the pepper. To Max, every chile was a bottled genie, a complex structure in a shiny skin awaiting liberation, an unrealized potent life force. Peppers were, for Max, a link with humanity, the fruit that had spread across the world and unwittingly united it, where a billion people on a given day spiced up their food because it made life a little better.

The Kyrgyz closed his eyes and extended his tongue, onto which Max poured a single gram of the Chimayo pepper sauce. Gasanov took it in with a strange slurp, causing it to run onto his lips and gums in a clumsy attempt to appear like a gastronome. He sat back, eyes still closed, anticipating an experience of savor and delight. After three seconds, his eyes opened wide, and fear began to overtake his facial expression. By ten seconds, he was grabbing his throat in an attempt to stop any more sauce from finding its way down. His eyes were watering profusely as he looked to Max for some sign that he was not being assassinated. After twenty seconds, he took a breath, which seemed to fan the flames within, as he swayed, mumbling unintelligibly, and his lips began to swell. He was going down hard.

Max reached out, grabbed his jaw with a single hand, and yanked Gasanov's mouth open, wherein he dumped a big shot of cheap tequila. The man's eyes were bloodshot red and wide with terror. Max then stuffed a lime wedge between Gasanov's teeth and pushed up on his chin to juice the lime.

"That ought to help," said Max thoughtfully. "You'll be alright in a few minutes."

Gasanov was drenched with sweat as he downed the other two tequila shots and grabbed for more limes. He swayed back and forth, mumbling unintelligibly, and Max heard a word that sounded like *mama*. This went on for some time. Ten minutes later, Gasanov returned somewhat to normal, evidenced by his asking what his new status in the Ring of Fire now meant.

"A badge, perhaps, for undergoing this horrific ritual?" he pleaded, massaging his face. Max had broken him down and helped him recover, and now it was time to get serious before Gasanov fell apart completely on tequila.

"Nickolai," Max said. "Why is the Kyrgyz mafia sending hitmen over here?"

"Not now, Max," pleaded Gasanov. "Can't we forget about them for a while and enjoy this place?" He was getting loopy.

"I won't enjoy anything until I know what's going on," said Max. "Time to come clean, Amigo."

"Agricultural espionage," Gasanov said.

As Max sipped the vintage San Matias tequila, Gasanov reluctantly spelled out the situation. The mafia boss Ruslan Bakiyev, who controlled the southern region of Kyrgyzstan, had heard of the Agriculture Ministry's find of a new, undiscovered agricultural product that could make whoever controlled it potentially rich, or in his case, richer. People had taken notice of the rumors that had been coming more frequently from the southern mountains. Word had spread to the markets of Osh, where Bakiyev had many ears. He also had ears in the Agriculture Ministry itself, Gasanov feared, and it was rumored that the Minister of Agriculture had been bought. When the rumor of potential involvement by the Americans emerged, Bakiyev dispatched his operatives to thwart the effort or steal whatever they could.

"Then who sent you?" Max demanded. "I thought it was the Minister of Agriculture."

"He sent me to America," said Gasanov, cringing, "but only to steal recipes and information about production. He and Bakiyev, I fear, are colluding to exploit this. I am now on my own."

"Why me, Gasanov?" Max was getting angry. He grabbed Gasanov's shirt with both hands and shook him. "Why me?"

"Easy, Max," the bartender said, gently bringing him down. "Sounds like it's going to be better for you if this guy's conscious."

"For my people," said Gasanov. Wheezing and whimpering, he looked about to cry. "For the people of Kyrgyzstan. We have been conquered and dominated for centuries. First, by the Mongols and Chinese, then the Russians. Now, the corrupt government and crooks are trying to steal our only new resource. You have a reputation for helping regular people, so you must aid us, Mr. Max. We have no one to trust. Bring my people into the Ring of Fire. I beg you!"

Gasanov collapsed onto the bar, his head in his arms, sobbing. Not long after, the sobs faded into snores. Max paid the bill and carried the man out over his shoulder, across the street to his room. He tossed him onto the bed and took an evening stroll down along the creek to clear his head. It was a starry New Mexican night, with the scent of pinon pine in the breeze.

Though loosened by tequila, Max was able to wade through his thoughts. Somewhere, two Kyrgyz mafia employees looked for Gasanov and had at least seen him visit Max's store. He had to assume they would have him checked out and realize his connection to the chile world. Would the Kyrgyz mafia, abetted by a corrupt Minister of Agriculture, deduce Gasanov's intent to contract Max to develop the mystery pepper into a cash crop? It appeared Gasanov was acting on his own for the benefit of his countrymen, but Max couldn't be sure. And if the criminals caught up with them, what would they attempt to do? Was this far-fetched caper worth it?

Max let the questions lie and headed back to his room to sleep.

The next morning, Max returned to the Laughing Lizard, plowing through a plate of fried pork machaca and eggs smothered in Chimayo Orange hot sauce. His first move had been to steam out the previous night's drama at the bathhouse, and the ablution and a large plate of food were setting him right again. As he was soaking up the delicious juices with a tortilla, he heard a pained grumble in the doorway.

"*Salamatsyzby*, Mr. Max," Gasanov offered as a greeting, clammy and unsteady on his feet. "*Maga dogdurdu chakyrgyla*," he said foggily. "Uh, I may need a doctor. I feel like a herd of Tien Shan oxen has used me as a doormat. This Ring of Fire is a dangerous place."

"Have a plate of machaca," said Max. "It's the local medicinal cure for such ailments. And it ain't the chiles you're hurting from, it's the tequila. If you still need a doctor, we can find you a healer in Santa Fe."

"Santa Fe?" said Gasanov wistfully. "The legendary western city? We are going there?"

"Yes, we are," said Max. "There are a few people I need to visit."

Gasanov had taken a taxi to Jemez Springs from Albuquerque and now rode beside Max in the pickup. The breakfast helped him to function, but he leaned against the window, breathing heavily and staring at the passing New Mexico landscape. Once on Route 126, they passed through the Jemez Mountains and crossed the Valle Grande, site of the magnificent Jemez Caldera, an extinct volcano fourteen miles across. Cotton ball clouds marched across an impossibly blue sky as they cruised across the high plain aided by a Van Morrison soundtrack.

"Your country is as beautiful as my own, Mr. Max," said Gasanov, "though our mountains are more grand."

"So I've heard," was all Max offered, and they rode on in silence down the mountains and east into the Rio Grande Valley, with the peaks of the Sangre de Cristo range looming gold in the afternoon light.

The crisp morning melted into a lazy daylong road trip, and as they pulled into Santa Fe, Gasanov's head craned to take in the distinct pueblo-style architecture, ochre terraced structures of molded earth.

"Amazing," he said. "Many of these buildings, the smaller ones, remind me of the ones in my village in Kyrgyzstan. But the larger ones, they are like palaces, growing out of the red earth."

They wound their way through the Old Town and around the historic Plaza, stopping in front of the grand adobe Hotel La Fonda. "Tonight, we'll stay here," Max said. "You can take a nap while I attend to some business. Perhaps by dinner, you'll feel better."

Once in his room, Max called his friend Chuck DeWindt, director and head botanist of the New Mexico State University Institute of Chile Pepper Research. He needed an honest, realistic opinion.

"A completely new and undiscovered variety of chile pepper in Kyrgyzstan? Hmmm," Chuck had responded. "Could be. But there are many people out there hybridizing varieties to stake a claim to new strains. Still, if you think about the Old Silk Road routes, pepper varieties could have come from both the east and west and met in Kyrgyzstan. A unique strain could have developed and survived all these centuries in a protected environment, but I would be highly skeptical of the probability. It's a heckuva long way to go to check it out, but I may have a motivator for you."

The university had been trying to send someone over to remote northeast India for months to get some viable specimens of the much-hyped *Naga Jolokia*, the reportedly one million-heat index chile from India's Assam province. If Max were willing to make a side trip and collect some fresh heirloom samples in their native environment, the university would split the cost of his trip. Max had assisted the Institute before on heat-seeking missions and though not a botanist, was regarded as a trusted resource. Moreover, Kyrgyzstan was just up the road from northern India, albeit a long and dangerous one. Max agreed to consider the trip but let Chuck know he had more fact-finding to do before undertaking such a venture. He did not tell him about the Kyrgyz mafia and Gasanov.

Max next ventured out into the Plaza neighborhood in downtown Santa Fe. He had people to see, and winding through the narrow streets and seeing familiar sights made him feel at ease. He was back in pepper country. First, he stopped in at Josie's Casa de Tamales to have some blue corn tamales and green chile sauce the place was famous for. Josie was a veteran chile head and a repository of information in the world of things spicy. Santa Fe was rightfully chile central, and while the subtle New Mexico chile famously ruled, peppers from around the globe were cultivated, marketed, and packaged here. Max saddled up to the bar and asked the bartender if Josie was in the house.

"Yeah, she's in the kitchen rolling out tamales," he said.

He quietly poked his head in the swinging kitchen doors to see Josie and two of her employees in a tamale production line. One of them hummed a Mexican love song. The first person portioned thick purple corn masa dough into palm-sized balls, which she then threw with a splat onto a section of trimmed corn husk. The next used her hands to spread the corn dough evenly across the corn wrapper. She then used a wooden spoon to distribute the tamale filling, red with crushed chiles and dripping cubes of green from a large bowl. Josie, supervising, folded one end of the masa-covered corn husk, now gleaming with filling, and rolled it gently before tying the loose end with a corn husk string. Max felt his stomach grumble, anticipating a plate of four of them.

"What's in the filling today?" he asked the production line.

Without looking up, Josie continued her task, not wanting to slow the team. "Roasted then fried carnitas, chiles three ways, grilled nopales. Green chile gravy on top." She looked up, and when she saw Max, she showed a wide smile. Then her smile turned to concern.

"I heard about the explosion at your store, Max," Josie said. "And Clyde. Everyone's been worried about you. What brings you here? Shouldn't you be back in Laguna getting open again?"

"I've got my guys working on it, and Clyde is in good hands," said Max. "I just needed to get away. I need some information, Josie."

Josie leaned in close over the counter. "What gives? There's been a rumor that your store was deliberately blown up, Max. What possibly for?"

"Some of my overseas dealings might be ruffling some feathers, I guess," was all Max offered. Then he asked, quietly, "Have you gotten wind of any new strains of peppers arriving on the scene?"

"Other than all the hoopla over that Indian *Naga Jolokia*, no," she said. "Except that, I heard a rumor that old Jesus Jones down in Louisiana is cultivating some strange new varieties."

The mention of Jones caused Max to start. Josie squinted her eyes. "What are you into, Max? Ring of Fire stupidity? Who blows up stores over a new pepper?"

She was sincerely concerned now. "Get your ass home to your dog and your store and drop whatever it is you think you're going to do. I mean it."

"Excellent!" exclaimed Gasanov as he tasted through what was for him a transcendent meal. He had enjoyed a long nap, and the sun was about to set. Flavors he had never experienced danced across his palate. "What is this food? It is not American food, I think."

They sat in the classic La Fonda Hotel's main dining room and sipped margaritas until the oversized platters of food had arrived. Dining there was a quintessential Santa Fe experience, and Max thought Gasanov would appreciate the ceremony of a La Fonda feast. Golden, late-day light filtered through the opaque amber panels on the ceiling, and the muffled sounds of eager diners had a calming effect on Gasanov. Though filled with a thousand overlapping thoughts, Max felt able to unwind a bit as well. The margarita cleared his head of the noise.

"Chile Rellenos," he answered. "Cheese-filled, breaded, and fried poblano peppers topped with sweet green chile gravy. Ceviche, fish marinated in lime with jalapeno peppers. And Carne Adovada, a traditional red New Mexico chile stew. Typical local dish."

Two wanna-be cowboys, probably Texans, sat at a table near them, burying their faces in the menu. Their boots and jeans were new, and their hats matched. *Santa Fe is such a magnet for cowboy posers,* thought Max.

"If we were in Kyrgyzstan, Max, my friend, I would take you to a restaurant in Osh that would forever change your opinion of delicious," said Gasanov. "We would drink *koumiss,* the fermented milk of mares, and eat like kings. The *shashlik* and *besh barmak* are spectacular. Nevertheless, it is the local *paloo* that would, as you say, 'blow your mind.'"

Having become a willing connoisseur of world cuisines, Max was always open to a discussion about food. Even as he took large bites of the smoky hot rellenos. "And why is that?"

"The secret ingredient. The *Fire of the Valley,* my friend," said Gasanov wistfully. "Paloo is a mutton stew with rice that has been perfected by the people of the Tien Shan Mountain region. The flavor is utterly unique, with a sauce made from local ingredients known only to the tribes of the mountains. It is magnificently spicy and incredibly difficult to obtain."

In his culinary rapture, Gasanov had let loose the secret that now bound the two of them. "Alright, Gasanov," said Max. "Time to come clean. Tell me exactly what you know of these peppers and why they're so important."

As he dipped into the large bowl of snapper ceviche with tangy diced jalapenos that had been placed between them, Gasanov drifted away. After a few moments, he shook and seemed to return.

"Things in my part of the world are different, Mr. Max," he said. "Culture, traditions, tribal bonds. For eighty years, the Russians took that from us. They brought Cossacks and Ukrainians in by the thousands to dilute our ethnicity. They stole our best land, our resources, and our brightest minds. When they left, we had virtually nothing except for our culture and our clans. Our food is undeniably part of our identity, our *qishloq*. And now we have a chance to get some of our identity back." Another round of margaritas arrived, and Gasanov sipped while he talked.

"When I first discovered these new peppers, I heard they were from Tajikistan, where most of the region's peppers come from. And those are usually bland and lifeless. Most of our country is too cold and too high in elevation. However, the ones in the market in Osh were unlike any I had ever seen. Or tasted. And they were fresh, so they had to be from Kyrgyzstan."

Tribes in the Tian Shen mountains' foothills had developed their customs and cuisine in relative obscurity due to the region's remoteness. They had famously fought off Genghis Khan's hordes in the 10th century by hiding in the remote valleys and randomly raiding the more significant force. This had kept most conquerors at bay and allowed the nomadic tribes to thrive in relative peace. Out of these nomadic tribes had come a particularly unique culinary tradition that suited a rough terrain and a hard life, influenced by travelers from other lands.

The Fire of the Valley was the base for this cuisine, a rich, smoky, searing blend of spices that these people kept secret, given a deep distrust of outsiders. Some said it was fermented, some said it contained hypnotic herbs, some described it as an aphrodisiac. Still, others said it was cursed, for it imparted a euphoric satisfaction that made eating such a pleasure as to seem mystical. Yet, no one had ever discerned the ingredients or their origin. It had become part of the Kyrgyz myth, until now.

"When I sampled the product I discovered in the Osh market, I was stunned," said Gasanov. "The fruit was rich in taste, not overly acidic. Addictive and vividly hot. These were not Tajik peppers, I determined. They were something else completely. I consumed fourteen of these, and I could not stop. The heat and flavor combined to create a taste sensation I have never experienced. I slipped into a state of incredible satisfaction that I could not remember ever having, and I have not been the same since. I had to find their origin."

It had taken Gasanov months to locate Adilet Buntun, the pepper seller he had encountered in the Osh market. The trip to the Naryn valley was a difficult one, and the people there distrusted outsiders. In the village of Dostuk, he knew he would stand out and likely receive little help if he began asking questions. Though a Kyrgyz, he was from the city, and village people were wary of his type. He had hired middlemen to act as traders, bringing pots and pans to sell, and in this way had located the Buntun family.

"In the village of Dostuk, along the valley of the Naryn River, Adilet Buntun and her family run a small riverside inn for travelers, villagers, and nomadic folk needing shelter," Gasanov began. "It is the only place to buy a meal for many miles around."

Gasanov's undercover traders returned with information on her whereabouts as well as tales of food so fiery and delicious they were compelled to stay an extra week. Yet, they could not gather more information on "the Fire," and Gasanov realized he would have to seek answers personally.

"I commandeered an Agriculture Ministry truck and driver, had a donkey put in the rear, and set out for Dostuk," Gasanov continued. "Three kilometers outside the village, I put on a nomad's garb and mounted the beast. I was now a seller of knives and blades and did not shave or bathe for a week to authenticate my false identity."

Gasanov had arrived on a fall day in windswept, forlorn Dostuk and had experienced little difficulty identifying the Buntun Lodge. Other than some small shops and a rural clinic, only houses lined the main street, which was dirt. A handmade sign identified the inn over the door, and once inside, Adilet Buntun, plump and rosy-cheeked, stood before him with her hands on her hips.

"Food or bed?" she demanded.

"Both," replied Gasanov, using a brusque voice he associated with tribal peoples. "I am here selling knives and blades of the finest quality, and not from China. These are from Germany."

Adilet narrowed her eyes. "Why would a seller of German knives come all the way here to the Naryn valley?" she asked. "We are simple people and make our own tools. My husband happens to be the local metalsmith in this village."

"I travel the country seeking out chefs and cooks, the kind of people who would care about using the finest blades. I have heard that delectable food comes from the kitchens of the Naryn valley," he responded.

Adilet grunted in reply. "We are hungry, we make food, and we eat. Why should people anywhere else talk of this?"

Gasanov knew it was time to cut to the chase. "Well, let me sample some, and let's find out. Perhaps a bath first."

She led Gasanov through a low doorway on floors of worn planks, the establishment simple yet clean. They headed down a narrow hall that led to the rooms, where they passed an open door, revealing a small kitchen. Atop a wood-burning stove sat a collection of pots, contents steaming. A tiny, round woman stood over a cutting board, chopping herbs. In a wood bowl sat mounds of chopped, dark meat, glistening, and baskets of vegetables in multiple colors. Gasanov bathed in scents that, for just a moment, created an utterly rapturous fragment of time. His mood lightened, and he experienced a keen desire to eat and drink as he arrived at his domicile.

Adilet opened the door to his small room and said, "I will bring hot water for your bath. Dinner is in one hour."

Exactly one hour later, Gasanov sat alone in the small dining room. Long tables hewn from logs and chairs with stretched leather seats appeared to be the only furnishings. There were few windows, and the walls showed recessed places for candles that burned with large flames and too much smoke. Adilet offered vodka, beer, or Kyrgyz fermented mare's milk, called *koumiss*, to drink. He chose the local option, working to fit in, and took a long draft.

"Your koumiss is outstanding, woman," he said to start a conversation.

"We take milk, we ferment it, we drink it. Perhaps our mares are happier than others," Adilet replied.

Gasanov sat alone, sipping the cloudy bitter brew, recalling the peppers he had found in the Osh market, and wondering about the Fire of the Valley. It was rumored to be a blend of spices and herbs known only to the Naryn River region clans. His further research had led him to this same village. With the Buntun Lodge Guest House being the only establishment that sold prepared food for many kilometers, it was clear he had reached his destination.

The Buntun woman returned, balancing a tray atop her shoulder. From it, she placed an array of plates and bowls in front of Gasanov. There were grilled mutton and goat meats, slick with oil and covered in herbs and spices. Wild rice, yellow, brown, and black, steaming. Green, leafy vegetables sprinkled with garlic. Fluffy yellow dumplings, under a towel. The largest bowl was filled with a cloudy, pungent broth, and he saw onions, chopped peppers, and herbs floating in it. Finally, she placed a small, covered earthenware jar off to the side along with a bowl of dried spices.

"Most people just make a paloo stew," said Adilet in Kyrgyz, "but here in Dostuk, we make it *kuurdak*-style, grilling the meat rather than boiling it. The dumplings are filled with mushrooms from our cellar. We cook the ingredients alone to retain their flavor and let you make your own dish. It is fresher that way. Not like the slop they sell you in the city."

Her gruff demeanor abated as she spoke of the food, a change not lost on Gasanov.

"Now stop looking at it and eat," she said.

Over the rice, he spooned the grilled meats, dumplings, and spiced, leafy greens. Then he ladled the meaty broth with onions and peppers, making a stew for one. Upon removing the top from the small earthenware jar, he found an orange sauce comprising many ingredients. He scooped up a bit of the mixture with a small wooden spoon inside the pot and passed it under his nose. Gasanov was immediately reminded of the peppers he had tasted before. A wave of sensations overtook him, intense hunger among them.

While the host described the food, groups of tired, grimy, and stone-faced people had begun to come through the door, aware of the lodge's opening time. The tables were soon filled with an array of truckers, workers, and families, and Adilet delivered tray after tray of food just like Gasanov's. The air began to fill with the sounds of eating, the clinks, clanks, slurps, grumbles, and belches of hungry, hard-working people. Gasanov noticed that as they began to eat, their collective mood lightened, and the conversation flowed. He remained alone, however, at his small table in the corner.

Gasanov was intrigued, trying to guess the composition of the orange condiment before him. He was sure that its scent evoked the same fresh, hot peppers from the Osh market, but this was complex. He caught the sour of vinegar, the strong-sweet of garlic, and the grassy tone of herbs. That it was heavily spiced was certain. He put out his tongue and let five thick drops fall onto it.

A rush of flavor overtook him as the concoction flowed over his taste buds. First came the awareness of mellow, roasted, soft vegetables, then the clean spring note of freshly-picked herbs. Next were acids of fresh peppers, fruits, and vinegar. These were followed by a distinct mineral quality that he had not experienced before in food. The acute sensation of the ground, soil, and rock crossed his tongue. A clean, clear heat, not like a flame, but like the expanding light of morning sun. The heat grew, yet in a pleasant spreading flow. These sensations combined to take over his mouth, and when the entire production passed his palate and slid down his throat, he became overcome by satisfaction, well-being, and comfort.

He spooned healthy amounts of condiment over his bowl of food and, for a solid forty minutes, took bite after bite of the most delicious food he had ever tasted. He did not hurry. When he finally sat back to take a deep breath, he saw that the entire room had stopped eating and conversing and was watching him. Unable to stop it, a healthy belch found its way up from the depths of his belly and exited his mouth of its own accord. He sank into his seat, wholly consumed by the experience, while the observers resumed their meals, satisfied.

Ten minutes later, Adilet came to clear the plates and bowls that covered the small table. "More?" was all she said.

Gasanov swiped at his mouth with his hand. "No, dear lady, I have had enough, though I must say that in all my travels, which have been many, I have not had my table set with better food."

The woman grunted. "You did not make use of our dried spices. Is something wrong with them?"

"No, there is not," Gasanov said. "I was simply too excited to get to them. Tell me about this mixture."

"It is the dried version of the sauce you see in the clay jar that we sell to other villages," Adilet explained. "We use it mostly to take with us when we travel, but it makes a good table dressing. Try it next time."

"And what of the fiery liquid that graced my food? From where does it come?" Gasanov demanded.

"Right here, of course," replied the woman, insulted. "Do you think we buy the things you eat? There is no market for many kilometers. What is on your table, we make."

"Then tell me what it is, how it is made," said Gasanov, "and perhaps I will give you a German knife at a spectacular price."

The reply was curt. "You will leave this village without a sale, knife peddler. My husband's blades meet all our needs. Why don't you have more mare's milk and relax?"

The women and children had left the inn, and only the men remained to drink and sort out the world's problems. Gasanov had been delivered a jug of *koumiss* and sat alone in the corner of the lodge sipping from a clay cup. Smoke began to fill the room, and the voices rose. Emboldened by the mare's milk, Gasanov decided to mix with the locals. Dressed surreptitiously in his trader's garb and beard and convinced of his own façade, he ambled over to the local men.

"Forget the government's price controls!" and, "If I see another ministry flack, I'll shorten his legs!" were some of the protestations Gasanov overheard.

"Salutations, comrades," he said by way of an introduction. "Might I join this lively discussion?" While he felt confident, he wobbled noticeably as he crossed the room.

"Your comrades, we are not, traveler," spoke the largest of the men. "We are the proud men of the Tien Shan Mountains, whom not even the hordes of Genghis Khan could subdue. You are obviously a soft-skinned merchant from the city. Which?"

"I am from Osh," responded Gasanov, "and I am traveling the countryside selling knives of the finest German quality."

"Then you have traveled far for nothing," said the monstrous man, whose ears hung like steaks on the sides of his head. "We craft fine blades of our own. I am the town's forger and the owner of this inn."

Gasanov realized with whom he was dealing but was nonplussed, as knives were not what he cared about. "Very well," he said. "Then let us speak of other things. I will try and sell no cutlery here."

"Then what, merchant?" said the Buntun man. "What shall we speak of?"

"Food!" said Gasanov. He immediately sensed eyes narrowing around the room. "And drink! And the hunt!" he added to soften the mood.

Murmurs of agreement came from several of the men. When Gasanov ordered enough jugs of mare's milk for everyone in the room, a cheer went up among the village's men.

"Very well merchant from Osh, we will speak of these other things," said Buntun. "What do you hunt?"

With the village horde now in his pocket, Gasanov entertained them with tales of hunting valor he had seen only in old Soviet training and ministry propaganda films. He sat in the center of a circle, surrounded by listeners. The *koumiss* flowed, and he received a few healthy slaps on the back. An hour later, he felt he had sufficiently convinced these hard, suspicious men of his authenticity.

"And what good is hunting a mountain stag if you cannot cook it?" he said in segue.

A collective assenting grunt came from the tables around him.

"The food of this village is among the best I've ever had," continued Gasanov. He was addressing one particularly glassy-eyed candidate directly in front of him. "How is it that I have traveled across this country and find the best in all of it right here in Dostuk?"

"You are fortunate enough, merchant, to have experienced the Fire of the Valley," blurted the man.

"And what exactly is the Fire of the Valley?" Gasanov asked.

The large hand of Nazaat Buntun clamped the other Kyrgyz man's shoulder, causing him to wince and go limp. "Ozmat here is an overzealous fellow," he said. "He gets himself into trouble sometimes. Tell us more about yourself, merchant."

Sensing the need for a diversion, Gasanov launched into the speech he had prepared that would further convince these suspicious nomads of his authenticity.

"I grew up in the kitchens of Osh, by my father's side, a cook. I became a man working in the famous market there and tasted the world's foods. My specialty became the cutlery chefs use to ply their trade. I have traveled across this entire country eating in its kitchens, and I have heard the Fire of the Valley whispered in hushed tones by cooks and lovers of food. Now perhaps I have found its origin, yes?"

"You have found an inn in a small village in the valley of the Naryn River, merchant, nothing more. My wife cooks what she is given to cook with, and that is all," said Buntun, growing suspicious.

The extreme satisfaction after his meal, combined with an entire jug of koumiss, threw Gasanov over the edge. He stood.

"I know this is the origin of the Fire of the Valley," he announced, "and I have come to claim it for the Ministry of Agriculture and proud people of Kyrgyzstan!"

He finished with an exaggerated wave of his arm, which knocked his Genghis Khan-lookalike mustache just enough out of place to expose him. As he stood before the men of Dostuk with his arm outstretched, awaiting a response, Gasanov realized he was finished by the circle of narrowed eyes he now faced. And, a dozen shining blades pointed at him, no doubt forged by his host.

The Kyrgyz man took a long sip of the salty-sweet margarita in Santa Fe. "They strapped me to my donkey, tied up like a chicken, and pointed it west, back toward Osh. They kept all my knives. It took the beast two full days to reach the next village."

"So, you didn't actually find the source, nor even evidence of the existence of this new pepper variety supposedly unique to Kyrgyzstan," said Max. "I don't understand what all the fever is about, Gasanov. There's more you're not telling me. Out with it."

"Isn't their response enough to convince you that I had found the source, Max?" pleaded Gasanov, "That these villagers would kill to keep their prize secret, as I nearly proved?"

Max tried to connect the dots, and Gasanov kept things vague, either by cultural divide, innate treachery, or fear. Something wasn't adding up. Other diners gorged themselves, talking loudly and being tourists.

"Gasanov, why did two goons try to blow up my store and Gus? So you found some good hot sauce," Max said, getting more and more agitated. "Get over it. *Why is the Kyrgyz mafia after us?*"

"Shhhhhhhhh, Max!" squeaked Gasanov, gesturing nervously for Max to calm down. "Why must you display these outbursts? There is no need to arouse suspicion!"

"Then fill in the puzzle, Gasanov," Max said, "before I start shooting tequila and telling all of Santa Fe what's going on."

"Alright, alright, Max," said Gasanov, who had broken out in a cold sweat. "But please, you must control yourself. Much is at stake here."

After returning from his failed mission to Dostuk, Gasanov had immediately reported his experience to the Minister of Agriculture in the capital, Bishkek, and his opinion that the villagers in Dostuk were knowledgeable about the location of a new, or yet undiscovered, strain of chile pepper unique to their country. They no longer had to steal and try to appropriate varieties from other countries. Gasanov was mystified when the Minister told him not to waste any more valuable ministry time on a foolish treasure hunt and was promptly switched over to the livestock division.

"It was then I realized that the Minister of Agriculture, my respected superior, could not be trusted. He had been bought off," said Gasanov. "By whom, I did not immediately know."

Using his many contacts, Gasanov had the Minister trailed. Three days later, the Kyrgyz Minister of Agriculture altered his usual path home. The tail remarked that the man had sent his driver off early. He then boarded an electric trolley across town, disembarking across from the central train station. It was not long before a black vintage Lincoln Continental with tinted windows picked him up and sped him away. The tail, a somewhat questionable man himself, recognized the sedan driver as someone in the employ of the notorious mafia boss Ruslan Bakiyev.

"Great. And now the Kyrgyz mafia wants the Fire of the Valley all to itself," said Max, more confused than angry. "As a cash crop to control. If it even exists. And you've brought them here, to me. This will not end well, Gasanov. For you, I mean."

"I did not know they would send those bad men!" whined Gasanov. "I came to enlist the aid of your own Department of Agriculture! They had security escort me out of the building. Then I had to find you, my only hope. Bakiyev was never in the picture until just before I came here. He sent his men to scare me away from pursuing this." He was now highly agitated, gulping his margarita. "Max, please, let's get out of this place. I need air!"

Max needed air too, so they walked in silence, and a warm, dry breeze accompanied them through the old town and up to historic Canyon Road. It was a late spring evening, and the cottonwood trees bloomed lush and green, their rustling leaves making hypnotic music. A perfect evening for gallery-hopping, which Canyon Road was known for, but their mood was dark. Gasanov was miserable, kicking stones in the road, his hands thrust into his pockets.

Max had been in more than one dicey situation in his life, but his easygoing charm, quick reflexes, and a healthy dose of good karma had kept him mostly out of trouble and in one piece. He'd been in a few jails, held mostly under false pretenses or by corrupt officials expecting bribes, but had never knowingly broken the law. There was that one time in Rosarito Beach in Baja, though. He had no way of knowing that woman was married. In Mexico, married women who happened to be sipping tequila alone in hotel bars were off-limits, especially if betrothed to the local police chief.

However, the prospect of dealing with trained bad guys was disconcerting. These thugs were in the business of making bad things happen to people. How far would they go? Max played out the infinite number of scenarios that could develop from a confrontation with these nefarious fellows, as guys usually do. He had decided not to tell the Laguna Beach Police what he knew about the store explosion. Why? If he thought hard enough about it, it would have been because his sense of impending adventure got the best of him. Now, he would have a hard time getting anyone in law enforcement to believe him.

He knew several tough hombres from his travels but wasn't the kind of guy to ask for help. What would he say? That he needed a bodyguard? He realized that he'd have to find a solution independently and decided to break the silence.

"Nickolai, how far out on a limb are you? Are you doing this alone? Without help? Is there anyone you trust? What are we up against?"

"We?" asked Gasanov, noting the use of his first name. "Perhaps I am not your enemy anymore, Mr. Max?"

"I don't think you're capable of putting together an espionage operation against the U.S. government with the intent to pilfer agricultural information, and I don't think you intend me harm. But you will lie and deceive to achieve your ends. Plus, you have dragged me into something out of your control, and I need to get the control back."

It was not the response from Max for which Gasanov had hoped.

They strode, side by side, up the meandering path of Canyon Road, lit now by bright art gallery windows. Gasanov jammed his hands into his pockets, obviously troubled. His cowboy hat was too large and fell onto his nose, and to Max, he looked like a child in a costume.

Gasanov pushed his hat back up. "That I am alone here in America and acting without support is now obvious. I have been putting all my will and effort into this matter since I came across some unique peppers in the Osh Market. I discovered what I believe to be something of great significance to my people, the people I am dedicated to bettering. For many months, I had the support of the Minister of Agriculture, who had been pressing me for years to develop new cash crops for our country. I gathered seeds from around the world to find the ones that would grow in the harsh climate of my country, and none successfully adapted. I collected sauces and spice mixtures to use as models for the products we might develop. This is how I found you, Max."

"Found me? How?" demanded Max, shocked.

"The Kyrgyz Ministry of Agriculture has been a client of Little's House of Fire for two years," said Gasanov, even more surprised. "We have purchased your complete collection of products through your website. Did you not know?"

Max didn't handle the order fulfillment of his products, which were sent straight from the Laguna Canyon warehouse. He knew, of course, that he had customers from around the world. Max also realized that some of those customers bought his products to replicate them, so his recipes and processes were kept secret. He gave his Mexican co-owners a significant share of the company for their loyalty and confidentiality.

One buffoon in Florida had gone so far as to approach Max's Costa Rican partners with the intent of creating his own, cheaper version of Mocha Lava. Burt Hornby offered them a considerable payoff. But his slippery sales pitch and bad cologne raised the Costa Ricans' suspicions, and they immediately alerted Max back in Laguna. Three days later, Max drove directly into the man's Orlando warehouse, where he was bottling cheap leftover sauce from another producer after watering it down. In the bed of Max's pickup truck was a 55-gallon drum of Mocha Lava Sauce.

"I have something for you from Costa Rica, Burt," Max said after walking right into the man's dingy, messy office.

Thinking it was the first installment of product from a deal he never intended to make right on, the man jumped from his desk to inspect the goods. As Max opened the lid to the drum, Hornby peered down inside as spicy sauce scents filled the room.

"Smells dee-lish," said the man. "When do I get the rest?"

"Well, don't you want to taste it first?" asked Max.

"Sure, why not?" replied the slippery Burt.

Max clamped him by the ear, twisting the lobe just enough for the man to shriek in pain. He then forced the man's entire head into the barrel of Mocha Lava and let him percolate for a few seconds. He brought him up, sputtering, and sent him down again for another round.

Once released, the poor fool lay sprawled on the floor, flopping like a fish and bawling like a terrified mule. Max then grabbed him by his collar, holding him close to his face. "You try and horn in on my turf, pal, and your entire world will feel like your head does right now."

He then kicked over the barrel and let the contents spread across the man's office, filling it with potent pepper fumes. With that, he left Orlando and drove home to Laguna, making a few spicy stops along the way. Word had gotten out, and people knew not to try and get in Max's business. Having an entire ministry of a foreign country working to deconstruct his products was another story, however. Possibly backed up by the Kyrgyz mafia. Things were becoming convoluted.

The quick thinking that had aided Max throughout his life kicked into gear. He stopped and turned directly to Gasanov, looking him in the eye.

"Here is what is going to happen, Nickolai. You have one opportunity to achieve your goal. You and I are going to be partners. But to have this occur, you will be my subordinate, and you will do as I say. We're going to have to combine our efforts to solve this dilemma and get the forces flowing back in our direction."

"Partners? For this, I am most ready, Max," said Gasanov with delight.

Wondering what his hasty decision would mean for the future and witnessing the Kyrgyz man's response, Max suddenly craved clarity. He needed the sanctuary of a bar. And good tequila.

"Follow me. We're going to see Genovevo at El Farol."

The restaurant and bar in the building that housed El Farol on Canyon Road had been operating since 1835. It was among Max's regular haunts when in Santa Fe, and the people there knew him well. Needing to gain some perspective on the events unfolding in his world, some grounding, he knew he could find some peace, and rare tequila, at its bar.

Two bars in two days, Max thought as he worked his way across the room, headed for the only empty barstools. It was typical when he was running from something or when the world outside was getting crazy. Both were at play here, and the cocoon of the El Farol, Max thought, would help. But then, he still had his new partner to deal with.

"What a wonderful place," said Gasanov. "I will like it here."

The low, timber-beamed ceiling and soft, adobe walls painted with El Virgen de Guadeloupe's murals enclosed what was for Max the perfect sanctuary. For Gasanov, it was the ultimate image of western America. The bartender, Amber, had served Max on previous visits, so she knew what he wanted.

"Looks like a rare tequila night, Max," she said with a smile. "Word has it that your world is a little wacky right now. That right?"

"Just wackier than normal. But it's all good. Or soon will be. Right, Nickolai?"

"You betcha, partner!" Gasanov crowed.

Amber raised an eyebrow at the would-be cowboy but offered him a drink anyway.

"I'll have what he's having," said Gasanov, with John Wayne swagger.

The bar was full but not crowded, being a bit before the dinner rush. Scores of tequilas lined the shelves, as El Farol was known as one of the country's best tequila bars. Max had two solid meals in his belly and felt ready to make the comfortable place his home for the night. The small room had the low-key energy that all genuinely good bars have. Gasanov sat smiling, taking in the scene, pleased to be bellied up to a western saloon.

"Let's have the Fortaleza Reposado to start, Amber, if we may," said Max. He planned to sit and sip and allow the evening to take its course. "And tell chef Genovevo I'm here too if you would. I've got a few chile-head things I want to run by him. Thanks."

With a nod, Amber went off to the kitchen.

Gasanov was inquisitive. "Max, what is tequila? It's allure?"

"Now that, Nickolai, is something I'm happy to talk about," replied Max, settling into his barstool.

Crisscrossing the globe in pursuit of peppers and sauce had afforded Max intimate knowledge of a few delectable things. The distribution of the plants, spices, and sauces he sought often found him in Latin America, and he had become quite familiar and fond of the beverages and drinking customs there. Tequila ranked high among Max's areas of expertise, and his passion for fine, aged, and rare tequilas had opened many doors, brokered many deals, and rescued him from several sticky situations. He was extraordinarily knowledgeable of the myriad indigenous cultures of Latin America and their rituals and reasonably well-versed in the world's women, particularly the Latin kind. Although the more he interacted with them, the less Max realized he actually knew. He had learned to accept that with each encounter, he was learning about women again for the first time, for they were all so vastly, wonderfully different.

"Well, since you asked, Tequila happens to be a town in the Jalisco state of Mexico, where people in the 16th century began to distill the roasted hearts of the agave plant. The *jimadores*, or harvesters, come from generations of families who have done this very same thing, by hand, for hundreds of years. I've been there for the harvest and worked in the fields, hacking out the center of the agave, which they call 'pineapples,' with a special long-handled knife called a 'coa.' Roasting the agave hearts turns the starches to sugar, and then the juices are pressed out, fermented, and distilled. Sipping tequila where it's grown and made is a remarkable thing."

Some years back, Max took a trip to Mexico to meet with a botanical research team searching for the origin of *Capsicum annuum*, the pepper family that includes bell peppers, jalapeno, Anaheim, and cayenne. Besides the Amazon basin and the Andes mountains, Eastern Mexico and the Yucatan had long been believed to be the birthplace of several chiles - or where they were first cultivated. In contrast to the other main staples, corn, squash, and beans, which originated in the area, various chile pepper varieties have much more biological diversity in the Yucatan. This proved that the seeds had traveled less far and were less homogeneous, suggesting they were closer to their place of origin. It was the kind of news that got Max to throw some things in a duffle bag and catch the next plane. He wanted to be at ground zero when a species' birth was discovered and taste the fruit.

On the way, he stopped to check on the status of a new, tequila-based sauce he was developing with the Camarena brothers at La Escondida Distillery in El Arenal. They had agreed to co-develop the sauce but needed him to choose which tequila would be the new product's base. As it was harvest time, Max had been invited to experience firsthand the process of making tequila. He was met at the airport by Felix Camarena, and they drove together the 40 miles to the estate.

"Have you ever seen the agave harvest, Senor Max?" asked Felix.

"No, I haven't," said Max, "But I sure have been on the receiving end of your efforts enough times, Felix. I commend your *jimadores*. Your tequila ranks among the best I've ever had."

Choosing which tequila would be the base for their sauce took many days. Max was invited to stay in the estate house and be part of the extended family during the harvest. There were elaborate, hours-long meals and many nights tasting tequilas straight out of the oak casks in which they aged. Desiring to solidify a relationship with the

Camarenas, Max worked in the fields and learned the art of harvesting the agave hearts. Working with the *jimadores*, the idea came to him to blend in the sweet agave pulp as an ingredient in the sauce they would make.

Fully ten days and much tequila later, their El Arenal Roasted Agave Fire Sauce was born. In addition to tequila and agave pulp, it employed achiote, the rich, orange Yucatecan spice, and roasted *Xcatik* chiles, also from there. But Max had missed the research team in Merida. Fortunately, no earth-shattering chile pepper discoveries were made, and Max made a promise to go down and conduct further research.

Max slid a bucket glass of gold-tinted Fortaleza Reposado in front of Gasanov. "Take just enough to cover your taste buds, then let it sit a minute. The strong burn of the alcohol will diminish, and you'll find the taste of the agave remains, smoky and even sweet."

This the Kyrgyz did, with extreme concentration and force of will. Gasanov looked straight ahead as he took the first swallow and then closed his eyes as he tilted his head back. He took a long, exaggerated breath through his nose and then swallowed. There was no jerking reaction to the alcohol, no wide-open eyes, no sputtering.

"I am amazed," said Gasanov. "There is no liquor in all Central Asia which compares to this. I could sense the agave pineapples and the roasting fires. I even saw you in the fields, proudly engaged in the harvest, Max. I will have more."

They sat together, quietly sipping the smooth, smoky golden tequila as Amber brought out hot tortilla chips and a small bowl of pureed sauce.

"Genovevo is busy in the kitchen, Max, but he says he'll come out when he can," she said. "In the meantime, he says he wants you to try his Ten-Pepper Mélange and for you to guess which ones he used. If you do, the bar tab is free."

This was the kind of challenge Max could not possibly resist, what made chile heads chile heads. Knowing it would take time and concentration to deconstruct Genovevo's sauce, he ordered more tequila and asked for an entire bottle of the sauce. Amber returned with a squirt bottle full of the mixture.

"He says it's 'way hot,' so don't touch anything you don't want on fire, Max."

This was meant more for Max's guest than himself, for Max had learned early on that the heat in chiles travels; touch a cut habanero and then touch your face, and you'll be begging for mama.

Amber's warning had given Max a clue he needed to begin deconstructing the sauce. He dipped a spoon into the liquid, and taking it out, looked at it closely. There were flecks of yellow, three shades of red and orange, green and purple, which would be the chiles.

There were also bits of black, meaning that Genovevo had toasted some of the ingredients over an open flame. Bits of white were onion and garlic, while anything green and leafy signified fresh herbs, probably cilantro. There had to be a base liquid to hold the ingredients, which in bottled sauces was usually vinegar, to act as a preservative. However, in a fresh sauce made in a gourmet restaurant kitchen, it meant something else. He saw small oil pools, which looked just a shade green; *cilantro oil*, he deduced. And with his nose, he caught a few other clues: a hint of black pepper, which tended to mellow other spices, and fruit. Max was getting the distinct note of strawberries as he passed the full spoon under his nose.

He then put the spoon in his mouth and left it there to let the ingredients do their work on his palate. Anyone else would have felt their senses overloaded by the cacophony of flavors and heat sensations that bombarded Max's taste buds. Still, he had learned from countless tastings to go slowly, to separate each level and wave as they came. Gasanov and Amber watched him closely, and others at the bar began to take notice of the guy tasting scorching sauce with a spoon in his mouth. Max settled into a trance, shutting out all other stimuli, and felt his senses come alive. He separated the herbs, fruits, vegetables, and black pepper while the mixture still sat on his tongue. There was no vinegar; the base Genovevo employed was simply strawberry juice and cilantro oil. *Nice*, thought Max, *an unexpected disguise to all the savory and spice.* He tilted his head back just enough to let everything slowly pass all his taste sensors and down his throat. There were fresh chiles of different acidity and spice level. Some were sweet, others more vegetal. Others were either young or more fully ripened. Still, others roasted and blistered in flame. For several moments he didn't breathe or move at all. Then, he took in a long deep breath and held it before slowly breathing out. Again, he sat in a state of trancelike stillness for a full minute before opening his eyes.

"Aji Amarillo, Filius Blue, Chocolate Habanero, Black Cuban, and Hot Banana," he announced.

A cheer filled the bar. "And," he held up a hand for quiet. "Bolivian Rainbow, Dong Xuan, Goat Horn, Little Nubian...and..."

As he searched for the identity of the last chile, a movement and flash of color down the hall by the bar caught his eye. The tasting of hot peppers always keened his senses. He caught a glimpse of the two over-dressed cowboys from the La Fonda as they each tossed something round toward the bar. As he started to yell, the room was shattered by a concussive blast, a flash of light, and then smoke. Three long moments of silence were followed by mayhem. People screamed and scattered. Grey smoke clouded the air as glass broke and chairs toppled.

Max was instantly blinded by facing the blast, and the concussion had knocked him over off his barstool. He lay on the ground of the bar, swiping at his eyes to make them see.

Through the smoke, he heard Gasanov shrieking, "Stay away! No! You cannot do this!"

In his temporary blindness, he heard grunting and heavy footsteps. The moment he focused, he saw a shiny cowboy boot just in front of his face as he lay on the floor. It had a smiling iguana embroidered on the toe. He grabbed it with both hands and twisted as hard as he could.

The man was large and fell to the ground with a roar. With his free foot, he swung a kick at Max's head. Fueled by a rush of adrenaline, Max rolled as the hard tip of the boot whooshed by his face, barely missing his temple, and he saw the grime on its sole as it passed by his ear. He rolled again and saw another man with his arms locked around Gasanov, whose eyes read terror as he was dragged across the room. Then, at the foot of the bar, Max saw the fallen squirt bottle of Chef Genovevo's Ten-Pepper Mélange. In one well-calibrated sweep, he grabbed the bottle and leaped on his attacker's back. The larger man jerked and swung his arms backward, trying to dislodge Max, rodeo style. Max clamped the man's neck with one arm and used his other to jam the plastic bottle into the brute's nose. He squeezed it hard.

In his terror, the man bucked Max to the floor on his back, screaming and clawing at his face. He turned in slow motion and looked down at Max as he howled. Ten Pepper Sauce ran out of both nostrils and oozed from the attacker's mouth. His eyes were more red than white, and Max could make out the veins in his eyeballs, which seemed about to burst. Enraged, the cowboy swung another vicious kick at his head. Max recoiled, avoiding it, and scrambled painfully to his feet. He was greeted by a flung barstool, which broke across his face. As he staggered backward, he felt himself falling, and the room went black.

Max rocked back and forth, hugging his knees as he sat under the ancient oak. Images flooded his mind, pulling him away from the present. He could taste a salty breeze and saw the fields of chiles stretch out clearly before him, but his awareness was elsewhere, distant. Then a clear voice broke the spell.

"So, what happened, Max? What did you do?" It was a voice he knew, had heard before. In Louisiana, Lilah beckoned him back to the pepper fields of Jesus Jones, where his past and present collided.

"Do where?" he responded, enveloped in his fog.

"In Santa Fe!" she said, "What happened?"

Max was still weak from passing out, and now, having been revived by Lilah's splash of icy water, was disoriented and his mind doing strange things. The wound on his head throbbed, and he was suddenly overcome by exhaustion.

"I think our friend here needs a hot bath and some rest, Lilah. Let's get him sorted out, and we can hear his story later," Max heard old Jesus Jones say.

Max Little was raised in Long Beach, California, in a tidy house not far from the ocean near Signal Hill. His father inherited a small auto repair shop from his father, who had retired from Southern California's momentous aircraft industry after World War II. Max's first vehicle was a 1955 GMC pickup inherited from his grandfather at age twelve, which he worked on until he could drive it at sixteen. Max grew up hanging around the barely surviving business – his father had not inherited his grandfather's industriousness – and as a result, he was raised as much by the colorful characters that rotated through the operation as his own parents. Hippified Vietnam vets, old-timers from the black community in Inglewood, tough Samoans from Hawaiian Gardens, and extended communities of Latinos were his family friends, evidence of a changing Southern California.

Max was a mixture of European nationalities, mostly French, with some Croatian and Scottish on his father's side. His mother, a teacher, was a vibrant woman who imparted a keen interest in geography and maps to the young Max. Cartography of all types covered the small house's walls, hand-me-downs from his mother's school district, and a Polynesian theme colored its décor. Strings of lights spanned the small but well-used backyard, an oasis in the homogenized suburban sprawl. Max spent hours studying the charts, drawing pictures in his mind of the places he learned to identify. More tattered and worn than the rest, one depicted the Mongol Empire of Genghis Khan and the routes of the Great Silk Road.

Max's father was better at celebrating than working, seeming to find any occasion to throw a party or backyard barbeque. Every holiday, American or otherwise, became the catalyst to dust off the tiki bar and fire up the small suburban backyard's charcoal grill. Max got a unique education at these events that opened his eyes to a larger world than he experienced in Long Beach. There were luaus with roasted pigs, Cinco de Mayo parties, Southern barbeque cookoffs, moon launches, presidential debates, ball games, and birthdays. The auto shop staff brought their extended families, making the Little's home a colorful place, and Max was exposed to a variety of cultures no school could provide.

Vietnam and World War II vets told stories of the wars and brought along with them the flavors of Europe and Southeast Asia learned from tours of duty, pointing out on the house's maps the locations of momentous events and where foods originated. With their extended families, the Latinos always brought *comida*, made in their home kitchens: tamales, rellenos, tacos, menudos, and ceviches. Max learned from them about the Incan, Mayan, and Aztec civilizations and their lasting mark upon the lands they inhabited. The Samoans traveled in large groups and were large themselves, tattooed and with sweet island foods. They gave Max his first pukka shell necklace in 1977 and taught him to surf. The Callaways from Inglewood, natives of Mississippi, brought barbeque and stories of the old South, slAcadian, and the Civil War. Every famous battle from that struggle was marked with a pin on Max's big United States map.

Max grew up in this environment of shared ethnicities and cultures, possessing an understanding of the world much deeper than the kids at school or in his neighborhood. The knowledge gained from these experiences made Max a wise-beyond-his-years, easygoing young man who found interest in many things. Music was always a vibrant presence in his younger years, and the Seventies soundtrack that played through his adolescence became the soundtrack of his life. Though they did not play an instrument, his parents knew the lyrics to any song from that decade that carried a harmony. Max knew every verse of Don McLean's eight-minute-and-thirty-six-second anthem "American Pie." Poetic singer-songwriters crooned daily, even when there was no celebration. Max's parents taught him every song by Harry Chapin, Jim Croce, Gordon Lightfoot, Bill Withers, Joni Mitchell, and Simon and Garfunkel. The Samoans introduced him to island music from Cecilio and Kapono and reggae from Bob Marley. He learned Otis Redding and Muddy Waters and blues and zydeco from the Callaways, and the multigenerational Latino families brought him Norteño and salsa music and ballads by Ruben Blades and Juan Gabriel. He became an excellent dancer by default, a skill carried through life that helped him easily integrate into communities around the world. The mixtapes he created and albums he collected stayed in his truck and home, played on his parents' old tape deck and turntable.

Max developed a taste for ethnic food that kept his mother busy when there were no backyard parties. He carried salsa and tamales and samosas and chutney and gumbo in his lunchbox at school before other kids had ever heard of them. And he learned to cook and handle a knife, how to sauté and grill, by the time he was twelve. He was also agile and strong, surfing Seal Beach from the age of ten, accompanied by the Samoans. Long Beach was becoming a rough town in the Seventies, and Max had a large extended family who looked out for him and taught him to be tough. The Samoans showed him how to remain focused, handle himself in tight situations, outsmart adversaries, and stay above the fray. He fought when he had to but never started a fight.

Once his father walked away from the shop and his family in 1986, the fun times ended, his mother darkened, and the music stopped. Max was on his own in the world.

Max awoke fourteen hours later to the licks of a beagle. No, *two* beagles were licking his face, he realized. He was in an upstairs room in Jesus Jones's southern farm-style house, with open windows and a soft breeze blowing through the curtains. It was the next day in Louisiana, and the beagles had waited at the foot of his bed until they got bored and decided to revive him. He missed Clyde, but these were good dogs, and they had taken to him immediately.

A hot bath steamed down the hall, and he soaked in it for a full hour before throwing on fresh jeans and a faded Traveling Wilburys t-shirt. The now-familiar rows of pepper plants stretched across the horizon, and the air felt lazy and peaceful. Time progressed at a slower pace here, he thought, and the place had a magical sensation to it. Downstairs, Jones and Lilah sat at the kitchen table, where a hot cup of chicory coffee sat waiting for him.

"You sure are a deep sleeper, Max," said Jones. "I guess you had a bunch of highway and a few explosions to sleep off."

Max noticed that Lilah was regarding him with a wary, questioning look. "Yeah, I guess I am a little stretched from it all. Things are stacking up, and I've gotta figure them out. But put me in a pickup on the open road, and I'll never be tired," Max said, projecting nonchalance.

Glancing at Lilah, he knew the time had come to finish the story of Santa Fe.

"While the bar at El Farol was a big mess, it turns out the explosions were made by cheap fireworks you can get in Mexico. One flash and one smoke, a buck a piece, and I fell off the stool trying to get out of the way. No one else saw the two fake cowboys except me since they went right back out the rear door. The bartender stayed ducked behind the bar through the entire thing, and everyone else cleared out as soon as the fireworks went off. Santa Fe PD was there in minutes, and of course, asked me how my head got cracked open," Max said, then paused in thought.

With a shudder, he continued. "I told them I slipped on some of Genovevo's pepper sauce. There was a pool of it where it had drained out of the guy's nose. When it became clear that only I had seen the thugs, I told the cops that it must've been a couple of drunken convention-goers. I had seen that the International Brotherhood of Plumbers was in town, two thousand strong, and figured there would be some hijinks associated with a bunch of hard-drinking tradesmen. Turns out I was right. They bought it."

"But why, Max?" implored Lilah, "Why didn't you tell them?"

"That's what I spent many hours and many miles of road trying to figure out. I mean, they kidnapped Gasanov, right in front of me. And yet, I got a strong feeling that they weren't out to hurt me, only to get Gasanov and perhaps scare me off. Maybe get information. The only reason I got the barstool to the head was the hot sauce injection I gave that thug, you know. You should have seen his face." Max shook his head. "When I asked the police about a man named Gasanov that was sitting next to me at the bar, they ran a check, and nobody had a record of him ever being in the country. It's like he didn't even exist, so I couldn't report him missing. The whole thing got written off as a plumber's prank."

Realizing he was lucky no one in Santa Fe could officially tie the events in Laguna Beach and at the El Farol together, Max had retreated to his room at the La Fonda for some much-needed rest. Of course, there was the very distinct possibility that the Ring of Fire folks would get wind of another explosion occurring in Max's vicinity. Josie and his other chile head friends would be distraught, but he would have to deal with them later. On his nightstand, he had found a hurriedly handwritten note. It was in Gasanov's script.

Max, pepper partner. If anything should happen to me as we continue our journey, it will be at the hands of those in my country that seek to thwart my efforts to better my people. There is a man named Jesus Jones in your state of Louisiana. Go find him.

After a few stitches and some new clothes, Max called Chuck DeWindt at the university. He wanted to find out more about Jesus Jones and the new peppers he was growing and figured it might prove promising to find out what he could in Louisiana. He felt there may be answers there yet had no idea what to do about Gasanov, and how he knew about Jones.

"Jesus Jones is pretty much as old-school a pepper farmer as there is in this country, Max," said DeWindt. "His farm goes back many generations, and he's in the heart of the Louisiana pepper territory. Funny thing is, the Jones farm has been organic since day one and has produced the most consistent fruit in the entire region. One of the universities is interested in what Jones is doing and sent a professor and Ph.D. researcher to conduct a study. Rumor is that Jones is working with her to grow heirloom varieties and cultivating some new strains, top-notch stuff. No one knows how he's managed to collect all these new varieties. A visit down there will get your sniffer activated, Max, if I know you."

Max studied his coffee as he recounted the conversation to Lilah and Jones in Louisiana.

"So, here I am, talking to the two of you, and this mystery keeps getting weirder. Your work here has generated some outside interest, it appears, Lilah. It seems obvious that Gasanov, or someone he was working with, sent you the seeds in question from Kyrgyzstan, plus probably all the others. Have you planted them?"

Lilah had a startled look on her face. "The latest ones, direct from Kyrgyzstan, have been in the ground a week," she said, "half an acre on the northwest corner of the property. All the others you've been feasting on already. But why me, and why here?"

Max pondered her question. Somehow, Gasanov in Kyrgyzstan had found Lilah and Jones and knew they would cultivate the heirloom seeds.

"Have you published any work to date about what you're doing here? Or perhaps something on developing small farmers?" he asked.

Like Max, Lilah shared a strong belief in cultivating and empowering small farmers. Industrialized agriculture was denuding the land and killing the oceans, she believed. The farmer's markets she had set up in Baton Rouge and Shreveport were among the most popular in the entire state, and the family farmers that benefited from her efforts thrived. While her Ph.D. focus was studying the organic methods and new heirloom varieties on the Jones farm, her master's degree research and professorial curriculum had been on cultivating small organic farmers both in the U.S. and abroad. Lilah's "Blueprint for Success of Small Organic Farming Cooperatives" thesis had been widely distributed in educational and agricultural circles. It spread ubiquitously on the nascent internet, where she enjoyed a much more extensive following than she realized, even overseas.

"Well, yes, I guess I have," Lilah said, "but again, why me?"

Max's deductive reasoning kicked into high gear. "Gasanov told me he'd been buying heirloom seeds and sauces from my website for more than three years, thinking he'd cultivate the different varieties and copy the sauce recipes. But then he discovered that there was a potential heirloom variety right in Kyrgyzstan. Your research on developing small farmers surely would've caught his eye if he looked at ways to develop a local economy. From what I know of him, he probably thought he could get you to do the work that he was unable or afraid to do, given that his ministry had been compromised."

"Well, it worked," Lilah said. "I've already planted them for him, and we'll be cultivating them organically. But I would imagine the soils and growing conditions are substantially different here and in Kyrgyzstan. What could he hope to gain?"

"There's a ton of money in the spicy foods industry, especially here and in Europe," said Max. "Gasanov is hoping to cash in on that for his country, but first, he needs international verification that theirs is unique. That would be big news in the pepper world and have enormous potential. And it's obvious now that others are looking to cash in on it. Those people have kidnapped Gasanov, and I can't begin to imagine where they've taken him."

Jesus Jones had been mostly silent through Max's storytelling but now looked at him with deepening concern.

"Max, I can tell that you're an earnest and thoughtful man. But there is bad juju around this whole thing, and you do not see it. You need help. I think it's high time for you to get some protection and to arm yourself."

Max was startled at Jones's take on the situation. "Hold on. I've never carried a weapon. And I've always figured my way out of things. I'll grant that this situation looks pretty dicey, but I am not going to arm myself. We're talking about vegetables and hot sauce, Jesus."

Jones persisted. "Not arm with weapons, Max. You need armor. And someone watching your back. It's time to start the wheel turning in your direction, man. Lilah, call your Aunt Delphine and tell her to set things up."

Bayou Des Allemands

Southern Louisiana has long been a crossroads of humanity, with races and cultures mixing there for generations. The original inhabitants, the Atakapa, Choctaw, and Chitimacha, saw their territory diminished at the hand of the colonial powers: the British, from the north and east; the Spanish, from the west; and the sea, the French, who ultimately made their base near the mouth of the Mississippi River in 1718, at New Orleans.

Slaves from West Africa began appearing in the Caribbean basin and French Louisiana shortly after, bringing their own culture, language, and traditions. So new was the colony that slaves outnumbered whites two to one by 1732. Louisiana was still a young and evolving society, allowing African culture to flourish, unlike the land under British, Spanish, and later, American control.

The Africans, to survive and retain their own culture, continued their brand of worship and ritual called *voudou* in the *Fon* tongue of West Africa. Based on the worship of animistic entities and ancestors, it employed trance-inducing ceremonies to communicate with spirits. Charms, amulets, and special herb potions were used in these rituals by voodoo priestesses called *Gris-gris*. Over time, elements of Catholicism were incorporated into the rites, as Christianity was forced upon the slave population.

Though Jesus Jones had grown up on Chicago's South Side, he explored and fully embraced the culture and traditions there upon his arrival in Louisiana. He learned that his mother, Iris, the Belizean woman who had worked the pepper fields there for Jones's grandfather, had come from a lengthy line of voodoo priestesses among the slaves in the former British colony.

Jones related this information to Max as they rode east down Louisiana Route 90 in Jones's pickup on their way to a farm outside of Bayou des Allemandes. Lilah rode between them, the beagles in the back, gulping in the air, ears flopping in the wind.

Max noticed that Lilah had been mostly silent during the ride, looking straight ahead at the road, deep in thought. "So, we're going to visit a relative of yours?' he asked gently.

The question reached into her fog and partially pulled her back to the moment.

"You could say that," she said. "Delphine has been part of my family for so long that I've thought of her as my auntie my whole life."

Max turned to look at Lilah as she spoke in a faraway voice, hands folded in her lap, remembering her past. Her green eyes misted as Lilah stared ahead, unblinking, and she continued from within a trance.

"Our family is from outside Des Allemands, here in the bayou, where we've been for generations," she said, wringing her hands. "Not long after I was born, my mother was forced to go to New Orleans to find work after losing our alfalfa farm to the local bank. Times were hard, and my father, much older than her, died of a broken spirit the following year. I don't even remember him."

She sighed deeply and continued. "Mama was young then and on her own, and the community that adopted her was itself a collection of orphans, outcasts, mystics, and misfits. She found work in the voodoo parlors of old New Orleans, where it was practiced as a matter of life, not a tourist attraction, and my childhood became infused with rituals and spirits and spells. Delphine was by then a widely-known voodoo queen. She took Mama in and put her to work collecting herbs, making potions and amulets, and preparing for the ceremonies that Delphine was regularly called upon to perform within the community."

Though she stared out the window, her face softened with a faint smile. "She was highly sought after for her fortune-telling skill and amazingly effective curses, both good and bad. Delphine later said my mother had 'the keen sense' that would someday make her a formidable voodoo queen herself."

At this, Lilah paused, again deep in thought and instantly far away. Jones picked up the tale.

"I met Delphine Anjou in New Orleans, back in '77," he said, "where I had gone to find out what I could about my mother. I went to Belize and was told by people on her island of Caye Caulker that she left the country for New Orleans around 1963 to further her training in voodoo practices. I often went to New Orleans, asking questions and seeking clues about a voodoo queen named Iris from Belize. It's a tight-knit community there among the voodoo practitioners, suspicious of outsiders. I'd almost given the whole thing up when finally, in a bar in the Algiers quarter, I met an ancient Creole fella who told me to look up a voodoo queen named Delphine in the French Quarter. When I finally found her little apartment, she opened the door and told me not to say a word. She sat me down and looked into my eyes for what seemed like an eternity. 'You must be Iris's son,' she finally said. 'I can see it in your eyes. I've been waiting for you. She was my apprentice but taught me more than she ever learned from me. She spent her life praying and working her magic for you. Before she disappeared, she told me she knew you'd found peace.' She'd returned without warning to her family in Belize, just after I'd gotten to Louisiana. Delphine believed she'd encountered some powerful black magic that spells could not remove."

To Max, hearing this story brought a deepening sense of fondness and empathy for Lilah and Jones, realizing their connection, losing their mothers, and to Delphine. But there was a sadness Lilah evidenced that colored the moment. "What happened to your mother?" he asked her.

Again, she returned to the present with a slight shudder.

"My mother worked in Delphine's parlor for four years and was there the day Jesus showed up at her door," she said. "She decided to become a voodoo queen herself and was undergoing the intricate training under Delphine's tutelage. She would send home the money she earned to help us back in Des Allemands, where my older sister raised my brother and me in a one-bedroom apartment. Then one day, the calls just stopped. A month later, Delphine showed up at our door. She came bearing the news that Mama had died of a fever that the magic could not cure, and she'd come to take care of us. She promised her she would so that mama could die in peace. Delphine helped us reclaim the house, moved in, and we've been family ever since."

Delphine had continued her voodoo practice out of the DeVillier's old house near Bayou des Allemandes, which she bought back from the bank, and paid Lilah's way to college in Baton Rouge. The house turned out to be an ideal setting for Delphine's work. Lilah went on to earn a full scholarship at the University of Louisiana for her graduate degrees in agriculture, agronomy, and botany, then becoming a full professor.

"I owe her everything," she added.

Creoles, like Lilah and her family, were the result of Louisiana's hodgepodge of cultures. Attributed initially to French settlers born in the Americas, the term meant all people of mixed descent in the Louisiana Territories. Lilah alone was a mixture of French, African American, Spanish, and Native American, who carried attributes of all those peoples: strong, soulful, connected to the earth, and a beautiful blending of races and spirits. And while she was open and confident, Max sometimes sensed a closed-off distance that clouded her brightness.

Route 90 wound its way through the LaForce and Grosse Tete bayous of Terrebonne Parish, and the trio passed in silence the miles of moss-covered oaks and mangrove swamps. Max split his mind between what recently occurred in his life and what was to come, especially what awaited on a Bayou des Allemandes farm. In the company of Lilah and Jones, he felt at ease, despite his predicament. They were kindred spirits who had quickly taken a genuine interest in him, even though they had just come into each other's lives.

From among his many world travels, Max had experienced his share of unique cultural experiences. Tribal rituals and rites were familiar to him, and he immersed himself in the cultures of the people he met and cultivated business with, as the purple Bere-Bere tattoo on his arm could attest. He traveled widely in Latin America and the Caribbean, partaking in the savory edible offerings, the cultural and the beautiful. There was ayahuasca in Brazil and peyote in Guatemala, shared with ethnic people. With his Mayan friends in Mexico, he was invited to partake in an ancient Olmec tradition of drinking cacao spiced with the native chiles, vanilla, achiote, and allspice in the state of Tabasco, a recipe and ritual dating back to 1800 BC, a hot chocolate on fire. The Olmec peoples predated the Aztec and the Maya cultures and were among the first humans to domesticate chiles, a ground-zero experience for a chile-head like Max. Nonetheless, he knew he was about to encounter something entirely new and ancient at the end of the dirt road their truck now traveled.

The truck turned onto a side road bordered by a canopy of moss-draped willow and cypress trees that dampened sound and blocked light, creating a thick air of mystery, even dread. No one seemed eager to talk. As they rounded a bend, an opening in the canopy appeared before them. They passed through and into a large clearing, brightened by sun and covered with grass. An old but tidy two-story estate house stood in the middle, encircled by porches, the arbors laced with vines. A trio of massive oaks, preserved obviously for their cover and stately presence, shaded the grounds. Lilah lifted her head and smiled at the sight.

"Home," was all she said.

As they opened the vehicle doors, they were met by the deep baying of hounds. The beagles leaped from the truck's bed, bounding off to be met by a bloodhound and shaggy sheepdog. The ensuing reunion, group chase, and rolls in the grass instantly lightened the dark mood. Max was immediately moved by the homestead's beauty, with cultivated fields stretching out in three directions from behind the house, thick with alfalfa. To the east stretched watery bayou, reflecting the afternoon sun. Thick woods bordered the farm, secluding it from the surrounding world, and the sense of privacy was striking. A stately Creole woman stood on the porch, obviously waiting for them.

"How long have you been standing there, Delphine?" Jones called out. "We didn't tell you when we'd be comin'."

She wore a white, long-sleeved dress, down almost to the ankle, and was barefoot. Her head was wrapped in a green scarf, and she observed the trio smiling warmly.

"I knew when you were coming, Jesus. I could hear your creaky bones a mile off. And Lilah, I saw your cloud come over the horizon, girl."

Delphine waited atop the stairs as Lilah ran into her broad embrace. They held each other tightly for a long time. Jesus followed, and the woman pinched his cheek as she looked into his eyes. "Older, but no wiser," she said to him.

Sheepishly out of place, Max remained at the foot of the stairs, hands in his pockets and kicking the wood. "Come here, young fellow," Delphine demanded. She spoke with a distinct bayou patois, infused with French. "Let me take a look at you."

As Max climbed the stairs, she held out both her hands for him to take. She clasped them firmly, and her gaze stopped him unexpectedly. She had intense green eyes and caramel skin, with arms that jiggled when she spoke, and wore a gold amulet much like Lilah's. Her teeth were perfect and white, and her voice forceful yet reassuring. Max figured she must be near seventy. She exhibited a vibrant, palpable power, and Max became aware of his inability to break her gaze. For what felt like a full minute, Delphine held him there. He had the sensation not of being judged but of being explored. The green fields at the edges of his sight collapsed inward until only Delphine's face occupied his view. She closed her eyes and breathed deeply. Then she looked at his hands, turning them over and back again. She smiled just a bit as she looked again into his eyes.

"You are one wildcat," she said, "a wildcat on the run. This cat requires claws. And his tree needs roots. Let's have a mint julep."

They sat on the spacious porch looking out through the giant oaks and across the fields while Jones and Lilah updated Delphine on the goings-on at the farm. Max absorbed the view and serenity that the site exuded, and the relaxation of the minty julep was distinctly enhanced. While the other two talked, however, he could feel Delphine's gaze upon him. Inevitably, the story turned to Max's arrival and the strange tale he had told.

"Food is an amazing thing," Delphine said after Max had related his version of the events. "It fuels life and brings us all together. Wars have been fought over it. Food is history, and food is the future. Along with our traditions, it's the one thing that helps us remember where we came from. No wonder people are getting passionate about your peppers."

She stopped and took a long sip of her julep, and the opening compelled Max to add his insight.

"I've eaten all over the world and in the company of many unique people," he began. "I've been part of growing and harvesting crops that not only feed people but make them whole and proud. I've eaten food in the bush and dined in palaces. And because of food, amazing people and experiences have populated my life. It's also introduced some of the craziest nut jobs on the planet and sparked my unique global adventure. Chile heads or not, spicy food makes for good company."

Max felt that summed it up adequately and leaned back in the wicker porch chair.

At this, Lilah turned to Max, and for the first time in a long while, looked directly at him.

"But Max," she said, obviously confused, "how can you reconcile this with the recent events going on in your life? Is your passion for what you love blinding you to the obvious threats that you face? I feel the strong pull of the earth, too, but I know Mother Nature and passionate foodies won't throw bombs at my house. Why the nonchalance? Maybe it's something else you're running from. Or into."

Her probing question threw Max for a loop, unlike her usually carefree demeanor. All their eyes were upon him as he stared into his glass. He hadn't factored in the wave of emotion that arose as he spent more time in Lilah's presence. Was it genuine interest he registered from her, or simply curiosity? Typically, he would either charm his way from the spotlight or duck out. Now, in the company of her powerful aunt and in her family home, he felt weak and confused - out of place, wondering if he should be there at all. Max looked out over the lush fields and understood it was necessary to look deeper than he had before. He found that he desperately wanted Lilah, and all of them, to know what was hidden in his depths, including him. Unused to having his emotions publicly on display, it was becoming clear that something unearthed had to be explored.

For as long as he could remember, Max had taken care of himself, had worked things out. The day his father left in 1986 to live his Tacoma bar dream, and his mother receded into shadow, he had been on his own, driven by necessity to carve out his place in the world. The adventure and passion Max experienced in the world of his creation defined his life. The living he made was a good one, and his business always grew profitably, but not significantly so. He had been able to care for his mother for years. The nest egg, though small, was getting fatter. He was well-regarded in the fiery foods industry and had walls covered with pictures and characters from adventures in faraway places. People in Laguna said hello to him on the street. The global adventures and growing business filled his time, and soon, years had gone by. Now forty sat fat on his horizon.

As the four of them sat on the porch in Bayou des Allemandes, Max could feel water nearby, in the swamps beyond the thick wood that ringed the farm. The air hung so moistly he could taste it in the breeze. They were deep in the bayou, removed from the chaos outside and he felt his walls receding, much as Lilah had as soon as they arrived. There was a powerful aura to it, the misty and mystical Deep South, wrapping him in its embrace.

Max believed himself as much a ponderer of life as the next guy but had spent most of his life in motion, attached to new projects or adventures since he was forced into manhood at sixteen. Deep thoughts came and went, sorted with a basic understanding of how to live. He always figured the answers to the big questions would come with time and age. Suddenly, Max felt entirely lost, clouds obscuring his future, hiding a coming reckoning. What was it that he ran from? Where was he going?

He closed his eyes and began to trace the course of his life. It played like a frantic, fast-reversing video, stopping abruptly at the day he had come home to find his father's letter. It had been addressed to him rather than his mother, reflecting the man's shame and cowardice, even though he abandoned them both.

Max, I know this is gonna be hard to understand, but I have to leave. My dreams, I guess, lie elsewhere. Turns out I now own a bar in Tacoma. Won it in a card game over in San Pedro last Friday, so I'm headed straight there. Working on engines simply ain't my thing anymore. Your mom's never gonna get it, and I don't have the guts to break it to her, so now you're the man of the house. The shop is yours if you want it, the keys are in the kitchen drawer. Dad.

The shock, anger, and fear born in that moment were quickly buried. Max had just turned sixteen, the only son. He took the rest of the year off high school and immediately worked full-time in the shop. There were bills and a mortgage to pay. He was deeply scarred but never cried. His anger had been channeled into survival, both his and his mom's, for she had crumbled instantly. Her husband was the force, albeit a scattered one, that she had used to feel whole in life, and now she was unable to find her strength in the absence of his charm. Max quickly formed a partnership with the Samoan, the Vet, and the old-timer from Inglewood, with equal shares in the business, and by the time he was eighteen, it was profitable enough that he could step away and take the test for his high school diploma. His share of the business profits helped keep him and his mother in their home and Max out of trouble.

To Max, his response to these events had always been the right ones, and he had survived. His mother was away in a distant place, but she was safe, if unwhole. He had been the man he needed to be and bore that task with quiet dignity and determination. He hoped for a day when he could have his mother back, to share their lives and their music once again.

He never looked back after he put himself through college, with degrees in history and business at Long Beach State. From the first surfing trip he had taken to Baja with the Samoans, Max knew he wanted to see and experience as much of the world as possible. In the summer of 1988, he drove the classic VW microbus that he had restored at the shop the length of South America to Tierra del Fuego, and looking out at the Strait of Magellan, was a man of the world.

Through traveling, he developed an even greater passion for food and grew to relish the experience of dining with strangers and finding new friends. On the way, he collected all the hot sauces encountered in every cantina and bodega and had started his collection. He could not see the destination, but he knew he was on the journey of life.

With several pitfalls and missteps, balanced by many successes and fantastic adventures, he had stayed on his course, and the path had been a rewarding one. But a cloud hung over Max, staring at the southern Louisiana alfalfa fields. And at that moment, he understood that he had been robbed of his youth. He never went to a prom, played on a team, never experienced graduation. He ran so fast into manhood that the anger of being abandoned never had a voice, a place to scream. Life became about survival so quickly that the image of his father had been pushed aside. He believed he had simply written the man off, canceled his memory. Yet it became clear to Max that he ran not to survive but away from his father, unlike him at all costs. By leaving, his father had shaped him. He made sure there was as little room in his life for betrayal as he possibly could, and as a result, was alone much of the time but not lonely.

Constantly on the move guaranteed that. Max had never allowed himself lasting relationships other than the ones he cultivated in business. Since nineteen, he had lived alone. He preferred casual romance, and life had been abundant with that. Camaraderie and adventure had become preferable to commitments. It was the reason he took in people like Gasanov; they guaranteed the continuation of the adventure that kept him moving, unattached. He was, as Delphine had surmised, a wildcat on the run. Max perceived that he needed to find the fuller meaning of his life at that moment, an emotion buried deeply in his bones, called forth by Lilah's question. It was time to discover his journey's real purpose and share what he had learned about the world. Doing it alone suddenly felt empty, with diminished meaning. And certainly less fun.

Lilah had been looking closely at Max, watching him as he escaped into memories. She could feel that his mind was far away as he stared out over the fields of her family farm. The man presented an enigma, and she had become entertained by and wary of him, a surfer with a vocabulary, good manners, and success in business. He was charming, easygoing, and worldly, yet there was a lack of caution about him, and danger was on his tail. He preferred to go it alone. Their shared passion for things from the earth enticed her, and his efforts to help the people he interacted with were admirable. His rugged good looks and take-it-easy attitude were attractive, she thought, as she looked him over. The boots and jeans were worn to just the right point to be sexy rather than messy, and he always wore clean band t-shirts. His hands were elegant, like a pianist's, but had scrapes and cuts on them. He was earthy and cultured at once. Sitting next to him in the truck, she had caught the scent of him, and he smelled good, like juniper.

Max had come all the way to southern Louisiana to meet Jesus Jones, to talk about his farm and his peppers, and hitchhiked half the way. Jesus obviously liked him. That their lives had intersected amidst a wild tale over chile pepper seeds seemed somehow magical. He hadn't talked about any women in his life other than his faraway mother. The offhand way he spoke of the violent men he had encountered was at once unnerving and enthralling. She found him a mystery, though a pleasant one. And something in her shifted; she was happy he was there, in her home, where she felt most safe in all the world.

"Max," she said softly, "Where are you? Come back."

Though they had spent mere days together, it was a gentle and intimate question. The softness of Lilah's voice flowed into Max's stupor and lifted it from him like daylight through evaporating clouds. He looked over at her, and she was smiling. There was just a bit of mist covering his eyes as he took her in, and in that moment, something happened to both of them. A passageway between their spirits was opened.

The moment was not lost on Delphine (or Jones, for that matter), who sat through the entire span of Max's mental wandering and awakening.

Before Max could respond, the voodoo priestess said, "I think it's time for healing. And strength. Tonight, there will be a ceremony for you, Max. That's why you have all come. Are you prepared to take part and without fear?"

Max was raw, his mind awake, and his emotions flowing. "Yes, Delphine, I am. It's why I'm here, and I'm grateful to be in this place, with all of you. May I rest a bit before? I'm feeling kinda worn out."

Delphine stood, smiling, and took Max by the arm. "Come with me, my boy. There's a nice room with a view of the fields upstairs waiting for you. We have preparations to make, and that will take us a few hours. Plus, I want you rested for tonight's journey."

A strange sound stirred Max from his deep sleep. He thought he had heard a distinct animal squeal. Twilight had arrived outside, and the sky was purple, turning to black, exposing faraway stars. He had rested fully, making him groggy. Candles were lit all over his room, incense burned, and apart from a simple bed and dresser were tables adorned with all manner of random things: pictures, amulets, objects wound with string, dolls, bowls of herbs, feathers, and bottles of liquor that hadn't been present when he had gone there to rest. Other assorted objects hung from the canopy of his bed, making for an eerie but sensuous view. Max felt and smelled magic in the air.

A pair of loose-fitting, white cotton pants and a matching shirt were laid on the dresser, with a note that he should wear these and proceed barefoot to the house's backyard. As he opened the bedroom door, he was met by the beagles, who had been sitting just outside. *For how long*, Max wondered. He knelt to scratch their ears and let them lick his face. The three descended the stairs, led by the pair of ears-flopping hounds, and as they did, he saw that the entire house was lit by candles, casting an ethereal golden glow. Then, Max caught the rich scent of cooking food enveloping the house. His senses immediately awakened, and he realized he was intensely hungry.

He opened the rear door, where he saw a long table set with twenty places. Torches ringed the yard, casting light off the trunks and boughs of the ancient oaks. A Creole woman, her hair piled up in a white turban and who looked quite like Lilah, walked backward around the house, scattering orange dust in a wide circle. Mingling about was a mixed group of people; black, white, Creole, young and old, men and women. The entire group stopped talking and looked up at him. He felt very much on display, a notion that faded when he made out the smiling, white-bearded face of Jones, who was dressed in white, and Delphine, also dressed in white, as before. Everyone was in white. It made for a surreal sight, especially in the fog after sleep that he carried with him. He did not see Lilah.

A temporary outdoor kitchen had been assembled, with a grill, stove, and propane ovens. On a spit over hot coals smoked several animals, and Max could hear them sizzle. A man and woman worked the outdoor kitchen, and he could see and smell various things sautéing, baking, and roasting, the smells fragrant and rich. The Lilah-like Creole woman met him at the foot of the rear stairs and offered him rum to drink, straight.

"It's Cuban," she whispered, smiling, "but don't tell anyone."

He sipped the gold liquor, which instantly warmed him as it found his stomach. He strode into the group, making his way straight to Jones.

"Quite a party, eh Max?" said Jones, lifting his glass with a smile.

He looked entirely different to Max in his white attire, completely relaxed, a smile accentuated by his white beard. *Almost like a holy man of some sort*, he thought.

"You'll find that this is truly a unique place, full of magic and power. Delphine loves to entertain, and these people are serious about enjoying it," Jones confessed.

"Oh, I know it's unique. You should see my room," said Max, to which Jones only winked. "Where's Lilah?"

"Haven't seen her in a while, but she should be joining us soon. There will be good Creole cooking to enjoy and a slew of people to meet before the real fun begins. Come on," he said, gesturing for Max to follow him.

Friends and relatives of Lilah and Delphine introduced themselves, all of whom Jones seemed to know. They nodded their heads when meeting Max, and he got the distinct impression that those he met knew everything about him. Max noticed a few understanding, even concerned looks from some of the guests.

One elderly fellow with wide, seeking eyes responded to meeting him by shaking his hand and saying, "We are so fortunate to have you here. Thank you."

Lilah's older sister, Angelique, had the same features, but her hair and eyes were darker, and while she seemed hardened by life, she still hugged him like an old friend. They toasted with the same rum she had earlier given him, and Max asked her about the powder she had used to ring the house.

"It's called hot foot powder, what we use in voodoo to ward off undesired energies and people," she explained. "And if you scatter some on the doorstep of someone who's wronged you, they will have a restless, wandering life. The famous bluesman who met the devil at the crossroads, Robert Johnson, wrote a song about it called *Hellhound On My Trail*. The legend says one of his many lovers used hot foot powder on him and caused his wandering life. Down in this part of the world, he's regarded as a very mystical and powerful figure, still."

"What's it made of?" asked Max, intrigued.

Angelique thought about it for a moment and responded, totally frank. "Concoctions vary, but generally, it's black salt, ground cayenne pepper, black pepper, chile flakes, wasps' nest, ground sulfur, and graveyard dirt. Preferably from a fresh grave."

Another man was introduced as Lilah's cousin, and his grip was substantial as Max looked up to take in a veritable giant. "This is Othello," Jones said with a serious look on his face. "He played ball at Tulane."

Delphine looked at him from across the lawn, smiling, and she seemed brighter than the rest of the crowd, even larger somehow than before. She had added jewelry to her ensemble; rings, bracelets, and necklaces adorned every possible place, and big hoop earrings hung from her ears. She looked like a venerable queen, and it was evident to Max that she commanded respect in this group.

His agreement to come here was not surprising, given his open-minded nature and the ease he felt with Lilah and Jones. Nonetheless, even for Max, things were bordering on the surreal. The rum warmed him and helped him feel at ease, but he had difficulty understanding why these people were there and how they fit into his experience. Suddenly, Delphine spoke above the conversation.

"Friends, as you know, we are gathered here at our *lakou*, our family compound, for the purpose of cleansing and fortifying our new friend Max, who is on a journey. One that is being diverted by some bad *boko*, the left-hand magic. We have offered a goat, a pig, and some chickens to satisfy both our souls and the *Loa*, who we will call forth this evening over in the *ounfo*, the ritual place. Let us begin by feasting."

This became the signal for platters of food to be set along the length of the table: roasted pig and chickens, a red stew with goat's meat, shrimp in black pepper sauce, okra, rice, roasted peppers, and peas. Baskets of sweet, freshly baked bread were pulled from the ovens. Bowls of red and yellow sauces smelling of hot chiles and vinegar dotted the busy table. Max felt his uneasiness subside as he was offered a seat next to Othello and commanded to eat heartily.

It was evident to Max that these preparations had been going on for much longer than the time he slept. The breads, sauces, and sumptuous dishes all had been made fresh and with care. Othello took it upon himself to explain to Max everything on the table as it passed them by, and they helped themselves generously. The pig had been marinated and brushed with citrus juices and spices while grilling, falling apart as he lifted it from the platter. He covered the perfectly roasted chicken with the yellow and red pepper sauces and ate them with sweet white bread. Max's nose cleared, his head tingled, and his ears popped with the fresh, tangy heat. Gulf shrimp as big as plump sausages had been sautéed in dark beer, butter, and molasses, with handfuls of black pepper, and people fanned themselves as they ate it. Bowls of rice turned brown with Cajun spices arrived, then okra, boiled with gumbo file, sweet with sassafras, and four different roasted peppers that ran from mild to sweat-inducing hot.

It was the kind of meal that put Max at ease anywhere in the world, food being his barometer of memorable places and good people. He felt more at home as he took in the smacking, slurping, and exclamations that came with a table set such as this one, a group of friends and family gathered deep in the country.

Then, heads on the side of the table opposite him began turning and staring at something to the house's rear. He turned to see Lilah at the top of the stairs, looking out over the whole affair and smiling at the gathering she beheld. She was dressed in white along with everyone else, wavy hair pulled back, her shoulders exposed. Max took note of the long, curvy figure silhouetted through her gauzy dress, halting his eating for a long moment. If Delphine was a queen, Lilah certainly looked like a princess.

She took a place at the table in a seat of honor, next to Delphine. The feast continued for another hour, during which Max engaged in a polite discussion of agriculture and food and adventures by those nearest him. In particular, Othello proved to be a fountain of information on the hot sauce industry in Louisiana.

"I worked as a doorman at a club during college in New Orleans, where oysters and beer were the main staples," he said. "We stocked every hot sauce from Louisiana except for Tabasco. There was Red Hot Creole Pepper sauce, Trappey's, Crystal Pepper Sauce. But the big favorite was Frank's Red-Hot Cayenne Pepper Sauce, created by one Popie DeVillier, a relative. Probably because I pushed it," he added, grinning. Max could understand why people followed his lead. He was overtly genial and soft-spoken but truly imposing.

In time, Delphine stood and spoke to the guests. "I hope you have enjoyed your repast, my friends. Now, it's time for us to come together and summon the Loa for our friend Max. First, he will have the *Lave Tete*, washing the head before calling upon the spirits. Please follow me into the ounfo. And I will ask the *Hounsis* to prepare themselves as well."

Silently, the assembled guests rose from the table and began to head toward a dirt area beneath the ancient oaks, covered by a latticework canopy laced with vines. Max tried to make his way toward Lilah, but she was deep in conversation, with Delphine and herself grouped alongside the guests addressed as the "Hounsis." He felt the massive paw of Othello leading him elsewhere, toward the center of the ounfo.

He spoke quietly into Max's ear.

"The Hounsis are Delphine's apprentices. It's a great honor." Max realized that this meant Lilah as well, and his mind began to spin. *A voodoo apprentice?*

The ounfo was ringed by bales of hay, where the guests seated themselves. At the center of the ounfo stood a large pole, which Othello called the *peristil*. Coiled around it swirled a giant, carved white snake. At the four corners of the ounfo sat what looked like elaborate, brightly colored dollhouses. All manner of things sat around them; the same trinkets Max had seen up in his room.

"Those are the shrines of the spirits we are calling upon tonight," said Othello, "and the serpent on the peristil is called *Damballah*, the father of all the voodoo spirits, the father of creation." Othello had become quite serious, and it occurred to Max that he had been appointed his guide for the ceremony about to begin in his honor.

Othello led Max to the center of the ounfo, near the serpent pole, and was directed to sit in a chair facing outward to the assembled group. A number of the guests had taken percussion instruments and prepared to play them. Torches were lit, painting the faces staring back at him with an eerie, surreal glow. From the shadows, Delphine emerged, followed by her ten apprentices. Lilah was the last into the square, head bowed, carrying a large bowl in one hand and massaging the gold amulet around her neck with the other. She seemed to be chanting, quietly. Delphine, in a commanding voice, addressed the gathering.

"Before the Lave Tete, we will appease the four spirits with the creation of the *Veve*, the beacon for the Loa. The cornmeal patterns you will see drawn on the ground are specific to each of these spirits and are used to call them to our lakou, an invitation."

Silently, four of the apprentices began creating intricate patterns in the dirt using the cornmeal directly in front of each of the shrines. There was almost no sound, except for crickets and frogs off in the distant swamp. Max sat still, focusing on the intricate emerging patterns, and the quiet and otherworldly setting began to work him into a trance. The flickering light and glowing faces proved powerfully hypnotic.

Lilah began to walk toward him, her head still bowed. Delphine called for Max to kneel on a mat laid out on the ground before him.

Lilah knelt and did the same, directly facing him. Their eyes did not meet. She placed the bowl on the ground between them, and in it, Max could see water that had been infused with a mixture of herbs. It had a strong, sweet smell. Delphine commanded him to lower his head and face the ground. Silently, Lilah cupped her hands and poured the medicinal mixture over his head seven times. It was a superb sensation, the cool, scented wash, and he breathed in deeply. As his hair dripped with the sweet liquid, Lilah wrapped his head in a large, gauzy kerchief, and raising him, their eyes met, taking Max's breath entirely away. She had mist in her eyes but smiled sweetly, from far away. Max bit his lip so hard it almost punctured, and she rose and retreated to stand with the other Hounsis. A lot was happening at once in unfamiliar territory.

Then, Delphine walked to the center and stood before Max, carrying a large oil candle. "Light this flame and focus upon it, Max. It is the light of the spirits which we call upon tonight."

He did as instructed, and a lone drum began to beat slowly. The flame and beat combined to further entrance him, and as he focused upon the fire, Max's peripheral vision drew closer, blacking out all but what he saw before him. Delphine then reached out and placed a leather thong around his neck, attached to a small amulet bag.

"This is your 'garde,' Max. Its contents are sacred, and they represent the Loa we call now on your behalf. And this is the blood of the sacrificed animals, thinned out with some rum. Will you drink it and imbibe the spirits?"

She held out a clay bowl before him, which he took and paused before swallowing it all down. It was heavily laced with rum and not at all unpalatable. She wiped a large drip from his chin before he softly belched.

Then, louder so that all could hear, and raising her hands high, Delphine called out, "*Papa Legba*, I call upon you now to open the *gat* between the spirit world and this one. I call the Loa to come forth and grace this gathering with their presence: *Ayza*, the Protector, *Ogou Balanjo*, the spirit of healing; and *Zaka*, the spirit of agriculture and the earth."

She turned and walked toward the seated group. As she did, she said quietly, only to herself, "And *Ezili*, the spirit of devotion." Then she was handed a bottle of clear rum, and this she poured on the ground four times, in a circle around Max.

"Send our offerings to the houses of the Loa," she commanded her disciples, as large platters of food and bottles of rum were placed before each altar.

Another drum took up the beat, and Delphine began to hum softly, the sound coming from deep within her. Her voice slowly rose as she chanted and sang in Creole French, along with other tongues Max could not understand. The drums grew louder, their intensity moving the air. She produced a snake from a basket on the ground, which she held up and shone to the four directions. Then she started to dance, slowly and deliberately, with the snake held aloft. Drums and chanting joined in a mystical gumbo of sound. All the Hounsis, including Lilah, took up the dance as the entire group began to clap and chant to the drums' rhythm. Max felt the intensity rise as he focused on Delphine and her gyrations, and the snake. She moved like a much smaller and younger woman. Lilah danced with her eyes closed, chanting and twirling with trained focus, her white skirt spinning out like a dervish.

Above the cacophony, Delphine took up a loud invocation, "Loa, Loa, spirits that guide and protect, we ask you to present yourselves here in this ounfo. We ask you to heal and nourish our friend Max."

Max heard several in the crowd exclaim, "Ho!" as the drums and chanting grew even louder.

"We ask you for protection for him on his journey," she proclaimed, speaking to the dark night, "for he is on a warrior's path. And we ask you for bounty from the earth that will strengthen him!"

"Ho! Ho!" he heard the crowd respond.

The drums, dancing, and chanting combined to create a wild, pagan-intensive ritual. It reminded Max of Africa and the Bere-Bere ceremonies with the Amhara, whom he considered family. That this was all meant for his benefit had a profound and moving effect upon him. As Delphine repeated the invocations, he found himself calling out "Ho!" each time she did. He closed his eyes and let the magic wash over him and could still make out twirling bodies and flickering flames through his closed eyes, reaching a feverish pitch.

The spell was broken by a high-pitched "Aiyeeeee!" Max opened his eyes to see one of the dancers stopped, with his arms outstretched and head bowed. The other dancers made space for him while the drumming and dancing quieted, and all eyes were upon the lone disciple. He began to dance in odd movements, chanting and calling out, with his eyes closed. Max made out the words "Ogou Balanjo," which he remembered was the spirit of healing, and the crowd took up the chant. Again, it rose in intensity, accompanied by the participants' collective percussion on the hay bale fringe. The man acted clearly outside of his body. He shook violently, and with his eyes rolling back in his head, fell to the ground, at which point the others took up the dance.

This happened two more times with other dancers. Max sat still and kept his eyes closed, hearing the words "Ayza" and "Zaka" as each dancer fell to the ground. The spirits of protection and earth had taken possession of the dancers and made their presence known. And then the drumming stopped. Everyone sat still, anticipating.

Slowly, Lilah began to move. Her eyes were shut, and her head bowed as she slowly moved to the rhythmic chant. Only the group's women took up singing a single song, French in the Creole patois.

Ezili! Ezili! Guide Esprit d'amour, Entrer dans ce lieu et laissez votre esprit libre.

Nous vous honore, et de vivre votre étreinte, Viens ici, l'un de nous, et montrer votre

beau visage. Avec vous Ezili, dans notre maison, L'amour sera résident, et dans

ta lumière, Les ombres se dissipent.

Max was transfixed on Lilah as she danced. She moved in a way not unlike the tribal women of Africa but with more grace and femininity. She arched herself backward, then touched her head almost to the ground and spun in circles. Lilah, too, seemed possessed, and her abandon felt to Max at once hypnotic and erotic as her white dress flowed and spun with her movements. As the song reached its crescendo, she reached up her arms and looked to the sky. In a voice that didn't seem to come from her, she yelled, "Ezili! Ezili!" and fell to the ground.

Max watched intently as Lilah lay motionless. Other disciples surrounded her, gently picking her up and carrying her over their heads toward the house, with her long hair hanging down beside her arms. She appeared unconscious. They chanted "Ezili, Ezili" as they slowly marched. Max believed the ceremony had concluded and got up to follow Lilah, wanting to see her revived.

Delphine gently blocked his way, placing her hand on his chest. "Max, your purification is complete, and you witnessed for yourself the presence of the Loa in this place. To complete your spirit connection, and for the purification to keep, you must sleep here in the ounfo tonight, alone. The light of the spirits will remain with you to guide you through the night."

Slowly, the entire gathering shuffled into the night without a word, and Max was left alone with a blanket and the single, flickering light. His ears rang, and his mind raced as he wrapped himself in the blanket, staring at the flame of the spirits.

Max's dreams, when he finally slept, were vivid and chaotic. There were drumbeats and flashes of faces: Gasanov, Clyde, Delphine, Jones, Othello, the red-faced Russian attackers, and Lilah, each parading through his mind. They all danced in a circle around him, voiceless and without expression. Though the world outside was silent, drums and chants played in his dreams. The faces swirled, faster and faster, to the intensifying tempo of the soundless drums. He became dizzy, reeling in the other realm and unable to break free from a circle of confusion. And then it all stopped. He awoke with a start, lying on the ground, still wrapped in the blanket, shivering and breathing hard. It was deep in the night, and the only thing Max could see was the flickering flame directly before him. A dark sense of dread hung in the air, and he lay motionless in the circle, unclear whether the menace he felt was external or from the chaotic dream. No sounds came from the fields and woods, and even the frogs and crickets were oddly silent. From outside the circle of the ounfo, lurking in the dark, something had broken through to his consciousness.

Straining to hear anything at all through the cloak of the black night, he registered only his own labored breathing. Max willed himself to inhale deeply, to calm his thoughts and nerves. Nothing, it seemed, threatened in the dark. He lay back down and began to replay the events of the evening over in his mind. The image of Lilah succumbing to the ritual's intensity and being carried aloft by a group of chanting voodoo disciples dressed in white replayed vividly in his mind. He had not anticipated her participation in the ritual and was disoriented by her performance. It added a layer of mystery and complexity to her image, and he wished he could see her and hear her voice. He felt very alone, lying in the dirt and staring at the eerie flame that embodied the spirits' light. If the spirits called forth that evening were with him, as Delphine had proclaimed, he was not comforted.

Then, almost imperceptibly, a twig snapped off in the distance. Max stiffened where he lay and listened with every ounce of his concentration. Nothing. Stillness and a flickering flame at which he stared for what felt like many long minutes. Then, out of the darkness, he heard whispers.

Two distinct voices hissed at each other in the dark, thirty yards away, from the fringe of the woods, and one voice reprimanded the other as they moved out of the brush toward the ceremonial ounfo where Max lay. It was maddening that he could not see anything beyond the glow cast by the spirit lamp. He realized it would allow anybody looking to see him clearly, so he slithered to the edge from the center of the hay bale-encircled space, trailing the blanket behind. Taking cover under one of the four house shrines and covering himself again in the blanket, Max retreated into the shadow, listening.

Now that he was aware of their presence, Max could follow the faint sounds of the interlopers' movements as they made their way around the outside of the ounfo and toward the darkened house. He figured out their path would take them right past his perch and began to look for something to defend himself with. The smell of rum wafted powerfully all around him. Drop by drop, Max noticed the clear liquid coming off the table above that served as the shrine's base, and food items, four bottles of rum placed among them. He quickly reached over the edge and followed the moisture to the nearest bottle, which he grabbed. In the bottle's neck, stuffed to the waist, protruded a small cloth doll, resembling a white male. *Him.*

The bottle happened to be an extremely volatile 151 proof rum, and Max instantly searched for ways to make that work to his benefit. The soft footfalls were much nearer now, and he followed their route, trying to picture in his mind who these people might be. The steps stopped directly behind him, on the other side of the hay bale wall.

"Izz crazy devil vorship place," he heard one voice whisper. "Thees voman has the name DeVillier, French witches."

The strongly accented voice was now right above Max's head. The other, lower and more menacing, responded.

"There vaz some type of ceremony here tonight – look at all zee liquor bottles - and now they are zleeping. She must keep dee seeds and her research in this place, and vee must find zem before we go back, Antony. Bakiyev will have our heads eef we return empty-handed."

Max heard them begin towards the sleeping house.

A chill overtook his entire body as he held his breath for what seemed minutes. It was clear who these men were and what they were after. Lilah was their target, and Max felt anger rising from within. Staring at the bottle in his hand, an idea came to him. He turned the rum bottle over and let the high-octane alcohol soak the small cloth doll that was his likeness. Then, he rolled the bottle across the soft dirt of the ounfo, directly toward the flame of the spirits.

The next thirty seconds evolved in slow motion. The Molotov cocktail rolled directly next to the flame, and Max watched intently as it licked the head of the doll, then caught. Captured within the glass prison, the highly flammable liquid had nowhere to go. The bottle exploded, sending flaming rum thirty feet in every direction. Soaked in rum, the shrine above him burst into flame, and he realized he was in a horrible place, trapped below it. Max had to act. Rising with the entire shrine atop his shoulders, screaming, he stood and encountered the faces of the intruders, pale with fear. And as they saw him, their expressions turned from fear to menace. Max leaped atop the hay bale wall, still screaming, and ran toward them, ejecting the entire flaming apparatus in their direction. Other rum bottles broke as the shrine crashed to the ground, spreading intense flame in a wide arc around where it landed. The intruders became caught in a spreading circle of fire and shrieked in unison, their boots aflame, and they began to dance. Max stood, heaving, and looked into their eyes, which glowed with both fear and rage.

At that moment, a massive, blurred figure appeared from the shadows of the darkened house, roaring toward the Russians. Dogs began to bark, and the beagles, sheepdog, and bloodhound issued forth from the kitchen doggie door. Terrified and risking the fire, the two men leaped the flaming barrier and began to run back toward the woods, crashing into the brush as the unknown defender chased them with a prolonged scream. The dogs followed, braying, on the hunt.

Max raced with adrenaline, disoriented. A rum fire burned all around him. Lights began to turn on in the house, and he heard alarmed voices. He needed to think quickly. Something, someone, was engaging the intruders, so he did not have to. Rather than take part in the chase, he grabbed a hose next to the house and calmly began spraying down the flaming bales of hay and the torched voodoo shrines. By the time Jones reached him, he had looked like a man watering his lawn.

"Max, have you gone crazy?" Jones said, "What in Jesus' name happened here?'

"Not crazy, and no need to invoke your name," Max said. "We had some visitors, and I think someone and the dogs are chasing them off. But I guess I did start the fire." He offered nothing else, and Jones did not ask. He knew who the visitors were and the implications.

Max calmly put out the fire, which, left untended, would have consumed the ancient Louisiana oaks and engulfed the DeVillier home. The thought that dangerous men knew who Lilah was and where she lived began to smolder inside him. As he swept the stream of water over the remaining flames, remembering the hissing, accented voices, he felt a hand on his shoulder. Max turned to see Lilah, barefoot and still in her white dress. The look in her eyes showed serious concern, but Max could not tell if it was a concern for him or herself and her home because of what he had brought upon them. He bowed his head, ashamed at not having dealt with the men who had been tracking his movements. He understood that his cavalier response had brought them to her home, looking for her, not just him. A lifetime of responsibility only for himself worked well enough for a lone wolf, but other people entering Max's life required greater care.

"What happened, Max?" Lilah asked softly.

She had watched Max as he embraced her home and the people in it. The openness he showed while partaking in their rituals had not been lost on her, and the visible impact of Delphine's words upon him was moving. Though he lived on the run, to her, he did not come across as reckless. Rather, he was fluid, intelligent, and moved like a cat through the world, she thought. But when he looked up at Lilah, there was fear and confusion in his eyes.

"The men from Laguna and Santa Fe were here. They were looking for you," he said, "and me. This is my fault. I think it's time to go."

The shock of this froze Lilah. She gripped Max's arms as she stood facing him, needing to keep her balance. Again, he looked at the ground. She breathed deeply, trying to clear her head and reason. Her mind worked quickly. She reached out her hand to his chin and raised Max's head to face her own.

Looking directly into Max's sad, confused eyes, she said, "They want to get a hold of the research. As you said, Max, these guys are looking to make money on new pepper varieties. If I've done the work already, especially if one of these varieties is unique to their country, then, of course, they would want that information. But the funny thing is, we've only just planted those seeds, and there's no data yet."

She was getting irritated. "I would have told them that myself if they'd given me a chance. I don't understand what all the clandestine crap is all about. If a few more women were playing parts in this charade, things would be a lot simpler."

With a huff, she turned and walked back into the house, leaving Max stupefied.

At that moment, heavy footfalls could be heard crashing through the brush underneath the forest canopy, accompanied by dogs' barking. As he turned, Max saw a towering figure lumbering towards the house. Othello, the former football star, had pursued the invaders. The four hounds circled him as he walked directly up to Max.

"We chased them for half a mile through the woods and across fields before we hit the bayou. Their feet were on fire. They went right in, with the dogs hot on their tails. It's thick with gators and water moccasins in there, so I imagine they'll be having an interesting morning, and they won't be back. The interesting thing is, Delphine knew something was gonna happen. That's why she had me sleep on the front porch and keep an eye on you. And the hot foot powder seems to have worked." He paused, looking at the devastated ounfo, and then grinned. "Quick thinking with the rum, though."

The beagles circled Max, and he knelt to take in their affection. As he scratched their heads, he saw dawn breaking and was suddenly overcome with fatigue. Too much had happened, and he needed a bed.

With the rum fire out, Max returned to the house. Delphine sat in the living room, calmly, in an oversized chair in the corner.

"Aren't you a sight," she said. "Sit down, son."

Only then Max became aware his white garments were covered in dirt. He looked like he'd escaped from a bayou chain gang, and he smelled like rum.

He sat across from her on the edge of the couch, as he did not want to soil anything, looking at her for a long moment. She said nothing, staring out the window at the torched ounfo and the rising dawn.

Delphine then sighed, coming to some conclusion. "I guess it was time to rebuild that thing anyway," she started. "I've always thought it should be farther from the house."

She looked at Max, quite serious. "I hope you realize the power of last night's ritual. I sensed that danger was on your tail. A danger that was kept at bay. You passed your first test, my friend. You're on the warrior's path."

Max sat, tired and confused, overloaded by the events of the last twelve hours. "I almost burned down your house. I've put you all in harm's way. How does that make me a warrior?"

Delphine leaned in closer and spoke in earnest. "You were protected in many ways. The Loa, the hot foot powder, Othello. Your path is to make this whole thing right, Max. As old Jones said, it's time to get the ball rolling in your direction, and tonight you did. Now you must pursue the path to its end. You have been purified and are protected. Your life is your own, as well as your journey. Though you will now have support."

Max still felt bewildered, guilty, and continued blaming himself for the mess he believed he'd brought with him. If there was support, he did not feel it. He looked up at Delphine.

"How did you know those men were going to come here?" he asked.

"I knew a challenge was near," she said, "and that you would overcome."

A long pause ensued as she looked into Max's eyes, smiling.

"I got a call from town that some men were asking about Lilah and figured it out. Some local boys kept an eye on them for me, so we assumed they might be waiting until dark to snoop around. I asked Othello to keep an eye on things, just in case. Part of your protection," she said with a wink.

The realization that she knew something might happen and that his actions could have been different in a dozen ways made a lead weight land on Max's shoulders. He felt sapped, raw.

Delphine was circumspect. "There's an old Creole proverb that tells us 'Pushed times make a monkey chew pepper,'" she said, looking out the window.

Max turned to her with a confused look, bewildered by the pepper reference.

"Challenging times require unique actions," she said.

"I need rest, Delphine," was all he could say.

She remained bright and energetic. "Go ahead, my boy. Rest. You have much planning to do."

Max slowly climbed the stairs, numb, casting a wondering look at Lilah's bedroom door before he stripped off his clothes and fell into bed.

When Max awoke, it felt late in the day, the light cast at a low angle. He dreamt of the voodoo deity Ezili, though he did not know why. He and the specter had been climbing a cliff, thousands of feet high, and at its top, Lilah stood, dressed in white, waiting. Despite his desperate efforts, he could never reach the top. Again, the smell of food had found its way into his dreams and stirred him to consciousness, and he awoke genuinely ravenous.

He had found another hot bath waiting and returned to find his clothes cleaned and laid out on the dresser. As Max slid on his boots, Delphine's words came back to him. *Tested. On the path. Planning. What did she mean?* He couldn't see through the fog of confusion. *And what about Lilah?*

Again, the beagles waited outside his door to escort him down the stairs, and their allegiance brought a weary smile. As he reached the top of the stairs, Lilah's door opened, and she stepped into the hall. She, too, was dressed in her original clothes, jeans, and a yellow blouse. Yet the image of her in white, silhouetted by the light, flashed in Max's mind. He blinked back to reality.

"Hi," was all he could say.

"Hi," she said back lightly while scratching the beagles. "You slept all day."

Then she walked down the stairs, leaving him there, fumbling for words. He could not find any, so he merely followed, with the beagles in tow. She remained a mystery. In the dining room, a set table awaited. Lilah sat, joining Jones and Othello, as Delphine ferried platters in from the kitchen.

"'Bout time. Cajun meatloaf with pepper sauce, fried oysters, and crayfish bisque," Jones said as he tucked a cloth napkin into his collar. "And smoked alligator sausage, a bayou delicacy. We weren't gonna wait much longer. Now let's eat."

The five of them ate as if nothing had happened, with the meal accentuated only by perfunctory table talk.

"Jesus brought some fresh peppers and some of his sauces, which I understand you quite like, Max," said Delphine.

Max only nodded, having charged into the heap of food he had served himself, enhanced by pepper sauces, relishes, and chile-infused oil. He had to force himself from slurping the creamy bisque, heavily fortified with sherry, and the fried oysters tasted firm and salty as he dipped them into a vinegary bayou pepper puree that balanced their briny deliciousness. The massive slice of meatloaf had been dusted with a mix of Cajun spices that made a fiery outer crust, then topped by a sauce of sweet roasted peppers reduced in a thick glaze. He doused the garlicky alligator sausage in Louisiana pepper sauce and found it sweet and savory at the same time and used doughy homemade bread for dipping, humming as he worked through another plate. His head began to clear as he retreated deep into the dining groove. After the third plate, Max pushed his chair back and, looking up, realized that the others were all staring, especially Othello.

"I was hungry," seemed all he could think to say.

"True that," said Jones with a chuckle, "You gave Othello a run for his money."

Delphine cleared the plates, then brought a silver platter with a crystal bottle and matching glassware. The liquid had a green glow to it, and in each glass was a single ice cube.

"Absinthe, *La Fée Verte* 'the Green Fairy,'" she said. "From France. It's vintage 1910, before the war, and before it was illegal. I found it in the attic of an old French Creole I was treating who couldn't afford to pay." The seal had remained unbroken.

Delphine poured a few emerald ounces into each glass and then placed a sugar cube on a small, slotted spoon. She poured icy water over the sugar from a pitcher, and the mixture blended with the absinthe, turning it cloudy.

They raised their glasses in unison as Delphine looked at Max and toasted, "To the future," which they all echoed. Max took a small sip of the cloudy liquor and immediately identified the anise flavor that identifies absinthe. He also detected overtones of nutmeg and juniper. It tasted intense and sweet, and he felt it settle within his depths, warm as it found its home.

"Jesus, I've yet to ask because I believed you'd tell me when the time was right," Max suddenly said. He wanted to know a vital piece of the puzzle while they were all still together. "But I need to close a chapter on my journey. What makes your peppers so unique?"

There was a long silence as Jones stared into his pool of absinthe. Lilah looked first at Max with surprise and then back at Jones. She sat back and folded her arms, waiting.

"People have wondered that for generations, Max. They've even sent spies to try and unearth my secret," he said, and then looked directly at him. "It's the apples."

Max looked at Jones expectantly, waiting for him to expand on the statement, his discovery radar on high alert.

"Those apple trees have ringed our property for as long as the fields have seen cultivation. I believe the apple trees impart their character into the soil here, what the French call *terroir*. It seems my great grandfather had a taste for applesauce, and part of the farm was originally dedicated to its production. What remained, the pulp, got infused into the composted fertilizer that was made right there on the farm, which we keep in its locked building. The peppers became sweeter. They started getting sugar cane pulp from the local sugar refinery and added it to the mixture to sweeten up the fertilizer. With Lilah's help, we've sourced byproducts from other organic fruit farms and local canneries. It all goes into the mix with uncanny effect. Pure chance, but pure nonetheless."

As Max digested this information, a sense of completion came over him. *Answers to mysteries are always more straightforward than your mind wants them to be,* he thought, returning to his essential nature.

"As always, the people who have a connection to the land are the ones who understand how best to make it bear the sweetest fruit," Max said. "Everywhere I go, it's the same thing. Love, and care of the land, and what you put into it make the best farmers. And some tasty tricks. No wonder McIlhenny and Ivins can't duplicate your peppers, Jesus. There are generations of you in the soil."

As he looked into his glass, he didn't see the smiles of the others.

The five of them sat in silence, taking in the nearly hundred-year-old spirits. Max's mind, now grasping the secret it sought, began to wander once again.

The chaos and confusion that had led him here weighed upon Max as he sat in Delphine's parlor, accentuated by the many miles he had traveled. Louisiana and these people felt like an oasis in the random, chaotic world he now inhabited. Usually a solo operator, he had allowed people deep into his life, which seemed to be changing the landscape. Gasanov had found his way further into Max's world than he should have, and danger and chaos were the results, though he was affected by the man's desperation and actually feared for his safety.

Since landing in Louisiana, these rare characters had entered his usually solitary orbit, and the tumult of his world was beginning to touch theirs. He felt a kinship to Jones and Delphine, as though they had been a part of his life forever, a family that he didn't have. His mentor had been the wide world in which he moved. Lilah entered as a strong, intuitive, independent, and mysterious woman whose draw upon him grew more powerful by the hour.

Max's comfort became restored by the sound of Jones launching into tales of life on Chicago's South Side and the heady days of life in a blues quintet. He regaled them for hours with remembrances of smoky lounges, roadside honkytonks, Odette Washington's cooking, and Otis Pepper and the South Side Five. Listening to the stories, Max made a mental note to see the world from which Jones had come. Then, bowing to conditioning, his mind began to focus on the road ahead.

It became clear to Max that resolution was the rope that would bind this new world of his together and keep everyone safe, including himself. The resolution lay in following the story to its end. To do that, he had to find its beginning. And in Louisiana, he already had. The journey to the end was a path further afield.

Chicago

Miles of rolling countryside stretched out from the window that constituted Max's view of the world. Long periods of pondering were broken by naps and half-hearted attempts at reading the pile of material he had brought along for the ride. In May, Southern Illinois exploded in layers of cultivated green, and the trees lining the full waterways, tributaries of the Mississippi, were plump with foliage. With the countryside flowing past his window, Max thought back on what had transpired in Louisiana.

To an outsider, the cascade of events could easily seem overwhelming. He had become awash with emotions after the extraordinary bayou experience. That he was freshly voodoo-blessed lingered in the air like incense. Images of Lilah, chanting and dancing as if possessed, were bright flashes in Max's mind, yet now she was behind him, farther away with every mile. He wondered if the magnetism he'd felt, she shared. She mystified him, yet she felt familiar. He held onto the small leather pouch Delphine had given him, and he rolled the contents of the voodoo "gris-gris" bag around in his fingers. There appeared to be a chicken foot. Some stones. The scent of frankincense. Yet he did not open it, preferring to keep the magic within contained.

The "City of New Orleans" had traveled north up the Mississippi River Valley, through plantation country, and Max scoured the landscape for the occasional antebellum mansions that still dot the countryside and allude to the South's complex history. He was journeying by train, needing the time and passing scenery to gather thoughts. A stack of journals and reports sat in the empty seat next to him, including Lilah's dissertation He had chosen to take in the world through a window for twenty hours, to contemplate as it passed him by.

Max was bound for Chicago, where he would pick up a flight to New Delhi via London. Rather than fly to the Windy City, he had bought a ticket on the two-day train, hoping the time alone would afford some clarity and much-needed reflection. The intensity of his Louisiana experiences had given rise to a need for solitude. For this reason, he had booked a private, two-seat roomette. Plus, he loved trains.

At New Orleans' small station, he had sat, watching the passing crowds and taking in the conversations and dialects of other people's lives. They crisscrossed the station's dull light, bound for important places, some with expectant chatter and others quiet, with faces strained by worry. He felt at once a part of the sea of humanity, yet alone within it.

Train stations are a crossroads of stories, he thought, *each journey an individual universe, alive with anticipation.* Max's journey, too, had become a world unto itself, spreading out before him.

After a night of storytelling in the velvety absinthe haze of Delphine's parlor, Max had awoken early for a drive along the bayou waterways. Carrying a thermos of potent, chicory-infused coffee, he parked atop the levee holding back the black swamp waters from the farmland on the other side. He rolled down the windows of Jones's old pickup and leaned against the driver's-side door, with his feet stretched out across the long bench seat. The air was still, mildly humid, and a morning fog hung over the swamp.

He followed the fervent tap-tap-tap of a woodpecker high in the boughs of a moss-laden tree that grew right out of the murky water, catching the red flash of the bird's crown. Frogs croaked in the waterways. A visible splash in the distance led his eye to a water moccasin, which dropped out of a tree and slither-swam towards the shore of a small island. In bayou country, those small islands were called hammocks, he remembered, and closed his eyes.

When he stirred, the sun was high, and the mists had burned from the swamp. The frogs and woodpeckers were silent. He hadn't dreamed, surprisingly, but upon waking, felt a wave of certainty wash over him. He shifted directly into a familiar gear, and rubbing his face, Max decided it was time to make the future happen. He fired up the truck and chased down a payphone to call Chuck DeWindt in Santa Fe.

Agreeing to undertake the Naga Jolokia fact-finding trip to northern India, Max requested to embark from Chicago. Chuck had agreed to fund half the plane ticket and hotels in Delhi and Tezpur, where the unverified peppers waited. He would also need all the information DeWindt had on the ridiculously hot Indian chile and what he was supposed to find out. DeWindt agreed that he would make the arrangements and would email a slew of background files. *More reports to read on the 17-hour flight,* thought Max. DeWindt also added a note that the chile world was abuzz with rumors of Max's situation. Some chile-head conspiracy theorists even claimed they had news he was involved in a nefarious scheme to monetize the new hottest peppers on the planet as a battlefield weapon. Chuck closed the correspondence by adding, "Seems you've become the James Bond of hot sauce, my friend. Be careful."

Max had arrived back at Delphine's house to find the three of them, Jones, Lilah, and the voodoo priestess, sitting in the living room, talking, which they continued to do despite his arrival.

"You may say it makes no difference, but you know it does," he heard Jones say.

To which Lilah replied, "It'll make a difference, either way, Jesus, but this may be the thing that matters more."

That left Delphine, whose input became, "The road you will take you have already decided. You just don't know it yet."

The talk was cryptic and left Max wondering what their words meant. "Ahem," he coughed in the doorway.

The three of them looked at him neither as if he were interrupting nor his arrival mattered. "I'm taking

the train out in the morning and heading to India," he said flatly.

"Helluva way to get to India from Louisiana," said Jones.

"I'm taking the train to Chicago and then flying to India," Max said, a bit irritated.

He expected the announcement to carry more weight, but they just looked at him; Jones, nodding his head and scratching his scraggly beard, Delphine smiling and looking at him knowingly, and Lilah, looking past him with an air of indifference.

"Going to India gets me to Kyrgyzstan, where the answers are," he said, with a forced certainty that he knew was not lost on them all.

"I was just telling these two that you'd be leaving soon, Max," said Delphine, "and that your journey must continue. You are ready."

He looked at Lilah, hoping to see what response his departure might have on her. She met his gaze, and seemed to look right through him.

Then she simply said, "It sounds like this is where your journey must go, Max. It will be a great adventure, I'm sure. And that's how you see the world, as an adventure."

Then she looked away. Though he knew he had to leave, Max hoped for more of a sendoff.

"Well, I hope I see you around," was all he could think to say, looking at Lilah.

Still looking out the window, she said, "Perhaps you will."

Max had one day in Chicago before the flight to London, and as he disembarked at Union Station, he began to make a mental list of the things he wanted to see and the food to seek out. He checked into the old Silversmith Hotel by the station, where a pile of faxes and email documents from Chuck DeWindt awaited. After tossing his duffle bag and a satchel full of reports on the bed, Max set out for a much-needed city stroll. While he felt sure about his journey's forward momentum, Lilah's casual response to his departure had left him in a funk on the long train ride. He wondered if she thought about him.

Like New York, Chicago was a city best seen on foot, but unlike New York, Chicago remained amazingly clean. The clever folks who laid out the new Chicago after the great fire of 1871 had the good sense to build alleys behind the new buildings, keeping trash and the trucks that hauled it off the streets.

Max headed straight up La Salle Avenue to the famous Newberry Library on the north side of town. The Newberry had a renowned collection of maps, atlases, and manuscripts, and Max wanted to see in detail the routes of the old Silk Road for himself before heading to Asia. The Newberry Library Center for Renaissance Studies was a stellar repository of that era's information and collaborated with over fifty universities' knowledge and efforts. Of the Center's half-million maps, most were published before 1900, one of the main reasons Max wanted to travel via Chicago. Chuck DeWindt had arranged for him to visit, as New Mexico State was one of the museum's affiliated universities.

The librarian, alerted to his arrival, had selected three specific maps for Max to view. They had been securely stored in humidity-controlled cabinets and presented to him on a wide viewing table. First, he looked over an early fourteenth-century masterpiece by Swedish adventurer and cartographer Otto Lumens, who was in the employ of the Portuguese in India at Goa. Then, the historical atlas of Abraham Ortelius, published in Antwerp in 1592. And last, the famous Tabula Rogeriana of 1154, a copy of the priceless original by Mohammed al-Idrisi, the famous Arab cartographer to King Roger of Sicily.

The oldest map, by Al-Idrisi, was the most accurate map of the known world for hundreds of years. On it, routes were traced from China and over the mountains into present-day Kyrgyzstan and Uzbekistan, one of the first depictions of the Silk Road. The Lumens map, dating from before Columbus (and hence chiles from the new world), clearly traced a route east from Samarkand and Fergana through the Naryn Valley. At the town of Naryn, the course turned south, passing the ancient Tash Rabat caravanserai on the way to the Torugart Pass, Kashgar, and China.

The latest document, the 1592 atlas of Ortelius, showed the clear link between the Silk Road's eastern end, at Xian in China, west to Kashgar, and over the Tien Shan Mountains. After that, it linked with three other routes, all headed for the Uzbek city of Samarkand, called the "gem of the east," then Asia Minor, and finally, Europe.

Though the Silk Road took many routes across Asia, and later, by sea, Max was interested in the ones that went through Kyrgyzstan. And while there were multiple interpretations of the routes, what was unmistakable was that the Naryn River Valley, where the peppers

Gasanov was so excited about might have come from, figured prominently as a Silk Road route.

Max closed the sixteenth-century atlas and sat at the large library table, scratching his weeks' worth of beard. *The possibility exists*, he thought, as he pictured pack trains bearing the goods of east and west and the centuries of trade and interaction. *Time to go and see for myself.* He was intrigued, excited, and hungry, sensations that rekindled his latent adventurer's spirit.

Nearby the Newberry was the Twin Anchors Tavern, a stop he made every time he was in the Windy City. The tavern had been a Chicago fixture since 1932, in a building dating from 1881, and was known for sweet, spicy, and sticky pork ribs that he enjoyed right at the bar with a pint of Joseph Huber Premium, one of the oldest beers in Chicagoland. The light was low, they always played Sinatra on the jukebox, and a visit there gave Max the instant feeling of a vibrant downtown. The midday crowd was talkative but not overly loud, serious about eating and drinking, his kind of people. It was good to be back in a city, and Louisiana and its voodoo fires felt far away, smoldering in the back of his mind.

With a full belly, Max emerged on the street with a healthy belch as the late afternoon light cast skyscrapers' lengthening shadows. A long walk would take him along Lakeshore Drive and across the Chicago River to visit the Chicago Art Institute. Max was a fan of the straightforward American school of art embodied by Grant Wood's *American Gothic* and Edward Hopper's *Nighthawks*, and he never tired of their evocative simplicity. He identified with Wood's benign prairie resoluteness and the loner's prominent place in Hopper's works. The hour he spent sitting on a bench and quietly contemplating the domestic masterpieces, so unlike the grand displays of Europe, plugged him into the essence of his particular proud Americanism.

Then, Max decided to head for the South Side, taking the South Shore train to explore Jesus Jones' old neighborhood. On East 75th Street, between South Chicago Avenue and the Dan Ryan Expressway were clustered the places that once had been the center of Jesus Jones's world. Jones had spent a stretch living in the old Buick just off 75th and South Michigan, right near Odette Washington's place, and down the block from Army & Lou's Fried Chicken. Blues legends played on the same street at venues like Willa's Fifty Yard Line, The New Apartment, and nearby Lee's Unleaded Blues.

Wanting to experience this world, Max found 75th, hoping to poke his head into a couple of the joints. Jones had said to check in at Lem's Barbeque, a Chicago institution, and ask around for Odette, who he had not heard from in years. Washington's Smoke House had closed, Jones understood, sometime in the early Eighties.

"Jesus Jones," said the fifty-ish man working the counter at Lem's. He was Lem's nephew Isaac, who inherited the barbeque joint after Lem's passing in 1986. "Now, there's a name I haven't heard in a long time. He got a letter one day and was gone the next. Was living in his car right down the block in front of Odette's place. Word has it he's growing marijuana down south somewhere."

Max shook his head, thinking of the acres of peppers. "Oh, he's growing good stuff, alright. The sweetest around. I just left him a few days ago," and left it at that. "How about old Odette?"

Isaac wiped his hands on a sauce-stained apron and plucked a polaroid image off the wall.

"She's still going strong, must be ninety now, and living down in Sarasota in an old folks' home. She sends a card every Christmas and complains each time that there ain't no barbeque worth eatin' in Florida."

"And what about the South Side Five? Any of them still around?" Max wanted to know.

Isaac shook his head. "Other than Jones, all gone, except for old Otis Pepper. Otis inherited his uncle's joint, Pepper's Hideout, up on 23rd, near Congress, but it closed just a few years back. Otis took off for Bermuda for good after he closed it up, but I hear he's playing joints up and down the East Coast still."

"I ran into Otis in a beach bar in Delaware about three years back," said Max, remembering their oyster and pepper sauce shoot-off with a chuckle. "He's one spunky old fella. I'm glad to know he's still kickin'."

"You tell that old cheat Jones he still has an unpaid tab here and a couple of others along 75th. My uncle kept all those things in a shoebox in the office," said Isaac.

Max turned to leave. Then a thought came to him.

"Say, do you think you could find me that old tab? I want to give it to Jones."

"Be glad to," said Isaac, taking off the apron and heading in back. "Don't want these things sittin' around forever, piling up."

He returned with a stained, handwritten restaurant check that showed lines of charges covering different dates. Some had been crossed out as paid. More were not. Isaac handed it to Max, and he chuckled when he saw the total, $47.65, followed by a note scrawled in bold letters: PLUS INTEREST, it said.

"How much do you figure twenty years of interest is on that total?" Max asked.

"Hell, total's gotta be at least twenty bucks by now," said Isaac.

"Twenty?" asked Max, surprised. "What's the interest?"

Isaac responded a bit indignantly, assuming Max thought Jones had been overcharged.

"Interest is a dollar a year, and Jones agreed to it, so there ain't no negotiating," he said, with finality.

"Alright, alright. Here's what I'll do," Max said. "I'm going to give you a couple of hundred bucks. Will that pay off the tab here and the others on the street?"

"Better make it three," said Isaac. "Jones liked to drink more than he liked to eat."

With all debts settled, Max strolled 75th down towards Chicago Avenue. The South Side was gritty but vibrant with life and community. He popped into a few of the legendary blues joints, soaked up the soul of the city, and grabbed some of the famous fried chicken at Army & Lou's before heading back to his hotel, walking under the regular rumble of the elevated "L" train. He could almost feel Jones walking there with him and realized he missed the man.

Booking last minute for Max had forced Chuck DeWindt to find a seat on the only available carrier to New Delhi. Air India had courteous, even deferential service, but like its host country, it was chaotic. The boarding process was comical, with everyone charging the gate at once. Being the Indian national carrier, nearly all the passengers were from India and other parts of Asia.

Max waited until the melee died down, boarding last, just before the doors closed. Better, he thought, to let them all get settled. Managing to score an exit-row seat, he knew he would need the extra room to stretch out his legs on the long flight. The trip had a scheduled stop in London with a four-hour layover, where he would have enough time to get out and stroll the Heathrow terminal and move his body, which was going to be stiff. And to eat.

Unlike most commercial flights leaving the U.S., Max was a passenger on one that had a distinctly different air. Literally. Over the richly perfumed scents of sandalwood and patchouli worn by both the men and the women was the unmistakable scent of curry. Not wanting to suffer the airline food, many Indian passengers had prepared their food for the flight, and Max wished he had too, awareness growing that he traveled in a flying bazaar.

Once aloft, Max settled in and looked over accumulated background material on India and the Naga Jolokia pepper he was traveling to research. He opened the New Mexico State University report.

The Agricultural Ministry of India asserts that the chile peppers grown in the country's northeast region are the world's hottest. Genetic sources of chile pepper varieties in northeastern India have not been accurately documented, but a few names mentioned include "Naga

Jolokia," "Bhut Jolokia," and "Bih Jolokia." The Assamese word *"Jolokia"* translates as Capsicum pepper. Mathur in India in 1998 reported that the *"Naga Jolokia"* might be a variety of Capsicum frutescens and to have an exceedingly high heat level, possibly approaching 855,000 Scoville heat units (SHUs). There are indications that the military laboratory in Tezpur may be attempting or has been able to assess the actual heat value. The hottest chile pepper currently on record is the Capsicum Chinense cultivar Red Savina habanero, with a heat level of 577,000 SHUs. Based on its reportedly high heat level, the Jolokia may be a member of the chinense, rather than frutescens, species, a determining fact that has yet to be verified. However, no documented native cases of C. chinense have ever been reported in India. It may even be possible that both species are present in the pepper, which would be a global first. The Institute has been unable to obtain eyewitness reports of the fruit growing in its native habitat. Plans for a research junket are desired yet not possible given current budget constraints.

Max - I have arranged a meeting with you and the military scientists in Tezpur, in Assam, who are the ones claiming the Jolokia's discovery. With the military involved, I would make sure they understand we have to verify the findings in our labs, not theirs. So we need to obtain specimens. Good Luck.

Now I get it, thought Max. *They're getting their research done cheaply.* Then, he thought, *all I can do is examine the torturous things, though, maybe eat one.* He tried to envision the experience but couldn't. What then? He figured they trusted his palate enough to send him. Chuck had stressed that they would need a botanist and a lab to get an accurate reading on the chiles. And to get a hold of a specimen.

India itself had dozens of cultivated chile varieties, called *chillis*, in varying shapes and heat levels. However, the Jolokias were capturing the chile world's attention because of the ridiculously high heat factor. As the world authority on chiles, it was strategically important to have the New Mexico State University Chile Pepper Institute's final analysis and stamp of authenticity before the proud Indians could claim they were home to the world's hottest chile pepper.

Max's research was further challenged by the numerous incarnations the Jolokia pepper had acquired in India. Near Tezpur in the far northeast, the *Naga Jolokia* chile was named after the ferocious Naga warriors, inhabitants of Nagaland in Assam, one of India's most fertile and remote regions. The Naga were notorious as headhunters until the 1940s. Other names for this variety were *Bih* "poison" *Jolokia* and *Bhut Jolokia*, meaning "ghost pepper," so hot it could drive away ghosts. In Bhutan, they were called *Bhutias*. Another variety from Bangladesh, the *Dorset Naga*, also vied for the title, as did the *Naga*

Morich, the "snake or serpent chilli," which was reputed to have a "bite like a snake."

Max learned by further reading that the unique peppers in Assam were reportedly used as a cure for stomach ailments and as a remedy to transcend the summer heat, presumably by inducing perspiration. *Only in India*, he thought. *Beat the heat by going hotter.* In the northeast, the peppers also were smeared on fences and used in smoke bombs as a safety precaution to keep wild elephants at a distance. There were reports that the Indian Army was looking at methods of weaponizing the fiery powder into artillery shells to burst over battlefields and riots like mustard gas and immobilize opponents. *The Ring of Fire rumors weren't that far off,* he reasoned.

Assam had experienced years of an extended separatist uprising, which, along with a global decline in demand for Assamese tea leaves and governmental neglect from Delhi, had shattered the regional economy. It was easy for Max to see that being home to the world's hottest pepper could significantly impact the hard-hit northeast, where it could become a valuable cash crop for export and tourism draw. Then Max paused in his thinking. It was the same view Gasanov had expressed about his country. The parallels between Max's current assignment and the one he planned to undertake to Kyrgyzstan were suddenly obvious. He was embarking on the dry run for the mystery that waited a thousand miles north, over the Himalayas and a half dozen other ranges.

At Heathrow, Max disembarked and walked the entire length of the vast, crowded, and chaotic terminal to work out the stiffness and plug into the international energy he always felt in airports. The sounds, faces, and colors were truly global, with London being one of the most important hubs on the planet. The terminals offered foods of every type and an outpost of Harrods. An English breakfast of bangers, potatoes and eggs, and a pint of Bass Ale at the Tin Goose, overlooking the busy runway, helped to set things right on his four-hour layover, reading reports. Watching the takeoffs and landings, Max felt far removed from the Louisiana bayou, Santa Fe, and his beach home. He missed Gus, the bulldog, but knew he was in good hands. The faces of Delphine, Jones, and Lilah reflected back at him in the windows as planes taxied outside. He had abruptly left them behind to embark on a quest and though resolved, felt empty, removed from their presence by his decision. He wished he could smell Lilah, hear her voice.

Once back aboard the 747, an even more international crowd accompanied Max on the trip to Delhi. More Indians, assorted Arabs and Persians, Indonesians, and Africans. He managed to have a window seat's luxury with no one sitting next to him, but a distinguished Indian gentleman presently took the aisle. He turned to Max and introduced himself.

"Hello sir, I am Rajdeep Singh, from Jaipur, in Rajasthan. I would like to make your acquaintance."

"My name is Max Little, Mr. Singh, and I am from California," he said.

"Ahh, Califorrrrrnia. Hollywood, the Golden Gate Bridge, and Palm Springs. I have always wanted to go there. Only our film industry turns out more movies each year than Hollywood. Do you like Bollywood films, Mr. Max?" he asked.

Max had always held a particular fascination for the lavish, over-the-top productions which played on the screens at the Kashmir Palace Restaurant in Laguna, where he went to satiate his spicy curry cravings. The owners, Anil and Letaya Kapoor, had educated Max on Bollywood and became friends, as they all loved spicy foods and sharing stories.

"To be honest, Mr. Singh, I am a fan. Watching your stars Sanjay Dutt and Aishwarya Rai together onscreen is mesmerizing. I think Bollywood films will become a global phenomenon someday."

Mr. Singh became visibly excited that Max knew about Bollywood. Indians were incredibly proud of their thriving film industry.

"Ahhh, you pick your stars well, Mr. Max," he said thoughtfully. "Sanjay Dutt is Bollywood's true bad boy, and Aishwarya Rai is the most beautiful woman in the entire world, not just in India."

"Please, call me Max. I agree wholeheartedly with your assessment, Mr. Singh. And you say you are from Jaipur? I haven't yet been to your city, but I hear it is one of the most enchanting in India."

Singh showed thorough delight. "Then you must visit soon, Max, and stay with my family. I will show you the real sights of Rajasthan, where I work as an exporter of textiles and tour guide. And please call me Raj. Are you married?"

Max shook his head. "No, I'm not Raj. My love seems to have been the world itself."

"A lover you can never truly know, then, Max. She will always mystify you. You have chosen this?" asked Raj.

Max was thoughtful, scratching stubble. "No, it's just worked out that way, I guess. I've been moving around a lot, and no one has been right to bring on the ride."

"Well, perhaps India will be the place where you find love," said Raj. "We've been specializing in it for thousands of years, and obviously with exceptionally satisfactory results. A billion of us can't be wrong, Max!"

"Perhaps Raj. You never know where love will find you, I guess," was all Max could think to say. It occurred to him that perhaps he was the one not looking. The wide world was a tantalizing mistress, and Max had spent years attempting to know her. They went on to talk about India and its burgeoning economy, with the new call centers sprouting across the country to service the needs of the West.

"India is ancient and modern at the same time," said Raj, "vexing and magical."

Inevitably, the conversation turned to food, as usually happened when Max engaged fellow travelers. Like most Indians, Raj was passionate about it.

"I have traveled much of the country. The amazing diversity of food in India reflects our nine-thousand-year history, our interactions with invading and conquered cultures," he said in a voice that bounced along, "and the vast physical and climatic differences of our regions. Plus, over two thousand ethnic groups exist in our country, each with particular traditions and customs. There are more than thirty main languages and many more sub-dialects. Trying to put Indian food into a single category is simply impossible. It would take more than one lifetime to experience them all," he expounded, holding both hands before him for emphasis. The man was an eloquent observer, Max discerned.

One unifying theme, however, in Indian cuisine was spice. India's spices spawned the first global trade, and the continent was the origin of many of them. While the Portuguese were the first to bring chile peppers in the 1500s, they spread quickly across India and developed their own character in many places. Peppers became identified with each region, infused over half a millennia into every one of their cuisines and ethnicities.

Raj became curious. "What is it that brings you to India, Max? Is it business or pleasure? You seem quite interested in our foods."

"I guess my pleasure is my business, Raj, or perhaps the other way around. I'm a spice collector, you might say."

Again, Raj became excited, shifting in his seat like a salesman to face Max. "Well, in India, you will surely do great business. India is the historic kingdom of spices, like no other in the world. Spice is in the land and our blood. Songs and long poems have been written about it, and battles fought over it. It is part of the fire of life."

The fire of life. These words resonated with Max, and he understood that rather than just a necessary step to get to his destination, India was a place that would again only deepen his link to the Ring of Fire. He could feel its unstoppable mystical force.

They disembarked together in Delhi, chatting amiably. Once out of the plane, the undeniable sensation that he had entered another world overcame Max. Indira Gandhi International Airport had the feel of all of India, barely controlled chaos. Delhi smelled like it was burning even in the terminal, as millions of small cooking fires were at work across the teeming city. The air was hazy and thick with the sweet scent of burning wood and cow dung. Vegetarian Hindu India had adapted a surprisingly sustainable resource by not slaughtering its ubiquitous cattle, which roamed the streets of every village and city in the country freely. Their dung was eagerly scraped off the ground and formed into patties, which became fuel for the fires that burned day and night after drying in the sun. India's was an unforgettable smell of life in the process that Max sometimes remembered in dreams.

Raj accompanied Max to the baggage claim, where he would depart for the train to his home in Jaipur. Max planned to make some strategic visits in Delhi and had a connecting flight in three days to Guwahati, the Assam province's central city.

"Please come to visit me in Jaipur, Max. I will show you food that will blow the winds of your mind," he said, handing Max a white business card.

"It would be my pleasure, Raj," said Max, smiling, "and someday I will take you to Universal Studios in Hollywood and then introduce you to Mexican food."

The Indian's eyes opened wide. "Really? You would do that, Max?"

"I would, and I will, Raj. I would very much enjoy being your host. We must stay in touch."

They walked through the hectic terminal and were preparing to make their goodbyes when Raj stopped and said, "Perhaps India is doing its work quickly, my friend."

Max paused to inquire what Raj meant, then followed his gaze down the breezeway where a striking woman stood in their path. Taller than most Indian women, she had similar olive skin and lined eyes, hypnotically green. The woman wore a shiny green kurta, the typical knee-length Indian embroidered shirt with long, flowing sleeves, and white silk pants with sandals. Gold bangles jingled on her wrists. Hair tied back in a ponytail, she looked very much the modern Indian woman but strangely familiar. Perhaps from a dream Max had.

Lilah waved to them, smiling, without a trace of surprise.

INDIA

Max and Lilah stood, staring at each other in the chaotic terminal. Adrenaline coursed through Max's system, who was shocked at the apparition before him. They were an island of three in a sea of India.

"Amazing, your plane was on time," Lilah said, entirely too comfortable. "What a wonderful circus this city is. Seething with life, I can feel it on my skin. Oh, and Namaste."

Raj placed his hands together in response and bowed. Max could only stare, dumbfounded. Lilah was upbeat but calm and appeared as if she had been in India a month.

"Mr. Max didn't tell me he had friends in India," said Raj, bowing. "I am Rajdeep Singh from Jaipur."

Lilah laughed lightly. "I am not from your spectacular country, Mr. Singh, but the kurta I just bought perhaps makes me fit in a bit more. I am from Louisiana in America."

"Ahh, Bourbon Street, Cajun cuisine, Dixieland Jazz, and the Mississippi Delta! I have always wanted to go there," said Raj eagerly.

"Well, perhaps you will, especially if you have a friend like Max here," said Lilah, aware of Max's continued look of disbelief.

"*What's the deal?*" Max blurted out, and not what he wanted to say.

His ears were red, which often happened when he was flustered, or experiencing elevated levels of chile heat. Max hoped she would not notice.

"You're looking a little overheated, Max," said Lilah with a laugh, "Why don't we get out of here and find a cool tea? Raj, would you care to join us until your train departs? We're going to the Imperial."

"The Imperial!" said Raj, with awe. "This is the most famous hotel in all of India, Miss Lilah. I am honored, but this is an expensive place."

"Then come as our guest," said Lilah. "We would love your company, and you can tell us about your country." She then turned to head for the taxis outside.

"*Hold on!*" Max blurted out. He had dropped his duffle bag and refused to move while Lilah and Raj turned and looked at him quizzically. "What are you doing here? and I am not going to the Imperial Hotel," he said, refusing to move. "I have travel documents to arrange, and my hotel's on the other side of town."

As soon as he said it, Max thought he probably looked and sounded like a complete idiot. The chaos of the airport swirled all around them as they all stood looking at each other. Sweat beaded on his forehead and dropped off his nose. He was trying to make sense of the situation, but flight grogginess and India itself made clarity elusive. Max was both excited and confused at Lilah's sudden appearance, halfway around the world. The humidity did not help.

"Oh, just come on, Max," Lilah said, chuckling, very much at ease.

She looked unnervingly natural in her tied back hair and bright Indian attire. "I'll tell you why I'm here when we've settled at the loveliest hotel in India, where we'll have tea with our new friend Raj."

Baffled, Max shook his head and followed the pair to a waiting car at the end of the lengthy line of taxis. Lilah had secured a driver, having already experienced Indira Gandhi International the day before. Bags found the trunk, and the trio slid into the ancient Hindustan Ambassador, the workhorse car of India. Sonia Gandhi, the widow of slain Indian leader Rajiv Gandhi, himself the son of Indira Gandhi, chose to travel only in the native auto for purely nationalistic reasons. As they exited the airport, making their way to National Highway 8, which would take them into Delhi proper, a grouping of tall glass towers loomed on the southern horizon.

"Those are the modern towers of Gurgaon," said Raj, assuming the role of a tour guide. "Since 1997, when your General Electric Company decided to open a call center there, it has quickly become the call center capital of the world. Outsourcing, I believe you call it. When the rest of India sleeps, the lights of Gurgaon burn bright, taking customer service calls from America." He was undeniably proud of India's meteoric rise in the international arena.

They entered a highway unlike any in the ordinary sense. Buses, innumerable overstuffed and swaying trucks, motorbikes, three-wheeled tuk-tuks, taxis, bicycles, and bouncing tractors vied for position on the four-lane thoroughfare. Potholes the size of small meteor craters appeared without warning, obstacles whose avoidance required uncanny skill, or pure luck. Possibly divine intervention. Nothing made any sense, to a Westerner at least, though Lilah smiled blissfully. Cattle that found their way onto the highway were miraculously avoided while entire families sprinted across the road, dodging death. The ridiculously crowded road was in the process of being rerouted for the construction of a new elevated expressway, a significant development that was to last five years. Everyone in India seemed headed into Delhi, already stuffed with twelve million souls, yet their driver somehow negotiated the mayhem. One could not create a video game with more moving obstacles.

"I learned after arriving yesterday that riding in a car in India is an exercise in acceptance," interjected Lilah. "You accept the possibility that this may be your last journey. You also accept that there is, at least in India, amazing poetry in the chaos. So you lean in, and you let go. Then you really arrive." With the window down, her hair blowing in the breeze, Lilah appeared to talk to the chaos itself.

Max looked at her, again suddenly aware of her ease and way of seeing the world. That she sat here with him, riding in a taxi in Delhi to the Imperial Hotel, was mystifying. She seemed to enjoy the effect it had upon him. He decided to relax and let her have control, something he was not used to allowing, but the feeling of simply wanting to take in her presence was overpowering his conditioning. While watching her, he felt that things were going to be interesting at the very least, possibly perplexing, even as he worked them out and pursued his destination.

The Imperial Hotel had been, since 1931, the location of a significant part of India's history. It was the first among the legendary "Four Maidens of the East," which included The Strand Hotel in Rangoon, Raffles Hotel in Singapore, and the Great Eastern & Oriental in Calcutta. The Imperial was historically the only place where British and Indian royalty could meet on equal ground. It had been designed by architect D.J. Bromfield, a student of Edward Lutyens, the man who inaugurated his design of the new capital in Delhi that same year. Delhi had replaced Calcutta as the capital, and The Imperial was an icon of both British and modern India. Pandit Nehru, Mahatma Gandhi, Muhammad Ali Jinnah, and Britain's Lord Mountbatten would casually meet at The Imperial to discuss India's momentous partition and Pakistan's creation. The hotel embodied visual, tangible history.

Turning off the delirious Highway 8 onto Ashok Road and then onto Janpath, "the Queen's Way," the venerable Ambassador pulled down the palm-lined drive of the regal hotel. A clutch of liveried attendants opened all three doors of the car at once. Bearded and turbaned Sikhs, dressed in black, satin-embroidered coats of the finest quality, opened the doors to the hotel in unison. Even Max, used to more lowbrow digs, was impressed with the ritual and the unmatched impression of entry to the place.

"Welcome to the Imperial, Mr. Little," said the attendant who opened his door. "We will take your bags to your room, and your tea has been set in the Atrium."

Max corrected the fierce-looking yet utterly professional man. "We're just coming for refreshments, my friend, and will be moving on to another hotel. If you would be so kind as to store my bag for a bit."

The attendant politely nodded, sending a sidelong glance at Lilah, who smiled as she had the whole way into the city. Max wondered how they knew his name, but with his mind focused on lounging in the grand hotel's cool marble, he let it pass.

Newer hotels than the Art Deco-inspired Imperial existed, but this felt most like India. High tea there, served in the lofty central atrium, has been a ritual of well-to-do Indians and travelers for decades. In the center of the skylight-lit room, a fountain played water music accompanied by four other groups' soft conversation. The sunlight overhead cast a yellow glow on the white marble floors and walls, creating a pleasant escape quite cool in contrast to the daytime heat of Delhi. Max, who usually headed for a simple guest house and looked and felt rugged after eighteen hours of travel, took in the room and then slumped into a tall wicker chair.

"Water, iced green tea, and a bunch of those little finger sandwiches, please," he asked the waiter while Lilah and Raj went a more traditional route, ordering English tea with milk and sugar. Sandwiches and cakes arrived on metal carriers that stacked the plates three high.

Raj and Lilah talked about their lives and homes while Max devoured sandwiches. He thought about the many documents he would need to travel in Central Asia, an often-daunting task in itself, and which way to go. His mind was moving forward now that he was relaxed and fed, though the intervention of Lilah's presence made the immediate future suddenly askew.

Max looked over at her, and as he did, she turned from her conversation with Raj, apparently about chile peppers, and asked, "Do you know how the Scoville Test determines the relative heat of a pepper, Max?"

Surprised by the technical question, Max stammered an answer. "It measures the heat of a pepper by, uh, determining the level of capsaicin after diluting it in water. Somewhat subjective based on the palates of the human tasters. I trust my own sniffer, actually."

Though he was an authority on peppers and successful at crafting them into varying forms of fiery delicacies, he gave little weight to precisely how other people determined their actual spiciness. He opted to trust his super-refined palate to tell him how hot things were, which served him well, and trusted the chemists to give him the Scoville rating numbers that were a mandatory inclusion on the hottest of the hot sauce labels. Chile-heads demanded to know when crossing the high tolerance threshold, and the higher the number, the greater the endorphin rush. Hot sauce makers generally included the rating with a warning for the uninitiated, and for heat junkies, it was a highly effective marketing tool. It was safe to say that Max, himself, was an addict.

"It's actually very straightforward, Max," Lilah said, confidently at ease. "The Scoville rating is the number of drops of sugar water required to completely dilute the capsaicin extracted from a chile until there is no heat detectable by a panel of five separate tasters. It's been the accepted method of determining spiciness since Wilbur Scoville developed his Scoville Organoleptic Test in 1912. The problem lies in the test's subjectivity to the testers' sensations, you're right, and palate fatigue after tasting too much spice. New laboratory tests and advances in high-performance liquid chromatography will soon make the Scoville Test obsolete, but for now, it's the definitive benchmark for assessing heat levels in chiles." She completed her short dissertation with a satisfied smile and resumed her afternoon tea enjoyment, though both Raj and Max regarded her with raised eyebrows.

"I had no idea there was such a passionate interest in chiles, even universities dedicated to their study," Raj said.

"Yes, a huge interest," said Lilah, looking directly at Max. "And to some, an obsession. You see, when capsaicinoids come into contact with the nerve endings in the tongue and mouth, the brain is tricked into thinking that they are burning. The brain jumps into action, increasing the heart rate to get rid of the invasive substance. Then, the mouth salivates, the nose runs, and sweating occurs. The brain secretes a strategic natural painkiller, endorphin, which acts like morphine, perceiving it has been injured. This is the fabled chile high for which Max and his strange compatriots are constantly searching. And like morphine, people slowly build up a tolerance to the effects, always seeking out hotter and hotter chiles. It's a cycle of pain and pleasure disguised as food."

Max stared off into the distance, pretending not to pay attention. It was clear he represented the obsession, even to Raj, who skillfully and diplomatically provided Max with a way out.

"Mr. Max, why such a focus on where chiles came from and how they got to where they are?"

Sensing a timely opportunity to remove the focus from himself, Max inserted what he believed was a wise nugget. "Apart from the fact that spicy foods comprise a multibillion-dollar industry worldwide," said Max, "tracing the migration of chiles from their origins in South America has had a clear impact on the study of history and botany worldwide. Since 1492 and Columbus's arrival in the New World, it took only fifty years for chile peppers to migrate across the world and become infused into nearly every culture, so much so that the Chinese believe the origin of chiles is in the south of their own country. It's the story of humanity, wrapped up in pods of chiles."

With his short dissertation delivered, Max glanced across to Lilah, raised a single "Well, how about that!" eyebrow, and resumed his tea sandwich feast. She merely shook her head.

"I can't imagine an India without them," said Raj. "They are part of our culture."

Their lighthearted and pleasant conversation drifted on for an hour while Max and Lilah peppered Raj with questions about his country. Now fully slouched into the wicker chair, Max was particularly interested in the Assam region in India's far northeast.

"Nagaland," Raj called it. "Home of an ancient warrior culture with a history going back two millennia or more. One of the last areas to be brought under British colonial control and a reputation for being fiercely independent. If I recall, the tea plantations of the Assamese Himalayan foothills were gems in the colonial crown. An active separatist movement thrives there to this day, I understand. Since independence, the Assam region provinces, called the Seven Sisters, have felt continually marginalized by the central government so far away in Delhi. The mystical region is bordered by Myanmar, China, Bhutan, and Bangladesh, and those countries have as much, if not more, of an impact on the area as Delhi." Raj spoke crisp Indian-inflected English and proved an educated India observer.

Max considered that the unearthing of possibly the world's hottest chile pepper could bring newfound notoriety to the often-overlooked region. He imagined the train station packed with chile heads from all over the world, making the pilgrimage to the source of the hottest fire on earth. And the other half of his mind drifted off to Kyrgyzstan, and Gasanov, and his pleas for Max to help its people. To uncover a mystery much the same as he was now attempting. He knew now that he had to go, to unravel the puzzle there. But threats and dangers remained, in the form of Bakiyev and his henchmen. Returning to the present, Max tried to focus on the immediate journey ahead.

"What do you know of Assamese cuisine, Raj?' he asked, adding, "Are the foods there particularly spicy?"

Raj squinted in thought, then added, "An interesting question, Max. While my travels have taken me to northeast India to discover the tea plantations or venture into the Himalayas, the cuisine is a mystery I've yet to unearth. The influence of Burmese, Bhutanese, and Himalayan cultures has created a distinctly unique cuisine that is often hard even for Indian nationals to decipher. As to spiciness, all I can offer is that the Naga Warrior myth has become so infused into Assamese culture that some dishes and foods are named after them, including, I believe, the local chile."

The Naga Jolokia, Max thought.

"Are you planning a trip to Assam?" Raj asked. "For if so, you must take the train. Flying will cause you to miss some of the most amazing sights in India. The train follows the Ganges most of the way, goes right through Agra, home of the Taj Mahal, and the ancient holy city of Varanasi on the Ganges. They are not to be missed!"

Max liked his new Indian friend increasingly more. Raj was the perfect guest, with a curious mind and a happy, eager demeanor, and he was a fountain of information.

As he considered his new friend, Lilah interjected, "Why don't you come with us, Raj? We know so little about Assam and could use a guide. I think we can afford it, right, Max?"

Max paused, dumbfounded. *What is Lilah doing here?* He thought. Her presence was causing his equilibrium to falter.

"Us? We? What are you doing here? What's going on!" he demanded.

Lilah looked at him and laughed.

"You really are silly," she said, biting into a sandwich. "How are you going to know if you've found the hottest pepper in the world? One that may be a completely unique variety? Are you going to eat it? What then? Chuck DeWindt sent me to back you up, to give you and the university credibility on this caper. The university's bankrolling this part of the trip, and they want qualified verification. You've got a renowned palate and may be a famous chile cowboy, but I've got the credentials, pal, so I'm coming along. If that's alright with you, or even if it's not."

She looked Max straight in the eyes, making sure he got the point. He felt blood pressure rising straight to his ears, which he knew were beginning to glow red. The fact that she was right sent flashes of realization through his brain and into his blank and blinking eyes.

Max felt undermined, frustrated that DeWindt had not let him know of the change in plans. He questioned who was in charge of the Indian quest they were now on. They would be pursuing the Jolokia together, another wave that crashed into his reckoning. Realizing he was thinking the same thing as she regarding Raj made it somehow less frustrating, however, something to agree on. After furrowing his brow and faking some mental calculations, he said, "Sure, I suppose we could use a guide. I was thinking the same thing myself."

Lilah again had a knowing smile subtly cross her face. Max felt as if he was merely acting out motions that she already knew and understood, that he was part of something he had less control over, and she somehow more. Yet he was humbled by her strength, her conviction, and the realization that she was eminently capable of running the Jolokia operation without him. At the same time, he managed to be soothed by her presence, her voice, easing the pressure in his head. She looked so natural, at ease in India, and he was aware of a sense of, perhaps, comfort in her presence, something he did not recall feeling before. The shock of seeing her had become eased by India, Raj, and the Imperial.

Raj sat up straight, and his face brightened. "If such an arrangement is desirable to you, I could make some adjustments in my schedule. I would be honored to be your guide in India."

Despite consummate professionalism, it was difficult for the man to contain his excitement. He wrung his hands and bobbed up and down in his chair, though only slightly. "However, I must travel to my home in Jaipur to see my wife, Ambika, and kiss my son. I can be back in two days' time if that is acceptable, and there are trains every hour."

Max assured him that it was, as they confirmed the plan and took their leave for a few days, Raj shaking Max's hand vigorously and giving Lilah a courteous bow. He walked briskly out of the hotel, his pleasure evident.

'What a charming fellow," Lilah said. "He'll make an excellent chaperone."

Max wanted to agree but became confused by the word *chaperone*. It was evident Raj would be an excellent resource on their journey and good company. He understood that he and Lilah would be traveling together, working together. An intimate set of circumstances for two people just beginning to explore one another and who had shared and experienced much in a brief time. She mystified him, a new sensation, and perhaps having Raj along would help cushion the emotions Max was experiencing. Again, it was as if she had already known that Raj would come along and that he would be joining them on their journey. He stared at her as he worked through things and was shaken out of his thoughts by her question.

"Won't he?"

Max was able to merely stammer, "Uh, yes, he certainly will."

Another of Lilah's sly smiles made him blink hard and return to the present. She proved one maneuver ahead of him, it appeared, every step of the way.

Properly nourished and cooled, Max made it known that he was ready for his guesthouse room across town and a shower. After a signal from Lilah, an attendant approached. "Your room is ready, Mr. Little. May I escort you there?"

"That's mighty generous of you, considering my room is on the other side of Delhi," said Max.

Seeming only slightly confused but with the utmost professionalism, the attendant courteously responded. "Actually, Sir, your suite on the third floor is directly across from Ms. DeVillier's. There is a bottle of champagne compliments of Mr. DeWindt from New Mexico. Your bags have already been taken to your room."

Too tired to protest and finally realizing the reason for Lilah's smug smiles since the airport, Max allowed himself to become a guest of The Imperial's legendary comforts. The brightly liveried attendant led him to the third floor, where a small anteroom with a couch and two chairs acted as the waiting area for two adjacent suites, Max's being on the right. The attendant then escorted him into a large, bright room overlooking lush gardens and palm trees, swaying in the light breeze. A billowy king-sized bed faced a couch and reading chairs, while the sound of fountains trickled in the slightly open windows, and a ceiling fan turned lazily. It was seriously sweet digs, far from Max's usual mode of beatnik travel, and he felt out of place in his faded jeans, scuffed boots, and travel-worn Johnny Cash t-shirt. His battered duffle bag waited in the corner, looking entirely forlorn, yet the graciousness of the attendant put him at ease.

"Enjoy The Imperial, Mr. Little, and contact me directly with anything at all you may need. My name is Anush." He handed Max a personalized card and backed out the door, quietly closing it.

On the small table by the room's yellow couch and chairs was a silver tray with champagne on ice and a handwritten note in a cream-colored Imperial envelope. There were two glasses. The message had been transcribed per the sender's instructions.

Max, if you're reading this, you must have made it to Delhi. Enjoy The Imperial! It's the least I could do for sending you on a trek across India just to go and burn your tongue for the university. And sending Lilah was almost all my idea. She proposed it, and I agreed. I thought having a reputable botanist would lend the expedition some credibility. Plus, from what I've heard about your exploits in Louisiana, I gathered that you wouldn't mind having her around. Now find that damn chile. Cheers! Chuck

Realizing that being here and surprising Max was Lilah's idea spun his gears. The expedition certainly had a compelling scientific and historical appeal, which would motivate a keen botanist like her. And that Chuck DeWindt, one of the field's most respected authorities, had not only endorsed but bankrolled the venture, made it all seem to fit together easily. *Too easily*, Max thought. There had to be a catch, and he couldn't put his finger on it. He needed a bath and made his way across the room.

The expansive space was more of a tiled spa lounge than a bathroom facility. An Art Deco-inspired room included a vanity and large mirror with a velvet upholstered stool and a cushioned bench directly below an open window overlooking the lush gardens. A deep porcelain tub stood ready with bathrobe and slippers draped over the edge, as though Anush knew Max would soon be needing them. He ran the water hotter than usual and sank into a steamy trance enhanced by the trickling of fountains and the scented breeze of smoke and spice, of India.

After nearly an hour's soak, Max emerged, feeling rested and fresh. The old jeans and boots returned, graced by a new t-shirt commemorating the musician Gram Parsons, a brilliant artist gone too early. Atop the table in the corner sat a picture book of elaborate size titled *The New Delhi: Edward Luytens' Vision of an Imperial Capital.* Max settled onto the couch and thumbed through the pages.

The metropolis now known as Delhi had been the seat of empires stretching back over a thousand years. Originally the home of the Indian Rajput emperors, the city was known as Indraprastha until its conquer by the Afghan warlord Muhammad of Ghori made it the first Delhi Sultanate in 1192. In 1398, the legendary Tamerlane, whose vast empire rivaled Genghis Khan, arrived with his Persian armies to end the Delhi Sultanate. After Tamerlane, the city-state passed from sultan to sultan, ultimately falling to Babur in the battle of Panipat in 1506, heralding the beginning of the Mughal Empire, which would leave profound marks upon Indian society, and architecture. Though the Mughal emperors favored Agra as their actual capital, in 1638, the emperor Shah Jahan built the walls of Old Delhi, establishing it as his new capital city. Finally, after generations of decline and excess, the remnants of the once-mighty Mughal empire fell to the British in 1803.

The British made Calcutta their initial capital, given its convenient location on the sea and easily protected by the British navy's overpowering force. However, a hundred years later, needing a more centrally located government, the British decided on a new capital in Delhi, the old capital. After the rebellion of its people in 1857, the British largely destroyed the city, renaming many of its ancient monuments after British heroes and monarchs, and in 1911 King George V and Queen Mary laid the first stone in the foundation of New Delhi. Desiring to co-opt the former power of the Mughal dynasty they replaced, the British plan for Delhi was intended to project the immense power and reach of the British Raj. A new city design stretched across vast marshlands outside the traditional city center to visually solidify this power. It became the most remarkable British building project since London's rebuilding after the Great Fire of 1666. The project, which required 26,000 laborers and almost two decades, has been called the most magnificent architectural achievement in all of British history.

Upon seeing it for the first time in the 1930s, the British writer Robert Byron said, "People don't realize what has been done, how stupendous it is, and such a work of beauty, so unlike the English."

It was also the last British construction project in India, as it passed to India's people in 1947. The British controlled their grand capital city for only sixteen years.

As Max leafed through the pages with images showing the layout and construction of Delhi, he drifted off into a deep and relaxed sleep. When he awoke, the sun was noticeably lower and the light more diffused. Something had roused him from his slumber. Rising, he noticed an envelope placed under his door. On cream-colored Imperial stationery, he removed a beautifully handwritten letter.

Max Mi Amigo and Pepper Confidante –

My sources inform me that you are in India on an Indiana Jones search for the hottest chile on the planet. What an endorphin rush you must be having as the executor of such a historic and groundbreaking scientific chile pepper journey.

I was convinced by Bakiyev's friends in Santa Fe to return to Kyrgyzstan (via New York, where I went sightseeing with my captors, who for some reason dressed like rap music professionals), and where I am a de facto prisoner of my office in the Agriculture Ministry. Fortunately, the building has a commissary where I can eat and a gym where I shower. My family believes I'm living with a mistress here in Bishkek and will not speak to me from our home outside the city.

The mystery of the peppers from the Tien Shan foothills deepens. The farmers I procured the original samples from have gone underground and have not reappeared at the world-famous Osh market. Bakiyev may have people looking for them. My deepest fear is that unless we can locate and make contact with them, the Naryn valley people who possess knowledge of this remarkable fruit will either keep it hidden forever or eradicate it. The proud people of Naryn and the Tien Shan Mountains have no love for the central government nor the criminal gangs from the cities.

Max, being that you are nearly next door in India, I implore you to come to my country and unravel this Fire of the Valley mystery for my people's benefit. Its exploitation by the central government and its partner crooks will be an incalculable loss. The Indiana Jones of spicy things in you, I know, wants to be the one to make this discovery. If you come, I must caution you: DO NOT arrive by air at the airports in Bishkek or Osh. The Minister of Agriculture is wary of my connection to you and has placed you on a watchlist. You will have much better luck at the land border crossings. If I were you (and right now very much wish I were), I would travel to China and venture to Kashgar in that country's far west. Kashgar is the original endpoint of the Silk Road and could provide some substantial background for the concept of the migration of chiles in Central Asia. From Kashgar, arrange to enter Kyrgyzstan via the Torugart Pass in the Southeast of the country. This route will take you directly through the Tien Shan Mountains and down to the Naryn River valley and the hamlet of Dostuk, where I would seek out a man by the name of Nazaat Buntun. But be forewarned: he can smell a rat a mile off and had me pegged the minute I walked through his door as a well-disguised cutlery salesman. He's exceptionally good with a knife and is known to make the finest of those for miles around, a fact I witnessed for myself. On the way there, you will have an opportunity to visit Tash Rabat, an amazingly well-preserved caravanserai from the Silk Road era and a place I have a feeling figures into this entire escapade. I beg you, please come, Max. Help me. Help us.

A footnote: While you are in Delhi, you should visit the Manuscripts Division in the Central Asian Antiquities Section of the National Museum, at the intersection of the Janpath and Rajpath. Locate an earnest young man in that department by the name of Rudra. He will have some materials gathered for you that you may find helpful. You're welcome.

A Second footnote: It's very possible my two always inappropriately costumed friends are in India, looking for you. If I was able to unearth your plans from halfway around the world, then others certainly can. Use cash whenever possible, and make sure your back is watched.

Also, please tip the lovely young lady at your hotel who transcribed all of this while on the phone with me so many mountain ranges away, imprisoned in an office with a sad excuse for a view.

Until We Meet Again in Happier Times, Gasanov

After rereading the letter from Gasanov, Max sat in thought. Whenever the man entered the picture, Max's world became somehow altered, often for the worse. Yet it was difficult to dislike him, and Max was moved by his pleas for aid. Somehow, Gasanov was convinced that Max was the only person in the world capable of solving the Kyrgyz puzzle and getting him out of trouble. If he could escape the same trouble himself.

He dialed Lilah's room. "I have champagne on ice from Chuck DeWindt and a letter from Gasanov. Want to come over?" Precisely twelve seconds later, there was a knock on his door.

"Well?" Lilah said, "What gives?"

She was refreshed and wearing a shining gold kurta and sandals, as Indian as any Indian woman he had ever seen. Max couldn't help himself from sending a long, silent stare.

"Oh, this?" she said as she twirled in a circle. "A gift from Chuck. To help me acclimate, he says. Isn't it fun?"

Fun wasn't the word that struck Max. She was refined and relaxed. "It's perfect on you," he managed to say. "The gold brings out your green eyes."

It was the first time Max had openly commented on Lilah's appearance, a revelation not lost on either of them, and the effect was immediate. By making this simple observation, Max not only let it be known but became fully aware of his attraction to this person on many levels. And for the first time with a woman, Max did not know what to do. His emotional framework had become scrambled, and the loose, nonlinear but controlled path of his life disrupted.

Lilah's refreshing ease never faltered. "Let's open the champagne! What's the word from Gasanov?"

Max handed her the letter and worked on opening the champagne, pouring Lilah a glass, which she took and sipped, eyes never leaving the document before her.

"Lovely and crisp," she said, scanning the correspondence, "and perfect for a balmy Delhi evening." She summed up the situation coolly, sipping effervescence. "So Gasanov's a prisoner, and you need to go to Kyrgyzstan to spring him, and to find a mythical pepper sought by a corrupt government official and his underworld partners, who are looking for you already, correct?"

"Essentially, yes," Max replied. "With a short side trip across India to identify the hottest chile pepper in the world. And we can't forget that they know who you are as well. You are now in the club, for better or worse."

Lilah regarded Max. He was calm, casual, boyish, a surfer with a vocabulary, a successful entrepreneur, and worldly. Confident, not arrogant. Give him a hat and a whip, and he could be *the* Indiana Jones of the ridiculous chile pepper world.

"Certainly for the better. This is an interesting world you live in, Max," she said, "What is it about chiles that makes you people so crazy?"

Taking a long draw of the champagne, Max leaned back and absorbed her query. He let his mind clear as he heard the gurgle of fountains and the rustle of palm fronds, felt the warm early evening breeze on his face. He considered "us people."

"Chile heads, heat freaks, endorphin cowboys, we're called lots of things," he said. "We're a specific and unique subset of the human race. A finely focused classification of humanity linked only by a passion, no, obsession, with the heat generated by this fruit of the earth. We come in all shapes, sizes, and colors from across the globe, chasing a fire that will scorch our flesh as we bathe ecstatically in a pleasure and pain delirium caused by something we choose to eat. We can identify each other in bazaars, festivals, and cantinas like vampires. Often a simple nod acknowledges one another, a knowing smack of the lips that follows a moment of something imbibed that approaches hot lava, willingly and with relish. It's a fraternity of incendiary consumption. A near-religious order of epicurean fanatics."

Finishing the speech, he drained the glass and folded his arms behind his head. Lilah stared at him in disbelief. He thoroughly believed it, even personified it. Max was an enigma, a palace of many doors, for all his outward simplicity, she thought. The adventure was going to be interesting.

"I need a city walk," Max said decidedly. "And some food. Are you ready to explore the Queen's Way and experience the Janpath People's Market? Certainly, a vibrant Delhi baptismal."

Lilah had been ready for hours. "Absolutely. Let's get out and see Delhi."

As they exited the stately hotel, the liveried doormen bowed formally, jeweled turbans sparkling in the twilight.

"Enjoy the magic of Delhi, Miss DeVillier and Mr. Little," they said in unison.

They took a path that led across the verdant grounds and emptied them onto Janpath Road, one of the main thoroughfares of Delhi. Designed initially as a perpendicular counter to the Rajpath, or 'King's Way,' Janpath was the 'Queen's Way.' India no longer found importance in kings and queens after independence, and Janpath became, democratically, the People's Way. And to the people, it certainly belonged. Each side of the broad boulevard hosted a long row of countless businesses on the ground floor, topped by many offices and other concerns. A canopy of trees dotted the median and curbs, creating a breezy, shaded avenue with wide sidewalks. Off the main road, numerous smaller alleys branched off, each with its thriving market. Janpath always played host to a sea of people, more so as the evening progressed and temperatures dropped, and became undeniably the most colorful avenue in all of Delhi.

The road hosted innumerable touristy curio and trinket shops and vendors hawking everything from miniature *hookahs* and Taj Mahal magnets to handmade bags from Gujarat, Hindu statuary, tiny bookstalls, jewelry, tapestries, scarves, and of course, saris. The stalls became brightly lit with evening falling, while gas streetlamps burned atop Art Deco poles. Music of all types echoed over itself, creating a chaotic, festive atmosphere. Janpath was an eclectic riot of haggling and commerce, a mix of families, couples, merchants, and serious shoppers. Over one small lane hung a sign reading "Tibetan market" in Sanskrit, Tibetan, and English, and music and incense smoke wafted from the lane.

"Oh, let's go down there," Lilah pleaded.

Tibetans had fled their country by the thousands after China's 1950 annexation, and this small market had been their home in Delhi since the exodus. Lilah found beautiful red coral and blue lapis bracelets in hammered silver, and Max picked a strand of prayer flags, the style traditionally flown in Tibet. *Nag Champa* incense burned at every stall, creating an ethereal scented fog. The loud music of the main boulevard became replaced by recordings of Tibetan chanting and simple, stringed instrumentals. The narrow avenue felt as magical and mystical as Tibet itself, and the spell worked on them. The new travel partners strolled a bazaar halfway around the world, far from their own lives, as mutual attraction crackled statically in the air between their bodies. Max felt an overwhelming urge to take Lilah's hand in his but then admitted how little he knew about the magnetic woman, her past, loves, hopes, and dreams. He felt her specialness, yet she remained a seductive mystery.

They strolled the avenue, without hurry or a destination, in casual silence for an hour. Not usually at a loss for words, Max spit out a question. "Any boyfriends?" was all he found to say.

Lilah looked at Max quizzically. It wasn't an odd question. But the timing was, and she had not expected it. "Why yes, a few," she said and continued walking.

Her face became clouded. Max waited for her to continue, but she let her response float in the air, challenging Max to clarify. "I mean currently," he said, "the past is just the past."

Lilah sighed but kept on walking. "Growing up on our farm, we were quite isolated," she replied. "There were bayou boys and school heartbreaks, but for the most part, I stuck to home. By the time I was old enough to begin thinking about the future and my place in the world, I'd gotten pretty heavily involved with the son of a wealthy landowner who'd been courting me since I arrived at the local parish high school. For generations, his family owned the farming property and were known in southern Louisiana as descendants of former slave owners. But Mitch didn't appear to share his family's conservative Confederate yearnings. He asked me to marry him at one point, but I'd already been accepted to Baton Rouge to study botany. He wasn't used to hearing 'no' and turned vile and mean. He told me a woman's place was in the home, his big antebellum mansion, of course, and that science was a man's profession, that I'd ultimately fail and spend my life alone. I set out to prove him wrong."

"I just meant currently," Max said.

She seemed not to hear him. "In college, I had as much fun as anyone else but focused mainly on my studies. There were boyfriends, but no one serious. Most weekends and holidays I spent at home, helping on the farm. After my mother died, there was a lot to do. Fortunately, we had Delphine, and she never pressured me one way or another. It was as if she knew I'd find my way. My last boyfriend was a professor in the master's program who got jealous when my work received more recognition than his own. I realized that age is not a guarantee of maturity. Since then, teaching and my doctoral work have been my passion."

Lilah kept on walking, lost in thought. She had been vague on whether or not there was anyone presently, yet Max appreciated her story, even though he hadn't asked her to tell it. It was as if Lilah wanted him to know who she was and why. Then she stopped and looked straight at Max.

"I'm a blank book with only some of the pages filled in. And I'm here, filling in pages, walking in India. With you, Max. I called Chuck DeWindt, and here we are. Delphine told me that my journey lay here, alongside you, and that's why I came. Where it leads, I don't know, but I'm here with eyes wide open, ready to embrace whatever comes. It's going to be an adventure, that is certain, and you aren't bad company. Now let's buy some of those pointy genie shoes I've always dreamed of having."

Her answer was as heartwarming as it was disarming. Max had no response to it, and it seemed clear that Lilah didn't need one. Yet it brightened his mood even as it left hazy the question of romantic entanglements. She proved honest and open, and Max vowed to approach the adventure and their journey with the same "eyes wide open" mindset. His mood lifted, and his heart was light.

"The shoes are called *jutis*," Max said, smiling.

Then he perceived his palate craved sensation, a typical response to a change in mood. For Max, food had become an emotional barometer, with meals celebrations of positive outcomes. And everything else.

After they had located the stall with the best selection of Rajasthani Jutis and picked out a pair for each of them, Max proposed a meal. Lilah, too was ready to dine, having bathed in the scents of Janpath street food for an hour, and agreed to follow Max to a place he knew from previous visits.

The family-owned Nair Kerala Tamarind House had been operating for three generations. Since their arrival from Kerala along the south Indian coast, Nair's had been a sought-after outpost of the best fruit and spice-infused foods from India's tropical south. Sunil Nair ruled over the kitchen and had a heavy hand with the spices in his tropically inspired foods. Located on a narrow side alley, Nair's hid behind a thick hedge from the Janpath melee.

Wafts of coconut, curry, mango, and tamarind greeted them as they entered, and waiters carrying whole fish steaming in banana leaves scurried past. Sunil's wife, Areetha, smiled broadly as soon as she recognized an old friend.

"Max!" she said, approaching with open arms. "Sunil will be so excited to see you."

A tiny woman with round, warm eyes and a lilting, cheerful voice, Areetha acted as if Max had been there only yesterday. She led them to a table in the corner, private but with a full view of the room. Indians of all types and very few foreigners patronized Nair's, always a good sign for Max.

Areetha brought them cold and thick yogurt-based mango lassis to start and asked, "Shall I just have Sunil send out what he feels like, as usual, Max?"

"Absolutely!" seemed all Max needed to say. Then, considering he wasn't dining alone, said to Areetha, "Perhaps tone down the spice for my guest."

It was more a question than demand, and Lilah interjected, "Absolutely not! Please ask the chef to prepare everything exactly as he wants us to have it."

Max felt instantly relieved, sending an approving wink to his alluring dining companion. Heat was on the horizon, and he had found yet another fine attribute to attach to her. Shortly after, a steady parade of waiters began to appear at the table.

First were served an array of chutneys, the ubiquitous, all-purpose Indian condiment. On a tray sat the standard mint, coriander, and green chile chutney. Then sweet coconut milk chutney spiced heavily with black pepper, spicy tomato chutney laced with dried chile flakes, and *Pacha Manga Chammanthi*, the tart, sweet mango chutney flavored with tamarind, for which Kerala is known. Also, a large bowl of "gunpowder," a special fiery southern chutney made of roasted lentils, ground red *Kanthari Mukalu* chiles, and an array of pungent spices, coarsely ground and blended with melted ghee.

That was just the condiments. Then began a presentation of dishes brought by various waiters, each with a brief but professional description. First, with tamarind sauce, *Chaat Pakora Kachoris*, fried dumplings filled with potato, peas, and fresh hot and citrusy green chiles. In a hammered brass bowl came *Pandhi* curry, tart and blisteringly spicy from the Coorg region, a rich dish of small pieces of pork in a thick, spicy, hot, and sour yellow gravy. The pork had been marinated in fruit vinegar and cooked with three treatments of chiles. Flecks of red pepper flakes and green chile wheels hinted at its latent heat. The food and smells were ethereal, sensual as they dove into each dish.

Then appeared *Sarson Murgh*, mustard chicken, simmered in the seven Indian *Garam Masala* spices, basted in mustard oil and mustard seed, and cooked in a clay tandoori oven, which offered the nose a heady mustard greeting. It revealed layers of cardamom, cumin, clove, cinnamon, coriander, and nutmeg as they peeled it apart. A whole large squash on an oblong platter followed, called a *bottlegourd*, hollowed out and filled with its meat, dried smoky *Goan Gavti* chiles, lentils, coconut milk, and curry leaves, and baked in a tandoori oven. Alone it could have fed a family of four. Sweetfish curry sauteed with coconut milk, grated coconut, and *kokum*, a sour fruit native to Kerala. Notes of the tropics and dancing levels of spice infused the food throughout. A bowl of *Sorpotel* followed, cubes of lean pork cooked in fiery red gravy thickened with pig's blood, dense, rich, and deeply hot. Wafts of cinnamon and chile powder perfumed the air as it arrived. And finally, fish *Kolivaadi*, Barramundi fish rolled in coarse cornmeal and an array of spices and dried ground chiles, then fried. It came to the table still crackling from the hot oil resting on a bed of banana leaves, flaky and tantalizingly spicy. Each dish varied in nuance and heat, and with the array of chutneys liberally applied, it represented a sumptuous feast with textures and combinations unique in the world. They became immersed in the flavors and ample levels of spice, speaking little, each of them focused on new taste sensations and the piquancy of many layers.

Sunil made his appearance along with the sizzling fish, round to his wife's petite frame but only slightly taller. His apron covered a healthy belly that bounced when he laughed, which was often.

"Max! It's been too long, my friend!" Sunil followed with a hearty hug. He smelled of curry and cinnamon. "How is your dinner? And who is this?" he said with a jolly laugh.

"Your food is as delicious as ever, and this is my, uh, business associate, Lilah," said Max. "It's her first time in your country."

Lilah stood and offered her hand and became immediately embraced as well. "Lilah! What a lovely name. It sounds like a flower," Sunil said. "How did you enjoy your first meal in India?"

"Why thank you, Mr. Nair, this has been a most memorable meal. One I shall never forget, I assure you." And Lilah meant it, fanning herself with her napkin. "I am intrigued by the strong presence of mustard in Indian cooking. Is it the same all over India?"

"I am Sunil, and my wife is Areetha, Miss Lilah. And any business associate of Max's is a friend of ours," said the chef. Then he turned serious, projecting his passion for his country's cuisine.

"Most cooks in India will not cook without mustard oil, especially in the northeast and south, though cheaper vegetable-based oils are now available. Such has been the case for all of known history. The Vedas mentioned mustard oil five thousand years ago, and Ayurveda practitioners have been using it since then, along with cooks. It has a very high smoking point, so it's perfect for frying, and it stands beautifully on its own. More importantly, mustard adds another level of complexity to Indian food that other cuisines often lack. It adds layers and depth to the flavors. Cooks have abundant seasoning and spice with the various interpretations of garam masala, the Indian spice blend. Being from the tropical south, we use fruit for sweetness and acidity, then coconut milk, and coconut meat for a creamy texture. Mustard has a strong flavor that does not linger." Sunil spoke passionately with his hands. "I believe that along with curry, mustard is the flavor of India."

"The complexity of the food transfixes me," Lilah said. "And your evident embrace of history. I am your new biggest fan."

"Excellent!" he bellowed, followed by yet another of Sunil's embraces and a belly-jiggling laugh.

With a wink at Max, Sunil then said, "I assume you are on the hunt, Max? Following your appetite around the globe, as usual? Have you any new chiles for me to try?"

"You guess correctly, my friend," said Max. "We are in search of the hottest peppers on the planet, which may be here in India, in fact. Next, we are off on a train to Agra, Varanasi, and Assam in search of the earth's fiery delights."

Sunil approved. "Bring me some when you find them! You must see the sunrise ceremony at the banks of the Ganges and the cremation ghats. Not to be missed!"

"Then we shall," replied Max, "and I hope we find meals as delectable as this one. Nair Kerala Tamarind is world-class, my friend."

After more embraces, they set off into the Delhi night, strolling the market back to The Imperial and their separate suites.

"Tomorrow, we're going to Khari Baoli," said Max as they strolled the People's Way. "It's the biggest spice market in the world, and I have a good friend there."

KHARI BAOLI

I saw you green, then
Turning red as you ripened.
Pleasant to look at and tasty in a dish,
But too hot if excess is used
Savior of the poor, enhancer of good food.
Fiery when bitten, this makes it difficult
Even to think of the good Lord himself!
– Purandara Dāsa, 16th Century Indian Poet

They had both slept soundly following the previous night's feast and met for coffee and croissants in the Imperial's atrium café. Despite the notorious Delhi smog, a sunny day greeted them, and the doorman summoned a cab for the ride to Khari Baoli.

"Would it be possible to take a tuk-tuk instead?" asked Max, to raised eyebrows from the attendant. "We'd prefer to be closer to the energy of your wonderful city. Plus, we need to negotiate the alleys of Khari Baoli."

The request obliged, they set off for Old Delhi and the Khari Baoli market in the city's Chandni Chowk district. They darted in and out of traffic in the enclosed motorized tricycle, smelling fumes and burning cow dung, braking for camels and oxen, and swaying to the crosstown venture. Lilah laughed out loud at what she now called the Indian "poetry of chaos."

Entering the Khari Baoli district, Max's level of excitement palpably grew. Late morning showed the spice economy already in full swing. The wholesale market started as early as four a.m., with the merchant storefronts opening their doors at ten. Sitting on the edge of the small tuk-tuk's seat, Max craned his neck to look down alleys at the mass of spicy business conducted under every storefront. Pungent aromas of turmeric, curry, cardamom, and dried chiles wafted through the windows, overpowering even the thick smell of exhaust. Lorries and buffalo-drawn carts unloading colossal burlap sacks of spice clogged the roads, and Laila watched as Max turned back and forth, following his sensitive olfactory like a dog. She was fascinated to observe him, wrapped within his ultimate element, an entire section of one of the largest cities on earth dedicated to all things spice.

"Please get us as close as you can to number five-seventeen, Katra Ishwar Bhawan," Max implored the driver.

He said to Lilah, "We're going to see my friend Kashi Prakash, one of the finest spice and chile merchants in all of Asia. His family has been in Khari Baoli for five generations."

In 1996, Max discovered the legendary Khari Baoli in the ancient Delhi district called Chandni Chowk during his first trip to India. His friends and competitors had all spoken of the place in rapturous terms, and it was Mecca for any serious pepper-head. The market emerged in the 17th century in the neighborhoods adjacent to the Fatehpuri Masjid Mosque and was bordered on two sides by the ancient, fortified wall of Old Delhi. Far off the usual tourist map, it hid in alleys so thick with spice that it hung in the air. To go there was a journey back in time, with little changed over the centuries, and the district exhibited an almost medieval essence. Weathered, leather-covered ledgers were the accounting record of choice, and yellowed portraits of ancestors hung in every stall and office. Max had spent a week three years before wandering its tight pathways and dark corners and came out a changed man, baptized in the innumerable spices of India.

The tuk-tuk turned off Khari Baoli Street and entered the warren of alleys, beeping its tinny-pitched horn and swerving in and out of stopped and moving conveyances of every type. The narrow streets had no posted names, and Lilah began to wonder how anybody could find anything or anyone in the maze. Then they stopped at a large, gated compound. "Prakash and Sons," said the driver. Over the gate was an ancient, weathered, but proud sign that read *Prakash and Sons, Purveyors of Fine Spices, Est. 1828.* The gate was open.

On his first visit, during that enlightening week in Khari Baoli, exploring the alleys, meeting merchants, and hearing their stories, Max emerged part Indian. Experience had taught him that a good story makes a better product, and he searched for a collaborator to create a relationship. Over a series of days, he sampled and shopped and discovered the universe of spices in India. Max had wandered through Prakash and Sons' arched gate by chance and met the current proprietor, Kashi Prakash, the family's fifth head in Delhi. A rapport quickly grew as Max plied him with earnest and intelligent questions not only about chiles but about the Prakash family.

"My family comes originally from Goa," he had told Max, "and were merchants there when the Portuguese arrived in 1510 and claimed the city for themselves. The Portuguese wanted the East's spices, of which my forebears were purveyors, and they brought with them chillis newly arrived from South America. A long and profitable relationship began. In the early 1800s, our family came to Delhi after hearing of Khari Baoli to open our headquarters, and here we have thrived for generations."

Over the five hundred years since their introduction to India, chiles had taken on a life of their own and become so ingrained in the culture and cuisine that it was impossible to imagine India without them. Chiles infused and often defined the foods of every corner of the country. Through crossbreeding and distinct environmental conditions, they had evolved seemingly on their own, unique to the vastness of the Indian subcontinent. The pace of their spread across India from the late 15th Century to the mid-16th Century was so quick that several noted European botanists - Fuchs in 1542, Dodoens in 1554, and Gerarde in 1597 - described chile peppers as part of the native flora of India. Dodoens wrote of Indian chiles that:

> The Indian pepper is hot and dry in the third degree. Indian pepper is used in diverse places for the dressing of meats, for it hath the same virtue and taste that the usual pepper hath. Furthermore, it coloreth like Saffron, and being taken in such sort warmeth the stomach and helpeth greatly the digestion of meats. The same doth also dissolve and consume the swellings about the throat called the King's Evil [scrofula], all kernels and cold swellings, and taketh away all spots and lentils of the face, being laid thereunto with honey. It is dangerous to be used in too great a quantity: for this pepper hath in it a certain hidden evil quality, whereby it killeth dogs if it be given them to eat.

At Prakash and Sons, Max had encountered a new world of chiles that he never knew existed. He proved such a passionate student that Kashi had spent an entire day sampling him on an array of chiles from across India. For Max, it became a baptismal bordering on paradise.

While sipping on Kingfisher beers and nibbling on crisp *chapattis* and *rotis* with fiery chutney, Max and Kashi sat at a table in the courtyard's center as samples of whole chiles, both dried and fresh, were brought to them. Though most were identifiable as relatives to known peppers, some were entirely unique. As Kashi cut them open to sample and examine, Max discerned each one intently and listened to their stories.

Kashi introduced *Kaddi Byadagis* from Karnataka and Goa on the southwest coast, which the Prakash family had initially brought to the markets of Delhi, descendants of the first Portuguese seeds. Bright red and seven inches long, the Byadagi was elemental in Goan Masala and cleanly hot. Short *Mulaku Curd* chiles, also from the coast, soaked in yogurt and salt and dried in the sun for a week, were sweet and mildly hot and unlike anything Max had ever tasted. The ubiquitous *Dhanis*, clearly *Capsicum frutescens* like the African Devil, were small and intensely hot. They chewed them dried and red and cut into fresh green, yellow, and even purple specimens. From Tamil Nadu in the south were *Ramnad Mundus*, or "fat chilis," spherical like the *Rocoto* of South America and possibly a cousin, fundamental to Chettinad cuisine. *Guntur Sannam*, from Andhra in the south, a *Capsicum annuum* and extremely hot. Narrow green *Jwala* chiles from Gujarat in the northwest, Jwala translating as "volcano" in the local language, akin to a Serrano. Dried fat *Kashmiris*, apparently in high demand as they were difficult to cultivate in mountainous Kashmir's fertile valleys. The ground version, a delicacy across India, proved dark orange and dusty sweet. *Kantharis*, an ivory white chile from Kerala in the south, bittersweet in its heat. *Moru Mulakus, Nellores, Reshampattis, Nalchetis*, and *Punjab Puyas* followed in succession and were *annuums and frutescens* varieties, each a story unto itself.

It was the single most extended and varied tasting of chiles Max had ever experienced in his life, a thoroughly indulgent day in the Delhi sun, drinking in the stories and the Kingfisher beers. He and the Prakash family partnered on the spot for a turmeric and curry-infused sauce called Khari Baoli Jwala, made from the family's peppers and spices. It sold famously in the Indian markets of America, and now Max was back to check in with his friend and business partner and to see if word of the Naga Jolokia had reached Kashi's well-informed ears.

As they exited the tuk-tuk, Lilah became hypnotized by the intensity of aromas that enveloped them, an onslaught of turmeric and curry and clove and dried chiles. Over the alley they entered hung a fog of spice as sacks were filled and emptied, loaded and unloaded, orders fulfilled, and purchases made. Locals wore bandanas over their faces amidst the piquant cloud, and there was no Westerner in sight.

"Follow me," said Max, leading them through the arch and under the ancient Prakash sign. Once in the courtyard, the spice fog subsided, yet the intense aromas remained. Stacks of bags on pallets spread across the small square, where workers moved back and forth, calling out to each other, carrying loads, and conducting business. Goans were famous for singing while they worked, and tunes echoed through the yard.

Prakash and Sons housed a combination spice market, warehouse, and living facility in a building hundreds of years old. Business took place on the ground floor, in alcove offices and storerooms staffed by family members, each expert in the various commodities. This specialization made the Prakash operation more competitive in the crowded Indian spice marketplace. If turmeric or curry were sought, Uncle Govind Prakash and his son Rudi would be your guides in all things relative to them, while other family members worked various spice alcoves. Kashi and his sons Mandad and Kashi, Jr., were the chile pepper experts, and business had been conducted this way for generations. The second and third floors of the building housed the extended Prakash family, forty strong.

With the sun not yet at its apex, the courtyard was cool but humming with activity. Lorries came and went, loading or unloading spices from all over India at their designated spot in the yard. Signs above the alcoves marked each spice specialty, and Lilah saw the ancient placard for "chillis" in a far corner, hand-painted in Sanskrit and English. On a stack of burlap bags under the sign sat a slim man, with coffee-brown skin and oiled black hair, jotting down figures in an ancient, leather-backed tablet, wearing the traditional white kurta shirt. As Max and Lilah approached, he looked up and grinned broadly, his teeth stained red from a lifetime chewing betel nut. He looked as if he'd been punched in the mouth but broke into song at the sight of his American friend.

"*Orsanchi amizade re amchi, amizade re amchi (Our friendship of many years), Zaunchi sasnachi. (Should last forever.) Zaunchi sasnachi. (Should last forever.)* Max Little, you are a surprise! A fine day has become finer!" he shouted. "I never know when to expect you, halfway across the world!" They embraced like old friends, and Kashi looked him over. "You look the same. But wiser, somehow, in your eyes. Has the world brought you good fortune?"

"Some wisdom may have found its way in, my friend. Time will tell. You are looking well. And Prakash and Sons appear to be prospering, as always," said Max, whose smile was genuine, seeing an old pepper friend.

"And who is this?" said Kashi, opening his arms to Lilah, "A beauty from a foreign land you've brought us."

Lilah accepted his affection before replying, "I am Lilah, from faraway Louisiana, Mr. Prakash."

Kashi's eyes widened. "The legendary home of McIlhenny and Ivins, largest purveyors of hot sauce in the world! They buy chiles from my competitor. I have always intended to go there and see for myself their fields, but I hear they are demanding partners and don't pay market prices."

"Then go, you must, and I can show you those fields myself," Lilah said. "I've been in them many times. But there are other fields nearby that would impress you more, and I know the grower well."

"Excellent!" Kashi said. "I'll have to decide how many of my family to bring."

Prakash begged them out of the dusty courtyard and into his office/storeroom. A fan blew the scent of dried and fresh chiles in circles, creating a mesmerizing perfume as a row of fading ancestral photographs lined the walls.

"Sit, please! And Mandad! Bring us tea!" he said. "So what brings you back to Delhi, Max? I get your monthly reports on the Khari Baoli

Jwala sauce. It's doing so well! Are you here to create another winner with Prakash and Sons?"

Max became thoughtful. "Yes, our sauce is doing well, and we should develop another, without a doubt. But I'm here to talk about new varieties of peppers. Something so new that the world has yet to hear of it."

Kashi leaned in closer. "New varieties? Well, as you know, we are among India's premier brokers of chiles in our vast country." And turning to Lilah, he embarked on a short history. "Our family was in Goa when the Portuguese arrived in the 16th century, bringing with them the newly discovered *Capsicum annuum* and *frutescens* from the Americas."

Kashi paced for effect, using his hands while he talked. "My forefathers were already trading in clove, nutmeg, and cardamom that the kitchens of Europe so desperately desired and were among the first Indian companies to domesticate and sell the new fruit that became the Byadagis, Dhanis, and Jwalas that are all over India today. Chiles are forever linked with the Prakash name!" Then, to Max, "So, what are you looking for, my friend?"

"I'm interested to know if you've heard of anything new coming from the far northeast of the country," Max said carefully, "particularly from Assam." He left the statement hanging in the air.

"Nagaland," the Indian replied, scratching his chin, "Hard to get to or from, logistically difficult, and beset for years by a separatist rebellion, so it's thought of as a dangerous place to sell, or buy. A historically fierce and insular people, with a palate that favors extremely spicy foods. They grow their own chilies, Nagas, which seems fitting, so we sell nothing in all of Assam state. They don't like outsiders trying to do business there." He sat back and folded his arms. "And this is the thing that brings you to India, Max? What do you know?"

Max was usually secretive with information, but in the company of his trusted Indian partner opened up. "There is word of a pepper in Assam that is exponentially hotter than anything else on the planet, and an American university has sent me to see if it's true. I also plan to go to China and a couple of other places to sniff around. But I figured I should see you first, with your expertise in all things India." Everything he said was true, though he left out Kyrgyzstan.

Kashi was thoughtful, searching his mind for information. "If there was something new, I should have heard about it," he said, scratching his chin. "Unless, of course, the Indian government has become somehow involved. Our behemoth bureaucracy can be amazingly compartmentalized and secretive when it wants to be. And Assam is tricky. Are you going there? Shall I send one of my sons with you?"

"I am going," said Max, "and no need for you to send a son away from the Prakash family business. I promise to tell you what I find. Plus, my traveling companion here is a professional botanist who can help me verify any findings."

The Goan regarded Lilah admiringly. "Traveling with a professional you are, Max? I would have thought that your legendary taste for chiles might have been enough, but apparently, you need an even more expert expert for this. It sounds serious."

"It's serious enough, especially to people who track and catalog all the varieties on earth, like the university we're working with," Lilah responded, "and of course fanatical pepper freaks like Max here, who I realize there are more and more of."

Kashi beamed at the description of his friend. "Mr. Max is among the most passionate and dedicated repositories of the spicy life, that is certain, Miss Lilah. His palate and his integrity are at the top of his field. I trusted him with my family's generations-old reputation, and he has preserved it and enhanced it on the international chile pepper stage. You are in good company for such an important junket. Now, let's have some tea. Mandad!"

Served by Kashi's son, they continued with easy banter about family, lives, and homes. Kashi was particularly interested in Jesus Jones and his farm in the middle of McIlhenny and Ivins' vast holdings. "I must go to this place someday," he said, "and meet this Jesus. He is the David to their Goliath!"

With midday approaching, Max let Kashi know that they had an appointment at the Chinese Embassy. As they walked out, something occurred to Kashi that Max might be interested to know.

"Vikram Ashwant over at Rajasthani Imports told me about an Englishman asking about new pepper varieties the other day. I didn't give it a second thought until just now when you came asking about the very same thing. Are there others on your quest, Max?"

"Not that I'm aware of," Max replied. "An Englishman, huh? I can't imagine who that might be. But thanks for the tip. Be well, my friend." He made a mental note to find out from his friends in the Ring.

Rather than flagging down a tuk-tuk for the ride out of the Khari Baoli maze, Lilah suggested they walk and work their way over to the Fatehpuri Masjid, Delhi's largest mosque. They wound through the alleys, sampling spices and bites of street food. The sky overhead had become a narrow strip of blue crossed by a spider web of electrical wires, and the streets a sea of oxcarts, lorries, honking horns, and turbans.

As they made their way down Tilak Bazaar Street, Max noticed two out of place figures: tall, Caucasian, and wearing matching long Indian shirts, kurtas in bright blue. Before he could react, they made eye contact across thirty yards of the crowded lane. Max immediately recognized the man's angry face he had pepper sauced in Santa Fe and another torched in Bayou des Allemandes. Seeing their prey, the men began walking purposefully toward them as Max stopped abruptly in mid-step.

"Uh, oh. Holy crap. Quick!" Max said. "Down this alley. It's our friends from Kyrgyzstan. Gasanov said they might be here."

Lilah was shocked but quick to react. "How in the world would they find us here, Max? What are the odds?"

They ran down the narrow lane, looking back over their shoulders as their pursuers fought their way through the crowd. Max spoke quickly. "Gasanov alluded that they might have assistance from the Kyrgyz Interior Ministry, meaning that our passports and travel might be tracked. In here, quick!"

They entered the edifice of a small-scale spice vendor, finding nowhere to hide, and were trapped. Lilah quickly scanned the shop.

"Sir!" she said, "May we have two five-kilo bags of your hottest chile powder? And quickly?" She paid for the two bags and said anxiously to Max, "Follow me, down the alley."

As they wound their way through the crowd, they could see the men gaining on them. The alley they had chosen was a dead end, a trap. Before them was a cramped nut vendor, last in the passage. Lilah hatched a quick plan.

"Max, see if you can get on that fire escape up there, above the alley. I'll hold their attention while you think of a way to stop them. Take these. Figure out something to do with them!"

As Lilah tossed him the two sacks, Max bolted, crouching low beneath the crowd, for the door that led to the nearby apartment building.

Max, on autopilot, buried his shoulder in the building's door, cracking it open. He entered a narrow hallway, with stairs leading to a second floor. A small window led to the iron fire escape overlooking the alley as Lilah faced the oncoming henchmen, alone below. She casually strolled out into the narrow passage, which provided little traffic or witnesses at this far end, and picked from a bag of nuts, looking entirely unconcerned. Turning back down the lane, she came face to face with the former Spetznaz commandos now in the employ of Ruslan Bakiyev, mafia lord of Kyrgyzstan. Under their stiff kurtas, they wore Levi's, Adidas t-shirts, and Nike hi-tops.

"Hello, boys," she said, stopping them in their tracks. "Fancy meeting you here. I see you have new shoes since the ones you were wearing in Louisiana somehow caught on fire."

The senior of the two men spoke, scowling. "Mizz Devvvilier, ve haff need to speak to you. Mr. Bakiyev has message for you. It iss verrry important."

Lilah was the essence of innocence, offering her pursuers a nut. "Well, Max is just inside buying another bag of these delicious nuts and will be out soon. Would you like to try one?"

Skeptical of a trap, the man peered into the store but was unable to see Max. "Vhere iss he?"

Lilah was calm as a cat. "In the back negotiating, of course. This is India, after all, fellas. Have a nut." She extended the bag out to them, and they both focused on it, trying to figure out the catch.

Max had slowly inched open the window to the fire escape and slithered on his belly with the two chile powder bags in each arm. Pulling out his knife, he gingerly cut a slice into the top of each bag, now perched directly above Lilah and their two assailants, breathing hard.

Lilah stepped toward the men, her bag of nuts in hand. "Now would be an appropriate time to go nuts, don't you think?"

It was Max's cue to act. As one assailant reached out for the bag, Lilah suddenly looked up and said, "What's that?"

The two hulking men followed her gaze and met a dense cloud of Rajasthani Red ground pepper so thick it completely covered their faces, including open mouths and eyes. Lilah quickly stepped back and let the cloud cover the men, who clawed at their faces clumsily, cursing in Russian while flailing to get a hand on her. Only lightly dusted herself, she issued a swift kick to the groin of one man who managed to grab her kurta and a shin of the other, sending them toppling to the pavement. The duo became a mass of chile powder, arms, and legs, roaring with rage, gasping for air, and unable to see anything. They quickly devolved into shrieking oversized victims, terrified and helpless.

"Max, run!" Lilah yelled, heading back up the alley.

Max leaped from the fire escape, landing close enough to the writhing men to see their faces. They were clearly in distress but furious. Running past, he said, "Geez guys, I thought you would've learned by now. Try washing with some goat's milk, and you'll be sorted out in no time."

They zigzagged through Khari Baoli at a fast clip, making numerous distancing turns and watching their backs. Breathing hard and stained with bright red chile powder splashes on their clothes and in their hair, they looked like pilgrims at a Hindu religious festival. Max and Lilah changed course regularly, putting time and many turns between them and their pursuers, distancing themselves from the danger for a half-hour until they felt safe. Eventually, they finally slowed and allowed themselves to relax.

Turning the corner of a narrow alley, Max stopped abruptly, shocked to spot another familiar face. Roy Fergus of Voodoo Hot Sauce, an edgy upstart Australian company, browsed the pepper vendor stalls looking out of place in khaki shorts, safari hat, and outback boots. Though not if you knew him.

Max and Roy had encountered each other more than once, sniffing around in the global markets and interacting on a level of pseudo-friendly competitiveness. Roy's sauces were highly regarded in the Ring of Fire, as was his uncannily accidental ability to discover new varieties. Roy edged out Max to uncover and market the rare Yucatan White Habanero with his famous White Hot Yucatan Habanero Sauce. In Merida, Mexico, where Max had been on Roy's tail for the White Habanero, they had engaged in a legendary showdown, matching each other chile for Habanero chile in what became known as The Gringo Standoff of 1997. They ingested to a draw after fifteen searingly-hot Red Savina chile pods caused Roy to blackout and Max's tongue to swell so large that he couldn't physically get anything in his mouth except cold beer through a straw. Max had to swing in a hammock by the sea for three days to recover, sipping coconut water to heal, while Roy exited on a stretcher. Even now, the memory made his tongue tingle.

Lilah, sensing Max's heightened awareness, looked around and said, "What gives, Max? You just tensed up like you saw a cobra. Is it *them?*"

"No, not them. That guy in the safari hat and khakis is one of my toughest competitors. And it can't be a coincidence that he's here, in India, at the Khari Baoli spice market. Maybe he's the one Kashi talked about. But he's an Australian."

Tailing him, they came close enough to hear Roy inquiring about "Spirit Peppers, or something like that, mate," at stall after stall, where he was met with confused looks and shrugged shoulders. *A possessed chile head on the hunt.* Max knew the type all too well.

But Roy was not asking about *Naga Jolokia* or Assam, which perhaps the Indian merchants would have heard about, making his information incomplete and resulting in dead-ends at each vendor he queried. Max knew he had the edge.

Slowly edging up next to him, Max said, "Fancy seeing you here, mate."

Roy turned with a start, visibly shocked to see his competitor. "Mm-Max Little! Crikey! Whatcha doin' sneaking up on me halfway around the world like that? You look like a chile dusted madman!"

Enjoying the moment and staying cool, Max said simply, "Just doing some shopping Roy. And opening a few bags to sample by hand, as you can see. Sniff out anything new?" He dusted off his shirt as Lilah brushed back her hair, freshly tinted red.

"Not really, mate," said Roy, who was a poor liar. "Just mountains upon mountains of *annuum* and *frutescens* pods, as usual. What about you?"

"Doing some traveling," said Max, nodding over his shoulder, "and showing my friend Lilah the India that I know. She's a voodoo priestess from the Louisiana bayou."

Roy looked past Max and regarded Lilah with an astonished look. She was glamorous even while disheveled, in her long orange kurta shirt, flowing hair tinted red, and sunglasses.

"Greetings, miss, I'm Roy Fergus of the Voodoo Hot Sauce Company out of Adelaide. Max and I go back a bit, you could say. Pleased to meet you."

Lilah looked Roy Fergus up and down as a sea of shoppers swirled around them, then said, "*Well I float in liquid gardens, and Arizona new red sand, 'Cause I'm a voodoo chile, Lord knows I'm a voodoo chile....*"

Roy shook his head in disbelief. "How do you know *that*?" The song had been the inspiration for the name of his company.

"I've always loved Jimi Hendrix. And his song *Voodoo Chile* happens to define two of the things I'm really good at," she said, aloof, and strolled off to browse the spice bins nearby. Max now understood the import of the necklace pendant she always wore. Lilah was training in voodoo alongside being a college professor, a tantalizing layer to her mystery.

Roy's look was quizzical. "Well, isn't she something? A chile voodoo priestess. Where'd you find her, Max?"

He smiled as he watched her walk off. "She's also an agronomist and botanist, who I chanced to meet in Louisiana, and she's tagging along on my shopping vacation."

"Shopping, huh? And with a botanist," Roy shot back. "If I didn't know better, I'd say you were hunting, not shopping." Then, he regained his usually cocky persona. "Caught word of some interesting things going on in your world, mate, even from way Down Under. Regarding Asia and some very unique chiles. And terrorists. Care to share a little information with a fellow pepper hunter?"

Though not unexpected from a player in the pepper game like Roy, Max was surprised that word of his experiences had traveled so far. And that the information was compelling enough to get the owner of Voodoo on a plane to India. But was it the Naga Jolokia or possibly the Kyrgyz peppers his competitor was after? Roy was a slippery character.

"Don't know what you've heard, Roy, but I'm here on vacation. Going to do some yoga and see the sights. And like you, I'm always sniffing around. But here's a nugget: there's word of some recently discovered hybrid varieties grown by the Hmong people in the Laotian highlands that has people interested. Very remote and unexplored. You can only reach it by longboat and oxcart."

He left vague whether he intended to track the entirely false but potentially groundbreaking information down. Roy's gaze narrowed as he attempted to decipher this valuable new lead, as Max was notoriously hard to read when he did not want to be. But he had a score to settle with Max.

"Laos, huh? Haven't heard about that one yet. I guess India's a smart stopover heading to Laos if you know your way around, which I figure you do. See you around, mate. I'm back to Australia. Nice to meet you, miss. And for the record, Max, I didn't pass out in Merida. I just overheated."

With that, Roy Fergus turned and disappeared down the narrow alley. Max heard later that he got arrested at the Laotian border with Thailand, trying to cross illegally with a band of Hmong freedom fighters. He sat in a rat-infested jail for a month before Max bailed him out.

After many turns, they finally returned to Khari Baoli Street and hailed a taxi.

"The Chinese Embassy please," said Max, as they settled, exhausted, into the now-familiar Ambassador. With chile-dusted commandos on their tail, arranging documents to leave the country had become a priority. The Masjid mosque would have to wait.

"You were quite effective back there," Max said to Lilah. "Smart thinking in a sticky situation. Sorry I keep bringing those bad dudes into your world."

"Our world, Max," said Lilah, looking out the window. "And if you think about it, it's the most logical place to find you. You reacted as quickly as I knew you would. This caper is our journey now, and we're in it together, whatever that ends up meaning."

The meaning of "meaning" hit Max like a wave. Did that mean that their coming together on this journey could end up meaning more? Or that they were merely coworkers on a mutual mission with anticipated results?

"It's time to get out of Delhi, I think," he said. "Raj arrives tomorrow afternoon, and we'll take a long train to Guwahati. We'll have lots of time to sort things out. Before that, we'll get our Chinese visas and pay a visit to the National Archives, where our friend Gasanov has arranged some reference materials for us."

They spoke little during the remainder of the ride, each drifting in their respective *What ifs?*

Arriving late from their spice market escapade, they failed to beat the notorious crowds. Getting visas to China was a challenge, and the embassy in Delhi had a reputation as a house of consular mayhem. The visa section was a sea of stress and despair, with not a chair in sight. Max was instantly agitated and blamed himself for not planning ahead.

"We're screwed," was all he could say. Meanwhile, Lilah scanned the room calmly, locating a Chinese national with a clipboard.

"Follow me," she said, confidently making her way across the chaotic room toward the man in charge. She pleasantly asked him for a Mr. Shin in the visa section and mentioned that she was expected.

"Expected?" said Max. "How the hell are we expected?"

"Just let me do the talking," said Lilah. "I have a connection."

The visa officer spoke into a small microphone on his lapel in Mandarin and got a crackling response. "Mr. Shin will see you now. He's on the fourth floor."

Mr. Shin, a Han Chinese, looked dubiously over their applications for visas to Kashgar, a thousand miles from anywhere and not a regular destination for Americans.

"Why Kashgar?" was all he asked.

"We hear the bazaar in Kashgar is one of the best in the world," replied Lilah, "and we are purveyors of spices." *Spice and Chile Broker* was the occupation they listed on the form.

"It is also the largest," Shin said. "What kind of spices? And how will you get there?"

"We intend to travel overland from India to China as we have business in the Assam region, and our specialty is chiles, of the hot variety," Lilah answered calmly.

The man was stone-faced. "Not possible to go overland because the border is closed. Your only option is to fly to China. If you want to leave via Guwahati, there are two options. Fly through Pakistan direct to Kashgar, or via Shanghai and Beijing, then to Kashgar. And you need a letter of invitation, which I'm sure you know."

"Then we shall fly," said Lilah, "and here is our invitation letter from Professor Lin Shaojou at Shanghai University, who also works in your Agriculture Ministry." She pushed a signed and stamped document across the table.

Mr. Shin regarded the letter skeptically. Raising an eyebrow, he said, "It appears you have the proper required document. You may proceed." The man's stamp thudded into their passports.

Lilah had left out that they would be using the Torugart Pass to get into Kyrgyzstan from Kashgar. They would deal with that challenge once in China.

As they rose to leave, the man added: "Chiles originated in China, which is why our food is the best in the world. Perhaps you know the *Capsicum chinense.*"

Not in the mood for a botanical history lesson, Lilah responded simply with a pleasant smile and, "Of course. And Mexican *Habaneros* came from Cuba, I assume. You would do well to learn your botanical history." They left the chaotic building, visas in hand.

Max, who hadn't said a word, was instantly baffled. And agitated. "What just happened in there? Who is Professor Shaojou?"

"A contemporary of Chuck DeWindt's," she said, smiling pleasantly. "Chuck knew we would try to get to Kyrgyzstan and might have to go through China, so he supplied me with the tools and a connection. Let's get out of here. We'll have just enough time to make the archives at the museum before closing."

Max merely shook his scrambled head. Lilah was proving to be a resourceful traveler, thinking ahead of even him. She represented an entirely disruptive and compelling new force in his journey.

They then commuted across Delhi to the National Museum. A massive block of a sandstone building, the museum sat at the intersection of Janpath and Rajpath, a location virtually at the heart of Lutyens's New Delhi. The Manuscripts Division was hidden in the basement, directly below the Central Asian Antiquities wing. It housed thousands of artifacts from across Central Asia, procured primarily by late 19th-and early 20th-century European explorers like Aurel Stein, Sven Hedin, and the Russian Max Prezhalvsky.

The late afternoon's waning light added to the aura of antiquity as Max and Lilah descended the stone staircase to the museum's subterranean halls. Horizontal light filtered through faded windows placed high in the walls. The visitors that thronged the main galleries were markedly absent, and the smell of antiquity was abundant in the still, warm air. Following signs to the archives, they reached the end of a long, dim hall, where they faced two large doors topped by a sign: *Archives of the Central Asian Antiquities Division.* The doors creaked as Max swung them open, releasing a gasp of dusty, musty air. A lone clerk in thick round glasses sat at a reception desk, the lamp upon it the only source of light. Behind the man and his desk, a gate spanning the room's width loomed, protecting rows of shelves holding thousands of manuscripts.

"The main galleries for tourists are upstairs," the clerk said, without looking up from his work. "The museum closes in one hour."

Lilah stepped forward, forcing him to acknowledge her presence.

"I am Lilah DeVillier, and this is Max Little, representing New Mexico State University in the United States, and we are here for research purposes at the behest of your government. Are you the director?"

The man's eyes narrowed, even as the thick lenses of his glasses enlarged them. "Research? I have had no notification regarding any researchers. And yes, I am the director of this department. We will be closing in one hour. Please come back tomorrow. Or next week."

Lilah bristled, but before she could continue, Max said, "I am here to see Rudra."

The clerk now regarded them skeptically, pushing the thick glasses up his nose.

"You know Rudra? I was not aware anyone knew Rudra. He never goes outside. His life is the manuscripts and this basement. Why him?"

"He has some things for me," Max said authoritatively. "Where is he? Please tell him Mr. Max Little has arrived. We don't have much time."

The clerk, clearly irritated at the intrusion and being directed to act, turned toward the stacks and yelled, "Rudra! Come out here. Someone's actually asking for you."

Following a short silence, they heard the shuffle of feet approaching from a far corner of the room. Emerging from one of the rows came a diminutive young man in pants too long and a sweater too baggy for his frame. A worried look wrinkled his face.

"These so-called researchers from America have requested you by name, Rudra," the clerk said indignantly. "Do you know Mr. Max Little and Ms. Lilah DeVillier?"

Hearing Max's name caused the man Rudra's face to transform from worried to astonished. "Max Little? The man from the Ring of Fire?"

Max was just as surprised at the question. "That's me," he said.

"Please, this way, quickly," said Rudra, his face suddenly a mask of anguish. Before closing the heavy doors to the gallery, he scanned the exterior hallway and led them through the archives' gate, which he locked behind them.

Max and Lilah followed the clerk in silence to the room's left, then down a long aisle lined with thousands of ancient manuscripts to a small office tucked into the corner. Atop a lamplit desk sat stacked piles of books, their pages separated by hundreds of notes inserted into various chapters. Rudra, the epitome of a researcher, closed the door behind them as they all crammed into the space.

"If Gasanov had not paid me so handsomely, I might not have acknowledged your arrival," he said.

"Why is that?" asked Lilah, surprised.

"Because the other men who showed up yesterday asking about you offered me more to show them what Gasanov had me gather for you," he said. "They were clearly not intellectuals and had a nefarious look, so I feigned ignorance. Then they said they knew where I live. It was terrifying. I live in a world of books, not thugs. What could possibly be so important that they would threaten someone over books?"

That Bakiyev's men had known to check the archives sent a cold rush through Max's veins. How much did these people know about Max's journey? They seemed to show up everywhere he went. Max's mind raced into survival mode, looking for angles. It was time to get out of Delhi.

He placed both his hands on the researcher's shoulders. "First, thank you, Rudra, for doing the honorable thing and agreeing to see us. And thank you for doing whatever it is that Gasanov asked you to do on our behalf." He paused, then added, "The Ring of Fire will remember what you've done."

Rudra brightened, and the color returned to his face. He became immediately excited and engaged. "Really? Might I be honored by the illustrious global network of spicy foods enthusiasts of which you are a major luminary, Mr. Little?"

The man's response, hilarious but sweet, broke the chill of their reception and softened the impact of knowing Bakiyev's henchmen were still on their trail. Max and Lilah looked at each other, sharing their surprise at Rudra's response, and then Lilah shrugged, deciding to go all the way in. *What the hell?* She thought.

"Your deeds will travel far and wide across the Ring of Fire, Rudra," she said. "And people will remember you for the essential role you played in aiding us on our quest."

Rudra's transformation complete, he became the eager and motivated researcher of which Gasanov had spoken. "Alright then," he said. "Let's begin."

Brushing aside a stack of volumes on India's partition in 1947, Rudra allowed them to sit by his desk. Turning, and from a locked cabinet behind, he produced three manuscripts. Though they did not look particularly old, he handled them with reverence. Placing his hands over the documents, he began his dissertation.

"The Central Antiquities Division is well known as the main repository for collections of artifacts found by explorers on the Silk Road in the late 19th and early 20th centuries. The Manuscripts Division houses these explorers' documentation and journeys, among many other things, and my area of expertise. Gasanov said you had an interest in the specific explorers that traversed what is now Kyrgyzstan, is that correct?"

"Yes," Max replied, relieved that the man was finally in his element. Though the realization that Gasanov was clearly leading them on with his too well-informed guidance of the research did not settle in.

Rudra continued: "The archive has collected numerous volumes that focus specifically on Central Asia, going back over five hundred years. However, I believe your focus is on Europeans who may have traveled the Silk Road or sought to uncover its history. Therefore, I have focused on a specific set of four explorers' manuscripts from 1629 to 1920. Does that sound acceptable?"

Max was impressed. "Quite acceptable," he said.

"Excellent," Rudra replied. "I will preface each of these volumes for you. First, we have Jean Baptiste Tavernier's exploration journal, *The Six Voyages of John Baptiste Tavernier, Baron of Aubonne, Through Turkey into Persia and the East-Indies, for the Space of Forty Years,* translated by John Chuckips in London, in 1677. Tavernier was a Frenchman and merchant who, in 1629, probably knew the overland trade routes through Persia and Central Asia better than any other European in the seventeenth century. Six voyages took him to the Ottoman Empire, Safavid Persia, Tsarist Central Asia, and Mughal India. His interactions with merchant communities gave him an insider's perspective on Silk Road economics and cultures." Max and Lilah, impressed by Rudra's concise delivery, listened intently.

"Next, there is the *Ledger of the Merchant Hovhannes Joughayetsi from 1682-1693.* He was an Armenian merchant who traveled and traded between Isfahan in Persia, Samarkand in Uzbekistan, Northern India, and Tibet. His commercial ledger is a bountiful source of information on products, prices, trading conditions, and the Armenian commercial network on the seventeenth-century routes involving the Safavid and Mughal empires. After that, I chose the Russian explorer Nikolay Mikhaylovich Prezhalvsky, *From Kulja, Across the Tian Shan to Lob-Nor,* published in 1879. Prezhalvsky's major interests focused on the geography and wild animals and plants of the regions he explored, and it was in these fields he made unprecedented achievements. Prezhalvsky amassed an impressive herbarium of more than 15,000 plants and 1,700 species, including 218 new species and seven new genera. His zoological collection consisted of 702 specimens of small mammals, 5,010 birds, 1,200 reptiles and amphibians, and 643 specimens of fish. He discovered and described a wild camel and a wild horse, which became named after him, and studied the growth conditions of plants and animals' habitats and habits. In October 1888, Prezhalvsky was in the foothills of the Tien Shan, at Lake Issyk Kul where he contracted typhus and died."

Rudra paused and looked at Max and Lilah eagerly. "Is this the kind of information you hoped to see?"

"Yes," they replied in unison, the information a bounty of historical reference.

Rudra was visibly pleased, wringing his hands. "Good, then. And finally, Sven Hedin, Swedish explorer. Hedin's autobiographical work, *My Life as an Explorer,* was published in 1926 and immortalized his many years crisscrossing Central Asia. In 1893, Sven Hedin embarked on a journey that lasted for three and a half years, traveling from Istanbul through Persia, Central Asia, Bukhara, Samarkand, Osh, Kashgar, Torugart Pass, and Lake Issyk-Kul in present-day Kyrgyzstan."

His presentation complete, Rudra pushed the four volumes across the desk toward Lilah and Max. "You are welcome to examine them here in my office, and we can stay for one hour past closing time, which is in thirty minutes. There is also an excellent section on maps just down the hall, which is open to you. And you are welcome tomorrow."

Max became instantly stressed. Realizing that their train to Assam was departing the next afternoon, he had to decide which manuscript held the most significant potential return.

"Rudra, knowing what you do about the Ring of Fire, which two manuscripts represent the most promising possibilities for our research? We don't have much time. The fellows who visited you yesterday are still looking for us, and we need to vacate Delhi tomorrow."

The man thought quickly. "Well, Joughayetsi never actually made it to Kyrgyzstan, though his merchant dealings may have brought him into contact with spices on the Silk Road, not foods, so I'd count him out. And Prezhalvsky and his 15,000 plants, perhaps too much information to grasp here today, so...."

"Lilah, you take Tavernier, and I'll tackle Hedin," said Max. "We only have ninety minutes."

"I'm going to the map section," Lilah said, "and I'll take Monsieur Tavernier with me."

Rudra sat silently, watching Max begin to pore over Hedin's 498-page work, beginning with the explorer's foreword.

I had decided to set out on a journey on the known roads via Turkestan to Tashkent, Kokand, Margilan and Osh, via the pass Toruk-gart to Kashgar. The expedition will start from Osh in Fergana, where the mail routes are stopped, and caravan ones are started through which I will have to pass almost 800 Swedish miles to the coasts of the Yellow Sea.

For an hour, Max scanned the pages, seeking references to food. As he thumbed through the old book, studying the author's twenty hand-drawn maps, he came upon chapter 13: *Into the Heart of Asia.*

In the bright moonlight our caravan went tinkling along to Osh. I had decided to go as far as Kashgar, the most westerly city of China, on the farther side of the mountain ranges that link the Tien Shan with the Pamir. Their highest pass is crossed by the caravan road running between Osh, in Russian Turkestan, and Kashgar, in Chinese Turkestan, and is named Torugart, or "the poplar pass." Its altitude is 12,000 feet.

The last caravans of the season had already left, the snowstorm season was due, and only those hardy Kirghiz who knew the road ever ventured over the pass. This was not sufficient to deter me. I bought provisions, a fur coat and felt rugs; hired four horses, for each of which I had to pay sixty kopecks a day; and employed three servants, Kerim Jan, the jigit, or postilion, Ata Bai, the groom, and Ashur, the cook.

Heavily clothed, and in valenki, or soft felt boots, we set forth on December 1. Traversing the River Naryn, we made haste east toward the town of the same name. The snow was falling thickly; and between the mountains, the landscape, white as chalk, revealed the kibitkas, or the big-arched blanket tents of the Kirghiz, looking like black dots. We lodged in the tents of the Kirghiz, and ate, rested and slept around their cheerful fires. At Sufi-kurgan there was an aul, a village of fifty tents at the base of the foothills of the Tien Shan. Khoat Bi, the old chief, received us amiably; and at his fire we had a soup called besh barmak (the five fingers) because it is thick enough to be eaten with the hand. It consisted of mutton, cabbage, carrots, potatoes, rice, onions, peppers and salt, all boiled in water. Once we were thus served, the old chief produced a bowl of dried spices which to the soup he added, signaling that we should also do as he did. The old man related to me that he called it Ot Boyanca Oroon, "the Fire of the Valley." The concoction added miraculous heat to a frigid evening, and the soup, prepared in a nomad's tent, was the best I could remember imbibing, anywhere. Our party, and our hosts, were in uncannily high spirits despite the gales and frozen passes ahead. Thus nourished, we enjoyed much koumiss, or fermented mares' milk, by the light of the fire, into the evening. We departed on 5 December toward Terek-davan, revitalized for the journey before us.

Max sat back, stunned. His heart rate spiked, and he began hyperventilating, as he often did when uncovering a mystery. Sven Hedin, the intrepid Swedish explorer of Central Asia, had experienced something locals called "the Fire of the Valley" somewhere in the Kyrgyz Tien Shan foothills as early as 1926. And though it was only a dried spice mix made by the locals, the fact that "fire" was referenced seemed to corroborate important parts of Gasanov's story. The heat had to come from something locally grown. He asked Rudra to copy the book's title page and the referenced passage and set off to find Lilah.

In the maps section, he found her with an oversize portfolio spread out before her on a wide table, Tavernier's memoir pushed to the side. He tried to tell her about his discovery, but she raised her hand, starting first.

"Tavernier has nothing relevant to say about foods, or Kyrgyzstan," she said, pointing to the map before her. "But did you know that one leg of the Silk Road went right through the Naryn Valley?"

Max tried to blurt out an answer, but she cut him off. "And that of all the well-known 18th and 19th-century travelers in Kyrgyzstan, Sven Hedin from Sweden passed through Naryn, and the Torugart pass more than once?"

Finally getting a chance to speak and too excited to form a sentence, all Max could say was,

"In 1926!" and shoved the copies he had made in front of her.

She scanned the text of Hedin's experience and then looked up at Max, steely-eyed. "It would seem that we have sufficient cause to go to Kyrgyzstan, doesn't it, Max?"

"Yes!" he said. "It's the verification I needed. Time to go. Rudra, you are indispensable."

Max awoke from a fitful night's sleep, sweating and breathing hard, even while embraced by the cool comfort of The Imperial Hotel. He had dreamt in unconnected threads of faraway people and places. Men in fur hats and short beards shuffled down alleys, carrying sacks of what might be peppers. Even in his dream, Max could almost smell them. He *felt* their presence, but the men were lost in the narrow tracks and pressing crowds. In the vignette, there was a long, broad, treeless plain bisected by a jagged river gorge stretching west into the setting sun. In another, he followed two cloaked men on yaks traversing a high mountain pass. Then Max found himself in a smoky room filled with travelers, silently eating bowls of steaming broth when a series of explosions obliterated the scene and rocked his subconscious.

The hotel room was dark and quiet. Max rinsed away the lingering shock of the dream with a long, hot shower, preparing to meet Lilah in the hotel's atrium for morning coffee. With their mission in Delhi accomplished, Max hungered for some diversion before their train's departure to northeast India and Assam.

In the atrium, the effervescent Creole beauty who was now his partner in a journey of discovery sensed a restiveness in Max.

"Who'd you wrestle with last night?' she asked. "You look grim for being in such a fine place."

Max grumbled something about peppers and men in hats and rivers and explosions as he slurped his coffee. "I could smell chiles in my dreams," was the only intelligible thing she heard.

Lilah let out a hearty laugh. "Go figure! Only you would be up all night with chile nightmares, Max. Leave your cloud behind, and let's go out and see some history. The handsome and ferocious-looking doorman says the tomb of Humayun is not to be missed."

Max nodded, coming around. "Coffee and crumpets, and I'm good to go."

After whistling down an impeccably maintained vintage Ambassador, the doorman sent Lilah and Max on their way down Ashoka Road and east to the Nizamuddin district. Despite the mid-morning chaos, their driver skillfully negotiated the route and its obstacles to ferry them to their destination five minutes before its opening. They were deposited at the arched gate of Humayun's Tomb on a verdant roundabout and stood in line for the ticket booth.

When the attendant swung the massive iron gates open at precisely 8 a.m., they were the first visitors through and entered a garden paradise. Manicured greenery and groomed fruit trees spanned the hundred-acre site of symmetrical gardens, crafted, they learned, to mirror the designer's vision of Paradise. A broad gravel thoroughfare led them to the east, where a monolithic structure sat in the center of the complex, silhouetted by the morning sun. The red gravel path was perfectly divided by a stone culvert designed to carry water across the grounds using only gravity. Ahead of them, a lone worker strolled toward the massive tomb, carrying only a broom and bucket. Mist hugged the ground, dampening sound, and finches chirped from among the hedges. They felt like the only ones allowed into a sacred place, an architectural icon designated a UNESCO World Heritage site.

Lilah quoted the handout they had received upon entry. "The mausoleum was a gift from Haji Begun, the widow of the first Mughal emperor in India, Shah Jahan, after his death. His son Akbar built it in the 16th century, and it's the first example of the Mughal architecture style, which blended Persian, Turkic, Arabic, and Indian elements. It was the inspiration for the Taj Mahal, sixty years later."

They stopped, taking in the spectacular structure. Built in red sandstone inlaid with white marble and capped by a white marble dome, the mausoleum sat atop a 20-foot-high arched pedestal over 800 feet wide on each side. The entire perfectly symmetrical structure towered nearly four hundred feet. Four water features located at precisely the four directions fed the stone culverts, which carried water to a shallow moat surrounding the vast tomb.

"To symbolize the four rivers in Paradise, which the Koran says run with water, wine, milk, and honey," said Lilah.

In a sublime moment, Max grasped the dynastic power of a place built purely as a memorial to one man, designed by his wife and built by his son. The majesty was intended to be felt on every inch of the grounds, not just in viewing the monarch's tomb.

Within minutes they were overtaken by crowds of tourists who had entered behind them, and for Max and Lilah, the solitary moment of discovering paradise was lost. Rather than climbing the tomb with the chatty hordes, Max and Lilah strolled the gardens, viewing the monument from afar and taking in the scents of fruit blossoms and cut grass. They reclined in the shade of a peach tree as the sun rose and the mists evaporated.

Lilah lay with her head in her hands watching bees, and Max contemplated the engineering required to construct the monolithic structure in the 16th century. As he did, a bright flash of light caught his eye from the southern corner of the elevated pedestal. Something was reflecting the sun.

Max sat up straight and shaded his eyes with his hands. Standing at the stone railing atop the tomb's foundation stood a man looking through huge binoculars, scanning the pathways and groups of tourists. He wore a red tracksuit. On instinct, Max followed the structure's line to the opposite corner, where another man, also in red, swept his binoculars across the complex.

"Holy crap," he said with a gasp.

Lilah was shaken from her reverie. "What's up, Max? I was dancing in paradise, and you sound like you saw a ghost."

"I have," Max said. "We gotta go."

Using the hedges and trees for cover, they exited the memorial's far gate, eyeing the spyglasses atop the tomb. Confident they hadn't been seen, they ducked into a motorized rickshaw and headed for the Imperial.

Max was incredulous. "Those goons are everywhere!" he said." They can't have known we would be there. And at Khari Baoli and the Archives."

Lilah seemed unaffected. "We meet Raj at the train station in two hours, so let's just hurry and get there early."

After quickly packing their bags at The Imperial, they asked the doorman for a taxi to the Old Delhi train station, where the trains departed for Varanasi. Just as they were closing the door to leave, a young woman from the hotel staff ran toward them, holding a single sheet of paper in her hand.

"Mr. Little!" she said, breathing hard. "A message for you came over the phone just an hour ago. I was told to inform you that it's urgent."

Max took the folded paper, thanking the woman, and directed the driver to the station. Once en route, he unfolded the message. On hotel stationery, it had been written in the same hand as the one he'd received from Gasanov upon his arrival, dictated from afar.

Mr. Max! Bakiyev knows you're encamped at The Imperial. It's not safe for you there. I bid you make haste for other environs, as I have heard about the hot dusting you gave his men in the spice market. They are even more greatly motivated to locate you and your lovely accomplice. I've heard they have as many questions for her as they do you. However, your repeated ability to slip through their massive criminal hands has the Bakiyev organization in an uproar, with orders to locate you at all costs. It all feels very "Casablanca" to me.

I remain encamped at the Ministry, where crooked locksmiths have changed all the doors in my office wing to lock only from the outside. I bathe in the basement gymnasium accompanied by a swarthy Uzbek guard (one cannot ever trust Uzbeks), and meals are sent to me. My wife and family have deserted me, thinking I am still away with a mistress. I am repeatedly asked about you and your mission and what you hoped to find at the Archives in Delhi. Apologetically, I found it expedient to divulge to Bakiyev your intent to locate the hottest pepper in the world, in Assam. But before you rage at me in absentia, you must know I did this to throw them off the scent of what I sincerely hope is your ultimate objective, here in Kyrgyzstan. Please come, Max. Your friend and confidante, Gasanov.

Max handed the paper to Lilah and looked out the window. The mayhem of Delhi's streets passed by as they crawled their way across town, and a man riding a camel in city traffic looked down at him with a childish grin stained red from betel nut. A symphony of car and truck horns punctuated the air, and the sweet smoke of burning cow dung once again snuck in the open windows. *India is baffling, yet it becomes fathomable once you accept it*, thought Max. The dragnet sent from Kyrgyzstan to locate him proved more challenging for his mind to grasp. And that Lilah was in their sights was an added variable that provided further stress.

Lilah broke the silence. "So Gasanov is trying to throw them off our tail by telling them why we're here, which is actually why we're here. So, what's the big deal if they know we're going to Assam for the Naga Jolokia? It has nothing to do with Kyrgyzstan."

Max, grasping the obvious, unscrambled his thoughts. "Because they want to know what we know, Lilah, and now we know quite a lot. We've traced the Silk Road routes through Kyrgyzstan and the Naryn Valley and seen evidence of the Fire of the Valley in Hedin's writing centuries later. We know about Gasanov's foray into Dostuk and his experience of the Fire. It's possible you could be growing strains of these chiles at Jones's farm right now from the seeds Gasanov sent you before we ever met. We're deeply enmeshed in this story and getting deeper still. If we get a hold of these peppers in their original habitat and ascertain that they are a unique variety, original to Kyrgyzstan, then Bakiyev loses. He either keeps us from physically doing that or forces us to do the work for him so that he can benefit. Most probably against our will. There is a certain danger in our pursuing this to its end."

Lilah understood his concern. But she didn't get a whiff of fear. "You want to go to Kyrgyzstan, don't you, Max? You're already there in your head."

"Yes," he said. "I do. I want to discover this magical specimen on an ancient trade route that saw the meeting of east and west centuries ago, in the form of a chile pepper very few people have ever experienced. And despite all his slipperiness, I want to help Gasanov and his people. Somehow. Yeah, it's all a tantalizing elixir, but if I can turn this into something good and help those people thrive, it'll be worth it, Bakiyev be damned."

At that moment, Lilah became vividly aware of who Max was, and it moved her. And she was all in for the journey.

The Old Delhi Railway Station was opened to the public in 1903. It replaced its smaller precursor, which offered only two tracks and had been in operation since 1864, when the first track was laid between Delhi and Calcutta. The new station, built like a fortress of red sandstone inlaid with white marble, evoked the nearby Delhi Red Fort and British colonial India's vast power. Initially servicing a thousand passengers a day, the station now was the starting point for 180,000 travelers on 190 trains to all parts of the country.

The taxi stopped directly before the station's main entrance, but Max urged the driver to continue around the corner of the building, cautious in case it was being watched. Entering through a side door, they stopped next to a column as a host of travelers crossed before them in every direction, chattering with worry and excitement. The air was a thick haze of diesel fuel, fried food, curry, bodies, and smoke. Alerts in Hindi echoed on speakers through the cavernous space.

Lilah was entranced by the level of anticipation in the air. It looked like the whole country was catching a train to somewhere. The mayhem was fabulous.

Max scanned the immense space as they waited, looking out for people who might be monitoring the crowd. Though they were noticeably taller than the throngs surrounding them, he and Lilah didn't stand out too much, he thought. Though in her shimmering green kurta and long, sun-tinted hair, Lilah looked more Bollywood beauty than a research student from America.

"We need to find the track for the 2559 Shiv Ganga Express to Varanasi," he said. "We should find Raj waiting there."

Weaving their way through the masses, they read the electronic signs at the end of each track, which displayed destinations across the country. They spotted the red lights at the far side of the station identifying their train, scheduled to leave at 3:50. Directly underneath the sign stood a beaming Raj holding a small suitcase and a package tied up in colorful fabric, which he held by an elaborate knot at its top. He was dressed smartly in suit pants and a vest atop a blue collarless shirt.

"Greetings, my friends!" Raj said as he shook Max's hand with both of his and gave Lilah a warm hug. "Your timing is impeccable, as our train is just about to begin boarding. I've secured us a first-class, air-conditioned cabin for our overnight journey to Varanasi."

On past solo visits to India, Max had always chosen second-class travel. It afforded significantly less privacy but was a sure way to experience India and its culture firsthand, even if he had to sleep with his arms laced through his duffle bag straps. Traveling now as a group and wanting to stay clear of prying eyes, the first-class cabin seemed a desirable choice. They employed a young porter to ferry their belongings and were escorted through the crowds to the third coach in the long train. The cars were colored a faded red and blue, with a yellow stripe running their length at chest height that read Indian National Railways. The trains were aged and, in many places, rusted, but the uniformed conductors wore their INR badges and captains' hats with authority and pride.

As they waited in the rear of the group pressing to board the train, Max noticed the women and men pushing carts holding pots of hot food and samosas for sale to passengers embarking on long journeys, and he realized they had not thought about food on their fifteen-hour trip. He asked Raj whether they should consider venturing out to find something suitable.

"No time," he said, stepping aside for Lilah to board. "Plus, I've got you all sorted out, Mr. Max. Up we go!"

Checking that their three names were in the plastic slot by the door, they settled into cabin 3A on the south-facing side of the 24-coach train. "So that we have the best view of the Taj Mahal at sunset," Raj said.

Padded benches on either side of the cabin were upholstered in red vinyl, and red curtains covered the window and the door. Two upper bunks fronted by short metal rails occupied the top of the cabin, while the backs of the benches they sat on folded down to make two lower bunks. A table for dining folded against the window wall and the air-conditioning vents, and a fan whirred from the ceiling. It would be a clean, cozy home for the overnight ride.

Lilah and Max stashed their bags beneath the seats and settled across from Raj. Next to him on the red bench, he cradled a fabric-covered cylinder about two feet tall.

"What's that, Raj?" asked Lilah.

"My wife Ambika has prepared a traditional Royal Rajasthani *thali* in your honor, which I have brought from Jaipur."

"What's a *thali*?" Almost as soon as she asked, Lilah began to catch delicious smells emanating from the container.

"Thali is a preparation of all the finest foods of my home province in portions suitable for travel," he responded, "and we will enjoy the feast with the setting sun over the Taj Mahal and Yamuna River from our train window. Precisely 1.5 hours from now."

The Shiv Ganga Express had been named for two of the most significant images in Indian life, Shiv for Lord Shiva, one of the three primary Hindu deities, and Ganga for Mother Ganga, the holy river their journey would follow. The express train left only five minutes after its scheduled departure time, a notable occurrence in India, causing Raj to put his hands together in thanks. Their journey would be charmed with good luck, he proclaimed. The train housed a full component of travelers, with every cabin occupied and the open cars jammed with more people than their seats allowed. Families brought trunks, boxes, luggage, and stacked *thalis* like Raj's. A visit from a stern-looking conductor with a pencil mustache and aviator glasses confirmed the group's tickets just before the train lurched out of the station.

It took a full forty minutes for the urbanization of Delhi to fall away and the arid countryside to open to their shared window view. Shantytown settlements lined the route, while it seemed to Lilah that the poorest people of India wore the brightest clothes, a vibrant palette contrasting the squalor and struggle of daily life. Women carrying loads atop their heads walked random footpaths that angled out across the landscape toward unseen destinations. Villages gave way to a broad landscape dotted by random trees, with a low-lying haze hugging the horizon. Soon, they eased into regular conversation like old friends as the countryside rolled past. Leaving out the events with Bakiyev's men, Lilah and Max recounted for Raj their Delhi experiences, and he was most impressed by their success at the National Archives.

"I am proud to know that our archives have represented such a resource for your international work, Max," Raj said. "Getting into them is reputed to be quite difficult, and your man Rudra appears to be an ace in the hole. In India, it is essential to have connections to get things done. And a good business card."

Raj's observation made Max think of Gasanov, pulling strings from far away in his Kyrgyz ministry prison. How was he able to stay so connected to their journey, he wondered?

After an hour of relaxed conversation, Raj proclaimed it time to unveil the Royal Rajasthani thali prepared by his wife. Placing the fabric cylinder between his legs and addressing the carefully tied knot, he exposed various brass containers of different sizes, each with a lid. The topmost was a lidded pitcher topped by three brass cups.

Raising the folded dining table, Raj began his thali presentation, pouring from the brass pitcher. "Rajasthan is a dry province, so historically we have made extensive use of milk, buttermilk, cream, curd, and yogurt to save water," he said, "and this *thandai* is a traditional beverage served with our meals."

As Lilah sipped the cool, creamy drink, she sensed notes of almond and cardamom. It had layers of flavors, and she inquired about the ingredients. Raj explained.

"*Thandai* is goat milk, almond, fennel seeds, ground watermelon seeds, cardamom, rose petals, saffron, and sugar. We serve it on religious holidays and special occasions, which this surely is."

Layered beneath the pitcher were three brass plates and stacks of small brass bowls, called *katori*, which he placed before them. Each dish was then ringed with six small bowls, leaving the center clear. He produced flatbreads from the next vessel, a flat round pan, *besan rotis* made of rich yellow chickpea flour, which he placed in the center.

"In India, the drier areas use breads more than rice as an accompaniment to foods as rice is grown in water and thus must be imported. Today being special, we have rice as well."

Lilah was mesmerized. Max leaned in, attentive due to his gnawing hunger. While he had eaten extensively in India, thali was never on the menu.

"Why is it called a Royal thali?" Lilah asked.

"The Maharajas and attendant families used to travel across their kingdoms in large processions of elephants, camels, and porters," Raj explained. "And feeding the royal family was a logistical challenge. Thalis evolved as the easiest way to feed these groups expecting the same lavish feasts they experienced in the palace. Over time, the general population adopted the practice, though in a much more compact arrangement."

Raj reached down into the fabric bag and produced a platter atop which sat six small, lidded pots and serving utensils. He described each of them and their preparation for the next ten minutes as he gingerly served portions in their little bowls. Each was undeniably unique in both appearance and aroma.

First, there were small round dumplings called *Dal Baati Choorma*, made of millet flour stuffed with onions, peas, and lentils, fried in ghee. Over these, he spooned a red lentil and yogurt curd gravy with flecks of roasted brown chile. Next, *Kairi Ki Subzi*, thick Rajasthani raw mango curry, tangy and spicy-sweet, seasoned with fennel seeds, coriander, fresh green chiles, and turmeric. Then, *Ker Sangri*, dried blackberries with thin green pickled beans of the flowering *Khejari* tree, soaked in mustard oil with caraway seeds and whole red chiles. A fiery *Laal Maas* followed: lamb slowly cooked with wild cucumber, yogurt, *Mathania* red chiles, mushrooms, and coriander leaves. And *Safed Maas*, wild boar simmered with masala spices, cream and yogurt, mint leaves, and almond cashew paste. Raj spooned into the remaining bowl *Lasan Ki Chatni*, a spicy and tart garlic chutney made with mashed fresh green chiles, lemon, and vinegar.

"My wife added extra chiles and cooked down the chutney for two days to make it to your liking, Max," he said, satisfied in his presentation.

Before them lay a colorful feast of textures and flavor combinations neither Max nor Lilah had experienced. They dipped and scooped back and forth among the sumptuous bowls using the chickpea flatbreads as a spoon. When the heat level rose, they sipped the thandai.

"Raj, your wife Ambika is a magician in the kitchen," said Max between bites. "Every dish is unique and exquisitely prepared. May I have more of the wild boar?"

Twenty minutes passed with little further discussion of the food, apart from deep sighs of satisfaction and the occasional "amazing." The buildup of inner heat demanded an opening of the window. Outside, the open landscape began to change, with buildings more frequent, the sun shining orange through the haze and the light angling from the west as they neared Agra.

As they approached the end of their feast, Raj implored them to keep their gaze out the window, to the south. The landscape suddenly disappeared, and a red wall seventy feet high took its place, thirty yards from the window.

"The Red Fort of Agra," he said. "Home of the Mughal emperors until 1638 when they moved their capital to Delhi. It took four thousand builders eight years to complete in 1573, working every day."

The Mughals were conquerors and required a palace imposing enough to subdue the population and repel frequent invaders. Virtually a small walled city of almost a million square feet, the fortress was constructed by the emperor Akbar from red Rajasthani sandstone and featured lofty gates and towering parapets. The tallest of these looked across the Yamuna River to the Taj Mahal, a mile away.

The fort's massive red walls instantly dropped away, and their train entered a bridge over a broad river plain. The Yamuna itself was highly venerated in Indian culture, its water slaking the thirst of 57 million people in Delhi after flowing from glacial origins in the Himalayas. Bathing in its sacred waters ensured devout Hindus a peaceful death. Normally flowing through a channel half a mile wide, the Yamuna became just a trickle thirty feet across, with water needs upriver in Delhi squelching its flow in the dry season.

As Lilah followed the river's course to a sweeping bend, a twenty-foot red wall abutted the river valley for a quarter-mile. Atop the buttress, across a mile of rivery mist and the orange glow of sunset, sat the massive white mausoleum, the Taj Mahal. They stopped eating and sat in silence, taking in the view of the incredible monolithic structure, its white marble turned pink by the setting sun. It was a hypnotic symmetry of minarets and arches and domes captured at a sublimely perfect moment of light and shadow.

"All in the spirit of love," she mused.

The complex of buildings that made up the Taj Mahal sat on five hundred acres of lush gardens. Raj told them of the great Mughal emperor Shah Jahan, who built the Taj as a monument to his wife, Mumtaz Mahal.

"It began construction in 1632," he said, "and is the preeminent example of Indo-Islamic architecture in all of India."

The structure's immensity came into focus only as groups of tiny people appearing as small ants became visible on the walls and in the complex's courtyards. Miniature pious bathers, dressed all in white, gathered at the river's edge below for absolution and guarantee of a smooth ride to the afterlife.

It took only a minute for the train to cross the Yamuna River Bridge, and the brief view became obscured by the commercial buildings and life of Agra. They sat in reflective silence as the city's density closed in upon them.

"I must say, your timing is amazing, Raj," Max said as the train entered the bustling Agra station. "I've always wanted to see the Taj, and you set it out beautifully before us. What a testament to love." The look in Lilah's eyes showed that he was speaking for them both, which caused Max to question when that had started happening.

After a minutes-long stop to board more passengers, the Shiv Ganga Express left Agra, with the conductor exclaiming over the loudspeaker that Allahabad would be the next stop, at midnight. Raj collected the metal plates and dishes from the thali experience and left the cabin to wash the remnants and repack the kit. Lilah and Max, alone, both stared out the window as the development of Agra gave way to smaller hamlets and then open countryside. The glow of the setting sun sprayed the landscape in horizontal orange light, enhanced by the smoke and dust of working villages and end-of-day commuting. Max observed Lilah's relaxed look, eyes and gaze soft as she took in the passing view, face glowing in the waning light.

While Max sat fascinated by Lilah, she sat up, and her eyes opened wide. "Look, Max!" she said, pointing south.

Turning, he saw a vast plain appear, dotted with clutches of women and girls in a dazzling array of colorful saris squatting on the ground, fabric draped over their heads. The ground was bathed in red as far as they could see.

Nearly fifty acres of dry land were covered in long shiny *Capsicum annuum* chiles, red as blood. The women and girls searched through vast expanses of fruit for specimens that had sufficiently dried in the hot sun, removing the stems, then tossing the chiles into huge piles. Others carried baskets of dried chiles over to a donkey cart driven by the lone man in the operation, and after dumping them in the cart's bed, returned to select more. Their bright saris shone in the pale light, pink, orange, and yellow, creating a vibrant tableau of color and humanity in a sea of red. The field's vastness was in vivid contrast to the group of women tasked with handling millions of chiles barehanded in a scene that occurred all over India each day, providing enhancement for a billion meals. While Max had visited such chile operations on the ground, the view from the passing train was striking.

For Lilah, the vision was revelatory, outlandish. "Wow, wow," Max heard her say, pressed to the window like a child. The connection of chiles to people worldwide was a vibrant one, motivating their passion and shared journey.

Raj returned with the cleaned and repacked thali kit and a tray of hot tea, which they sipped, watching nightfall and the moon rise over the parched Indian countryside. By eight o'clock, he suggested that they prepare themselves for bed.

"We arrive in Varanasi at four in the morning to catch the sunrise ceremony by the Ganges," he said, "and we will have a full day seeing the city. Overnight, we'll pass through Allahabad, another of India's holiest cities, where the Yamuna and Ganges meet and where the Kumbha Mela is held every twelve years. Over one hundred million pilgrims attend over two months to bathe in Mother Ganga when Jupiter, the sun, and the moon are in the correct position. If you have never witnessed it, it is extraordinary."

They prepared their berths, which folded down from the walls of the cabin. Raj insisted on the upper bunk, and after removing his shoes, climbed up, leaving Max and Lilah the lower berths. He opted to sleep in his jeans and t-shirt and could not help but watch as Lilah removed her green kurta and hung it on a hook on the door. After pulling the curtains on the cabin door, she turned out the light. Lilah wore a simple white shirt and white silk pants under the kurta, and in the moon's glow, she looked elvish as she climbed into her berth. While the train rocked and lights flickered through the curtains, she flashed Max a playful, girly smile and slid under the covers.

"Goodnight, Raj," she said.

From up above came, "Goodnight, Lilah. Goodnight Max. I feel that discoveries await you in our ancient city by the river."

Then Max said, "Goodnight, Raj, goodnight, Lilah." He wondered about what discoveries lay ahead other than those that had inspired the trip they were on.

Lilah finished. "Goodnight, Max. Tomorrow we see the holy Ganges. Nothing to do with chiles or commandos. Think about that!"

VARANASI

"Varanasi is older than history, older than tradition, older even than legend, and looks twice as old as all of them put together."
– Mark Twain

The legend of Varanasi dates back 10,000 years in Hindu culture, to the beginning of time, in the oldest epics of Hindu literature: the Puranas, the Vedas, and the Mahabharata. In a country where most cities claim at least two names, Varanasi elicits over a hundred, including *Kashi*, the city of "divine light." It was the home of Lord Shiva, who walked there with his goddess wife Parvati and where they created the "original ground." Here, ancient texts told that the god Krishna set fire to his nemesis Jarasanda, and Lord Rama descended to do penance after slaying the demon Ravana. Varanasi is said to be the spot where the first primal *lingam*, a fiery pillar of light controlled by Lord Shiva, burst through the earth's crust and flamed toward the heavens, establishing his position over the other gods. The Shiva Lingam is one of the holiest icons in Hinduism, and of the seven sacred cities of India, Varanasi is the most pious. Recorded history dates the founding of the metropolis sometime around 2000 BC, and to this day, the city is a nexus of culture and tradition - a spiritual mecca for Jains, Hindus, and Buddhists. The waterfront is a UNESCO World Heritage Site. For three thousand years, it has been a place of pilgrimage. And for all living Hindus, to be cremated by the Ganges in Varanasi delivers instant enlightenment and frees one from the cycle of death and eternal rebirth. It is the best place in all of India to die. And at 4 a.m., when the Shiv Ganga Express from Delhi arrived, the city was already beginning to come to life.

Going to the holiest city in India was Lilah's desire. In addition to being a practitioner of voodoo rites, she had gravitated to Hinduism's teachings after studying world religions in college. That their route to Assam and the Naga Jolokia was taking them past the ancient holy Hindu city on the banks of the Ganges was too powerful to pass up. The city was steeped in mysticism, history, life, and death, and Raj would be a valuable guide for their short foray into the city's cultural and spiritual melee.

They disembarked at the station before dawn, already swarming with pilgrims and all of India in transit. Once outside, music and lights blared, with hawkers touting religious icons and shiny fabrics printed with holy texts. Food stalls did a brisk business, and buses and rickshaws and tuk-tuks moved everywhere. The city was electrifyingly alive though it was pitch black in the dark of night.

Raj urged them to hurry as he hailed a taxi. They had one hour until the predawn *Aarti* ceremony by the river Ganges was to occur.

"There are eighty-four ghats along the Ganges in Varanasi," said Raj inside their cramped taxi. "Some are attached to temples and the multitude of sects within Hinduism, others affiliated with specific deities. There are ghats used only for bathing and those solely for meditation and yoga. People cook, play, sing, and conduct business on them. And, of course, there are the cremation ghats, which fascinate visitors from outside India. We have an open and visual relationship with death, and nowhere is that tradition more visible than in Varanasi. Here is where life and death exist side by side, equal parts of daily existence. It's a pilgrimage for all Hindus, in life and death."

The taxi weaved through pedestrians, buses, camels, vendor carts, and the occasional lounging ox. Most of the movement headed in their direction, to the old city, called Vishwanatha Khanda, and the warren of ancient alleyways that led to the Ganges. Finally, the taxi could go no further as the driver motioned toward a thoroughfare wide enough for three people.

"We will drop our bags at the Shambala guest house and find some chai before we make our way to the river," said Raj. "Aarti begins in forty-five minutes, and we will want to get an unobstructed view."

They followed Raj as he wheeled his small suitcase across the busy street and into the narrow alley's dark opening, going single file to accommodate the steady stream of humanity coming in the other direction. After numerous turns in the dim predawn darkness, they reached a quiet lane and a doorway with a hand-painted sign that read *Shambala Guest House*. Cupping his hands around his mouth for volume, Raj looked up and shouted toward the sliver of sky over the thoroughfare.

"Rahuuuuuuuul, Rahuuuuuuuul!"

Following Raj's voice to the rooftops, Max and Lilah looked up to see an ancient, faded-green building. A spider's web of flags and power lines nearly obscured the sky. Decaying wrought iron railings sat astride crumbling balconies. Peeling blue wood shutters fronted the windows, and laundry hung, dripping, from every available surface. From a window just below the roof, a round head appeared.

"I am here!" the man, presumably Rahul, called down. "Two seconds, please!" The clatter of footsteps racing down several flights of cement stairs followed until Rahul appeared in the doorway, already dressed for the day in an embroidered orange kurta.

"Welcome!" he said, struggling a bit to catch his breath. "Hello, Mr. Raj, and greetings to the eminent American scientists in his company! Please, let me take your bags, as I am aware you are attending the morning Aarti. You will find Shambala a perfect oasis during your stay in Varanasi. Enjoy the ancestral labyrinth that is our city! And remember, while this is where Hindus come to find enlightenment, it can be easy to lose your way."

Leaving their belongings with the buoyant Rahul, Raj led them further into the maze of Old Varanasi. The cobblestoned alleys all seemed to lead downhill, *toward the river,* Max guessed. Two complacent cows lay peacefully in their path, fearing no disturbance. Everywhere they looked, altars of varying sizes were built into walls and in corners, with ground floor windows enclosed to accommodate oblong pillars of polished stone, the revered Shiva lingams. The stones embodied physical representations of Lord Shiva, Varanasi's patron deity, and touching or bowing to them provided an instant connection to Hindu theology's supreme being. Phallic in shape, they also signify fertility.

Reaching a confluence of two other alleys, where a thick Shiva lingam stood atop a pedestal behind the community water pump, Raj raised his hand for them to stop as the stream of people continued around them. "This is a good place for chai. Come up in here and sit."

The establishment Raj selected was about eight feet wide, six feet deep, and two steps above the alley traffic. One half was dedicated to a bench and a narrow table for customers. The other half was the chai *wallah's* workspace, consisting of a concrete coal burner topped by an iron grill, a small refrigerator, an array of pots and pans, and tins of dry ingredients. The proprietor crouched atop a wood platform by the burner, the light from the single bulb above him refracted surreally by steam from the boiling ingredients. Sliding onto the elevated bench, the three travelers filled the business to capacity. Aromas of nutmeg and clove permeated the space, while Lilah picked up a hint of basil perfuming the air.

Raj ordered from the chai wallah, who he called Lalu, and he began by pouring thick milk from a tall canister into a wide pan eight inches deep atop the grill. The coals burned hot and yellow beneath the grates.

"Buffalo milk," said Raj, "thick and creamy, the best for making chai."

Lalu poured steaming black tea into the already bubbling milk from a metal teapot, releasing it from the farthest point of an extended arm above his head, per tradition, and hitting the vessel with perfect aim.

"Masala chai, spiced tea, has a history dating back five thousand years in India," explained Raj as they watched the man work. "It was ordered by a Hindu king as a beneficial health beverage for daily consumption. The mix of spices each has ayurvedic properties; cinnamon, for circulation and respiratory function: star anise for good breath; ginger and black pepper for digestion; cardamom to elevate the mood, and cloves for relieving pain. Tea was added only after the

British made it available throughout the country. Assamese black tea, the preferred type since the 1800s," Raj added. "Strong but not bitter if he's let it steep correctly."

Next were added the five traditional dry ingredients, the masala spices: cardamom, ginger, clove, black pepper, star anise, and cinnamon. Lalu reached into the various metal containers and tossed thick pinches of each chai element into the now-boiling brew. Ginger grated fresh from the root went in after a fistful of sugar. Lastly, basil leaves were torn and tossed into the mix.

"The basil is what makes Lalu's chai unique," said Raj, "and famous. No one did it before him, and now, many others are. But he's the first as far as I know."

Flecks of dissipating clove and cinnamon turned the liquid caramel brown as Lalu swiftly stirred foam from the edges with a wooden spoon. The smells of spice and basil, combined with the steam of sweet buffalo milk, created an aromatic cloud of anticipation in their tiny predawn alcove.

Lalu leaned over the small countertop and placed three earthenware teacups in front of each of them. Then he put cheesecloth over the top of a smaller saucepan and, lifting the boiling pan of chai, poured the tea and ingredients through the cloth filter. He removed the filter and transferred the tea from one pot to another five more times, always from the highest point of his extended arm in the cramped space. Finally, he emptied the full frothing pan into a large brass teapot with a curved foot-long spout. Standing above the travelers, and with perfect aim, he reached up high and filled each of their cups from five feet away, spilling not a drop.

Lilah closed her eyes and drew in a deep breath, holding it briefly before a long exhale. This moment of predawn street chai in India's holiest city was moving, and she wanted to give thanks for the beauty of it. Leaning over, eyes still closed, she inhaled a face full of steam from her cup and was immediately awash in cinnamon and clove and nutmeg and basil and ginger. She then placed both hands around the small cup and slurped the piping hot liquid. The holiday spices, clove, nutmeg, and cinnamon, were the easiest to identify, but the slight heat of black pepper on the tongue and ginger in the throat was unique in the sweet alchemy. She tasted the strong yet, smooth black tea and the abundant sweetness of sugar. However, the freshness of the basil added at the last moment brought the entire concoction to an elevated place. Spicy, sweet, earthy, creamy, with notes of the minty herb. Eyes still closed, she rested the cup and exhaled deeply, meditatively.

"It tastes as perfect as you just made it look, Lilah," said Max, "and yes, I felt it too, in this place. May I have more chai, please, Lalu?"

The chai wallah poured again. Then again. They slurped and

savored the milky brew and watched old Varanasi come to life from their tiny chai haven. Moped-driving delivery men wove through pedestrians, chased by barking dogs. Men bathed at pumps alongside the throng by the alley walls, and the metal doors slid open as businesses awoke. Barbers and their customers sat on crates as haircuts and morning shaves were administered. From an adjacent thoroughfare, a full-grown Brahma bull emerged, strolling through the old quarter without care. His horns nearly reached the walls of the alley, and sari-clad women and kurta-wearing men waited patiently for their chance to pass.

Then, from up the path echoed the sounds of chanting and percussion. Leaning out into the alley to look at the source, Lilah saw a group of six men carrying a white cloth-covered load atop their shoulders on a bamboo stretcher. They chanted to the beat of a small drum wielded by a follower dressed in white, his head shaved. As the party passed, Lilah focused on the load they bore. Covered in bright woven red silk, she saw the tips of toes under the cloth. She followed the form's length as it passed until she made out the point of a nose and the arch of a forehead under the fabric. The dead person's final journey was part of the daily flow of life here, she comprehended, and the shopkeepers didn't look up from their work. Some people stopped to let the funeral procession pass, while others made their way around the group in a greater hurry. As the procession passed, the air moved around them, and Lilah, sipping her chai, recalled Raj's statement of life and death existing side by side in Varanasi.

"They are heading to one of the cremation ghats by the Ganges," said Raj. "We will get to see it after the Aarti ceremony, which begins very shortly. So, we must continue. Lalu, *dhayanavaad.* Thank you!"

Max paid for the tea, and he and Lilah pressed their hands together in thanks, prompting a broad, red-stained smile from the chai wallah. They followed Raj as he wound through the alleys, dodging handcarts, groups of saffron-robed monks, and barefoot pilgrims as the crowd going in their direction swelled. Within five minutes, they emerged from the old city's labyrinth onto an expansive concrete platform, blinking in the bright incandescence of spotlights. They had reached the *Assi ghat,* home of the morning Aarti ceremony for three millennia.

People milled about everywhere. A hundred wide stairs descended to the river from their perch, an inky black sheet of glass in the darkness. Halfway down the cascade of steps stood another platform, where the crowd's energy was focused. Five rectangular wood stages, draped in red fabric, sat bathed in the spotlights. The throng packed in close around the platforms, and rooftops and surrounding balconies above became jammed with pilgrims and tourists eager to witness the morning devotion. A fleet of small boats bobbed on the river, their operators hawking a floating seat for the ceremony and a tour on the water thereafter. Max and Lilah followed Raj as they wound their way through the crowd, positioning themselves with a clear view of the stages and the river.

The morning Ganga Aarti carried great symbolic significance in Varanasi. With the ghats all facing east across the holy river, the sunrise held powerful meaning and ritual. The word Aarti dates to the time of the Vedas in India, almost 3,000 years, and comes from the Sanskrit *Aratrika*, meaning "ritual that dispels darkness." Presenting offerings and mantras to the gods, the ceremony celebrated the five essential elements of the Hindu faith: air, water, fire, wind, and earth. It also immersed participants in *pet ki puja*, true communion with the divine, and Lilah was ready not just to witness but partake in the spiritual ride. Max thought the whole thing extraordinary, a passionate spiritual melee. And he took note of the fact that since leaving Delhi, he had not thought nor talked about Bakiyev or Gasanov, nor Boris and Vlad, as he had begun calling the Kyrgyz henchmen.

At precisely 5 a.m., a resounding series of notes blown from a conch shell above them caused the masses to look to the top of the ghat. Called by the sounds, a group of five priests worked through the crowd and down to the red stages. The entire audience began to light incense and chant and clap as the air filled with sound and thick sandalwood smoke. Bells rang, and drums beat, just as they had for centuries. Around and atop the priests' stages were numerous shiny brass ritual objects, water vessels, bundles of flowers, bells, and long incense sticks.

Amid the chanting and clapping, the Brahmin priests ascended each platform, then assumed devotional kneeling positions, bowing toward the river to the east. They rose in unison to their knees, beginning a rhythmic chanting of mantras and spreading their arms to the river before them. Bells, gongs, and drums accompanied the priests, creating a fervorous din. The volume and intensity increased over five full minutes of prayers and blessings, then stopped. The priests then raised the conch shells and blew deep notes that echoed across the water while the crowd sat silently with anticipation.

Max looked at Lilah, seeing her green eyes wide with wonder. In her headscarf, she looked like a pilgrim.

Elaborate, multitiered brass candelabras were lit and offered by the priests to the four directions, their red and gold silk robes flashing in the light as they moved. They chanted, calling to the spectators, who answered in unison. Then, long, snake-headed lamps on chains were swung in circles over the masses and toward the river, and the smoke and perfume of incense floated everywhere, like ritual fog. After being offered to Mother Ganga, bundles of flowers were tossed into the crowd, with pilgrims clamoring for them as a hint of pale light grew on the eastern horizon.

Raj helped place the ritual in context. "Bear in mind that this same ceremony has been taking place here since the beginning of Varanasi's recorded history. After prayers and offerings to Mother Ganga, the priests are blessing all in attendance. We are participants in the ritual, and the priests recognize that holiness exists within each person here. As witnesses, you are agreeing to surrender your ego and transcend material desires. Varanasi faces toward the past more than the future. Are you feeling it, Max?"

Max noticed he was watching the events over prayer-clasped hands. "I feel the magic in centuries of devotion in this place, Raj. It's joyous and life-affirming, even for a non-Hindu. India is so infused with ritual and history it's hard not to get swept up in it. Maybe I'll get a dot on my forehead today."

More lamps were lit, and bundles of incense and holy Ganga water were tossed over the crowd as flames leaped from the priest's devices. Chanting and drums and clapping by thousands of devotees created a scene vastly different than any Western religious gathering, and it was dissonant, mesmerizing. Lilah, accustomed to rituals with deep history, felt right at home, awash in humanity's energy and beliefs.

Light grew in the east, profiling the dozens of small boats on the water, packed with devotees, and transforming the river from black to green to pink to gold. Max watched as the ancient city's layered waterfront became washed with pink and gold light. Edifices of stone seventy feet high, temples, palaces, and places of business, increasingly came into focus and glowed. From windows, verandas, and rooftops, faces greeted the coming dawn. The ceremony reached a frenetic crescendo as the sun broke the horizon. Then, everyone went completely silent, savoring the celestial beginning of another day.

With the ceremony complete, the crowds dispersed. Most wound their way back through the alleys of Vishwanatha Khanda. Many others descended the stairs to the river's edge individually or in groups to perform ritual bathing. Holy men unrolled blankets for blessings and debates, and astrologers set up tables with charts and cards for readings. Following Raj, Max and Lilah worked their way down to the water and commissioned a boat to show the city and ghats from the river's perspective. As they stepped into the vessel, two skinny Varanasi girls jumped in with them, smelling of the mustard oil that shined in their ebony hair.

"We come, we come, okay? Please no say no we help make blessing for river, okay?"

The urchins each carried a basket filled with candles and flowers to bless the river. Raj, thinking to shoo them away, was stopped by Lilah. "Let them come. They're so beautiful, Raj," she said.

The pair scrambled eagerly to the bow of the boat, cradling their baskets and making themselves very much at home. Pointing to them each, Lilah asked, "What are your names?"

"Name? I am Radhika. My little sister Gidla," the older of the two said. "We are Dalit, lowest caste." The identifying of their lowest status in India's hierarchal society came without a trace of shame.

Breaking free from the crush of boats by the riverbank, their oarsman took them out into the current, the flow north and east. Lighting the candles in their baskets, the girls handed one each to Lilah and Max. Called lotus candles, each set within a bed of bright orange marigolds, with the flowers atop green woven leaves that enabled them to float.

"Put, put," little Gidla implored them while gesturing to the water. "Make happy Ganga send prayer."

Placing them gently in the water, Max and Lilah were then handed more candles, as many as they wished to purchase, creating a flotilla of flickering lights illuminating the offerings. Short mental messages went out with each floating lotus candle, dozens in all. Lilah had purchased the entire contents of both baskets hoping to enrich the girls' day. No sooner had the last candle been placed and the money exchanged than the children grabbed their empty baskets and hopped into another passing boat, giving the captain money for a ride to shore to gather more candles. *Smart girls* thought Lilah. They smiled together, calling out, "Thanks, pretty lady!"

With Ganga's blessings administered, they floated downriver along the ghats a hundred yards from shore. The panorama was extraordinary, a cutaway view of life along the Ganges. The water's edge was a riot of color, as women in bright saris dipped fully dressed the customary three times in the river. Each of them held a brass vessel for collecting the holy water for later use. Entire bolts of neon-vibrant fabric thirty yards long had been washed and were laid out drying on the steps in the morning sun, a hundred patterns in every color imaginable. Cross-legged yogis meditated amidst the chaos, challenging their skills. Handlers with switches led groups of cows and water buffalos to the river's edge to bathe and let them drink, while any cow pies generated were quickly scraped up by bands of roving children to be dried and used for fuel. Goats trotted aimlessly, scavenging for scraps, and monkeys leaped from ledge to ledge along the rooftops. Children played games, screeching when they got tagged. The tableau continued as far as the eye could see.

Apart from the teeming humanity, the ghats' architecture enthralled them, encompassing buildings of every size and shape. Some edifices rose seven stories from atop the hundred stairs, topped by towers and balconies and minarets. Many were obviously in use, while others sat neglected and in decay. Max asked Raj to whom they all belonged.

"The ghats here have many identities, Max. Centuries ago, regional rulers, the maharajas, commissioned ghats to symbolize piety and power. Other powerful people financed ghats belonging to a particular religious sect to gain favor. Members of the wealthy merchant class built some of the most elaborate because having a presence along the Ganges projected influence and social standing. The Shiv Ganga Silk Factory has occupied one for three hundred years. I think that erecting a building above the Ganges is for Hindus what owning a home in the Hamptons is to New Yorkers. Many sit unoccupied for much of the year, only to be enjoyed during religious festivals and holidays or lent out like VIP boxes at a football stadium to family members and business connections. And the actual places where the ghats meet the river have other identities entirely."

They passed the packed *Someshwar*, or Lord of the Moon ghat, reputed to heal those who bathed in its waters of all diseases. The accompanying building was unremarkable and in complete decay. There was *Schindia* ghat, among the most picturesque, with its orange Shiva temple sinking into the river's bed, poorly engineered; the *Bhonsale* ghat, erected by the ruling family of Nagpur, an imposing hundred-room palace atop walls forty feet high; and the monolithic *Darbhanga* ghat, a towering pavilion built by the royal family of Bihar in the 1800s. And while all ghats included steps to the river and public access as part of their design, adjoining palaces were often imposing and unreachable.

Rounding a bend in the river, they encountered a much different scene. An ancient ghat, blackened with time and centuries of smoke, loomed before them. Groups of people clustered around burning fires of cross-stacked tree limbs. Piles of wood lay stacked in every available space and on long shallow boats tied up by the river. Porters carried armfuls of wood down the steps of the ghat, while others shoveled piles of ash. One important fellow weighed stacks of wood on a massive scale, handing out receipts to the buyers. As they got nearer the shore, Max saw two feet protruding from among one of the fires, as the ancient ritual of Hindu cremation unfolded before them.

"This is Manikarnika Ghat," said Raj solemnly, "where the funeral pyres have burned twenty-four hours a day for centuries."

He went on to tell them the story of the ancient ghat. "Its founding legend was that Lord Shiva passed the spot while walking with the goddess Sati, who lost an earring there, thus condemning it to host the pyres of the dead for eternity. After death, cremation occurs as soon as possible, managed by the eldest son, dressed in white, who shaves his head in mourning. He shaves the face and head of his deceased parent as well. After the silk-wrapped body has been transported through the old city to the ghat, it is submerged in the river by the son before being placed on the family's pyre of wood. After circling the pyre five times to pay homage to Hinduism's five elements, the son lights the funeral fire. It takes six to eight hundred pounds of wood and six hours to cremate a body, and the wood is not cheap. The *Dom Raja*, the traditional family of carcass-handlers which has run the cremation operation for centuries, is among the wealthiest families in the city with land holdings across the state."

The powerful images and haze from the cremation fires had an emotional, existential impact. Millions of lives had ended their journeys here, and one could not help but think what one's own feet would look like sticking out of a burning pile of branches. They sat in the boat silently, watching the flames and the gasps of souls reaching for the sky. Families huddled around the fires as spectators watched from balconies, while ashes of the dead were shoveled into the river, spreading in a grimy alluvium human cloud. The business of death continued with purchases of wood made upon the arrival of yet another body borne through the old city's alleys, as entire families bathed in the smoke of their loved ones, chanting prayers for the dead. In Varanasi the dead were everywhere, a constant reminder of mortality, balancing the collective spirit of the living.

Raj directed the boatman to the river's edge north of the cremation ghat. The sun crept high in the sky, and the rumbling in Max's belly was calling for a meal.

"Rahul will have lunch prepared for us at the guest house," said Raj. But first, we must walk along the ghats and return through the old quarter on foot. Too narrow for rickshaws."

They disembarked and worked their way along the Ganges waterfront, encountering the daily life of Varanasi and its grimy, colorful display of humanity. Packs of feral dogs picked at piles of trash by the river, while groups of tourists were led in yoga sessions by hired yogis. Holy men, *sadhus* of all types, chanted, meditated, and offered blessings for a fee. One of these sadhus sat crouched in a shallow alcove balancing on one leg, arms crossed, smoking a *chillum* of cannabis and tobacco. The sadhu startled them by plying Max with a question.

"Are you an ordinary person?" he said in singsong Indian-inflected English.

Max stopped and turned to face the man, who perched in the small opening at waist height. The position looked unbearably painful, and Max had no idea how long the man had been posed this way, yet he seemed completely relaxed and comfortable. His face was dark and smudged with ash, punctuated by yellow marks drawn under his eyes and down his forehead, and could have been forty or seventy. The man's slight frame was ash-covered, and he wore only a loincloth, teeth stained dark red by betel nut. Strings of carved mahogany *rudraksha* beads were woven into his dreadlocked, ash-matted hair, clacking as he moved his head. His eyes were strikingly golden, and he looked at Max intensely, wise yet feral, head cocked to the left as if attempting to view what was inside.

Max thought before responding, pressing his palms together.

"I am of the world but unique within it," he said. "My search is taking me down many obscure roads far from home, and the destination and result not quite clear. So, perhaps not so ordinary." Max bowed, smiling, and stood still, clearly pleased with his sadhu-like response.

The man regarded Max for twenty seconds with piercing owl's eyes. Perched on one foot in his balanced crouch, smoking a chillum, he raised his palm toward Max in a symbol of blessing, speaking in the lilting voice of India.

"Extraordinarily ordinary. Searching you clearly are, but the direction must change. You are from the West, where life seems easily defined because it exists primarily on the surface. Here in the east, things are not so definite, and it is here you are searching, so embrace the mysticism of *eastness*. One thing can often be two things, those two things then becoming one. Change your perspective before unforeseen events force you to do so. An ordinary person believes reality to be all those things that have come into their consciousness from their own selfish experience. This you must unlearn. Look beyond your definitions since those come from your own understanding, which is limited by your weaknesses and fears. Live by the rule of the universe within, which has nothing to do with the rules the world follows. This means following your heart and intuition once you have cast off your fears and attachments. A splash of Mother Ganga on the wrists and behind the ears is recommended. As is bowing three times while chanting *om* before the largest Shiva lingam you can find."

The brevity and depth of the man's statement were unnerving. Max struggled to formulate a comeback, but his mind immediately began to catalog a list of fears and attachments. The random sadhu had managed to flip a switch, pull him out of the tourist present and into the maze of his thoughts. He stood, staring past the holy man.

"Uh, thank you, sir," was all he could say, placing a wad of rupees at his feet, with a nod to the balancing holy man. They began to walk away.

The sadhu reached out and held his arm, looking directly into Max's eyes. "Your search lies over high mountains, I feel. The mountains of doubt."

Placing a garland of flowers over Max's head, the sadhu then proceeded to apply a bright red powder dot, a *tilak*, on Max's forehead as part of his blessing. "Now go and find your *pitta*, your fire."

They continued in silence, taking in the vivid sights and sounds around them. A yogi sat on a platform, meditating cross-legged in the sun. Boats navigated the river, voices carrying across the water. Pilgrims bathed, and children screamed, playing games until Lilah noticed Max lagging behind.

"You alright?" she asked. "Did your sadhu send you for a loop?"

He smiled halfheartedly. "Naw, just thinking, taking this all in. Do your thing. I'll catch up."

Max sat down and, with his chin resting in his hands, contemplated the river and the teeming life carried on and around it. The sun sparkled off the rippling water, forcing him to shield his eyes. *Over the mountains*, he thought. *Mountains of doubt. Find your fire.* He felt the flowers of the garland in his hands, releasing candy-sweet aromas.

He stood and walked to the water's edge. The river was clouded and brown, laced with streams of colorful chemicals and floating trash. *How could salvation lie in these waters?* he pondered. *Their belief in the river's mythic power supersedes the reality of what the river is.*

A hundred yards ahead, Lilah looked around a wall and observed Max sitting on a step by the river, looking east. She watched him scoop a handful of murky Ganga and pour it over his wrist, then rub it with his other. He dipped a hand again in the river and dabbed it behind each of his ears, chanting something, and Lilah could see his deep exhale as he stared across the water. A lone goat approached and nudged him for some attention, and she saw Max laugh and scratch the wretched animal's head.

Finished with the small ritual, Max rose and dusted off his jeans. He had a spring in his step as Max made his way to Raj and Lilah, watching a yogi bend his body like a pretzel. When he looked at Lilah, there was a sense of resolution she hadn't seen in him before.

"I know the yogi is mesmerizing, but if I don't eat soon, I'm going to sacrifice a goat," Max said, quickly returning to his former self. "What's on the menu, Raj, my friend?"

Lilah wondered if perhaps the resolution she had sensed was only his need for another meal.

"Rahul is preparing us a meal of Varanasi's traditional dishes," said Raj.

They retraced their route through the shadowed alleys of the old city, snapping pictures and listening to Raj's thoughtful and incisive explanation of things. Arriving at Shambhala after offering a passing hello to Lalu the chai wallah, they climbed the five floors of stairs to the roof, emerging on a patio set with tables and umbrellas swaying in a light breeze. Rahul greeted them with many bows and escorted them to a table along the roof's edge, where their view encompassed the entire Varanasi waterfront in both directions, fading hazily in the midday sun. Before them lay a canvas of ghats and temples and flags and minarets and a thousand boats on the Ganges, all infused with a sea of vividly attired pilgrims and tourists.

"Glorious, Raj," said Lilah. "What a spot you've selected for us."

"It is my favorite place to stay when I come here, which is two or three times a year," said Raj. "My wife Ambika and Rahul's mother Sucheta have become friends and share recipes. Restaurant dining in Varanasi can also prove challenging given the city's very traditional nature, with predominantly vegetarian establishments. But Rahul has a small tandoori oven he uses to make a fabulous and simple fish *Tikka*, which isn't on the menu, but that he makes for friends. And of course, we always like the view."

Rahul appeared, breathless from yet another five-story climb, which he clearly did dozens of times every day. "Welcome, Mr. Max and Mrs. Lilah! What surname shall I use for you both? DeVillier? Little? Both? Or something else, perhaps? Some people come here who wish to remain anonymous and often ask me to create a name for them, and I am quite good at it. Shall I do so for you as a service?"

Lilah laughed and said, "Yes! Make us something new."

Rahul looked each of them up and down and in the eyes, then, focusing on Lilah, surmised, "Your surname will be Khojakarta. It means 'Pathfinder.'"

Lilah looked over at Max, who simply shrugged "whatever." "Lilah Khojakarta," she said, pleased. "I like it. It's settled then. We are the Pathfinders."

Max's wandering mind flashed to an Indian wedding with him atop a decorated elephant and Lilah wearing a veil under charcoal-painted eyes. He snapped to attention as food began to arrive at the table, carried by Rahul's mother and younger brother from the kitchen.

Plates were set, with copper bowls called *katoris,* and brass platters began to fill every inch of the table. Prayers and sprinkled offerings were offered over the dishes as they arrived, and the gestures fueled the meal with a mystical air.

Rahul became introspective when talking about food, looking ot over his city. "Food in Varanasi is inevitably tied to religion and culture, and many of our dishes are centuries old," he said. "Dining here often borders on the spiritual, and the kitchen is actually a place of sanctity. When food is served, we sprinkle water around each dish, accompanied by a mantra, or prayer. This is meant to purify the food and make it worthy for the gods. Before serving, we offer the food to the five Pranas, the life forces, and Brahma, who lives in the heart. Everybody is supposed to do this, and here we do it for you. This is not just a restaurant. It is our home."

Max and Lilah became aware of centuries of culinary history and an ancient ritual infusion of spirit into the meal they began. Varanasi was famous for *chaat,* or snacks. They were presented with *palak chaat,* crispy fried spinach leaves dipped in chickpea flour, dusted with *deggi mirch,* dried chile powder, black salt, and toasted cumin. These were garnished with pickled red onion, fresh tomato, and coriander leaves with a sauce of yogurt, tamarind, and pomegranate seeds. Steam rose off the leaves as they dipped in the yogurt. Next came steaming *Pani Puri,* fried wheat flour dough filled with potatoes, moong sprouts, chickpeas, and sweet mango chutney with chopped coriander and mint leaves, ginger, sliced green *jwala* chiles, roasted cumin seeds, and *sanchal* black salt. Their aroma filled the air as they opened.

Plates of *Tamatar chaat* arrived, a mix of mashed tomatoes, potatoes, peas, onion, and ginger fried with red and green chiles, cashews, coriander leaf, and garam masala spices. It was served in a traditional clay *kulhad,* savory and wonderfully hot. The star of the day was the Fish *tikka,* marinated in lemon juice and sea salt, then coated in pureed ginger and garlic and roasted in the tandoor oven. Served with mint chutney, fresh *dhani* chiles, and Basmati rice with slivered almonds, the oven-roasted fish was crumbly and moist within its pungent crust. It was offered with *choora matar,* mashed rice cooked in ghee, and spices with green peas, raisins, saffron, and sweet cream, a thick and chewy mouthful. And a basket of *aloo tikki,* potato patties with chickpea curry, red garlic, pungent *Kashi anmol* chiles, and tart tamarind chutney.

The hourlong presentation of the feast rendered Max speechless, and Lilah spoke for both of them. "Rahul, this is spectacular, she said.

"The soul in this food is palatable, and your presentation worthy of the finest restaurants in America,"

They scooped, dipped, and crunched across a table teeming with food, each dish distinct from the others. Chutneys were generously spread over steaming fried dumplings and oven-roasted fish. Round wheels of green jwala chiles and tiny fiery dhanis laced everything, warming bellies and conversation, and the food felt infused with ritual and place. It was impossible not to stop every few minutes and drink in the view of the pink and purple and ochre buildings that lined the river, flags fluttering atop their minarets. Children flew kites from the rooftops of buildings, reveling in the breeze. The holy Ganges ran south following the city's curve from their vantage point, the ghats fading off into humanity's haze. The sounds of horns and drums and chanting wafted up from the ghats below, and the sun flickered on the water, making the ordinary world seem far away.

Rahul appeared with dessert, a dish he called *thandai*, served in the clay *kulhad*. "A fresh fruit puree," he said, "topped with reduced sweet buffalo milk, pistachios, fennel seeds, cardamom, and saffron." They dove into the sweet dish enhanced by the mint, thick cream, and sweet spices, which all three consumed to the clay bowl's bottom.

Rahul's mother and brother appeared as the dessert was finished. Sucheta at first seemed solemn, shy as she cleared their plates, and Rahul's brother, even more so, standing behind her. Lilah reached out and took the woman's hand, motioning for the two of them to sit at the table.

"Please," she implored, "join us and tell us a little about your world."

Sucheta glanced over at her eldest son, seeming to ask permission with her eyes, and he nodded his approval. The younger son followed her, shyly pulling up chairs to join the group.

With Raj acting as interpreter, Sucheta slowly began to open to Lilah's questions. In singsong Hindi, she told them about her life. Her Muslim family belonged to the Ansari weaving community, which for generations had worked in the silk factories of Varanasi, the women doing the delicate embroidery and the men on the looms. Varanasi silk was revered in the country for the saris it weaved, customary for traditional weddings. It was considered auspicious if worn, and girls across India dreamed of a Varanasi silk sari for their wedding day, creating a limitless market.

Cloistered as a Muslim girl and foreseeing a marriage to a man chosen by her parents, Sucheta began to wonder at the outside world. Dressed always in traditional hijabs, she longed to wear the bright saris made by her clan for other women and met her future husband in the marketplace while shopping for the family. Karun, a Hindu boy whose name meant compassion, was charming and kind and understood the complexity of traditional culture for girls. But he read the smile in her eyes that he could see below her veil and became smitten with the girl he often saw wandering the markets with her basket. When they proclaimed their intention to marry, it drove them both from their families in scandal. Karun worked as a boatman on the Ganges and Sucheta in guesthouse kitchens as they built a life hidden in the old city's alleys, away from their enraged families. She had worked in the kitchen where Shambala now stood for forty years, raising her sons there, and they scraped the money together to take it over when the previous owners had failed. Karun died young, cremated along the Ganges, and her sons grew into successful operators with her of Shambala. She had never been outside Varanasi, and when Lilah asked why not, her reply was simple as she looked out over the Ganges.

"My life is in these streets, in this building, and my sons will take it when I am gone," Raj interpreted. "I learned to cook from my mother, who learned it from her mother, going back generations. Cooking food for others gives meaning to life, and ours is full. Karun went down the river, and someday, I will follow him. Varanasi is a good place to live and to die, and I am happy here. Thank you for visiting our home." She stood, bowed slightly, and cleared the dessert dishes as her son followed back into the kitchen, her face a picture of contentment. Her story conveyed that a life lived simply in a single building in an old neighborhood by the holy river could be a good one.

Max felt supremely at peace settled in his chair, hands folded in his lap, breathing calmly. Lilah sensed this, saw it in his face and slow breathing, and pictured he was for the moment becoming his own brand of yogi. Perhaps the visit with the sadhu had triggered something.

"Well, Max, what's cooking in that brain of yours?" she said. "Is Varanasi rubbing off on you?"

He took a deep breath. "How can it not," he said. "You'd have to be dead inside not to feel the magic of this place. And yes, the holy fellows wandering around dispensing nuggets of wisdom are a bonus. That guy and his 'mountains of doubt' phrase were an awakening, I must say. Helped me get over the hump. I want to knock out this Naga Jolokia business in Assam and get over the mountains where mystery and knowledge await. We have to figure out first how to get to China, to Kashgar, where some answers may lie at the easternmost end of the Silk Road. And Kashgar is the back door to Kyrgyzstan, where Monsieur Bakiyev probably has the airports monitored. So, going overland seems prudent, traversing the Torugart Pass. It all seems clearly laid out before me now, and I'm ready, Vlad and Boris be damned."

"To get to China and Kashgar, you must go through Kathmandu," said Raj. "Otherwise, you have to fly through Beijing, a long trip. Nothing direct from India."

"Then Kathmandu it is," said Max. "Perhaps we'll get a good view of Everest as we fly over."

It was the first they spoke of Jolokias or Kyrgyzstan in almost three days, and Lilah welcomed the break. The path to which Max seemed now committed, she agreed, was the best.

With bows and thanks to Rahul, they made their way from the dreamy rooftop of Shambala down into the shaded alleys, through the old city to where taxis gathered.

"May I suggest that we explore a special Hindu temple near Vishwanath Gali and then locate a venue for traditional Varanasi music?" said Raj. "We can then have a late drink on the rooftop of Shambala and see the moon on the Ganges. In the morning, we catch the Shiv Ganga Express for Assam."

In the afternoon haze of ten thousand mopeds, they summoned a taxi for the trip. Though the roads were just as busy, the chaos derby seemed less apocalyptic, and they swayed in the back seat with blissful grins, weaving through measured mayhem. Their morning spent in Varanasi's antiquity, infused with sadhu wisdom, was timely for learning how to relinquish control and not try to see ahead to the end. Of anything. Raj asked that they be dropped at the northern end of Vishwanath Gali, Varanasi's central shopping alley. It was a single artery laced with wires and popup awnings of a host of businesses, and food stalls dotted the lane, a canyon between multistoried buildings. The street boasted a thousand shops and vendors selling Varanasi silk saris, religious idols and ornaments, Hindu books, cooking supplies, shoes, and spices.

They walked together in the waning day, the lane becoming lit by a thousand merchants' lights and increasingly teeming with people. Mopeds buzzed through the crowd as sellers touted their wares amidst a wash of bright light and color. Max found a t-shirt stall and picked out a colorful one with an image of the goddess Lakshmi with the four arms representing wealth and abundance. Lilah browsed until she stopped in front of a shop selling silk saris in a host of patterns and colors. A family of three generations was in the shop, voting on selections for the matriarch, who appeared not yet forty. It was run by a husband and wife, which suited Lilah's sensibilities of supporting women in business whenever possible.

As the man approached, Lilah gestured to the woman and asked, "I would like her to assist me if that's alright." With Raj's interpretation, the woman stepped forward, smiling shyly, and opened her arms to invite them into her tiny shop.

Like most street-side sari venues in India, it did business on a raised platform above street level, the floor covered in worn rugs. Shelves stocked folded saris of every imaginable color and pattern. Customers then sat on the floor while various fabrics were brought and placed on the carpets before them. Lilah pointed to several, which the woman brought and displayed across her open arms with a flourish before placing them gently on the floor. She handled each one and selected a purple one with gold embroidery, to which the woman nodded her enthusiastic agreement. The colors were brilliant and the silk shiny, with intricate hand stitching in a dizzying array of patterns. Varanasi embroidery was so highly regarded that its workers were called *karigars*, or artists, rather than *jullahas*, the weavers.

The lady spoke to Raj in Hindi, who said, "She thinks purple is an excellent choice for you. It makes your green eyes glow like emeralds. In India, it identifies royalty and is the reincarnated color of Krishna, one of the most revered Hindu gods. It also symbolizes mysticism, and she thinks you are very much that Lilah."

A gold silk tunic was suggested to match the embroidery. With the garment selected, Lilah was directed to go behind a curtain at the rear of the shop where the woman would teach her how to wind the fabric around herself.

Once behind the curtain, Lilah removed her kurta and blouse and replaced them with the short gold tunic, exposing her belly. Her white silk pants would have to work. The sari was a single piece of fabric three feet wide and fifteen feet long, and Lilah was told each one can take three months of weaving and embroidery. The woman gestured for Lilah to raise her arms and went to work, stopping to make sure she understood the various tucks and wraps. First, the sari was tucked into the waistband of her pants, wrapped around her waist and legs, then gathered and tucked again at the front, creating pleats. After another wrap around the midsection to create layering, it was then brought around just below the right hip and up over her left shoulder, the remaining length hanging from Lilah's left arm all the way to the ground. Looking in the mirror, she saw a different woman and had never looked or felt so resplendent.

When she emerged from the curtain, Lilah had released the ponytail and her hair hung in long waves off her shoulders. Her caramel skin and smooth stomach were exposed, and Max realized it was the first time he'd seen her belly button. She was the essence of a Bollywood starlet, and the sight made his *retas* buzz. *Or a queen*, thought Max. *Wow, I'm in for it.*

"Well, what do you think?" she asked, twirling in a circle.

"It's a perfect choice, Lilah," said Raj. "You could easily be a *Maharaja's* wife."

"Hmm. Were there ever any women Maharajas?" she asked.

"Well, yes, they were called *Maharani*, and India has had many notable ones," he responded.

"I'll take Maharani then, thanks, Raj. Well, Max?"

Max could not inject a pithy response, immobilized at her transformation.

"The seller is right. Purple is definitely your color," he said, though he had wanted to say more. He just couldn't figure out what.

Lilah smiled, seeing through Max's lack of commentary. "Purple it is then, and I will wear it only on special occasions. Off we go." She turned to the sari woman and bowed, adding a heartfelt "*Dhanyavaad*," thank you, in Hindi, after paying for the garment and the purely Indian experience.

Raj led them through the streets to their destination. Around the corner from each other were two of Varanasi's most famous religious buildings: the Hindu Kashi Vishwanath temple and the Gyan Vapi mosque, making the neighborhood one of India's most sacred places to two faiths. The smaller Annapurna Mandir temple was less acknowledged but eminently important, a block away from Kashi Vishwanath's bustling market. Raj had selected this particular temple for them to visit, and as they made their way through the streets and past the more significant temples, Raj explained their destination.

"Annapurna Devi Mandir is dedicated to the goddess *Annapurna*, the deity of food and nourishment, *Anna* meaning food, and *Purna* meaning complete, full, or perfect. It was built in 1729 AD by the Maratha Peshwa Baji Rao for his preferred deity, the goddess queen of Varanasi, Parvati. He was a great Hindu general who united much of northern India."

The temple was just off Vishwanath Gali and encircled in the ensuing centuries by support buildings to broaden its mission. Annapurna's was a small complex surrounded on three sides by businesses and other smaller temples. The temple housed three idols of the goddess, one in gold, one in brass, and one in stone, and worshippers from across India came to see them.

They rounded a corner and were soon standing under a sign in Sanskrit announcing their destination. Once inside, the din of the old city quickly dissipated. A sign instructed them to remove their shoes, which they placed in a rack in the entry hall. They passed through double doors and into a courtyard and saw a temple of red sandstone two stories high, surrounded by more modern buildings, themselves three stories high. With its two small towers, the temple was carved from top to bottom in human and animal figures and featured a viewing vestibule at the top of seven steps, which led to an inner sanctum housing the icons of the goddess.

The mahogany doors to the temple were covered in tin panels depicting the deity in various forms. They ascended the steps to enter the first chamber, its columns also mahogany and covered in ornate artwork made of tin. No one else appeared to be in the temple, though they heard voices echoing around the complex.

Inside the sanctum, they found three small alcoves. Rich incense smoke clouded the air. To the right was one containing the goddess's gold statue, covered in silks and garlands of flowers, locked behind a gate. It was brought out only once a year, on the major religious holiday of *Annakut*, the day before *Diwali*, the autumn festival of lights. To the left stood the brass idol, employed for daily worship, called *darsana*. Both statues depicted the goddess holding a porridge vessel in her left hand and a ladle in the right. In contrast, the brass statue was accompanied by Lord Shiva's figure, with a begging bowl in hand awaiting the goddess's generosity. These statues, too, were covered in silks and garlands and surrounded by hundreds of candles. Raj pointed out that the entire room would be filled with trays and platters of prepared foods on holy days, offerings to the goddess, which would be fed to the poor afterward.

They heard the shuffling of feet, and a portly, bearded man, his hair slicked back with pungent mustard oil, a priest, entered the sanctum. He motioned for them to approach the third statue, directly ahead of them. This one was in the standing position, two feet tall, carved from shiny black stone, and sitting on a dais of hammered tin surrounded by a stone culvert with a hole at its rear. From a ledge to the left, the priest produced a pitcher of water and another of milk, motioning for Max and Lilah to pour the contents on the stone idol's head, anointing it. As they did, he recited a ritual message in Hindi, hands raised to the statue. They looked at Raj for an interpretation, holding their vessels over the goddess's form.

Raj followed the entire incantation, then replied, "Oh Annapurna, who is forever complete, more beloved to Lord Shiva than life. Oh Parvati, give me the alms of your grace to awaken within me spiritual knowledge, inner freedom, prosperity, and spiritual attainment. My mother is Goddess Parvati, my father is the Supreme Lord Maheshwara, Shiva. My relatives are the devotees of Lord Shiva, wherever they are in the three worlds."

The man then turned to Max and Lilah, still speaking Hindi, and placed garlands of orange marigolds around their necks.

Raj continued. "He says, 'She is the Mother who graces food to all, especially the poor. For your blessing to be complete, you must perform *prasad*, or service to the community by serving food.'"

Without hesitating, the priest led them back out of the sanctum and through a side door. This door led to a long passageway, which seemed to run the entire first level of the complex surrounding the temple, the smell of food growing as they advanced. He led them through double doors to a room full of a hundred people, and the sounds of eating greeted them. He pointed to a buffet on the far side and gestured towards it, where space was made for them at three serving stations. For the next half an hour, the three visitors served the poor of Varanasi what was likely their only meal of the day.

Spooning lentils over roti flatbread, Max took in the faces as they passed. Grimy, blissful, mumbling sadhus and soot-covered laborers alternated with untouchable-caste families in rags. He saw hardship, but not suffering, in the many toothless and gold-capped smiles that greeted each serving. Lilah, spooning potatoes, nodded at wide-eyed men, women, and children alike. Her green eyes, warm smile, long, wavy hair, and Indian dress sparked amazement in them and earned her vocal thank-yous. While they had merely nodded at Max, they all thanked Lilah with bows of gratitude. Children reached out to touch her. She appeared familiar yet mystical to them, it seemed, and as he watched, Max realized her powerful presence. The experience of giving to those who had little or nothing at all was both humbling and inspiring. The priest returned at the end of their service, pressing his hands together and bowing in thanks to the trio.

"He says go, be well, and live in Annapurna's grace," said Raj. They all returned the gesture. "Now, please enjoy and be nourished by the blessed food which you yourselves have served to others less fortunate."

"Please tell him we are grateful for this moment," said Lilah, looking back across the room of simple people nourished by generosity.

They proceeded through the charity buffet, now staffed by other volunteers, and the simple plate of lentils and potatoes over flatbread was delicious and welcomed. A selection of chutneys and fresh chiles was at the end of the line that added some heat to the simple meal. They shared a table with a mother and her two children. She rubbed her belly and placed her hands together in thanks. After they finished and retraced their way through the complex, little was said.

Humbled and nourished, they left the food goddess's temple to continue their journey into the old city's spider web streets, their senses and awareness heightened by the temple experience. Night had fallen, the alleys packed with all kinds of people shopping, eating, commuting, worshipping, and sightseeing. A youngish sadhu sat outside the temple's doors on a woven mat, ignored by the throngs. Older holy men usually garnered more interest, with more mileage to wizen them. This one was slight and wore a wrap that had once been white in diaper-like fashion around his waist and thighs, another around his head, both splashed red. He wore glasses covered in a red powdery film, and his skin was caked with red powder that he grabbed from a bowl and tossed into the air above, dusting his entire area in a circle of brick red and orange. The man's evident commitment and embodiment of peace in the small space were oddly compelling, and they stopped to watch. Each time another cloud was created, he called out to the universe.

"*Bheetar aag ko saaph karo!*" he sang.

Between each exclamation, he reached into a large clay urn, pulled something out and bit it, then rubbed it on his body, leaving a wet smear. Another cloud tossed into the air covered him in red, sticking more heavily to the wet spots. As they got closer, the scent of chiles was unmistakable.

"What's he saying, Raj?" asked Max, as another exhortation filled the alley.

"Let's see, uh, 'cleanse the fire within,'" interpreted Raj.

Again, the man called out. "*Bheetar aag ko khojo!*"

Again, Raj interpreted. "Seek the fire within."

"*Aag se saaph karake bheetar aag kee talash karen!*"

"Seek the fire within by cleansing with fire."

"*Aag se shuddh karana! Vichaar ko shuddh karo!*"

"Cleanse with fire. Purify the thought."

"*Shareer ek bartan hai!*"

"The body is a vessel."

After each utterance, the man grabbed vividly red fresh chiles, biting off the meat and rubbing the caps on various points of his body, fervently smearing the juice and seeds. Then he reached into a bowl of bright red chile powder and dusted his entire body with it. Looking straight ahead, he neither flinched nor coughed from the cloud, as sweet and smoky chile pepper smells wafted about him. After he swallowed with a pronounced gulp, the exhortations began again.

"*Yadi app khade nahin ho sakate to garmee rasoee se baahar nikalana chaahie!*" he said, then winked at Lilah through smudged glasses.

Raj looked confused. "If you can't stand the heat, get out of the kitchen."

Then, "*Pita jee ramata jogee,*" and "*No vuman no kraee.*"

"Uh, 'Papa was a rolling stone.' Then, 'No woman, no cry.'"

Max began to shake his head. *This guy deserves an all-star profile in the Ring of Fire.* Either they had a crackpot on their hands or a college student hiding from classes. Lilah smiled and approached the young man, crouching in front of his powdery display of commitment.

"May I ask why the chiles?" she inquired.

The young sadhu took a break from his ablutions to answer. "They are a complete food, a gift from the goddess Annapurna, to help humanity free itself from a shallow and material life. They are a *rajasic* food in Ayurveda, meaning we become ambitious, temperamental, and egotistic if we eat them without acknowledging the gods. Thus, I cleanse and nourish myself with them, exalting the goddess and embodying humility in the process."

Lilah nodded in understanding. "And are they hot?" she asked.

"Quite," said the red-dusted man. "The sensation on the skin is incredible, and I have never felt more alive. I do this every day for two years now. The chiles are high in vitamins, and Ayurveda says that they stimulate the spirit and the blood. Like any other human activity, eating can be made into a sacrificial act to liberate the soul or a mere act of pleasure, leading to bondage and suffering. It is up to us to choose. The Bhagavad Gita says that 'The saintly persons get relief from all kinds of sins by partaking of food that has been first offered to gods as a sacrifice. But those who prepare food for their selfish ends eat but only sins.'"

"May I ask why you chose the life of a holy man?" Lilah followed.

"My father was educated in London as a chemist before our independence, and then he started our family business, fertilizer. My oldest brother will inherit the company, and my younger brother is lazy and pampered by my mother. Not much room for the middle child, so I chose the 'middle way' and devoted my life to Annapurna. I'm a reasonably good sadhu. My life is blissfully simple, and I go home for a nice meal once a week with my family."

"And what kind of chiles do you use for your ritual?" asked Max, gaining interest.

"These are *Kashmiri* chiles from the north. Quite rare, actually. They are donated to me by a spice merchant in Varanasi who worships here, as is the dried powder. Very red, best for rituals and extremely hot, for cleansing. Would you like to be blessed?" he asked them. "I'll spare you the entire dusting."

Without hesitation, they both knelt before the man, who produced a chile for each of them from his earthenware jar, holding them out for Max and Lilah to each ingest a healthy bite.

As they did, he proclaimed, "Goddess Annapurna bless these chiles and make these seekers of truth fortified on their journey."

He then offered the half-eaten peppers to the four directions before pressing them into their foreheads, between the eyes. "To open the third eye," he said. Then he rubbed his thumb on the moist pepper meat before dabbing it into the bright red chile powder and pressing it to their foreheads.

"Varanasi is difficult to navigate, but a powerful place for finding one's way. You are on yours," he counseled.

The Kashmiri peppers were bright red and cleanly hot, enough so that the spot on their foreheads tingled and their mouths hummed at a high frequency. Heat spilled down their throats, lighting a small fire in the belly.

"You will feel the chakras activating," said the man, touching his forehead, "the third eye, *Ajna*, the throat chakra, *Vishudda*, and *Manipurna*, in the belly. Since these chiles have been goddess blessed, you are infused with the *sattvic* qualities of detachment and balance. Though you are consuming heat, your judgment will be cool. Be aware also that your *retas* have been awoken, the sexual energy."

"Well, thank you, these are certainly powerful chiles," said Lilah, raising her eyebrows. "Anything else we should be aware of?"

Max continued chewing the chile, focused on the ritual. The *retas* part they pretended not to hear, though the seed was planted. The man thought for a few seconds.

"Yes," he said with more seriousness. "One of the four aims of life is *moksha*, the transcendence of being released from the endless cycle of rebirth, called *samsara*. It is not achieved without living the other three: *dharma*, or virtue, *artha*, prosperity, and *kama*, pleasure. You achieve *moksha* after understanding the nature of the others. Monks and ascetics study this and work towards it our entire lives, but you can also attain it by living playfully, seeking the simple beauty in existence. One need not suffer to live fully!"

"That's beautiful," said Lilah, who then pressed her hands together. "We are endlessly grateful. What is your name?"

"I released my name long ago," he replied, then added: "My mother still calls me *Vivaan*, which means 'first rays of the sun.'"

They turned, readying to leave before the man stopped them with another question.

"How long have you been married?"

Looking back at the man, they responded in unison: "Us?" Embarrassed shuffling and mumbled responses as to their relationship followed until Lilah finally said, "We've only known each other a brief time."

Unfazed, the man continued. "Whatever you think you know, you are destined in this lifetime to complete a journey together, as I sense that you have crossed paths before in another lifetime. Your only enemy is fear."

Speechless, they bowed to bid the man farewell and turned to join the flow of people in the lane. As they left, Lilah said "*Ezili*" under her breath.

"Love that guy," said Max. "Full of moksha."

Deeper down, however, he was jarred by the encounter and needed an outlet to the energies and emotions swirling around him. Wherever his *retas* were, they were twitching.

"Raj, you mentioned music," said Max. "Can we find some?"

"Yes, of course," said Raj, smiling. The peppered sadhu had just stated what Raj had believed since Lilah walked down the ramp at Delhi airport. "We can walk to Kabir Chaura, the Muslim area, home to many musicians. There is a place where they have nightly performances of traditional Indian music. And often dancing."

The route to Kabir Chaura, the Muslim quarter where the musicians and weavers historically lived, took them north, through neighborhoods and alleys less populated with tourists. Passing an unseen border, evidence of their emergence into the areas populated by Muslims began to show. Wide eyes peeked from behind doorways and curtains, and brilliant mandala tapestries hung from the verandas. Fewer Shiva lingam altars decorated alcoves and corners, and goats tied to door handles bleated in doorways, more Muslim food than Hindu pets. Saris and women became less frequent, with only the occasional burka-clad wife winding along the passageways, dragging children along. They registered the scents of fragrant curries and grilling meats wafting through the alleys, countered by the smell of fresh cow dung and clouds of burning incense. *Food and fuel and ritual, the cycle of life*, thought Max.

New sounds echoed down the lanes, including the wooden clack-clack-clack of handlooms and the singsong of workers communicating over the devices that marked the official entrance to the quarter. In an open doorway, two young artisans in white-knit Muslim caps worked a loom under a single light bulb, calling back and forth in ethnic Urdu, which sprung from the collision in the 15th century of the Persian and Sanskrit languages. Urdu music made up the background soundtrack as they wound through the lanes, echoing off the ancient walls. Rounding a corner, they came across the brightly lit counter of the Dhandara Lassi Shop. A bench in the front sat three Muslim men and their young sons, focused on their clay pots of lassi.

"Shall we have a street lassi?" asked Raj. "Varanasi is famous for it."

Dhandara Lassi was a hole-in-the-wall establishment they learned had served the same yogurt recipes for 100 years and across four generations. Kumar Dhandara prepared the delicacy the same way his great-grandfather had, using a big wooden hand churner called a *madani* to froth whole milk yogurt into a creamy spoonable dessert. Dhandara served its lassi traditionally in baked-clay terracotta pots, with the yogurt made from cow's milk and its creamy fat, then topped with a sweet buffalo milk cream, called *malai*. Kumar added mango, pistachios, almonds, cardamom, honey, and tiny edible flowers. Reaching into a glass jar, he presented them with a choice of small green cookies to add to the dessert.

"Bhang cookies?" he asked. "Lord Shiva's two favorite things are cannabis and cows, so this is a holy offering atop the best lassi in Varanasi. You make Shiva happy, and you don't have to leave it on an altar."

Max and Lilah shrugged with a "sure, why not?" and three laced Shiva wafers were added to their concoctions. They strolled, dipping the cannabis wafers and savoring the generations-old desserts with wooden spoons as families flowed around them. The green cookies were pistachio-based, sweet, earthy, and enhanced by herbaceous cannabis. Having sampled many of the earth's delicacies, Max knew what to expect from the ingested herb and figured Lilah knew her way around it with her experiences in the voodoo world.

She bit into the green wafer, nodded approvingly, and said, "Soylent ganja, how fun."

They slowly emptied the clay pots of their delicious contents while walking the narrow ancient alley, anticipating the onset of a cannabis-infused musical experience halfway around the world from home.

Raj led them through the winding streets to the Kabir Chaura neighborhood, named after a Muslim weaver and poet who challenged Hindus and Muslims' religious status-quo in India five hundred years before. His writings and poems became songs, and his followers were the first disciples of the Bhakti movement, which questioned religious dogma. Bhakti promoted individual choice when addressing religion and spirituality regardless of social standing or gender, quite revolutionary for a Muslim-turned-Hindu in medieval India. The neighborhood where he spent his life had attracted the finest weavers and most illustrious musicians in the centuries since, with many famous families among its residents.

Music in India has its origins in ancient history, religion, and myth, which are the pillars of its society. It would not be a stretch to say that music embodies India, and Varanasi, as its most holy city, is the home of many musical traditions. Chants and hymns beseeching and honoring the gods thousands of years ago became the *ragas*, the foundation of North Indian traditional music, combined with the synthesis of ancient Vedic chants. Ragas in Indian music are like the eight-note scale of western music, except that there are dozens of them, compositions capable of inducing powerful emotions or mystical journeys. Music is seen as one of the most straightforward pathways to self-realization and enlightenment, a spiritual exercise attempting to attain salvation through sound, and musicians are held in high regard as a result. Good ones can open a portal to nirvana, and Max was down for the ride on his cannabis carpet. Lilah glided along the lanes in her new purple sari, beaming smiles to all she passed, Muslim women and men included.

They arrived at the foot of an ancient *haveli*, or multistory home, a corner building wedged between others in a narrow lane of ancient havelis comprising the silk-weaving and musical neighborhood of *Lalapura*. Plaster had fallen from the façade, and the wrought iron railings were badly decaying, but the window shutters had beautifully faded blue paint on them. A sign above the ground floor entry read Gharana Maharaj Music and Instruments. The building's ground floor was a shop for selling instruments and rooms for music lessons and practice, and on the walls were an array of Indian instruments for sale that looked at once foreign and familiar. *Sitars, sarods, santoors,* and a host of guitar and dulcimer-like stringed devices; *shehnais*, flutes, and other wind instruments; and *tablas*, the traditional percussive device preferred across India. Sharda Maharaj, who ran the store, warmly greeted and told them about Maharaj Music and its history.

"This has been our family's *haveli* for almost four hundred years and is today the home of the seventeenth generation," Maharaj said. "Our ancestors came here to follow the prophet Kabir and became musicians to exemplify their faith. We founded our own *gharana*, a musical dynasty, passing down knowledge from one generation to the next and keeping alive the old traditions. We teach that practice and training are avenues to enlightenment and ways of honoring the gods and that music played for others is a blessing for both parties. Tonight, you will hear members of our family perform traditional devotional music in our open-air salon."

They ascended a narrow stair in the rear of the instrument shop, emerging into an open space thirty feet by forty feet. Several groups sat on cushions around the floor, facing a carpeted dais for the musicians. They looked to be Varanasi locals, pilgrims, and a few tourists from different nations. Two of the walls were open to the air, facing the neighboring buildings, the upper floors supported by thick stone columns. Rows of candles shimmered on either side of the dais, their light flickering off the ceiling. People sat in the buildings' open windows next door, families with front row seats for every performance, the music here being a spiritual act, listening as devotion. A *sitar*, a *shehnai*, and a *tabla* were on the floor, awaiting their masters of string, wind, and percussion.

After removing their shoes, Max and Lilah selected large, flat, and round cushions called *poufs* in the middle of the room, almost big enough for a child's bed. The bhang had entered their minds and consciousness, and they felt the bodily hum of its lazy high. Max sat cross-legged while Lilah lounged on her side, propped on one elbow, looking like a Maharani in her purple silk sari. Raj made himself comfortable on an adjacent pouf. After five minutes, two men and a woman appeared from a door at the rear of the room: a white-haired and elderly man, a balding, middle-aged man, and a thirty-something female with long, dark hair. They all wore flowing, baggy pants and colorful shirts, with the men in woven vests. They introduced themselves as three generations of the Maharaj family, Bismillah, Nazreen, and Shoori, and took places on the dais, sitting cross-legged as well.

Bismillah, the patriarch, began the evening's introduction. "Welcome to our *gharana*, our traditional salon of music and learning. Members of the Maharaj family have been learning and teaching traditional music in this building for many generations. Ram Maharaj, my great-great-great-grandfather, has been credited with formalizing the Varanasi style of playing the *tabla* two hundred years ago, and my son Nazreen plays it today. This style is noted for powerful sounds modulated by sensitivity and delicateness to put forth its musical message and express the rhythm in all of us. Indian traditional music is an experience shared between musician and audience, a universe of sound enveloping this room, and our collective expression of devotion. We offer an avenue for artistic and religious beauty to be shared by all who listen, and for us, it is a blessing to perform. I will play the *sitar*, and my granddaughter Shoori will be on the *shehnai*."

The stringed *sitar* has existed in India in several forms for eight hundred years. A resonant-sounding box, made from a large gourd, was attached to a wide neck almost four feet long. The oversized tuning keys looked comically large and challenging to master, with the body accented by elaborate metal inlays and silver filigree. Its shimmering sound was accentuated by the presence of up to twenty-three strings that travel over arched frets suspended above the neck, which resonated and hummed when their neighbors were plucked, creating a haunting and meditative voice. The *tabla's* twin hand drums were played together with the fingers and palms to form a complete percussive sound, the backbone of Indian music. The *bayan*, larger of the two and played by the left hand, generates the bass sound, and the *dayan*, on the right, creates a higher pitch and overtones. *Bayan* and *dayan* were male and female sounds, respectively, an essential aspect of Indian music. The *shehnai* was a double-reed wind instrument descended from the *pungi*, traditionally used for snake charming. As an ensemble, they composed an enthrallingly rich and varied sound.

The set began slowly and gently, with light notes dancing across sitar, shehnai, and tabla, primarily as solo introductions. The string and wind instruments played off each other as if hopping from one lily pad to another. The bhang wafers kicked into another level as Max and Lilah both swayed to the harmony of strings and wind instruments and soft undulating rhythm of the tabla, settling into the poufs and the night air in the open salon. This moment to them was the only one occurring on earth, focused entirely on the hypnotic and mystical performance unfolding at their feet. Sitar strings bent to stretch notes like the undulating voice of a Bedouin. The reedy oboe sang a song of desert palaces and epic love stories, haunting notes echoing off the buildings and seeming to flicker the candlelight. Heels of hands and fingers danced from the tabla, like popping bubbles and gurgling water in a language all its own. For half an hour, the instruments teased each other, back and forth, calling and responding. Any one of them could easily have comprised a standalone concert in the hands of their masters. Yet, they worked in unison with this family of generations, articulating old themes while continually improvising.

Then the pace quickened, and the notes' strength increased, with the musicians' energy impacting the crowd and generating movement. Nazreen, the percussionist, met Max's eyes and, with his head, gestured to the open space in front of the musicians, inviting him to dance. Max wavered, but Lilah caught the exchange and, without waiting, sprung up and over to the musicians, facing them and leaving Max behind. Moving in her sari, she seemed instantly possessed by the music, a flowing purple extension of the ensemble, and began to move to its rhythms. The musicians seemed to play to her, increasing the tempo and then slowing, invoking her to move.

Everyone in the room was watching Lilah dance, Max noticed. He took in her movements and perceived that the key to traditional dancing was less feet and more hands and body. He got up and joined Lilah before the ensemble, eventually succumbing to the rhythm and going full Bollywood. Though he wore boots, his feet moved like they were in the ceremonial curved jutis bought in Delhi. Lilah looked over and nodded her head enthusiastically, honoring his unique form of expression. So, he let go and let it flow, imagining himself in a Hindu saga, and once Max found his groove, there was no stopping him. They twirled and shook and let their arms and hands do the talking, following the rhythm of the tabla and sitar's pace, which sped up and slowed down and increased or lessened with intensity. Lilah was a whirl and splash of hair and color as they danced in unison and separately, consumed with the multilayered sound.

In his bhang-laced vision, she was all he could see, luminous and generating her own energy. Others in the audience got up to join them, dancing in their ecstatic style. Max felt a tug at the hem of his shirt and looked down to see two wide-eyed girls seeking to join the dance circle with him and Lilah. They made room, and the two little dancers grabbed their hands as they created geometric patterns across the open space. The musicians remained passionately focused, building to a crescendo, but occasionally looked up and nodded heads in support of Max and Lilah's group dance performance, dervishes whirling to the centuries-old compositions.

When the music finally completed its journey, the dancers were left panting as the musicians directed the small audience's applause to Max and Lilah. In turn, they bowed to the band, the audience, Raj, the girls, and then each other. Then they embraced, falling into each other's arms in unison and breathing heavily, both still abuzz. Max felt Lilah's body, her deep breaths pressing against his chest and the cool dampness of her arm on his cheek. His hands wrapped around the waist exposed by the sari's bare midriff, and her skin felt electrified, sparked by energy. She smelled of citrus and sage as he buried his face in her hair, his senses alive in the mystical and surreal experience they had just shared. Her face was a sweet broad smile when she pulled back, breaking into a laughter of joy, her green eyes punctuated by laugh lines. Then, their tiny dance partners demanded attention, drawing the adults down to their level for shared hugging and giggles.

With the evening's performance ended, they returned to the alleys after giving each musician thanks and purchasing CDs for all their American friends. Realizing that the day had started at 4 a.m. and taken them across Varanasi made them feel gratitude rather than fatigue in the many magical moments the day had brought. The mood was light in the tuk-tuk as they careened back to their lodging at Shambala.

"We have an eight a.m. train to catch to Guwahati, my friends, but I imagine you'll sleep well after our full day," said Raj, who seemed tireless. "Thank you for allowing me to share it with you. I must say, everyone was quite impressed by your dance performance, and Lilah, you could be a professional. Max, you are a surprising performer once you find your rhythm. Varanasi has found its way inside you."

They were dropped off nearest the alley that led them home to Shambala, and they made their way there through the quiet, late-night old city with strings of lights illuminating the path. Rahul was working reception and greeted them eagerly.

"Welcome home, friends. I trust the magic of our ancient city has rubbed off on you and that you caught even small moments of enlightenment. And Miss DeVillier, you look stunning in your Varanasi silk sari."

"Yes, Rahul, it was fabulous, and thank you," Lilah said. "The Khojakarta's have had an amazing day, full of pathfinding, beauty, and deliciousness. We're sorry we have to leave in the morning, but I, for one, will be back. There is no place in the world like Varanasi."

As they made their way to the stairwell and their fourth-floor rooms, Max noticed Lilah stop and whisper something to Rahul, who winked and gave her a thumbs-up. When they reached their floor and rooms, Raj stopped at his door.

"Thank you for a magical day. I know for you Varanasi is surely exotic and unlike anything you have ever seen. It is amazing, even for Indians but seeing it through your eyes has been a special experience, my friends. Good night." He ducked behind his door, leaving them alone in the hall.

Max turned to the end of the hall and his room, but Lilah touched his arm. "Max, let's go have a beer on the deck and see Varanasi at night." She took his hand and led him to the roof.

They were alone on the deck, and over in a corner overlooking the river, a single table was set with a candle and two large Kingfisher beers. From their seats, the Ganges waterfront spread before them for a mile in either direction. Many ghats were brightly lit and still crowded with life, while the far shore faded to black, obscure in the night haze. Other candlelit rooftops dotted the cityscape. Off in the distance, they made out the waving flames brandished by monks at an evening Aarti ceremony and chanting and gongs from the ritual carried across the water. On the river below, hundreds of candles floated, launched by pilgrims in the boats, and from the cremation ghats rose a ghostly tower of smoke. The memorable moment, shared only by the two of them, infused the air with dreamlike weightlessness.

For five quiet minutes, they sat, absorbing the view. Finally, Lilah spoke. "Max, I think you'll agree with me that we've got something going on here. Something way beyond the search for chile peppers."

Max sat silently, looking out over the river and the flotilla of prayer candles. *Yes, something*, he thought, but couldn't define what. She continued.

"Did you hear the red chile sadhu, Vivaan? He said, 'Make these seekers of truth whole on their journey.' Don't you wonder which part of the journey he meant? And what the truth is that we seek?" She, too, looked out over the water, seeing distant possibilities.

Max processed the unexpected statement. If the hunt for chile peppers had been his life, what was way beyond that? His riverside sadhu had told him to go beyond his own "mountains of doubt," which he took as a sign to get to Kyrgyzstan and unravel the Fire of the Valley, and Gasanov. Lilah showing up in India had been a shock, had shaken him from his equilibrium. He had been prepared to undertake the venture alone, return to the States, and maybe, to her, when all was resolved. Now she sat on a roof overlooking the Ganges, talking to him about "their" journey. He became overpowered by a detached, existential sensation, as though her words might change his life. Something was happening outside of his control, though he attempted to rationalize the moment. Having her along obviously had its professional benefits, and he was uncovering clear feelings for her, but there were other factors. A dive into the emotional river of romance and the blinding prospect of making love to this powerful woman would quite possibly throw off his pepper-head mojo, and other potential dangers lay ahead. But she was intelligent and capable and had proven effective in a crisis. Her insights always strengthened their position. And of course, there was the fact that she was alluring and his deepening enchantment with her. Was he ready to leap off the cliff and make it *their* journey? Change gears during the adventure of a lifetime? A new mountain of doubt suddenly loomed before him like a cinder block placed on his chest.

"We are two Pathfinders seeking out the origins of unique species, which will certainly be interesting," Lilah continued. "I think that on this journey, we just may end up finding a path for ourselves, together. Let's just not muck it up yet with sex. Perhaps just take it slow and deal with things as they come. Everyone else already sees our connection, starting with Jones and Delphine. So do Raj and the sadhus. Vivaan also talked about sexual energy, and I want you to know I feel that, too. That energy is strong from you, and I can see the desire in your eyes, and it makes my heart race. I want to harness that energy, like tantra, and use it to get us to the end of this journey so we can begin the possibility of the other. Are you game?"

Her proposition was shockingly transparent and honest, and also smart. She articulated both their thoughts in a way that made Max believe she understood and felt him. And it gave Max a way out without having to take a stance on his own.

"Sounds like a brilliant plan, Lilah," he said, sipping his beer. "The sadhu also said, 'live playfully and seek the simple beauty in existence.' I think I'd like to do that with you."

He reached out, pulling her wavy hair from her face, and rested his hand gently on her cheek. She met his eyes as he said, "I'm in. And you've still got that holy dot on your forehead."

For just having agreed to celibacy, he felt extremely light.

THE SEVEN SISTERS

Once upon a time, or maybe twice, there was an unearthly paradise called Pepperland, a place where happiness and music reigned supreme.
The Beatles, from the film *Yellow Submarine*

The train to Guwahati in Assam province would take a full day, following the Ganges until the city of Katihar. Traveling east, they would then skirt Nepal and Bhutan's borders to the north and Bangladesh to the south, passing through the Siliguri Corridor, or "Chicken's Neck." This twenty-mile-wide stretch of land with artificial borders, the result of treaties and the creation of new countries, was India's tenuous connection to the seven states of its eastern provinces, called the Seven Sisters. These provinces share only two percent of their borders with India; the rest is shared with Bhutan, Bangladesh, Nepal, Myanmar, and China, with historical ties to those countries. Nepalese and Burmese lords ruled over the territory for centuries, and unlike the rest of India, it was never conquered by the Muslim Mughals. Ancient trade relationships between the provinces and their Asian neighbors were disrupted by the arrival of the British in 1826 and the Treaty of Yandaboo; India's far-flung northeast territories were then the last to be consolidated into the British empire. Artificial borders cut the Northeast off from the rest of the world. The region was host to more than 200 of India's 635 known tribal groups, making it one of the most ethnically diverse places on the planet, and few Westerners ventured there.

They awakened early, though Max had barely slept. His mind was a whirl of conjured images of Assam, the Himalayas, sadhus talking, ghost peppers, and he and Lilah making love bathed in moonlight. She had rested well and emerged from her room, energized and ready for travel. After pre-sunrise chai with Lalu in the alley, they headed to the Varanasi Junction station and the Guwahati Express train for the 24-hour journey. They settled into a sleeper car on the north side of the train at Max's behest, as he hoped to catch a glimpse of the Himalaya if the skies were clear.

The Varanasi experience's intensity stayed with them, everyone uncharacteristically quiet, preferring to read or stare at the passing landscape. Max had university reports to digest before the Assam junket, and Lilah had thesis work to complete on her project with Jones back in Louisiana. Their late-night discussion on the rooftop had made things appropriately clear, and now they could focus on other tasks and challenges. Existential crisis averted.

Raj dove into *Gitanjali*, a book of works from the famous Bengali poet Rabindranath Tagore, for which he won the Nobel Prize for literature. Tagore was the best-known poet in Eastern India and its most renowned connoisseur and lover of food. As he hungrily scanned the pages, Raj interrupted the railroad silence. "Of Tagore, it has often been said, 'Tell me what you eat, and I will tell you what you are,' for he loved the experience of food. Max, it is my impression that you live that as much as any Indian I have ever met. Watching you enjoy food is a window into your soul, my friend. Food for you has a life all its own, and it inhabits yours."

Raj's vivid definition of him hung in the air. Lilah watched as Max continued to gaze out the window, taking in India's passing landscape, daydreaming most assuredly about chiles and the road before them. The enterprising Raj had thought ahead and put his *thali* kit to practical use, having Rahul and his family fill the containers with peppery Varanasi treats for the train journey. Max plunged into them shamelessly, fully exposed for the epicure he embodied, sweating happily, wearing a napkin as a bib.

The endless landscape around the tracks spread flat and grassy in both directions, with the occasional glimpse of the Ganges reflecting shafts of the sun. The flat plain spilled into rolling foothills in the hazy distance to the north, and Max imagined the Himalaya rising into the sky behind them. After an hour's worth of window staring, he shifted his focus to their destination and the riddle of the chile they sought.

Over centuries, Assam's people developed their own names for it, defined by tribe or region. "Naga," for the fierce headhunting warriors of Nagaland; "Bhut," for ghost, "Mirch," for serpent, and "Bih," for poison. No other cultures attached such powerful names to their chiles, particularly their neighbors in the rest of India. The rest of the country had been eating chiles for as long as they had in the remote northeast, if not longer. Why were the chiles coming out of the northeast provinces reputedly so much hotter?

Max thought about the isolation of the area to which they headed. His reports detailed its history, where he read about the Burmese Ahom dynasty that ruled the region now called the Seven Sisters for six hundred years, from 1228 to 1826, when the British arrived. The kingdom of Assam was the longest dynastic run in all Indian history, yet they were strikingly inclusive and multiethnic. They famously resisted the marauding Muslim Mughals' attempts to control the territory. As a result, they were primarily Buddhists and tribal animists, worshiping the earth, the seasons, and animal spirits. The Naga tribes did not cease headhunting until the 1940s, and there were elders who reportedly still wore the face tattoos of the headhunting tribes, further evidence of isolation. The Brahmaputra Valley of Assam and the territory it drained was one of the top seven most biodiverse places on the planet, and seventy percent of the world's orchids were found there. *Such isolation and rich biodiversity could be perfect for a fierce strain of chile pepper to evolve in quiet obscurity*, thought Max.

Coins from archaeological finds showed evidence of a thriving trade between Assam, Bhutan, Nepal, Burma, China, and Tibet, commerce the Mughals of India were willing to go to war over. Five known routes went from Assam to China and Tibet alone. As a result of Mughal invasions, no trade had been allowed with any regions to the south and west of Assam, eventually comprising greater India, for the entire Sixteenth century. They did not *need* India. It was the European trader Jean-Baptiste Tavernier, traversing the region in 1676, who observed in his *Travels in India* that: "The Kingdom of Assam is one of the best countries in Asia for it produces all the necessities of life and there is no need to go for anything to the neighboring states."

After Columbus, representing Spain, encountered the skinny *Capsicum annuum* and *frutescens* in the West Indies, that group of northern-oriented chiles found their way to India and ruled the continent. The Portuguese, whose trading influence went further, brought chiles from the Amazon region and their southern holdings in Brazil to Southeast Asia and China. Those were primarily the hotter lantern-shaped strains that would come to be called *Capsicum chinense*, and for centuries the Assamese had chosen to trade with China and Burma rather than the Indian subcontinent. Assamese chiles were reportedly very much hotter than anything else on the Indian continent. *Capsicum chinense* is known to be significantly hotter than *Capsicum annuum* and *frutescens. The Naga Jolokia could have its roots in China, over the Himalayas, or Burma,* thought Max. *Or it could be a unique hybrid. I won't know until I see one of the bloody ghosts.* He was eager to get to Assam and into the thick of things with the Naga Jolokia, his palate keen for battle.

The hours flowed by in the comfortable car, punctuated by easy conversation and thali treats from Raj's metal dishes. The energy between Max and Lilah was characterized by less angst, knowing not what lay ahead but that they would be together, determining what they were as they went. They were allies on an adventure rather than something to be figured out. Max shared his knowledge and opinions on the Assam situation, and Lilah agreed with his view that the Naga Jolokia could be something randomly unique. However, in her profession, such an occurrence was extremely rare.

"It would be unprecedented. However, the possibility exists," she said. "Nature is a powerful force. We just have to get there." Max agreed and relayed that they were scheduled to meet officials at the Tezpur Defense Research Laboratory the following day at noon.

The broad, open countryside of the Ganges plain, more brown than green, gave way to the low rolling hills of West Bengal as they ventured further east. At Katihar, their route turned northeast, and in the afternoon sun, Max could make out the line of the Himalayas and the towering peak of Kangchenjunga, the top of the world. By sunset, they neared the city of Siliguri, the heart of the Chicken's Neck, India's narrowest point. Occasional tea plantations appeared, blanketed in humid mist, while Nepal and Bangladesh loomed to the north and south, just out of view.

Max again slept fitfully in the train cabin while Lilah and Raj slumbered in silence. In his short dreams, there were images of Gasanov and the markets of Osh. They were shopping for peppers, with Nickolai urging him forward, prodding him with a Russian pistol. Then everyone in the market started to run, silently, away from a threat he could not see. Running, running.

When he finally awoke, Raj and Lilah were quietly having tea, watching the endless tea plantations of Assam stretch out across the countryside to the north toward forest-covered hills and south across the Brahmaputra, the only male river in India, named after the god Brahma. Max stretched and asked for tea himself.

"Well, good morning," said Lilah, looking entirely fresh and rested. "Who was chasing you last night?"

"What?" Max said through his fog. "I didn't see you there."

"No, I was right here sleeping, but you mumbled 'running' five or six times in your sleep," she said.

"You don't wanna know," he groaned.

"Let me guess, something about chile peppers. You're quite predictable, at least in this regard, Max. Did you know that Assam produces more tea than any place in the entire world? Not only are we in the birthplace of the Naga Jolokia, but also one of the world capitals of tea. We should visit a plantation while we're here."

Max was still groggy, rubbing both eyes. "Sure, of course. Since we're in the neighborhood."

As they crossed the broad Brahmaputra at Golpaya, eagles and hawks scanned the river for fish, resting in tall trees along the banks. Three hours' drive to the south, the wettest town on the planet nestled in the verdant hills of Cherrapunji, feeding the male river. Mawsynram, on average, received 467 inches of rain each year, an indicator of the climate they approached. Every direction was brushed with green, showing lush foliage and tall trees blanketing hillsides. Forty minutes later, they rolled into Guwahati, capital of Assam and the largest city in Northeast India, the gateway to the Seven Sisters.

True to form, Max expressed that he needed the uplift of food after the twenty-four-hour trip. Raj had been only as far as Darjeeling, hours to the west, so they had to explore to find what suited them. Their first impression was that the regional capital of over one million was incredibly clean by Indian standards. Carrying their bags, they walked the few blocks from the station to the Brahmaputra riverfront to stretch their legs. They came across the Guwahati Spice Route Restaurant in the Pan Bazaar district, offering breakfast, lunch, and chaat, the Indian small plates. Lilah and Raj ordered a typical Assamese breakfast called *Jolpan*, made of ground, puffed, flattened, and cooked incarnations of rice with brown sugar, mango, yogurt, and heavy cream, served in brass bowls. Max opted for a hearty local soup called *Khaar*. The *Khaar Dal* he ordered had sliced duck in broth with lentil, squash, papaya, green chiles, and garlic paste. The broth for the soup was rendered by passing water through the ashes of dried and burnt banana peels. It was refreshingly tart and high in alkali and antioxidants, with clean chile heat, a traditional Assamese picker-upper. They also ordered a platter of a dozen *Momos*, dumplings traditionally from Tibet, only fifty miles to the north. Some were stuffed with mushroom and others pork, with a fiery chile puree and a sesame and rice vinegar sauce for dipping. The sweet Jolpan, savory Khaar, and doughy dumplings disappeared with collective relish and hums of satisfaction, representing an auspicious landing in Assam.

Before hailing a car for the three-hour ride to Tezpur, they strolled to the promenade overlooking the Brahmaputra, a half-mile wide as it flowed through Guwahati. On a tiny island in the middle of the river sat the Umananda temple, dedicated to the tantric omniscient mother goddess of desire *Kamakhya*, who in prehistory emerged from the Himalayan foothills to the north. Raj described her as a powerful goddess with twelve arms and six heads of distinct colors, ornately dressed and wearing a red sari, sitting on a lotus flower. The island was a bastion of feminine power anchored in the mighty male Brahmaputra.

"I like her already," said Lilah. "With twelve arms and six heads, I would have feminine superpowers. I'll be back to light a candle over there on that little island."

"She sounds pretty important. Seems like I'd want to be in her good graces, too," said Max, "I'll light a bonfire."

Raj negotiated a car and driver for the trip to Tezpur, who loaded them up and weaved the vehicle out of Assam's bustling capital. From West Bengal, their driver and Raj spoke enough common language to take the slower river road through the province. Departing Guwahati, development gave way to an endless sea of tea plantations. Tea bushes cultivated in neat rows followed the topography of the land, much like vineyards. *And pepper farms,* thought Lilah. Skirting the Brahmaputra, they enjoyed a slower pace and no honking lorries on the highway. Looking north, out his window, Max could see the river's glimmer and hazy Himalayan peaks through the trees. The late spring harvest was just beginning, and bands of women worked the rows with baskets on their heads and bags slung over their shoulders to bring in the crop. The similarity to pepper country was striking.

"Seeing as we're rolling through the heart of tea country, how about we have some at the source?" said Lilah. Max shrugged in a *Sure, why not?* way that she was coming to recognize. "Raj, can you ask the driver if he knows of any authentic plantations where we can sample the local brew? I'm not particularly keen on the highbrow British legacy estates."

After a brief exchange, the driver shifted direction, heading northeast. He knew a tea operation owned and run by local people who made tea in the traditional style.

When a Scottish adventurer, Robert Bruce, encountered the native Assamese tribespeople drinking a beverage brewed from local leaves in 1823, India's tea movement began. Local lore had the region's people using the same leaves for generations in their brew since the 12th century. It was found to genetically vary only slightly from the ancient Chinese version, with *Assamica* tea exhibiting slightly larger leaves from the increased rainfall of what would become northeast India. Unlike Darjeeling to the west, northeast India's isolation worked in its favor, allowing room for indigenous people to grow and market tea alongside the well-connected British. Assam was now one of the largest tea-producing regions globally, known for its bold black teas with a particularly malty aroma and bright golden color. In Assam and all over Northeast India, tea is impossible to escape, an essential element of everyday life, and for the Assamese, it had been for nine hundred years. The more remote areas, especially approaching the Himalayas, infused it with salty yak butter rather than milk and sugar, with the river and hill tribes creating their own traditional fire-infused and smoky brews.

The road they took became a slowly winding path through endless tea plantations north of the Guwahati-Tezpur highway. Low hills rolled lazily toward the Brahmaputra, covered in a carpet of tea bushes like rows of braids. Tall Sissoo, Betel palm, Silk cotton, and Hollong trees dotted the landscape. The second of four harvests of the year was just getting underway, and groups of pickers were spread out across the fields, wearing wide-brimmed hats in the May sun. After an hour of the picturesque landscape, their driver turned left toward the river into a long, palm-tree-lined lane. A sign at the entrance read Ningada Traditional Tea Plantation.

The tea rows here were visibly less manicured, bushier, and the entire property was less "estate"-like, countering the British style. They entered a clearing in a grove of bushy Jutuli trees about a quarter-mile along the narrow track. Four structures on bamboo stilts six feet high sat in a line, facing north toward the river, a half-mile away. Called *chaangs*, they were built almost entirely of bamboo, which grew in clusters around the property. Standing out front was a man about five feet tall, wearing a bright red cloth sarong and white cotton vest with a long red bandana, the traditional garb of the *Singpho* people. The Singpho are a small aboriginal subtribe of Assam, the River Dwellers, descendants of the Aryan, Mongol, and Dravidian races, with traces of Indo-Tibetan, Indo-Iranian, and Indo-Burmese ethnic groups. They built their civilization as farmers in the Brahmaputra lowlands over eons, and dealing with the monsoon floods of the river for generations made building on stilts a necessary adaptation.

Mirip Lutong was the head of the family farming tea on the property since 1962 and spoke a working English learned in the tea trade. He shook their hands vigorously.

"Welcome people to home of traditional Assamese Singpho 'Coin' tea," he said proudly.

He explained that his tea farm was different from the traditional British style of growing, where tea trees can reach ten feet high and picking often done sitting on elephants. Feeding elephants was expensive, so they evolved to grow bushes lower for hand picking.

He led them across the clearing and through a row of bushy trees. Beyond stretched fifty acres of tea bushes, wrapping around the central complex. The air was thick with the sweet grassy fragrance of green tea. The plants had been left to grow naturally, though topped off, very much like the 150-year-old Zinfandel vines Max had seen in the Sonoma Valley.

"These plants closest to house almost fifty years old can live to one hundred. Older ones produce less but have richer flavor, like wine grapes. We pick youngest green leaves, just green tips and buds on every plant once a week, March to November. Brother and sister families come to help! All types of tea harvested this way but become different by processing. Green, white, black, Oolong, start here like this. Four seasons for tea, spring has green flavor, summer has stronger scent from heat, rainy season tea milder flavor from quick growing. Winter tea more expensive, grows slower less leaves."

"What about watering?" Lilah asked.

"More important good drainage," Mirip said. "Spring and monsoon rains enough sometimes too much. Sometimes river sends big floods so why houses on stilts. We dig many drainage troughs. Pick some tea and smell!"

They each picked a few leaves and crumpled them in their palms, smelling much like other green plants, with the robust scent of being freshly cut.

"Leafy," said Max with a shrug.

"Flavor in tea comes from drying, roasting, oxidation," Mirip said. "And aging. That where these green leaves get flavor and become delicious tea. Now we taste."

He led them back to the compound, where a group of women carrying bags of harvested tea leaves had just returned from the fields.

"Cousins!" said Mirip, pointing. "Important for our farm and important work for extended family. Come upstairs!"

He bounded up narrow bamboo stairs and onto the small deck fronting the thatched-roof bungalow. They were suddenly enveloped by the sweet and smoky smell of tea and fire. Inside, a woman roasted tea leaves in a wide wok over a flame generated from thin burning sticks. She wore a woven red skirt and a white blouse, with wide, shiny brass bracelets and tanned brown from work in the fields. Bamboo racks sat above the fire, lined with bamboo tubes, one foot long and three inches in diameter. A hard mud slab protected a bamboo-mat floor from the fire in the square room's center. It had been hand-formed with a ring to contain the log fire and a platform for heating water for tea.

"My wife! Called Bissa. Say hello!" The woman briefly nodded and returned to focus on her work. Along two walls were bamboo shelves for air-drying trays of tea leaves before roasting. "First, we bruise tea leaves by hand to start oxidation of enzymes, then air dry by fanning fire smoke. Then we roast over fire to stop oxidation before most crucial step. Please, sit!"

They took seats on cushions set across the floor. Tropical and floral scents filled the room, offset by smoke from the sweet-smelling wood. A second woman crushed the roasted tea leaves and stuffed them into the hollow bamboo tubes, which Max thought looked very much like bongs. Once filled, the bamboo tubes were sealed and placed on the racks above the fire for drying and smoking for two months. Newer cylinders began on the bottom and raised a level as the next tubes were filled. A hundred of them hung from the ceiling, suspended by bamboo-leaf cords, where after roasting, the tea was left to age for four years.

Mirip continued. "Next huts full of aging bamboo tubes. Four years minimum we age, but this tea can age for ten and preserve for one hundred. It's called *Falap Signpho* and gets better with age. I have some from our first vintage, 1965. You like to try?"

"Absolutely," said Lilah. "Why is it called 'coin tea'?"

"You see now," he said.

Mirip joined them on the floor after selecting a blackened, footlong tube from the ceiling. He pulled a bamboo plug from the end and slid out a brown cylindrical mass of tea only half a foot long. It had been sampled over the years, apparently. From this, he sliced a section a quarter-inch wide, like a salami, then held it out for them to see.

"Like a coin," he said, smiling with gold-rimmed teeth, and handed it to Lilah. It smelled woody and smoky as she inhaled, with slight overtones of spice, exotic and old.

Mirip placed the thick coin in the center diffuser of a glass teapot and added steaming water from off the fire. They watched as wisps of color began to infuse the water, still quivering from its boil. First green, then gold, and finally a rich brown color, the tea evolved with smells of sweet smoke and earth. After a minute, the tea was poured into clear glass cups with metal handles so the gold-brown tea could be better viewed. In the cup, the smoky aromas intensified, and spice and wood tones became unveiled. No sweetener was offered, or desired. Slurping the hot broth, they became aware of its almost creamy nature, malty, smoky, and earthy like nothing they had ever tasted. Thinking about its age increased its depth and allure, accentuated by sitting on the hut floor near the fire used to smoke the leaves and make the tea. For the next twenty minutes, they sipped the dark tea and compared impressions. Lilah thought she tasted roasted banana. Max, blackened vanilla beans, and singed sweet poblano chiles. Raj thought he smelled the desert after a rain, with earthiness and dusty minerality. *So much like wine*, felt Max. It carried the essence and development of time as a flavor.

For an hour, Max not once thought of Naga Jolokias or scientists and immersed himself in the exploration of tea at its source. As he drained his cup for a third time, his journey's purpose resurged. It was time to get to Tezpur and get his hands on the Warrior chile. *Ghost chile, Serpent chile, Poison chile, whatever. Let's do this.*

"Lilah, we have to get to Tezpur. I could stay here all day. This has been extraordinary, and we should take home a couple of tubes of that tea to savor over the next few years."

The next few years, she thought. *Interesting.* "Mirip, can we purchase some back vintages of your teas?" she asked. "We are your newest fans, for life."

"With pleasure," the teamaker said. Reaching up to the hanging tubes on the ceiling, Mirip selected three. "How about 1970, 1980 and 1990? You compare each decade, see how time changes tea." Dates were scribbled on the side of each of them.

Lilah was wowed. "Really? That will be an extraordinary honor, and we will remember you and this place every time we drink your tea, Mirip. And Bissa, thank you," she said to the wife, with her hands clasped in gratitude. Bissa bowed from her crouched position, still tending the fire.

They paid, bowed, thanked Mirip, and left with their bongs of vintage tea in tow. It was yet another hour across tea plantations and rice paddies to the military base in Tezpur. For his part, Max considered the implications of sharing the teas with Lilah, tasting from each decade, wondering where they might be in the coming years.

Thinking they were meeting scientists at the research laboratory, they were surprised to be told they were being transported five miles north to the Military Air Station, Assam, upon arrival in Tezpur. The general in charge, a staunch nationalist, oversaw all military activity in the region and desired to make a spectacle of the Jolokia's reveal to the world. The Indian military intended to capitalize on the planet's hottest pepper for public relations and strategic purposes.

They were escorted in a convoy of vehicles speeding across the runway to a massive hangar on the air base's east side. The convoy halted outside the hangar's monstrous bay doors, and all the car doors opened at once, with the military retinue exiting in unison. It was an entirely over-official event meant to impress or intimidate the guests, who were escorted into the cavernous building followed by the entourage of officers. A squadron of fighter jets stretched across the hangar, with long military banners draping the walls. India's powerful adversary China loomed just up the road, and there were still active border disputes that had erupted into war in the past, making the military a pervasive presence in Assam.

Strategically placed between the jets was a presentation table with four chairs, fronting another forty chairs meant for an audience. Four soldiers waited at the table, writing in ledgers. On a dish in the center of the table sat four bright red chile peppers. *A public discussion on chiles?* thought Max. *Is that all I'm here for?*

A reception commenced, attended by formally dressed officers, local politicians, and scientists in laboratory coats, with drinks passed. It became apparent that Max's arrival constituted a significant event. Lilah was one of three women present.

Off to one side, five scientists huddled around a table. One carefully dispensed drops of water from an eyedropper. Another counted the drops as they fell into a petri dish, diluting a red concentrate. A third wrote notes in a logbook, while the fourth manned a microscope. The fifth videotaped the entire process. They were administering a basic Scoville test with theatrically comic overkill. *Chuck DeWindt would get a kick out of this production,* thought Max. *Guess I'm just here to observe. A long way to go just to watch.*

An adjutant officer accompanied by a scientist approached and introduced them to an ego-bloated General Abhijeet Chatterjee, Commander of the Indian Armed Services, Northeast. The General stood broad-chested with a pencil mustache and ridiculously over-decorated with jingling medals. Black hair was slicked back with oil, and mirrored aviator glasses hid his eyes. "Welcome, Mr. Little," he said with a deceptive smile. "This is an auspicious day. Though I was expecting only yourself. Who are these unannounced individuals?"

Max could feel Lilah bristle at his side. "This is Lilah DeVillier, a professor in botany and agronomy, representing New Mexico State University, and Rajdeep Singh, our representative in India," he replied. "Ms. DeVillier is from Louisiana, the capital of chile pepper farming in our country, and she is an expert on pepper varieties and cultivation. Mr. Singh is our interpreter."

Without acknowledging Lilah or Raj, Chatterjee said, "Very well, they can stay. Let me introduce you to our chief scientist, Professor R.S. Gupta. He is the one who first identified this thing."

Max immediately realized that the general desired international verification without jumping through too many hoops, his elaborate operation notwithstanding.

"Greetings, Mr. Little. We are honored by your presence," said the scientist, bowing quickly. "Your reputation precedes you."

Gupta was slight, his lab coat two sizes too big and hanging almost to his ankles. Thick round glasses enlarged his eyes, and he blinked nervously. "We have been preparing for this day for weeks."

"We are honored to be here, and thank you," said Max. "Tell me, Professor Gupta, what do you think are the reasons for the elevated heat levels in this particular chile? Are there unique environmental factors?"

Before the scientist could answer, Chatterjee said, "We can get into details later. First, let's meet the important people and have a toast."

The general led them to a bar set up in the corner of the room, which displayed an array of bottles and jars filled with liquids of varying colors. The contents ranged from gold to green and brown, some opaque and others were completely clear. Some had formal labeling, while others were affixed with smudged, handwritten labels.

"In the far northeast of India, there are hundreds of unique ethnic tribes, each with their own dialects and traditions, including their methods of producing spirits," said Chatterjee. "To honor our role in uniting and protecting all these endemic peoples of the Seven Sisters, we have assembled some of the local spirits that represent them. My assistant will describe them to you."

The adjutant stepped forward and began a dissertation on the various liquors on display. First, cloudy *Apong* from Arunachal

Pradesh, a sweet, malty yet spicy fermented drink served in bamboo stems, and a container of the vessels stood at the ready. *Chuwak* from Tripura state, clear and potent, distilled from rice, herbs, and jackfruit leaves hiding in clay pots. Gold-colored *Judima* of the Dimasa people. *Kiaad* from Meghalaya was triple distilled and served with charcoal for tartness and fruity, sake-like *Zutho* of the Nagamese. *Sekmai Yu*, a fermented and distilled rice beverage from Manipur, clear and smooth as vodka. And finally, *Lali Gur*, a potent molasses-based liquor from Assam. With the introduction complete, a server offered the spirits to the guests. Lilah chose Zutho, Raj, Judima, and Max, the potent Chuwak. For ceremonial purposes, each beverage was served in a tall bamboo tube.

On the bar sat a basketful of doughy chapatis and some tamarind chutney for dipping. Max took six and quickly stuffed them down. If at some point he got an opportunity to sample the Jolokia, he'd want a cushion in his belly for the impending firestorm. Once accommodated, they were led to the assembled dignitaries, at which point the general launched into a long speech in Bengali, occasionally mentioning Max's name and the university. Raj interpreted that the Defense Research Laboratory, supported by the military, was proposing the Directorate of Horticulture and Processing to receive formal Geographical Indication Certification applied to the Naga Jolokia to ensure that only Jolokias from northeast India were sold as such. And that research was ongoing into the weaponization of the peppers. At its conclusion, applause broke out, along with a few boisterous military cheers, and everyone turned to Max with their glasses and bamboo tubes raised.

"To the fighting spirit of the Seven Sisters and Mr. Little, cheers," said Chatterjee. Everyone drained their spirits, and the Chuwak flowed like a warm river down Max's throat.

After the toast, introductions were made, including members of the PBJ, the region's ruling nationalist political party. Max shook many hands while Lilah and Raj stayed to the side. He thought the pomp of the ceremony and setting completely unnecessary yet endured the formalities. He wanted to see a damn Jolokia, hold it in his hand. While Max mingled, Lilah followed Professor Gupta over to the table of scientists and their Scoville display. She had seen the test administered but never with so many levels of control.

The scientist counting out drops said, "Six hundred twenty-five thousand, three hundred eighty-five. Eighty-six, eighty-seven, eighty-eight."

The man with the ledger took notes while the videographer filmed, and the microscope man stared. A sample was taken from the petri dish at intervals of a hundred and walked over to the tasting panel, whose members dabbed the solution on their tongues using cotton swabs. Each of them pondered the sensations they registered, looking for a sign of heat in the samples. They, in turn, recorded their responses into individual ledgers. All four then gave a thumbs-up, indicating that they still registered heat in the sample, and the test continued. Their eyes were bleary, and they looked exhausted.

"They've been at it since yesterday morning," Professor Gupta said.

Poor bastards. Totally subjective, Lilah thought. *I guess it's all they've got.*

She quietly approached the table and the lead scientist with the ledger. He seemed younger than the rest.

"Hello there. How is the test going?" The man did not look up from his data recording.

"Not good," he said. "It is our fourth test, and every time we have gotten different results. We have even resorted to changing the panel each time, but still no continuity. So, we just take the average of the four tasters. First, we got a reading of around 1,089,000, then 747,000, back up to 867,000. I think the first panel was terrified, new to the process, and registered heat where there might not have been any. Their tongues were scorched, and they were afraid to say so. The general has been livid. The others have been more prepared, eating green chiles for a week for conditioning. Hard to tell still. Who are you?"

"I'm a botanist working with New Mexico State University in the United States, here to observe. Quite a show you're putting on."

The man grimaced. "The general wants results and all the credit. He thinks this will make him famous. And rich." Then he whispered, "Professor Gupta is okay, but he's afraid to give the general unwelcome news. He makes me do it."

"Have you experienced these peppers yourself?" Lilah asked.

"All my life," said the man. "We forage for them in the valleys below my village in the hills of Nagaland. Yes, they are extremely hot. But we've had historically little to compare them to. The dried chiles that come from India proper are not good examples for comparison. So, getting this Scoville test right is the only method we have available to tell us the truth of the matter. For those to whom this represents such an important thing." He nodded toward the general.

"Well, if we can get a sample, there are liquid chromatography tests available now in America that can give a scientifically accurate reading," said Lilah. "Irrefutable results. And we can do all sorts of fun stuff with the genetics."

The man shook his head. "The general will not allow anyone to take the specimens. He says they represent the future and security of the region and should be protected. Samples are locked in the lab. He overlooks the fact that they are growing in backyard plots all over the Seven Sisters. And in many places, totally wild."

"How can we find some? I need to get a sample to the university laboratory in America."

For the first time, the young man stood and looked at Lilah. He was handsome, wiry, and a few inches shorter than she, with close-cropped hair in military fashion. To Lilah, his features were more Thai or Burmese than Indian.

"Whoa, Shiva," he said. "You are American? If you were not so tall, I would say you are from India. I am Jahnu, my family comes from Khonoma, in Nagaland, and we are of the *Angami* tribe. My father is one of the tribal elders."

"It is genuinely nice to make your acquaintance, Jahnu. What is special about the Angami people?" she said.

He filled with pride, standing taller. "When the British first came to conquer the hill tribes, our people held them at bay for almost fifty years, until 1880, when a truce was declared. The Angami of Khonoma were never subjugated by the British invaders, and we make good soldiers. We also famously helped fend off the Japanese in World War II right here in Nagaland, stopping their planned advance into greater India. You could say we saved India. I am a chemist in the Army, and my village and family are enormously proud."

"They must be proud," acknowledged Lilah, "and I'm sure you are an excellent scientist for the Army. Why such an interest by the military in the Naga Jolokia?"

"Interest in the powdered form of the chile is very high, to use as a deterrent both for wildlife and on the battlefield," he said. "The Army is already experimenting with artillery and grenades, and the concentrate can render a crowd of people helpless, even restricting the respiratory tract and blinding eyes for half an hour. Quite effective."

"Amazing," said Lilah, lying. She detested the thought of weaponizing food. "Where should we go to locate some of these chiles growing in a natural state? It would greatly benefit our research if we could see the soil and the leaves."

Jahnu did not hesitate. "The best places I know are in the hills around my village in Nagaland. I see them all the time. You should go there."

"Perhaps we will, Jahnu. Thank you," she replied.

She was already planning a foray to locate the elusive chiles in their natural habitat. This show with General Chatterjee looked increasingly to be a public relations scam.

While Lilah engaged with the young scientist, Max was being passed around the military/political/scientific crowd and bowing often, with Raj acting as interpreter. Catching Lilah's eye across the room, Max pointed to his bamboo tumbler. He made clear he wanted a drink and signaled to the bar.

They met like spies, sharing secrets over cocktails. "What'd you find out?" Max asked, looking nonchalantly over the crowd. "All I did was say my name fifty times and try to explain that Little is actually a name in America." He sipped his spirits.

Lilah spoke over the rim of her drink exaggeratedly, like Mata Hari. "They're running an elaborate Scoville production, mostly for the cameras. They haven't been able to get a consistent reading. The general has all the available specimens locked up in the lab, but I met a young scientist who told me where to find them in the wild. We need to go find them. Chatterjee is a pompous ass."

"Great work, Agent Lilah," said Max, smiling and waving to officers and politicians he'd just met. "And you're right, what a blowhard. I wonder when we're going to get close to one of these damned chiles. Chuck DeWindt couldn't even find a picture of one, but I sense that they're not skinny little *annuum* chile types. Now there's four on a table across the room. Let's make our way over there."

Halfway across the room, General Chatterjee intercepted them. "Mr. Little, what do you think of our endeavor, 'Operation Headhunter'?" he boomed. He did not acknowledge Lilah.

Still, she seized the moment. "Great operation name, but your Scoville test has mixed results, for starters," she said. "No consistency. What are the optimal growing conditions? What's its range? I don't imagine you've been able to make any determination as to what type of taxonomic variety they are? That's an important thing to know when working with genetics to breed the strongest specimens. Gotta make those grenades really pop, you know?"

The general's face immediately rushed with blood, and his eyes narrowed behind mirrored lenses. He was unaccustomed to challenging responses, particularly from a woman. He spoke through his teeth, restraining himself.

"Most of that information is already classified, Ms. DeVillier."

"Then what is the point of having us here?" she asked defiantly.

"That shall become clear, in Mr. Little's case, that is. In India, women are more useful in places other than laboratories," he hissed. "Why don't you have another beverage."

Max sensed her entire body tensing, coiled, and ready to strike. Yet her response remained calm and confident. "Perhaps in India. In my case, General, if you ever expect international verification of these chile peppers, then you should be kissing my professional female ass. I'm the botanist here, and the university won't do anything that I don't tell them to. Your lucrative military kickbacks, I mean contracts, might have to wait." She turned and walked away as Max and Chatterjee stared at each other.

The general was red-faced but played it cool, polishing his glasses. "Your associate exhibits strong character, Mr. Little. I hope you can see the benefit of keeping her restrained." He paused for effect. "The next phase of the operation does not include her, only true initiates in the Ring of Fire. Yes, I'm quite familiar with your little club."

He hammered Max on the shoulder and with him turned to address the room, first in Bengali, then in English. "Gentlemen, if you would kindly take your seats, we are about to begin the next step of Operation Headhunter. Scoville tasting panel, you may recess. Volunteers, please go to the front. Mr. Little, if you would please join the others at the judging table, we would very much appreciate it." Chatterjee took the middle seat in the front row of chairs, with the rest of the group following. Lilah and Raj stood behind the back row.

Max expected to be part of a panel discussion on chile peppers, the Naga Jolokia in particular, and took the far-left seat at the table. The others preparing to sit at the table weren't scientists or any other qualified types, and his suspicious nature engaged. With Chatterjee's mention of the Ring of Fire, he knew he had a true sadist on his hands. The guy had done his research, at least.

Three uniformed men took the other seats, and the bright red chile pods at the table were passed among the four positions. They were about to ingest balls of fire, Max grasped. Looking down the table, he observed that they were terrified and definitely not volunteers. The general began to speak.

"Now, gentlemen, we are here today because we are taking steps to verify if the Naga Jolokia is indeed the hottest chile pepper on the planet, Phase Three of Operation Headhunter. As you can see, the Scoville heat test team continues its work, Phase Two, and we hope to get a reading from them soon. Mr. Little, who has come all the way from America to join us, is an authority on chiles and has experienced them all over the world. Now we will have him find out for himself if ours is the hottest there is. Three enlisted volunteers from the Air Force will also be joining in the research. Sergeant Kholaavi, please start the video cameras. Gentlemen, whenever you are ready."

Understanding he was being railroaded into public immolation by Jolokia set Max's heart racing. The other victims faced separate terrors, having no idea what to expect. One shook uncontrollably, and all of them perspired through their uniforms. *Already,* thought Max. *These guys are screwed. I wonder if I am, too.*

Max did not possess an elevated tolerance to chile heat, unlike a few of the freaks he encountered at hot sauce competitions. He simply learned from hundreds of encounters how to deal with it. Max looked down at the pepper sitting naked in the middle of a small white saucer, drowning out the sounds and stimuli coming from the room. He reached down and cupped it in his hand like a gemstone or an ancient relic, inspecting it with an archaeologist's fascination. He was experiencing an Indiana Jones moment, finally grasping the Holy Grail. Everything else in the room faded from view as he fixated on the details of the incendiary fruit before him. It was more lantern-shaped than elongated but not nearly as round as a typical *chinense* variety, like habanero. It most definitely was not an *annuum* or *frutescens*, the long, skinny tabasco-type of peppers, but he could not be entirely sure. Somewhere in the middle, unlike anything he had ever seen. *Seeing the leaves would sure help for comparison,* he thought.

The chile glowed vividly red, its outside wrinkled, almost blistered as if the fruit was suffering from the heat it was forced to bear. The skin had a slick shine to it, and the possessed body twisted in tortured growth. It was mean, angry, menacing, like the face of a Naga warrior, daring you to eat it or die. Or die eating it.

Glasses of water had been set at each position; however, Max knew from painful experience that water would only spread the fire and double the misery. *Wish I had my bamboo cocktail,* he thought. He imagined what kind of stories his experience would create among the pepper-heads and knew there was no way he could back out now. This was going to be a rough road.

"Gentlemen, I urge you to sample the Naga Jolokia of Assam." Chatterjee exhibited a veiled smile and seemed to relish the impending pain as the cameras rolled. "India is proud of you."

Max looked down the table and saw three faces looking back at him, bewildered and terrified. They had not volunteered for this. He wondered what minor transgressions found them forced into such a ghastly experiment. Max pointed to his glass and said, "Water bad," shaking his finger back and forth in an attempt to assist. The concept that the lifesaving water could somehow be bad unsettled them even more, and they all watched him for a clue to the next move.

"Gentlemen, please," prodded the general. Max caught Lilah's look from the back of the room, and it registered concern.

Max took four quick, deep breaths, knowing he could experience difficulty with respiratory and swallowing functions in the next minute or two. He picked up the fruit by its attached stem and bit cleanly into the thick shoulder near the top. The meat felt softer than a jalapeno and thicker than a habanero, he registered as he bit down. Max pulled the chile out of his mouth, leaving the center veins and many of the seeds behind, a chile-head tactic for cutting the soon-to-register pain significantly.

He peered into the chile's crimson heart. Shiny, menacing capsaicin-laced oils lurked on the walls and placenta veins of the interior, dully reflecting the hangar's harsh light. Max imagined them silently assaulting his innocent taste receptors, immediately remorseful for the pain he was about to inflict upon them. But his desire for the impending rush was too overwhelming for him to stop. Before the heat kicked in, he discerned that the meat was moist and quite sweet, almost juicy, with citrus notes. Not at all bitter, but floral. He defined earthiness and minerality, a hint of sweet lemon, some bright acidity. Six seconds.

Then an explosion of molten lava spread across his tongue, a rapid volcano-hot introduction he had never experienced. The heat hidden inside the tiny orb of sweet red flesh was so potent it warped the laws of nature. It spread to his gums, and his teeth went numb. The inside of his lips swelled, and his salivary glands shut off. He closed his eyes, traveling with the sensation, knowing it was going to intensify, breathing as deeply as he still could. Circuits and receptors began to fire from his scalp to his toes, causing a buzzing sensation throughout his body. Endorphins shot off like fireworks. He rocked his head back and forth to keep his neck and jaw muscles from cramping, which happened once in Bolivia. Max was twenty seconds into the journey and had reached a point already hotter than anything he'd yet experienced. Then Armageddon arrived.

Max became overwhelmed by the sensation of the skin in his mouth falling away, replaced by raw sizzling tissue. Without chewing any more, he swallowed the fruit before his tongue swelled too much to allow it. *No sense in keeping a lump of hot coal sitting on your tongue,* he thought. *Here goes.*

He began to sweat heavily, in waves, even at the back of his knees. Max knew enough not to open his mouth and fan the flames, which could cause an esophageal contraction, so he breathed through his nose, using techniques he'd learned in yoga class, bypassing the nuclear fire in his mouth. It was explosively hot in emergency reports from every sensor station north of his pelvis. Reflexively, he thought about Laguna and Gus and how far away they were. He thought about his Mexican partners and his father pouring shots in Tacoma. The sweat poured like tears from his face and dripped off his chin. He had a vision of his mother swinging alone on a loveseat in the old house in Long Beach, where the lawn was on fire. Other random, chaotic images flashed before his eyes. If he hallucinated, he knew he was ascending to the next level. As a tactic, he mentally focused on snowboarding in a blizzard and that his belly burned with the fire of the Sun God Surya. In his vision, he melted the snow as he cruised along with his belly as bright as the sun. It had been one minute since he leaped naked off the cliff and into the jaws of the fire.

To stop the visions, he opened his eyes. Forty people sat transfixed, addictively watching men suffer. Looking to his left, he saw the three volunteers in various states of torture and agony. They were decomposing in unison, but differently. One had spit out the pepper and was moaning loudly, shaking his head back and forth, trying to yank his tongue out. Another fell back in his chair, clutching his throat and struggling to breathe. He crashed, writhing, to the ground. The poor soul next to him was mumbling with his eyes rolled back into his head, possessed. He twitched with hallucinations, his limp tongue dangling from his face. For the briefest of moments, Max was able to pity them. One minute.

Then the final attack came, an advanced layer of heat he had never believed possible. His lips began to swell, his throat to close reflexively. An oral supernova cascaded through his entire system, causing all seven of his chakras to fire off like rockets. The sensation of fireworks detonating inside him was real, filling his field of vision with starbursts, and he could feel the heat permeating through his skull as his hair became a damp, matted mass. The buzzing was so loud he was sure everyone in the room could hear it. Then his psyche kicked in and transported him to another realm.

He saw himself sitting at the table in Tezpur, Assam, eyes closed. Then his view rose, like a helicopter lifting off, as the Max suffering below grew smaller. Max's psychic birds-eye view of the earth expanded, seeing the vast Brahmaputra River Valley and its path south and east from the Himalayas and the Tibetan plateau. He saw the Seven Sisters, his mind drawing their loose borders in India's remote corner between Burma, China, Bangladesh, and Bhutan. Rising above the earth, able to discern its curve, and with his expansive vision, he traced the routes that could have brought the Naga Jolokia to the hills of Assam. Miniature Portuguese galleons sailed across the Arabian Sea, coming from Europe and the Horn of Africa, landing at Goa in India. From Goa, lines spread across India, even to remote Assam, the unstoppable migration of chiles. Others continued from Goa, south around Sri Lanka, to Malaysia and the Spice Islands, then to China's eastern shores, spreading west from there. Looking west across the round earth, he found the Caspian Sea, the Black Sea, and the Bosporus in Turkey. From Constantinople, now Istanbul, lines fanned out, the Silk Road's various paths, crossing Asia Minor, Arabia, Persia, and the five "Stans" of Central Asia. He observed tiny trains of camels and oxen on the paths, threading their way across deserts and over mountain ranges, ending at Kashgar in far western China. From Kashgar, the west and east lines collided in China, one of them going south over the eastern Himalayas using the great Brahmaputra to find their way to Burma and India. The line culminated in Tezpur, where he sat at a table hallucinating. The hallucination's silent film perspective gave way to a deep, visceral buzz as he re-entered the earth's atmosphere and his swaying body. Two minutes.

Max was certain that when he opened his eyes, his symbolic third eye would be wide open and blinking as well, in the center of his forehead, wondering just what the hell was going on. When he did open them, his eyes were bloodshot, scanning the room to understand where he was. Strange faces stared back at him. Flying above the earth had definitely been better. He began to hyperventilate, fully saturated by heat and unable to ward off the advance of the lava flow. He had no more defenses.

In the back of the room, Lilah watched with fascination, then mild terror, as she witnessed the pinnacle moment of Max's existence. This was the essence of who he was, or indeed a big part of it. She noted how he absorbed the sensations and his uncanny level of focus and commitment. He appeared very Zen-like, or he might have been hallucinating. He twitched ever so slightly. When he had finally opened his eyes, she thought she saw the beginning of fear as their eyes met across the room. The other candidates had checked out entirely, and he was the last man standing, or at least sitting, and conscious. It had been three minutes. And he needed her help.

Instinctively, she walked over to the bar and grabbed the bottle of Lali Gur, the potent Assamese molasses liquor. Taking a large swig, she filled her mouth with the flammable spirits and walked straight to Max at the torture table. Water streamed from his eyes. She grabbed his neck and threw his head back, planting her mouth on his, and ejected a stream of Lali Gur into him. Their eyes locked as she forced her tongue into his mouth and swished the liquor around, rinsing the capsaicin from its inflamed surfaces. Then she began to kiss him, passionately and intensely, and felt his burn become hers. She sensed the relief in him and then felt him give in to her. Four minutes had passed.

After twenty seconds, she released from him, her lips on fire. The crowd behind her sat wide-eyed, in shock. She whispered in his ear, and his streaming eyes went wide.

"Wow, that is some world-class heat!" she said as a distraction. "Congratulations, Max!" She pinched him on the cheek and returned to the back of the room, leaving him sputtering and gasping.

"How is he doing?" Raj asked. "That looked dangerous."

"I think I got him sorted out. He looks like he'll make it," Lilah said. "Today was a big day for him." Her mouth was numb with heat and the energy of Max's contact.

"Yes, I imagine it was. The general seems upset that Max is still conscious. The Ring of Fire will certainly be on fire now," he said, chuckling.

It took Max another three minutes to come completely around and regain clarity. His mouth and lips returned somewhat to normal, though he didn't know if he could actually speak. He was still in high velocity, with massive endorphin releases charging his body, pumping his heart. His system continued to repel the perceived threat of fire like a band of Naga warriors, getting him high off the battle. A vivid, audible hum echoed through his head, and his hands and feet tingled. Then, his vision became abnormally clear.

This was by far the best pepper rush Max had ever experienced, and he made a mental note to record every aspect of the experience. He shook his head, flinging sweat off in a wide arc. *Damn!* he thought, coming around. *I know an army of high-level heat junkies who would love to get a hold of one of those little devils.*

With the odd public display over, Max was issued a towel to dry his soaked torso. The audience applauded, believing he was the winner of a bizarre survival contest, and he bowed with a flourish and wave of his arm like a Musketeer. He was high as a chile pepper kite. A bamboo tumbler was placed in his hand, full of lifesaving flammable spirits, and he took a long draw like it was lemonade. It bathed his throat with a welcome, liquid heat. The three unlucky volunteers were escorted from the room under heavy assistance.

Max sauntered up to General Chatterjee, sitting motionless next to Professor Gupta with his arms crossed. He raised and drained his bamboo shoot tumbler again, silently toasting both military man and scientist, adding his best Paul Newman wink for the camera, which continued to roll.

"Well, we've come a long way, baby," he said to the crowd.

Chatterjee displayed a confused reaction to Max's colloquial statement, slightly tilting his head. The American was a vexing riddle.

"Certainly, the hottest chile pepper I've ever tasted, by a wide margin," said Max with a grin. "That's my expert analysis, and you can take that to the bank. Or the armory. It looks like an elongated *chinense* pepper, but *chinense* is not known to naturally occur in India. Given the historical links to Burma and China, it could have come from there, where *chinense* is prevalent, brought first by the Portuguese. It could be a hybrid, either naturally occurring or crossbred somewhere in centuries past. Until it's verified by liquid chromatography and genetic testing, no official validation can occur. So, we'll need a sample, if you please."

The general expected more drama from Max for his audience and the cameras, and he wasn't about to give him what he wanted. He had thought he could break the American and show Indian superiority in the spice world, becoming an instant international player in the Ring of Fire.

"We will ship a sample to New Mexico State University," Chatterjee said through clenched teeth. "A car has been arranged to take you back to Guwahati and the airport for the flight back to the U.S."

"That won't be necessary," said Max, smiling, weaving just a bit, enjoying his high and the general's discomfort. "I think we'd prefer to wander around and see the amazing biodiversity of the Seven Sisters on our own for a couple of days. So, a car to our hotel would be appreciated. Thank you, General Chatterjee and Professor Gupta. It's been a heat-seeking honor." He bowed again with a flourish, then spun on his heels to find his friends.

Lilah and Raj were observing the proceedings at the Scoville test table. As Max approached them, he felt strangely light on his feet. His ears and hands were red, and his lips slightly swollen. The sweat was almost entirely dry as he toweled off his neck and arms, and he released a deep-rooted, uncontrollable dragon-fire belch that felt like a visible, flaming-orange cloud. Lilah regarded him with amused respect.

"What's the report, Max?" she said. "That looked like quite a ride."

Max spent a few moments in thought. "The hottest thing I've ever encountered," he said. "What's unique is that it came in waves, unlike the frontal assault of a chocolate habanero. My teeth are numb. And I went progressively further out of my body as it dragged on. I felt the eyes of the entire pepper world on me, vivid visions. And Gasanov, watching me expectantly. Then I floated above the earth. Getting the chile out of my mouth and into my belly helped, and it's good I ate the chapattis before. The molasses liquor was a smart move. You're crafty, Lilah. I feel quite...alive."

"Well done, Max," said Raj, shaking his hand vigorously. "The last man standing!"

"Thank you, Raj, my friend. I'm glad you were here. Man, I could use a meal."

Lilah had rekindled her conversation with Jahnu, the young scientist, and brought him over to join Max and Raj. "Max, this is Jahnu, one of the scientists working on Operation Headhunter. He has some ideas." She winked at Max.

"Hello, Mr. Little," said Jahnu, shaking his hand. "That was an excellent performance."

Then he softened his voice, clandestinely. "Though I do not imagine that is what you came all the way here for. I can show you the Naga chiles growing in the wild near my village in Nagaland, in the habitat that spawned them. Though it will certainly anger the general, I have developed some data on the chiles in the wild, which has not seemed to capture Professor Gupta's attention. All he cares about is the heat index. The journey is half a day, and I can arrange lodging for you in a cabin in our village of Khonoma. My family and I would like to invite you for a traditional Nagamese meal tomorrow evening if you are inclined. I have already spoken to them, and they would be honored to host such important guests."

Max looked over at Lilah with an *Are you kidding me?* face, and she winked again.

"Jahnu, we would be honored, and thank you. We will travel to your village and go pepper hunting. Please tell your family we, too, would be honored to be in their home and that we desire to be of assistance in the cooking if they'll allow it."

"They will be happy for the extra hands. I will meet you at your hotel tomorrow morning, and we will drive together. Oh, and I will get you a copy of the video from today if you like," Jahnu added. Max gave him a thumbs-up. He wanted documentation of a first in the Ring of Fire.

As they made their way to the opening in the vast bay doors, General Chatterjee stopped them. "I hope you will convey the findings and impressions of your journey here generously to the people at the university, Mr. Little. The outcome could be significant to Assam and all of India."

Max did not make a move to shake his hand. "My impressions certainly, General. Actual scientific findings will take place in the laboratory, under the direction of Ms. DeVillier and the university team, where she commands a high level of respect."

Chatterjee showed no emotion, though his eyes narrowed a little. He was used to getting his way. "Very well, then, we are at her mercy. Incidentally, Ms. DeVillier, a telegram arrived directed to me for you this morning. From Kyrgyzstan. May your travels be rewarding and hopefully without danger."

He handed the sealed telegram to Max and, turning on his heel, retreated into the hangar.

"Well, that was fun," said Max, "but entirely inconclusive. Let's go find some Jolokias."

Outside, a car waited to take them to their hotel. Once inside the vehicle, they crossed the airbase and headed south toward Tezpur, called the City of Blood.

"Did he say Kyrgyzstan?" said Max, handing the telegram to Lilah. "I guess Gasanov did know we were coming here, but why send it to you?"

"I believe he did, how interesting. And yes, addressed to me." She looked down at the unopened telegram. *Why me?* She wondered.

"Well, open it!" Max implored.

Lilah ran her finger along the sealed edge and unfolded the document. It read:

Ms. DeVillier, I pose you this, as you are a worthy botanist,
to digest before the winter snows render the passes impassable.
Black seeds, white seeds in the same pod, Black seeds, white seeds,
isn't it odd?
A euphoric state these fruits impart, in your middle, below the heart.
How such a thing occurs is a riddle, at least, worthy of a closer look,
for a start?
Come to Kyrgyzstan and let's have a feast, to figure out this mystery
of the east,
In the enchanting house of Bakiyev.
Once you've found that ridiculously hot pepper, of course.

She read it through again and handed it to Max, who digested every word. She looked out the window at the passing tea plantations south of the airbase for three minutes while Max stared at the telegram, confused.

"This is from Bakiyev," he said, stating the obvious. "Why is he writing this to you?"

"Sounds like he needs a botanist to do some botany," she said. "Strange about the black and white seeds. I've never seen that. Maybe some sort of hybridization, but no one has ever cross-bred *pubescens* before. Quite a riddle."

"This is saying much more than that," said Max, his frustration growing. Though his pride was affected by not being the focus of Bakiyev's machinations, he felt fresh fear that Lilah was becoming more involved, or could be.

"How does he know so much about these peppers? Their physical composition? Even the strange euphoria they're said to impart? Either he or someone he controls has access to the information or the peppers themselves. Which means his people could have gotten to the village of Dostuk and forced someone there to divulge information, or Gasanov is conspiring with him. Either scenario is not a good one for us if we plan to sneak into Kyrgyzstan. Nor for those villagers. We have no allies, even among the people we're trying to help."

"Max, we're talking about chiles," Lilah said. "They could have bought them in the market. Let's just go and see what we can find out. What can they do to us?"

Max looked directly at Lilah. "Two of his men blew up my store. Then kidnapped Gasanov. In plain sight, in America. They followed us to Louisiana and invaded your home. They work for a known criminal. They've made it clear that you are somehow part of their plan. Followed us to India and stalked us in Khari Baoli. Now he invites you for tea?" The strain began showing in Max's voice.

"Well, we've never heard what Bakiyev's actual intentions are until now," she said. "Finding that misogynistic blowhard general wouldn't have been too hard since he's taking up all the oxygen surrounding the Naga Jolokia. Perhaps all Bakiyev's goons wanted to do was give me the note. But they keep getting stymied by you. Maybe they think I'll be easier to deal with. There's no threat in his cute poem, and first, he's got to find us. Doesn't it make you want to solve the puzzle, Max? There is a groundbreaking discovery to be made. Our staying involved increases the chances for a better outcome. Gasanov or not, don't you want to help those people in that small village, in Dostuk?"

Max stared out the window as endless manicured rows of tea faded across the shallow horizon. Lilah was right, and fearless. She analyzed situations quickly. His fear of outcomes he could not control and concern over her safety, he knew, could be clouding his perspective. But what would Boris and Vlad do when they were all in the same room? And what was Gasanov's role in the whole thing? What kind of monster was Bakiyev? Mountains of doubt again loomed large in his consciousness.

He sighed deeply, thinking how absurd the whole scenario appeared. "Raj, this must all sound ridiculous to you." He was riding in the front seat, respectfully quiet.

"It sounds like a fine adventure to me, and you are the perfect people for it," Raj said, still facing forward. "The Bonnie and Clyde of the chile world. You will be legends in the Ring of Fire, and people will tell stories about you in cantinas all over the world. It is a tale worthy of a book. Certainly, a Bollywood epic. Imagine the dance scenes!"

Max smiled and shook his head, but Lilah could read his uncertainty. "Look, we're here in the farthest corner of India, and we're going to find those Jolokias where they grow naturally, which is the most important part of this thing, not just how hot they are. How silly. Let's have this experience and figure out our steps afterward." She put her hand on his.

Max looked over at Lilah, and her face was calm, reassuring, firmly in the present. The fact that she placed a high value on their partnership and togetherness broke the cloud of his confusion.

"You're right," he said, "Let's go find some roadside food first."

Raj relayed their desire to the driver, who nodded and replied in broken English, "Seven Sisters Dhaba. We go now. Best dhaba in Tezpur region."

Dhaba was the Indian term for a roadside food joint, Max's preferred class of venue in every country. Outside of Tezpur, between the city and the Brahmaputra, the tea plantations gave way to rice paddies in the flat riverine terrain, fed by the yearly monsoon floods. Rice was indelibly part of the landscape here for all recorded history, even before, as wild rice was first domesticated in the regions between India, China, and Burma ten thousand years ago. They plied country roads built on berms and levees above a flooded landscape, with groups of farmers working the paddies in cotton pants rolled up to the knee. Raj relayed from the driver that the monsoonal floods deposited a bounty of nutrients and river fish that lived in the paddies through the seasons, regenerating the rice fields over thousands of years. They were en route to a particular dhaba specializing in the famed river fish of Assam, the *chital.* Called a clown knife fish in the west, chital resembled the delicate and flavorsome Nile perch. The place was also widely known for its preparation of the catfish of the region, called *hilsa.*

They came upon a small collection of buildings erected on stilts in the rice paddy along a remote backcountry track. Glowing with light in the rice paddy mists, they were connected to the dirt levee road by a bamboo bridge, and the car pulled up in front of the gangway to deposit them.

"Raj, please tell the driver to join us," said Lilah. "We want his tips on what to eat. If he's agreeable, of course."

Though the restaurant sat in three feet of water, it looked like an island oasis, perched on bamboo stilts and built of bamboo poles, teakwood floors, and woven bamboo wall panels. Wood and bamboo comprised everything, even the dinnerware, light fixtures, and the roof of thatched bamboo leaves. A covered veranda extended from the building's exterior, and every piece of wood had been lacquered and polished in yacht-like sheen. Along another bamboo gangway, a series of six small huts teetered on poles above the water, exclusive private dining rooms. It was the in-between time from lunch to dinner, and still, the place buzzed with energy.

As they crossed the bamboo bridge, their driver trotted up to join them, smiling. He looked decidedly more Tibetan than Indian, and he and Raj spoke briefly. Raj then turned to Max and Lilah.

"This is Maru, from the Jingpo people of Arunachal Pradesh, the province bordering Tibet. He thanks us for inviting him and wants you to know how excited he is to dine with us."

Lilah clasped her hands in greeting as they exchanged names. Max and Maru sealed the introduction with comical bows and a high five.

"Maru says the fish here is the best in the entire region, and there are numerous ways it can be prepared," said Raj. "He says he hopes you can tolerate spicy food. Most of the British tourists who come here cannot."

Max laughed. "Please let him know that Miss Lilah here is a witch who uses chiles in her potions and that we are protected by her spells from the things that British tourists are not." After listening to Raj,

Maru stopped and regarded Lilah with wary respect, opting to stay a few paces further behind her.

Before entering the restaurant's side door, they paused to view the rice paddies, stretching in every direction. Paths crisscrossed a patchwork maze of reflective green fields, trod upon by women carrying stuffed bags of freshly cut rice shoots. Others waded through the paddies in calf-deep water, planting new ones. The flat, humid terrain was decidedly reminiscent of southern Louisiana and pepper country. On the dhaba's expansive rear deck sat a hundred potted plants, a farm on stilts. Many had green and red fruit of varying shapes and sizes.

"It's a pepper farm, just for this restaurant," Max said. "How deliciously fitting, since all these flooded fields are used to grow rice."

Maru identified the chiles they passed as they walked the potted rows. Long, thin *Akashi* and jalapeno-like *Kajari* peppers, tiny and fiery *Dhanis* and *Mulakus*, fat black *Krishnas,* and string-bean *Balijuris.* Indian cooks can use four different treatments of peppers in the same dish. They begin by frying dry chiles in hot oil to set the base heat, and during cooking, add helpings of powdered chiles, spoonfuls of pepper puree, or slivers of fresh ones. This chile alchemy breeds incredibly complex and layered flavors. The potted peppers represented a tantalizing cornucopia for a single establishment and fueled Max's appetite, though there were no signs of Naga Jolokias.

"Let's give it a try," he said.

They swung open the main door, and after requesting a private hut, were escorted toward a side door to traverse the floating gangway. Passing a pair of swinging kitchen doors, Max poked his head inside, guided by the smells and sounds of a busy culinary operation. On a long table, red, green, and purple chiles were being deseeded and chopped into small cubes, then mixed with other ingredients before being rolled into white dough circles. A woman in a red bandana mixed the ingredients of neon-red chutney in a huge bowl, the air around her thick with spice and mustard. To the left sat a broad, steaming wok, bubbling with boiling oil, and through the cloud of smoke and steam reached a hand, dropping thick cuts of spice-dusted fish into the crackling liquid. Max inhaled deeply, relishing the smells and sounds of a kitchen firing on all cylinders. The fryer man gave Max a gold-toothed smile and enthusiastic double thumbs-up, which was returned as he ducked back out the door. Anticipation caused his palms to sweat. Heading down the suspended walkway, they were led to their cabana, where they slid around a cushioned teakwood table, expectant of a new dining adventure. Afternoon light spilled through open windows overlooking the horizon of rice and humid mist.

A waiter appeared and spoke in a local dialect to Maru, who in turn said, "I request for best fish and some other things. Good?" he signaled, with two thumbs up. They nodded in the affirmative.

Speaking through Raj, Maru explained that the chiles growing in the pots went into various well-known dishes of the Seven Sisters, like the sauce for the fried *hilsa*, the Pudina mint chutney, and the filling for the Burmese dumplings, called *hoentey*. They would be served a traditional rice beer called *nogin apong*, brewed with thirteen medicinal herbs by the women of the *Mishing* tribe of Assam.

First came the apong, served in a large ceramic pitcher. As he poured, Maru explained some of the traditions surrounding the white, cloudy brew. In timeless rituals, Mishing men consumed apong in the nude because consuming it "reveals the naked truth." Many Mishing families resulted from elopements due to drinking apong, and such unions were customary in the culture.

"Don't have too much, Max!" said Raj. "I told you India might get a hold on you, and this Apong could just seal it." Hearty laughter followed as they toasted with their traditional clay cups. The drink was not bitter or sweet, but slightly tangy and not overly alcoholic, almost like coconut water with a lime kick. It went down smoothly, and they ordered another pitcher before the food began to arrive.

The server began with the Burmese-inspired buckwheat dumplings, hoentey. From the *Bodo* tribe, the river people, he explained the dish to Maru, who presented it to Raj, who then described it to Lilah and Max. Every arriving platter required this lengthy but essential communication trail, which got more comical as the apong settled in and the afternoon wore on. The steamed hoentey were stuffed with a colorful mélange of chopped chiles from the pots outside, along with garlic, ginger, onion, crunchy turnip, and crumbly local cheese. These were served with a dipping sauce of crushed red Balijuri chiles, raw tomato, ginger, garlic, rice vinegar, and red onion, an Assamese salsa that instantly made noses run.

Next arrived a deep platter of golden Brahmaputra River catfish cutlets, the hilsa, dusted with turmeric and caraway seeds and fried in mustard oil. The server spooned a sauce made from mashed coriander root, garlic, and Dhani chiles with lime juice and brown sugar over the fried fish. It paired perfectly with the slight tang of the rice beer. Sweet, spicy, and savory at once, Lilah wiped her brow and proclaimed it delicious far beyond any catfish she'd had in Louisiana.

The highlight, saved for last, was chital, served on a teak platter. The small filets had been marinated in ground mustard seed paste, fennel, and cumin, wrapped in banana leaves with shaved coconut and fresh green chiles, then steamed for half an hour. It was served with heaping mounds of white rice and Pudina chutney made from crushed mint, ground black Krishna chiles, garlic, and ginger. They peeled open the dark green banana leaves and received a burst of pungent, peppery steam. Dark and minty chutney dressed the steamed fish perfectly with the Krishna chile heat, adding balance. Despite the recent flamethrower-like chile assault on his mouth, Max was able to relish the unique combination of coconut, mustard, and chiles as he swabbed a perspiring brow with his napkin. Side dishes of cubed eggplant in a sweet chile sauce and mustard-whipped mashed potatoes with diced green chiles followed. For Max and Lilah, these were utterly new flavor combinations that they consumed with healthy drafts of rice beer.

Enjoying his feast, Maru watched Max and Lilah's reactions throughout the repast. They used the chutneys and chile sauces liberally and concluded the long, pepper-laced meal, red-faced and happy.

Once they finally pushed their plates away, he asked, "You like Assamese food?"

"If this is roadside food, I'm going to become a trucker," said Max, which, when interpreted by Raj, caused Maru to crack up uncontrollably, his body jerking with laughter. Being far off main highways, the Seven Sisters was not a trucker destination, confusing the Jingpo man.

"If this is roadside food, I'll buy you a truck," Lilah chimed in.

Interpretive laughter ensued. They drank apong in their private bamboo casita, toasting many things as the sun lowered on the western horizon. The remarkable vision of sunlight shimmering on the rice paddies, silhouetting the returning farmers at the end of their long day, filled Max and Lilah with a keen awareness of the place. Being near the origins of tea and rice and Jolokias infused the experience with history, where thousands of years of isolated pastoral life had influenced the foods and cultures.

Maru ferried the crew toward their lodging in nearby Tezpur, the informal Hotel Kalash. After a short conversation with the driver, Raj turned from the front seat and said, "Hotels in this part of India are funny about nonmarried couples. When checking in, it may be better to use a married name like the Khojakarta given to you by Rahul in Varanasi. If they ask why your passports don't reflect that name, inform them that you only recently got married and are on your honeymoon in India."

"Sounds like fun," said Lilah. "What do we do about the fact that we're not going to be sharing a bed? We are here on business. For the most part."

"I'll bunk with Max, and you can have your own quarters Lilah," said Raj. It was a simple solution, leaving Max a blinking bystander.

They soon arrived on the outskirts of Tezpur, known throughout India as the "City of Blood."

"'Teza' means 'blood' and 'Pura' means 'city,'" Raj said. "A mythological battle between the gods Shiva and Krishna took place here, which drenched the region in blood. It is believed that the entire world would have been destroyed if not for the intercession of the three-faced Lord Brahma. A monument to the event is built atop Agnigarh Hill, overlooking the Brahmaputra. Enormously powerful."

After Maru deposited the trio at the Kalash, Max and Lilah were, as forewarned, grilled on their marital status by the skeptical, conservative hotel manager, Mr. Ali Ahmed. "How have you come by the name Khojakarta? It is not a typical American name."

"Mr. Khojakarta, thank you, which means 'pathfinder' by the way," Max said. "We took the name together in Varanasi when we were blessed by the *Kashi Naresh* of the temple Annapurna Devi Mandir, to who we are dedicated. He's the head guy there, by the way."

The man was suspicious. "And what is the prayer of your devotion to Annapurna?"

Lilah moved in front of Max and looked Ahmed directly in the eye, at his height. "*Oh, Annapurna, you are always full, complete, and perfect. You are the energy of the beloved Lord Shiva. For the attainment of perfection in wisdom and renunciation, please give me your nourishment.*" Ahmed raised his thick eyebrows and gave a begrudging nod. Satisfied, he handed over the keys. Max shook his head as they moved to the stairs.

"I saw it on a wall at the Annapurna temple and liked it," Lilah said with a wink, "and it seemed like a good thing to memorize. Looks like I was right, Mr. Khojakarta."

As they made their way to their third-floor rooms, Raj turned to Max and Lilah and said, "My friends, I think we have accomplished our goals here in Assam, and more. I'll be taking an early train tomorrow back to Jaipur and my business. You have more adventures ahead of you in Nagaland and a good host in the young scientist, Jahnu. I hope the rest of your journey is a rewarding experience and you find what you seek. Please come and visit me in Jaipur, and we will see the sights."

"Are you sure, Raj?" asked Max. "We'd be pleased to have your company in Nagaland."

"I'm sure it would be interesting, especially with you two. But Ambika awaits my return."

"Understood," said Max, extending his hand. "You have been a superb guide and excellent company, my friend. We will have more delicious adventures together." They shook hands and then hugged.

As they did, Raj slipped something cool and round into Max's hand "A Shiva lingam stone for you, my friend. To fortify your will on your life's journey." It would find a home in his voodoo amulet pouch, Max decided.

Lilah gave Raj a full embrace. "You are the best chaperone I've ever had, Raj. You can escort us anytime. Thank you for opening my eyes to India. See you again."

Raj looked her in the eyes. "You have a kind soul and adventurous spirit, Miss DeVillier. I am glad you and Max are together on this adventure, and whatever adventure lies beyond it. Be well!"

Max arose at six the next morning as Jahnu, their Nagaland host, was scheduled to fetch them at eight. He wanted to catch the sunrise at the spot where Brahma saved the world and used the opportunity for a jog up the fabled hill. One part of their journey had concluded, but Max felt distinctly unsatisfied with the results. A foray into the countryside loomed, finding the Naga Jolokia in the wild, exploring with Lilah at his side. Raj had already gone, departing silently before sunrise. From the hill's summit, he enjoyed a view of the mighty Brahmaputra River and the entire city of Tezpur, its twinkling lights diminishing before the rising day. Ornate statuary depicting the momentous bloody battle of gods ringed the red-painted circular amphitheater atop the summit, and the utility of there being so many deities in a culture with vastly varying ethnicities dawned upon Max. *Thirty-three million gods*, he thought, *allowed for a lot of specialization.* The sun crested the eastern hills toward Burma, igniting the broad river in shafts of gold, and it was impossible not to feel the pure ancientness of the place. To the south, the climbing peaks of Nagaland lay shrouded in mist and clouds, their pull magnetic.

Max and Lilah met before the hotel at eight, where Jahnu was already waiting with his tiny sedan, a Tata Safari. He had three days of leave from his military duties and was eager to get home to his village and family.

"The entire village has heard about the important Americans I am bringing home," he said proudly. "My family is preparing a feast as we have many relatives in Khonoma, and they have accepted your offer to assist in the preparation. They have asked us to forage for some of the ingredients on our way."

With six hours of highway time ahead, Max retreated into his thoughts. He pondered how two chiles from across the world got to separate places in Asia and traveled overland to the rich biological paradise of northeast India, then randomly collided to create a super-chile that represented headhunters, serpents, and scared away ghosts. It was undoubtedly one of the most fascinating stories in all of pepperdom.

If it could happen here, it could happen elsewhere, he thought. *Perhaps along the Silk Road in Kyrgyzstan. What a coup to discover a new, unique type of chile hidden for hundreds of years in isolation. Just like the Jolokias here in Nagaland and Assam. It's like I'm being prepped for the real pepper journey, which lies ahead, over the mountains.*

The challenge of unraveling a great mystery was intoxicating and seductive, as was his traveling companion, working associate, and passionate pathfinder partner. He turned to look at Lilah, staring out over the Brahmaputra's marshes. Her hands were folded in her lap, and she breathed in the moments slowly and deeply, turning the passing beauty into a waking, backseat meditation. Her kurta collection was growing, and she wore shimmering turquoise with white embroidery and trim, round Jackie O glasses, and hair pulled back in a ponytail. *She could be at home anywhere across the globe, a natural citizen of the world,* he thought. *I bet she'd love Laguna.*

A future lay hidden in mystery over the Himalayas, and he could not even begin to play out scenarios in his mind. To adopt a phrase of Lilah's, he realized he just had to "lean in and let go."

Max felt more at ease knowing he had an intelligent, quick-thinking, and willing partner on the quest who was fully committed. They would either uncover secrets in the Naryn Valley or would not, and they simply needed to follow their instincts and whatever information they gathered to the source. Together. *She seems to think I'm okay.* His mind journeyed back to California, to his store, factory, partners, and Gus. *Gotta call California from the airport, check on things.* He needed to prepare a report on his India experience for Chuck DeWindt. Was the Naga Jolokia a hybrid? *So many unknowns.* He thought about new hot sauces. *Tezpur Tears? Naga Warrior? The Headhunter? Holy Shiva? Maybe not Holy Shiva. Don't want to offend the Hindu folks.* He pondered whether the Australian, Roy Fergus, was making his way to a dead-end in Laos.

His thinking turned to what the future might hold after Kyrgyzstan revealed itself. If they came out the other side. *What if Lilah was my partner in business? It would certainly up our game to have a botanist and agronomist on staff. Partner, hmmm. What kind of partners?*

Max shook his head to clear the noise inside. He looked again to his left, where Lilah sat with closed eyes, letting the breeze from a half-opened window fan her wavy hair. *How does she stay so calm?* The air was humid, and the warm breeze cathartic. Twangy Indian music played on the radio while Jahnu hummed along. They were far away from anywhere and going farther still.

Four hours later, they passed through Nagaland's largest city, Dimapur, heading south. Ahead of them, the green Naga hills backed up to humid six thousand-foot peaks that spanned the horizon. A manageable two-lane highway became a windy, steep track heading into the mists of a mountainous beyond, where villages clung to distant hilltops. Groves of broadleaf tropical trees shared the steep hills and deep valleys with evergreens, giant ferns, and some two dozen distinct bamboo types. Hundreds of varieties of orchids hid in the groves along with abundant fruit and nut trees, the most in the world. Elephants, leopards, jackals, bison, wild boar, eagles, and deer roamed freely. So did giant monitor lizards and the king cobra. The powerful energy of ancient, shared cultures and primeval nature existed everywhere.

As they approached the state capital, Kohima, Jahnu related some of the area's history as the Angami Naga tribe's homeland. "There are sixteen tribes in Nagaland, and our people have been warriors throughout our history, which goes back seven hundred years," he said. "The Angami were never conquered, even by the British, though they tried for fifty years. And yes, my forefathers were headhunters. It was how we documented our victories over other tribes during conflicts. Keeping a row of skulls on your walls definitely commands respect. When the British finally arrived in 1879, after signing a truce, tribal conflicts decreased, and headhunting was outlawed, as were the tattoos that identified the headhunters. But sometimes it still happened, even up until the 1940s, and some tribal elders like my grandfather still have the face tattoos."

Jahnu maneuvered them through the warren of streets in the center of the city. "We need to make a stop at the open market here in Kohima, Keeda Bazaar, and pick up some silkworms for dinner." It wasn't only the "for dinner" part that caught Max's attention. He and Lilah looked at each other in the same "*What the hell did he just say?*" moment.

They parked a few blocks from the market, eager to stretch their legs after five hours of highway and winding roads. Tents filled with eager shoppers lined both sides of the street.

"Keeda Bazaar means 'insect market,'" Jahnu told them, "and people every day from all over Nagaland, Manipur, and Assam come for its delicacies." As they moved through the crowds, an array of insect and reptilian life was offered for consumption, and even the worldly Max was astonished at the display.

Different stalls specialized in various delicacies. One displayed hornets' honeycombs with their larvae still in place, ready to be picked out for frying, as pissed-off hornets still buzzed around them. Dry branches coiled with pink woodworm larvae were proffered by a pair of Angami twin sisters. Stands with dozens of flat baskets holding tadpoles, scorpions, and eels and buckets of snakes did a brisk business. Frogs were packaged like goldfish in plastic bags, destined for someone's cooking fire, and competing women scooped snails by the pound. Fat silkworm larvae tried to jump from their bamboo platters, only to be flicked back inside by their masters.

Jahnu located the silkworm stand run by an Angami relative, selecting full pounds, sequestered with cocoons. He also chose a dozen strips of dried eel.

"Anything you want to pick up?" he asked Lilah, completely serious. "No, I think I'm good for today," she said, thinking, *Just another day in Nagaland.*

At the non-comestible end of the market, she made an indulgent purchase: a beautifully embroidered bodice called a *kanchadi*, worn by the Ribari women of Gujarat, full of colored yarns and tiny mirrors sewn into the patterns. Light glinted off the clothing as she lifted it, and as she moved, Max could not help but imagine on her. *That will look amazing,* he thought, as she held it up to her torso. *I'll have to break out my pointy shoes when she wears it.*

They returned to the car and headed west up into the hills toward Khonoma village. Jahnu craned his neck, looking off into the bush on either side of the small car, attempting to locate something specific as they wound up the steep valley. Eventually, he stopped at a turnout that marked a creek running down from the hilltops.

"This is a good spot," he said and got out of the car. Grabbing a machete from the trunk, he bounded into the forest. Max and Lilah followed reluctantly at first, then ducked into the rainforest after him. Jahnu followed a wildlife path along the creek heading up the valley as the canopy thickened above, the sun now barely reaching the ground. Along the banks, hundreds of fiddlehead ferns hid in the half-light.

"Max, you have a knife, right?" Jahnu said. He then gestured to the ferns along the path. "Here's one for you, Lilah. Choose the fern stalks that have yet to unravel. They are the sweetest and most moist and curled up, are easier to cook." They harvested the curly fern tops for fifteen minutes, leaving them in a pile by the trail for packing into Jahnu's bag. Then, they ascended from the creek's ravine, hiking to where the canopy was less dense. They walked as Jahnu scanned the trees for a quarter-mile.

"There," he said, pointing. "Elephant apples."

He scrambled up into a tree with branches no more than a few inches in diameter. Soon, he was tossing down round fruit the size of grapefruit that bounced off the ground. Picking them up, Lilah discerned that their outsides were brittle, like a nutshell.

"Too hard for the other animals to get through, so they are favored by elephants, hence the name," called out Jahnu. "Tart and delicious!" A dozen of these went into another bag.

Not far off, Max called out. "I think I found something!"

Jahnu and Lilah followed his voice to where he crouched, twenty feet up in the top boughs of a broad-limbed tree. Green and gold fruit the size of russet potatoes hung individually on long, thick stems from its branches.

"Starfruit!" said Max proudly. "And there's ripe ones. Shall I pick some?"

"Absolutely, and a good find," Jahnu said. "Get a dozen. We will need them for one of tonight's chutneys. All we need now is *kothal*, bamboo shoots, and banana flowers."

Native to India and used in a host of its dishes, the kothal tree, or jackfruit, is ingrained in the culture, its wood prized for carving religious icons. Ayurvedic practitioners hail its many healing benefits, and it has a reputation for tasting like a blend of pineapple, mango, and heart of palm. They climbed further up the winding road as Jahnu scanned the treetops, looking for the jackfruit trees' telltale yellow limbs.

"Got one," he said, and out they climbed to forage. He led them through the brush to an area where the trees grew taller, and soon they stood before a twisted, knobby tree with broad, green leaves. Spiked oblong fruit the size of footballs dangled from its smaller branches. Jahnu put on gloves and slung a large cloth sack over his shoulder before scrambling up to reach the fruit, where he removed four with quick cuts from his machete. The jackfruit immediately began to ooze a thick, white latex, and he wrapped them in strips of cloth before putting them into his shoulder bag. The bag emitted a musky, wild animal smell when Lilah opened it to inspect the strange crop.

"Whoa," she said. "That is some potently pungent fruit. Can't wait to try it!"

As they made their way back toward the creek and its shaded gulley, Jahnu led them towards a stand of vivid green bamboo, some of the stalks fifty feet high.

"This type is called *vapuu* and preferred for eating because of its soft, sweet core." He knelt at the base of one stalk, using his hands to clear the carpet of yellowed leaves, where his work exposed young shoots of bamboo, purple and gold in their newness. Flipping open his blade, he used its serrated edge to saw through the new growth, separating a dozen from their bases. "We call these *khorisa*, the new shoots, and ferment, pickle, steam, and fry them. Grandfather pickles them with the Naga chiles in rice vinegar, and they're delicious if you can stand the heat."

Last on the list were the banana flowers, and they found the tropical trees growing in protected small groves where the wind could not shred the broad leaves. Ten-foot-long stalks burst out from the main trunk, with bunches of green bananas dangling below, reachable by hand from the ground. At the base of each fruit cluster, a bright purple conical flower hung, a foot long. The purple petals of the central flowers were dying off at the top, exposing bunches of tiny yellow flowers the size of wooden matchsticks.

"The little yellow flowers all become bananas," Jahnu explained, "and are loaded with natural sugars. Extremely sweet." Six of these purple cones he removed by machete and placed in another bag. With their foraging complete, the trio returned for the final climb to Khonoma.

They came across groups of adults and children carrying rifles and machetes, hoisting bags containing their efforts' spoils along the climbing road.

"Imagine living in a place where you could forage for so much of what you eat," mused Lilah. "Those places are disappearing, but life goes on here. How remarkable."

"Northeast India is unique in this way," replied Jahnu, "as is much of Southeast Asia. Our remoteness has certainly played a factor. However, population growth and corporate farming started changing that. In Nagaland, only ten percent of the forests are under federal management. The rest are controlled by local communities. When clearcutting of the forests by outside interests began to degrade our woodlands, we pushed back. When overhunting began to affect the bird and animal populations, we collectively agreed to limit the numbers each community could take. Sustainability means survival here. My village is not far now."

They rose farther into the green hills and, rounding a corner, were greeted with a breathtaking display. A thousand terraced rice paddies colored yellow and green dotted the mountain valley's bottom, a quarter-mile wide, giving way to lush woodlands that reached six thousand feet. Moist clouds crawled over the mountaintops, spilling into the valley before dissolving in the afternoon sun. Above, a village clung to a steep hill, the road they were on winding up to meet it. Jahnu pulled to the side so Max and Lilah could savor the view. They exited the car to the sound of chirping birds and waterfalls churning in the distance. Tall bamboo, giant ferns, and broad fronds of banana lined the valleys, and mist hung over the terraced paddies below, shimmering in the light.

"The Angami of Khonoma is one of only a few tribes who utilize terraced farming, a carryover from our Burmese rulers ages ago," said Jahnu. "Burma is just a few valleys away. Our village is seven hundred years old, and this valley has been farmed in terraces for as long as anyone can remember, even before. Three thousand people live in the village, which has six hundred homes and many extended families." They sat for fifteen minutes, silently absorbing the timeless view. Jahnu appeared to be enjoying it just as much, returning home from living in military barracks and the pompous General Chatterjee.

"There are dozens of tribes in this part of Nagaland alone, all speaking different dialects. Some of them still can't understand each other. But what is unique is that several do not have a word for 'hello.' The greeting is best interpreted as 'Have you eaten?' Which in my estimation makes for a much warmer encounter, anyway," Jahnu said.

As Max breathed in the air, the unmistakable aroma of growing cannabis wafted over them, part of the lush valley's elixir.

"Ingesting cannabis carries no stigma here in eastern India," Jahnu said, reading Max's reaction. "We've been cultivating it for thousands of years. Here it is called *ganja*, as you may have heard. Many people grow it, and many more people consume it ceremoniously, without fear of reprisal. We feed the plants to aggressive male hogs to keep them calm, which works quite well. It's part of life here."

A half mile before the village, they came upon a sturdy gate announcing their arrival in Khonoma, a massive triangular wood pediment perched atop huge stone blocks on either side of the narrow road. A monument on the road's side listed villagers who had perished while fending off the British in the Battle of Khonoma, the legendary resistance that lasted for fifty years.

The last stretch of road skirted the hillside as it climbed into the village proper, six hundred dwellings covering the crest of an entire hill. People were scattered along the road, ferrying baskets of items foraged from the nearby forests; fruits, nuts, herbs, chiles, birds, and small animals. A few carried long bamboo tubes six inches in diameter balanced against shoulders, the traditional method of transporting water. Dirt road gave way to cobblestones in the terraced village, where many homes had stacked stone foundation walls and steep block stairs. Narrow walkways threaded between the small one- and two-story houses, crafted of wood, bamboo, and tin roofs to funnel frequent rains. Every dwelling displayed a garden inside a fenced front yard, no matter how small, where flowers poked out of window boxes, and potted yellow orchids and purple agapanthus spilled color from every corner. Trellises spanned many of the rooftops, built for setting wide bamboo-grass baskets in the sun to dry herbs and chiles of an assortment of colors. The village was indeed old, but it looked and felt fresh and alive, cared for by generations of Angami. There were no stores or retail establishments, and people waved and called out to Jahnu as he passed. Winding up through the village, they reached the hill's crest, where the road ended, and only a few houses sat.

They parked alongside a terraced wall atop which sat a cluster of dwellings, Jahnu's family compound. Potted flowers lined the walls, splashes of red and yellow and orange. Purple turmeric flowers and pink rhododendrons completed the tropical display. Shouldering their forage bags and market purchases, they ascended a stone stairway cut into the foundation wall, emerging at the edge of a courtyard ringed by several structures. Numerous extended-family compounds like this, called *khels*, made up the village. Rust patina covered the tin roofs, where smoke smelling to Max like chiles curled from open vents. Every dwelling showed potted flowers and herbs in neat rows along walls and every available flat surface. Small cherry trees sporting pink blossoms were patronized by a cloud of eager honeybees, and vines of squash and cucumbers climbed beams and trellises. Stacked wood stood ready for the cooking fires, and clothes dried on lines strung between walls.

Max felt he was entering people's lives somewhere back in time, which he was, realizing the setting had been the same for centuries. The largest of the courtyard's structures, two stories high, was designed with two massive beams crossed over the front. The beams had been adorned with a series of painted tribal symbols, looking more Polynesian than Indian.

"These crossed beams are added to homes in Nagaland that have hosted a wedding," said Jahnu, "and my older brother and sister had their ceremonies in this square. It also means that you have hosted feasts for the village at least twice. My family loves to cook, no matter how many guests."

A colossal log drum sat in front of the primary home, a hollowed tree trunk three feet in diameter and eight feet long, supported on stone braces. Its exterior was covered with hand-carved tribal symbols, images of skulls prominent among them. Jahnu explained that every village in Nagaland held one of the ancient drums to warn other villages in time of danger.

"Up to six men beat this drum in a rhythmic, concerted effort. Hearing the deep 'boom' of these drums echoing down the valleys is very powerful," he said, "and these days does not happen very often. Only on ceremony days. It is the sound of the past."

They stood in the small square's center, taking in the setting. Wisps of cloud grazed the green mountaintops surrounding the hamlet. On the patio of one of the houses, a woman sat on the ground facing a simple loom attached to hooks on a wall. Her legs stretched out under the lines of spun cotton she wove together in stripes of simple black and white and red. She looked to be in her sixties and wore black hair in a long ponytail. Pots of growing lemon balm, coriander, and basil surrounded her. Seeing the guests, she merely bowed her head and continued working.

"My mother is weaving the traditional Angami shawls worn by the women, called a *lohe*, and the *mekhala*, the sarong worn around the waist by the men," explained Jahnu. "They hand-pull the string from local cotton dyed with natural pigments, and each garment takes four to six days. And that is in between working in the rice paddies, looking for food, and cooking. Each tribe has its own pattern, which is a source of identity and immense pride. Come and meet my father. He'll be at the fire."

Jahnu led them underneath the ceremonial crossed beams, where he slid open a pair of bamboo-framed doors covered in bamboo thatch. Everything was bamboo. Inside they encountered a room with a packed dirt floor bordered by benches on three sides. In the middle sat a setup for preparing tea, where four bamboo tubes stuck out of a mound of glowing coals, and a half-dozen low stools surrounded the small fire. A dark, shirtless man in a tribal sarong crouched before the apparatus, and when the doors opened, he stood to face his guests. He could have been sixty or eighty, with his frame wiry and heavily bowlegged. Boar tusks pierced his earlobes, protruding from half-inch-round holes. The tusks curved up and forward, with all except the points wrapped in red string, and bobbed and shook as he moved. He opened his arms and grinned, showing a patchwork of ivory, gold, and missing teeth.

"This is my father, Kriyo Angami, one of our tribe's elders."

Jahnu's father bowed to them, then shook Max's hand with both of his.

"*Teiso viwe!* Welcome to Khonoma! *Kedi puo mhie ga?* How are you?"

Max returned the bow and gestured to Lilah and then to himself. "We are both very well and honored to be in your home and your village, Kriyo." Lilah followed with a bow, hands pressed together in greeting.

Kriyo then stood before Lilah, taking both of her hands in his. She was half a foot taller and dressed in her bright green kurta and sandals. He looked into her eyes, then up and down before speaking to his son.

"He says you must be a Bollywood actress, Lilah," said Jahnu. "That you are surely a good dancer. He loves the elaborate productions and worships the actors."

"Please tell him I am flattered and may show off my dance moves later in the evening," she said. The interpretation caused a broad smile from the man and a series of short, excited claps.

Kriyo gestured towards the low stools by the teapot. "Please, tea, sit."

Handing them a section of bamboo tube cut down to serve as a teacup, Kriyo then plucked one of the longer green bamboo tubes out of the embers. From this, he poured steaming, strong brown tea that showed a rich malty nose, each cup emitting a vertical cloud of steam in the dim space. As they sipped in silence, Max and Lilah's eyes adjusted to the room's low light. They began to make out animal skulls of various types hung randomly on the walls' upper sections. Dozens of fat-horned oxen called *mithun*, yaks, deer, tusked boar, and smiling monkeys stared back at them, lifeless. A leopard skin stretched to its six points of nose, tail, and four paws while patterned snakeskins crisscrossed the bamboo-thatch partitions. Ancient, long-barreled hunting rifles sat on racks alongside double-tipped ceremonial spears, while straight-bladed machetes called *dao* and curved hunting knives in bamboo scabbards completed the display. The dao was historically the preferred method of taking heads.

Kriyo followed their gaze with a growing smile, nodding in understanding. Jahnu interpreted as he spoke.

"For many, many generations, we have hunted here, in the forests. But now we hunt less to keep the animals alive, more food for everyone, more sustainable. Jahnu says you are a famous hunter. Hunter of plants!" He broke down laughing, with the sharp boar tusks making circles in the air as he did.

"Yes, a hunter of plants," Max replied with a smile. "Here to track and capture the fabled Naga Jolokia and show it to the rest of the world. We hear the most powerful of them may come from right here in your village."

Hearing the name caused the Angami elder to consider Max with different respect.

"Naga people are warriors. Naga Jolokia is the warrior chile, red like our people's blood, hot like a band of fierce headhunting Naga warriors. Also called *Raja Mircha*, King Chile. For many generations, we have used this in our food. My son says it came across the ocean and over mountains. Good for pickling, good for heat in sauces, good for flavor, good for strong warrior blood." He gestured to a row of jars sitting on a shelf in the bamboo wall, filled with tender bamboo shoots and once-crimson Jolokias fading in oily spiced brine.

"You take some home, yes, please, thank you. Jahnu will take you hunting! Now you see our kitchen, the *akhol gor*."

Finishing his tea, Kriyo rose and slid open another set of bamboo doors, revealing an even larger space than the tea salon. At once, aromas of cooking fat and roasting vegetables greeted them, along with the unmistakable scent of roasting chiles.

"Cooking and food are center of our culture, and this most important room," he said. Its floor was also hard-packed earth and bamboo walls. At the center of the home's structure, the roof pitched higher and had a vented vestibule at its top. Two separate cooking fires, called *chowka*, burned atop earthen platforms that held flat stones supporting iron grates. On the smaller one, pots of several sizes steamed, monitored by an ancient, white-haired woman. A collection of twenty red-beaded strands dangled from her neck, and a red headband held back her long hair. She hopped around the pots in a squat position, talking to herself and adding spices and herbs she plucked from different bowls and jars. When she saw Jahnu, she barked a command at him, and he immediately deposited the bags of bugs and eels and fruit against the wall closest to her, a rudimentary preparation area of tree trunk-section chopping blocks and shelves with ingredients.

"My grandmother," Jahnu said, tilting his head toward the spry woman.

Pans and woks sat on narrow tables, where stone mortar and pestles awaited the dried and drying herbs hung from lines strung across the room. Huge handwoven bamboo baskets were filled with rice and other dried staples, and two oil drums contained herb-fortified rice beer, which Jahnu said the Naga called *zutho,* stood in the corner.

The other, more significant fire was the main attraction, its foundation thicker and grates stronger. Above it, hung from the rafters, was a multilevel bamboo rack system for smoking meats and fish and drying vegetables and herbs. Strips of pork and game hung from the upper rack while fish were laid flat, soaking up the sweet smoke. Fat dripped from the meats, sizzling as it reached the orange coals. Below, closer to the fire, a broad, flat-woven basket sat on a bamboo-cane shelf just above the flames, charred from a life in the fumes. Three dozen halved Naga Jolokias in the basket bathed in the hot smoke, their dangerous ruby red interiors on their way to turning black. Mounds of black tea leaves surrounded the chiles, adding their sweetness to the smoke. After enveloping the chiles and desiccating the tea, the spiced white fumes rose to cure and flavor the meats above before advancing to the sky.

"The pork ribs are brushed with tamarind, brown sugar, cinnamon, and orange peel before smoking," said Jahnu. "And they've been smoking for two days. This method is a specialty of my clan and this village. We call it 'fighting fire with fire' in Angami, using the fire's smoke to release the fire hidden within the chile and infuse it into the meats."

Max watched the slow process, filled with the tingling sensation he got when he was near to the source of things, and this kitchen in

Khonoma was undoubtedly that. He was overcome by the feeling that he approached a pivotal moment in his life, arriving in the fabled Naga Jolokia's ancestral home. The tendrils of smoke massaging the menacing chiles became a potent hypnotic, and he followed them as they wrapped the meats in their ghostly wisps of Jolokia heat.

As if in a trance, he took off his shirt, stepped toward the smoldering fire of the chowka, and leaned into the stream of smoke rising from the coals and through the split Naga Jolokias and mounds of black tea. He fanned the smoke with his arms, causing it to wrap around his body and head, a native smudging. The old woman cried out in Angamese, registering danger and trying to shoo Max away from her fire, but Max only leaned in further. Lilah thought to stop him, but for a reason she couldn't identify, she did not. She soon understood Max had entered the throes of a Holy Grail moment. *Very sadhu-like of him,* she thought, *bathing in the fumes of the warrior ghost serpent chile at the end of his quest.* The room watched in silence, aware of Max's energy, his total commitment as he leaned into the smoke, performing a primeval ritual. Hollow-eyed animals' skulls stared back from the walls. He still wore the necklace of dried Bere-Bere beads he had received after a similar smokehouse experience years before in Ethiopia. Closing his eyes, he inhaled, bathing in the scent of slow-roasting peppers, animal fat, and sweet tea. Capsaicin, rendered by fire into dried airborne molecules, enveloped and permeated him.

Max tracked the inevitable sensations. It wasn't as excruciating as eating a whole Naga pepper, diminished in the wafts of smoke, but the airborne chile was tangible and vividly hot nonetheless. He felt it coat his throat and fill his nostrils, tingling with effervescent white heat, then held his breath. It reached for and enveloped his skin, creating a sizzling sensation that was more sensual than painful, infused his hair, and licked at his ears. From behind, it appeared he was actually smoldering. As he turned in a circle with his arms up to smudge his entire torso, Lilah took note of his lean body, with muscles in the right places, noticing that his nipples were hard. His skin glistened with a sheen of moisture, and she traced a trail of soft hair from his chest to belly button, continuing to parts below. She realized she licked her lips as she watched, catching herself. When he opened his eyes, water streamed out of them, and it was difficult for Lilah to tell if it was an emotional or physical reaction, or both.

Max emerged three minutes later from the fire ritual a modern-day aboriginal, cooked down to his primeval state. He managed to capture and crystalize his essence by bathing in the fire and chiles, energized, reborn, and renewed by the vaporous baptismal. Jahnu responded first, employing a very western colloquialism after capturing the moment on his smartphone.

"Wow, that was quite awesome! I got video."

Max stood between his audience and the fire, breathing heavily. His skin glowed red, and his nose ran.

"What an amazing sensation," he said, looking at Lilah. His normally hazel eyes were bright green and bloodshot, and he twitched just a bit. "The tea with the peppers is an extraordinary combination. What a burst of clarity. Chile smoke filled my lungs, generated heat from inside my chest, and the skin from my waist to my skull tingles. I'm having the mother of all capsaicin hot flashes, a standing sweat lodge. Whoa." He played the part of an obsessed chile head to the hilt, manic with excitement and realization. And Lilah respected the fanaticism she saw in Max's eyes, understanding his essential nature.

Kriyo stood with arms crossed, nodding slowly at Max. "Big ritual you make, one *anusthana*. Fire with fire, Max Chota. You one real chile sadhu."

"*Chota* means 'little' in Nagamese," said Jahnu. "I think he likes you."

Transformed by the Jolokia-smoke ritual, Max toweled off with his Jefferson Airplane t-shirt, replacing it with another from his duffle bag. After emerging from the fire, anointed by the chief of a headhunting clan as a chile prophet, customary hunger tugged at his insides. Combing back his wild, smoked hair with his hands, he looked across the ancient room. The fanatical display now passed, Jahnu's grandmother continued her preparations, assisted by his father, calling out clipped instructions. Afternoon sun filtered through the bamboo thatch walls, casting a patchwork pattern on the floor. Light collided with the wafting pepper smoke, highlighting the wisps and puffs, creating an exotic dancer in the center of the room. The thought that this same scene had played out in this place, in this village, for centuries, overtook Max's mind. The air was thick with the ancient ritual of preparing food. He heard the words again, 'fire with fire,' realizing his purpose.

"Jahnu, can we go find the chiles growing wild?" he asked, the intention palpable. "I really need to get my hands on them."

"Absolutely," said Jahnu, "we can take an afternoon walk through the valley of rice paddies to get there, chile sadhu Max Chota."

Shouldering a canvas knapsack, Jahnu guided Max and Lilah across the courtyard to a stone stairway descending between the houses. They ducked their heads under a turmeric canopy wafting scents of candied ginger, emptying onto a narrow lane below the family compound. They wended down through the village, passing weavers and basket makers working on front porches, and reached a point overlooking the rice paddies five hundred feet below, where they stopped to marvel at the expansive view. A trail snaked to the narrow valley in long switchbacks from their position, with groups of men and women carrying tools and baskets in both directions. The paddies themselves were a thousand cascading handmade walls fashioned into shallow pools of yellow and green rice stalks growing from the water, shimmering in the light. Narrow walkways crisscrossed the paddies in every direction, while a frothing creek ran down the middle, fed by the rainforests above and traversed randomly by hand-hewn bridges. A multitude of stone diversions ran from the waterway, the constant source of the paddies' water.

"The best plants that have not been picked over are on the far side of the valley, in the overgrowth between the paddies and the rain forest," said Jahnu, pointing west. "It will take us half an hour to get over there."

Lilah raised her arms and pointed her face to the sun. "Well, this just sucks, doesn't it? We have to hike from an ancient village across centuries-old rice paddies to find blazing hot wild peppers below a rain forest in a biodiverse paradise." She started down the path, swinging her arms and humming to herself. Her ease and exuberance brought smiles to both the men's faces, and Max felt a keen desire to wrap her in his arms and kiss her face. In this magical place on a chile hunt, being with her embodied the greatest joy he had known, and his skin still tingled with pepper smoke. It was a day in pepper-head paradise.

Every person they passed on their descent stopped, placed whatever load they carried on the ground, and offered the afternoon greeting of *Khinhie viwe,* with palms pressed together. Many knew Jahnu, sharing short conversations: their eyes lit up when he introduced his illustrious guests. Lilah, in particular, was greeted with deference.

Toward the end of the trail, a set of ancient stone steps carried them to the verdant valley floor. The track met the paddies, and other courses fanned out along the narrow walls in six directions, where they connected to different paths accessing thousands of plots. Each division served to create a level pond a foot deep, terracing the valley's gradual slope in innumerable pools. Various groups of families from the village had worked different paddies in the same locations for centuries. Small stone-and-thatch huts speckled the landscape, storing tools, and offering shade to rest. Jahnu chose a well-traversed track that pointed west across the valley, pitching from south to north. Palms and Nepalese alder dotted the valley, the alder historically selected for its ability to return vital nitrogen to soils depleted from centuries of harvests. Warblers, thrushes, and finches called to each other across the fields as they negotiated their way through the paddies. A log bridge crossed the creek at the valley's center, the water much more substantial and frothier than seen from above. Mist matted their hair and clung to shirts, welcome in the afternoon sun and cooling Max's pepper fire. They stopped on the bridge, which afforded views both up and down the valley. Specks of people worked in the ponds, planting or harvesting rice shoots and mending paths and walls.

"It must be nice to come home to your village and be in a place where things don't change, Jahnu," said Lilah. "It feels timeless."

"Especially from the regimentation of military life," he said, taking in a deep breath. "Little changes here. The big news in the village is when a house finally connects to the power grid. As a younger man, I could not wait to get out and live in a city. Now, I cannot wait to get back."

Following the western path to the terraced plateau's edge, they encountered a trail that crossed tall, grassed fields and led into dense brush six feet high before meeting thick rainforest.

"In there, we will find the chile bushes," said Jahnu. "It seems to favor the mottled light created by taller brush. This side of the valley gets the best sun all year long. Constant warmth and humidity along with the steady rain here are factors as well." They marched through the grasses and ducked into the overgrowth.

Lilah watched as Max and Jahnu, in hunting mode, moved gingerly through the brush. The sense of impending discovery was palpable as she sensed how exhilarated she was to uncover this mythically hot fruit growing in the wild, unique in all the world. Max spotted a splash of color a hundred yards along, telltale pods dangling to the left of the trail.

"Over there. I think we've cornered a wild Jolokia," he pronounced.

Despite the joke, he was all business. Amidst a tangle of other greenery, they found a bush five feet high and five feet wide sporting a few dozen peppers of varying ripeness, from green to bright red. Similar bushes were spread through the growth. Being late spring, the chiles were still maturing, with numerous flowers left awaiting pollination.

Lilah knelt to inspect the plant. "Two white flowers per stem with five petals and purple filaments. Like *C. chinense*. Leaves are more crinkled than flat as well. But look at the fruit. It's longer than a habanero. Not as lantern-shaped, two to three inches long. And the riper ones exhibit that very wrinkled skin as we saw in the specimens at the airbase. It's like a habanero romanced a jalapeno, a *frutescens*, and this is the supercharged offspring, not like anything I've encountered."

"So, you think it's a hybrid?" asked Max.

"Based on visual inspection, yes," Lilah responded. "Though I can't wait to get it into a lab to test the genetics. Do you know how they pollinate, Jahnu?"

"They appear to do it naturally," he said. "But in years with more insects, there are always more chiles in the wild. And these wild bushes can often be perennials, with crops year after year for a decade. Under the right conditions, some produce two crops a year, and above four thousand feet, the yields diminish. I have been observing them for many seasons since my teens. I guess it comes from my grandfather."

Max knelt beside Lilah, turning the red and green pods in his fingers, still dangling from their stems. For five long minutes, he inspected the plant, deep in thought. It was wispier than a cultivated plant, with longer branches seeking sun in the thick brush. He crumpled the waxy leaves in his hands, then stuck them in the loamy soil and pulled up a small pile, letting it fall through his fingers, noticing bits of sand and veins of clay. Worms scrambled from the light. For a wild environment, the soil was extremely healthy, with good drainage and evidence of minerality. Fetching a woven cotton bag from his knapsack, he began to pick pods of varying ripeness. The airy knit bag would hopefully keep the fruit, with its high water content, from spoiling. He then pulled out a pocket knife to cut one in half. Inside were thirty to forty off-white seeds, with veins and membrane typical of a *chinense* chile. However, the membranes themselves were significantly yellower than any habanero he had ever seen, and slick with oils. He remembered that capsaicin in its pure form was yellow. *So much heat hidden in there*, he thought. *It can't just be in the seeds and veins. Has to live in the meat and walls themselves to hold so much fire, totally permeated with capsaicin. Such a unique creature.*

Lilah watched him, awaiting his reaction.

Max stood, looking at the sky, the sun's position, the surrounding mountains, and felt the air's moisture and latent warmth. He recalled his hallucinogenic journey above the earth, tracing chiles' path across the globe, the vivid sense of isolation and lush bounty of eastern India. In his hand, he held a single red Naga chile and spoke as he pondered it.

"The evolution of this type of potential hybrid chile pepper could have occurred in several places around the world with an elevated level of biodiversity, and where both host plants' pollen could have been at the same time. The Amazon Basin certainly, where chiles originally came from, and I'm surprised it hasn't happened there. Why not, I wonder? Central America's jungles, the Andean cloud forests. Central Africa, with its humidity and rainforests and all the trade routes going around the Horn, with the global competition between Spain and Portugal. The spice islands of Sumatra. Or anywhere else in India, for that matter. But it happened here, and I would wager that the cross took place centuries ago, allowing the Naga Jolokia to develop in solitary confinement for an exceptionally long time."

He looked out across the valley and paused for a moment in thought.

"The reason? Centuries of isolation and rich biodiversity coming together. This remote region was not on any major trade routes, and their trade was with their immediate neighbors only. Direct with the Chinese. Direct with Burma and Nepal, with the kingdoms of India. While northeast India is a very biodiverse region, the trade historically was not diverse, only local. The chiles didn't travel well, so they never left. Yet they grow wild here and have for as long as anyone can remember. So, it must have happened naturally, a total incendiary fluke. But the chile seeds had to get here, and *frutescens* from India and *chinense* from China both arrived in this place, either through trade or carried by birds, and something extraordinary happened. The sun and soil and humidity and isolation caused a shift, elevating capsaicin to astronomical levels to ward off all predators, possibly even birds, or it would have spread globally from here. Adapting to these unique local conditions allowed elevated amounts of cross-pollination to occur within the isolated area and created variants in the species. It happened in the rich soil, humid bug-plentiful climate, isolated environment, and biodiverse soup of Nagaland. And we are standing in the heart of it, Ground Zero."

Lilah regarded him with genuine amazement. "So that's what's been percolating in your brain," she said.

Max kicked the dirt. "It's the romantic version, I guess, enhanced by some heavy chile hallucinations. I had a lot of time to think in the car and had to see them for myself. Your lab work may prove that it's all bullshit. But my gut senses that's how it happened."

He folded his arms with finality. "Is anyone else hungry?"

With a dozen wild Naga Jolokias in tow, the three pepper hunters made their way across the rice paddies and up the switchbacks to the Angami village, accompanied by workers from the fields. People sang songs as they ascended, trading verses. Shards of afternoon light slanted across the valley, silhouetting swallows diving for their insect feasts. The light accentuated the bright colors of chiles, set out on roofs in broad, flat baskets, laid out to dry in the afternoon sun. As they reached the family's small plaza, they encountered an elderly man sitting cross-legged before the doors of Jahnu's family home in meditation. If Kriyo was sixty or eighty, this man was ninety or a hundred and ten. He wore a heavy woven cotton sarong of traditional red, white, and black stripes. On his head was a bearskin cap with crossed boar's tusks woven into the front, and in his earlobes were inserted red shotgun casings, brass firing caps forward, filling half-inch holes. His meditative position allowed for closer inspection of the old man's face, which showed faded blue-black tattoo ink around his eyes from brow to cheekbone, down the bridge of his nose, and then encircling his mouth. A heavy beaded necklace hung to his chest, laced with tiger's teeth and a brass amulet of four skulls in a line. His ensemble was completed by a V-neck sleeveless argyle sweater vest. Hearing their approach, he opened his eyes and gave a gap-toothed smile, greeting Jahnu warmly.

"This is my grandfather, Chudi Angami," said Jahnu. "Ironically, *Chudi* means 'king of chiles' in our language. As a child, he began to eat them whole, like apples. And still does to this day. He is a legendary hunter among the Naga, and why he prefers to wear the shotgun shells as adornment. To remind us often of what we already know because he's told us all our lives." The last, he added with a wide smile. "He has been told of your arrival and wanted to greet you both. He is extremely interested in your journey. Word that our chiles may be the hottest in the world has reached the village."

Chudi, nimble for his age and just over five feet tall, stood and pressed his hands together. He then said, "*Nomoskar,*" the Angamese greeting, with a half bow. Max and Lilah did the same. His elaborate face tattoo identified the man as a one-time headhunter. Not wanting to be invasive, neither of them opted to ask the obvious question.

Seeing the inquisitiveness in their eyes, Chudi spoke to his son in Angamese.

"My grandfather wants to know if you want to see his heads," said Jahnu casually.

Lilah and Max answered together. "Absolutely. We'd be honored." Meeting a headhunter in 1999 was beyond either of their respective bucket lists.

Taking Lilah by the hand and motioning for Max to follow, he led them to a small building on the other side of the plaza. Sliding open the bamboo doors, they were introduced to a home like that of Kriyo, Chudi's son, but scaled down. A small fire of yellow coals warmed a blackened teapot in a room exhibiting the same packed-dirt floor. Animal skulls hung everywhere. Dowels were driven into the bamboo beams, and on each a human skull hung, fifteen in all. One had an arrow through its eye and out the back, while another sported bull's horns strapped to its sides. Chudi took two off the wall and handed one each to Lilah and Max. They turned them, looked into hollow eyes, and thought about the souls that once inhabited the hard domes. Closer inspection revealed the elaborate etching of symbols into the yellow bone, retelling its acquisition story. Chudi pointed to the two skulls and then to himself, nodding his admission. He then pointed to the flat, two-sided blade he had used, displayed proudly above. Nonchalantly unbuttoning his sweater vest, he exposed a leathery torso and the faded images of five different skulls on his chest, shoulders, and back.

"Officially, headhunting ended in the 1940s," said Jahnu. "But intertribal conflicts lasted into the 1960s, and some were still settled by beheadings. Taking and displaying a head was a means of establishing superiority over other tribes. It was said to increase the fertility of that tribe's harvest and the one who took it. Probably why I have four aunts and three uncles. There are more in our village and others of Nagaland, but my grandfather and his forebears took the ones you see here. It was an unwritten rule that if someone had dined in your home, you could not take their head, so people had to keep track of their guests. Christianity, of course, outlawed the practice, but ritual and history are heavily embedded in our culture, and keeping the trophies is a matter of great pride to this day. Now, we mix quite nicely with our neighbors."

Max looked at the man, imagining him as a warrior in life-and-death battles over honor or land. And that a meal with this tiny, fierce fellow could save your life. Chudi then grabbed a glass jar full of clear liquid and beckoned them to follow, exiting the small home and walking around to its rear. In terraced rows built with blocks into the hillside were an astonishing array of vegetables, herbs, and small fruit trees. Across the entire middle row were twelve Naga Jolokia bushes, perfectly manicured, fat with pods. Chudi scrambled up three levels to the plants and plucked green and red chiles off their stems, returning to present them to Max. The old man spoke in Angami, with his grandson interpreting.

"Grandfather says that these chiles have been a part of our culture for many generations. He remembers stories of the chiles from these hills being tried by people from the south, in India, who said they were too hot for humans to eat. Then by the British in the early 1800s who tried to subdue our people but failed. They shrieked and cried after eating them, unfit for survival, like their pale skin burning in the Nagaland sun, but from the inside. The Japanese did not fare much better when they invaded through Burma in the spring of 1944, attempting to defeat the British forces. They reached beyond their lines and ran out of supplies. They picked our Naga peppers, desperate for food, and ate them on empty stomachs. Many of the men were immobilized by the chiles, stopping the advance on Khonoma. Some were shot by their own officers, unable to fight. We have always known the chiles of Nagaland were powerful, and now, here you are. I have been waiting for you all my life."

He motioned for Max to try the green chile as he tossed the entire ripe red one into his mouth, popping it with his bite. He chewed the ball of fire with an impish smile, the chile's pulp covering his teeth, with no other reaction. Never one to back down, Max bit off half the green chile and waited for the onslaught, now that he knew what to expect. Its flavor was greener, obviously, and more citric. But the heat never exceeded that of a habanero, still enormously spicy but bearable as they chomped fire together. Once satisfied that Max had fully experienced the taste of the unripe chile, he offered him the glass jar full of clear liquid, called *tengizu*, a potent spirit distilled from sweet hearts of palm. Max took an obliging gulp that showed its strength in widened eyes and a hard swallow. The exercise was meant to show that the peppers' latent heat grew exponentially as they ripened, a product of the unique soil, sun, and humidity of Nagaland.

Chudi spoke to his grandson briefly and motioned for them to follow him again. "My grandfather says it's time to help with the feast," Jahnu said. "Uncles and aunts and cousins coming tonight, in your honor."

Crossing the open square, they entered Jahnu's family home again, coals still smoldering, steaming the bamboo tea bongs. A dozen adults of varying ages and sizes sat on the benches sipping dark highland tea. Some peeled fruit or crushed spices as they sipped. They dressed in a mix of traditional and modern clothing, with the red, white, and black Angami colors prevalent in thick cotton shawls and sarongs. Their conversation stopped as the Americans entered the door. Jahnu addressed them in Angamese, and as he pointed to Max and Lilah, they heard him say "Max Chota" and "Lilah DeVillier." The two special guests bowed to the group, who took turns pointing to themselves and saying their names one by one.

Jahnu then led them into the akhol gor, the kitchen. Seven additional people were spread around the room, busy with food preparation, directed by Jahnu's mother and grandmother. One woman peeled the leaves from the purple bamboo shoots they had harvested earlier, removing layers until a soft, white core remained. These she then sliced and placed in water for blanching. Potatoes boiled in blackened fire-top pots while chiles and onions chopped by deft hands with broad blades were tossed into woks for frying. Aromatic herbs were plucked from stems and placed in small baskets as the end-of-day sun shot shafts of light horizontally through the bamboo walls. Smoke and steam blended to create a sumptuous fog that softened the sounds of familial conversation.

Jahnu's grandmother fished the silkworm pods they had purchased at the Kohima market from one of the steaming pots. She placed a pile of them in a shallow basket, handing one to Max with clipped instructions to Jahnu.

"She says to remove the cocoons so she can fry them. You can have a seat over there." Max sat on a tree-trunk stool and, placing the basket on his knees, peeled the silky exteriors from their contents. Inside were the inch-long ribbed worms themselves, halted now from becoming silkworm moths. Once he had cleaned all three pounds of them, handing them back to the Jahnu's grandmother, she tossed them into a wok's sizzling oil. She added chopped chiles, garlic, ginger, and onion to these, stirring all with a wood spoon and murmuring to herself.

Jahnu's mother, free of her weaving, approached Lilah. Her long, black hair was still in a ponytail, and her Angami shawl had been traded for a t-shirt imprinted with the Hindu Lord Shiva, though she was a Christian. Taking one of Lilah's hands in hers, she used the other to point to herself. "I am Kaisa. I show you how to prepare banana flower, okay?"

Lilah nodded and was led to a pair of stools beside baskets filled with the purple banana flower pods. Peeling the pod open like an artichoke, every leaf revealed a new set of pale-yellow flowers for harvesting. Kaisa demonstrated to Lilah how to peel back the purple and yellow outer leaves to expose the fragile inner flowers. These were gently cut and removed, then blanched in lemon water. They then minced the flowers and sweet stems before putting them aside to dry.

Kaisa next brought two large mortar and pestles, setting one before Lilah and herself. She fetched metal trays from a counter across the room where two aunts prepared herbs and spices, giving one to Lilah. On it was measured piles of spices: cumin, fennel seeds, peppercorns, garlic, and ginger, which they ground into a fragrant paste in the stone bowls. With a pile of dried banana flowers and the handmade paste, Kaisa gestured for Lilah to follow her over to the fire, where two log stools awaited them. She retrieved a bowl of dark duck meat from an uncle, slick with oil and marinating in cardamom, cloves, turmeric, bay leaf, and cinnamon. She then slid the duck and spices into a wok of hot oil, hissing and popping. After five minutes, Kaisa instructed Lilah to sprinkle in the banana flowers, their sweetness locked in by the hot oil, along with a handful of chopped onion. Three minutes later, she pointed to the paste mixture, which Lilah gently spooned into the wok with the other ingredients. *Koldil Paro Manghor,* Kaisa called it, as she moved the wok to a far side of the flame and left it to simmer.

Max watched as ten family members performed various meal preparation tasks, inhaling the rich aromas filling the space. A nudge on his shoulder came from Chudi, holding a bamboo pitcher and cups with frothy liquid, *zutho*, the rice beer, which he offered to Max. In his other arm, Chudi cradled six new bamboo poles, green and about three inches in diameter. He placed these on the ground before them, along with two flat and sharp blades, mirroring the headhunting machete on Chudi's wall. He showed Max how to cut the bamboo into footlong sections enclosed at the bottom joint. When twenty of these were complete, Chudi called out to his wife, Lotha, who, together with Lilah, brought bowls of ingredients, joining the two men on stools.

"I'd like some of that rice beer, fellas," Lilah said, holding out a bamboo cup.

Chudi exposed his gap-toothed grin and obliged, refilling Max's cup on the return pass. The bowls contained minced chicken marinating in a paste of ginger, garlic, tomato, onions, and tiny green chiles. To this, Chudi added the pickled and chopped bamboo shoot, which they had seen resting with red Naga Jolokias on the shelf, tossing a few in his mouth along the way. In unison, the four of them portioned the chicken mixture onto sections of green banana leaves. After spooning some mustard oil and lemon juice atop the meat, they wrapped it in the leaves before sliding it into the bamboo tubes, called *pongsen*. Jahnu crossed the room with Max to assist in placing the natural cylinders in the fire.

Jahnu's white-haired grandmother spoke softly as she handled the bamboo cookers, and they stopped to listen as he retold her words. "My grandmother and grandfather showed me how to do this when I was a child. They said their grandparents had taught them how to use our bamboo for cooking. All I learned about our history I learned here in this place of food and family, the akhol gor." She looked up and smiled at Lilah and Max, content to be doing the same with them.

The bamboo tubes were placed end-up in the red coals and shot tendrils of steam from their tops within minutes. With their tasks complete, Max and Lilah settled in the corner of the room and sat in silence together, sipping beer while observing the extended family at work. They watched as poppy seeds were pounded into a paste with cashews and used to coat the chital clownfish in a dish called *chital posto* before frying in mustard oil. The fish then simmered in a sauce of mashed raisin, tomato, and more poppy seeds, eliciting a sweet and savory cloud.

In another wok, curly fiddlehead ferns danced in the oil, joining forces with fresh bamboo shoots, white baby potatoes, mustard greens, and whole curry leaves. An uncle mashed yellow potatoes cooked with purple onion and green chiles, which he formed into balls called *pitika*, and seasoned before frying. Sweet, meaty, orange-colored jackfruit was cubed and stirred into a yellow curry with onions, potato, garlic, and ginger. Oversize elephant apples were split and hulled, then sectioned to add to the *masor tenga*, sour fish curry with mustard seed, and dried red chiles. Eel chutney was made by pounding the market-bought dried eel into a paste with tomatoes, onions, garlic, and mashed Naga chiles. Chickpea rotis browned on flat griddles while Burmese black rice turned purple as it boiled.

The culinary tableau, utilizing all locally harvested ingredients and traditional methods combined with the efforts of an entire clan, was extraordinary, even by Max's worldly standards. Smoke and steam clouded the air as daylight faded, and the cooking fires' red coals glowed as people shuffled about, chopping, stirring, and frying.

Finally, Kaisa ordered everyone into the front salon for dinner, pouring water from a pitcher for washing hands as they passed. Fat candles flickered in holders hooked onto the bamboo walls. Around the smoldering tea coals, twenty places were set on the floor. Atop thin metal platters sat broad banana leaves to be used as plates. Bowls of rice, baskets of flatbreads, and pots of curries were carried from the kitchen and placed on the edge of the warming fire. Bamboo tubes of zutho made their way around as family members took turns serving themselves with wood spoons from the various dishes. No eating utensils were offered, as the flat roti bread was used for scooping rice and sauces off the green banana leaf platters. Max and Lilah sat on opposite sides of the family circle, smiling at each other across the room and sharing the excitement of this otherworldly place in which they found themselves.

Max's grin was loopier, as he was in a culinary paradise, laced with Naga chiles. He was offered the platter of fried silkworms first, along with their frying sauce of mustard oil, garlic, chiles, scallions, and ginger, spooning a dozen onto the banana leaves. Max took one in his fingers and tossed it into his mouth. As he rolled it around, he felt the hard, crunchy shell, breathing in the sauce's ingredients. Hot, yet not overpowering, heavy with garlic and tangy with ginger. As he crunched down on the shell, it released its warm, soft inside. Removing from his mind what it actually was, he found the combination of textures and flavors tantalizing, the amuse-bouche of the evening, and followed it with a splash of rice beer.

A tray of small bowls holding a variety of chutneys was passed. Sweet yellow starfruit and coriander leaf chutney with flecks of dried red chile and roasted tomato chutney with cinnamon. The dark and heady salt-dried eel and Naga Jolokia paste, called *Xukan machor*. Fermented soybean chutney, strong-smelling, with lemon basil, green onion, and ginger. Mashed white poppy seed chutney with ginger, mustard seed, and green chile. And a brick red chutney made from salty roasted ants and dried tomatoes, slightly crunchy. Max spooned a pool of each around his platter, dabbing his finger in them as he did.

Arriving next was a stack of the two-day chile-and-tea-smoked pork on skewers, brushed with tamarind, brown sugar, and orange peel. The layer of fat on top had a sweet, crunchy exterior, and as he bit into it, Max saw himself bathing in the same chile-smoke cloud that had perfectly cured the meat. Smoky dark chile heat partnered with savory cured meat in a wave that again made his skin tingle in memory, senses alive. Salt, sweet, fat, and fire married with the vivid spice, creating a revelatory combination of elements and deep bodily pleasure. Max could feel his taste buds sending signals through his body, which in turn released a squadron of endorphins across his system, fomenting a euphoric food high. He paused, sighing out loud, chewing with his eyes closed, meditative. While the meal carried a poetic, mystical weight for Max, everyone else was busy eating, clanking utensils, and trading platters. Atop mounds of purple rice, he spooned the jackfruit curry, savory and sweet, with a hot green chile finish. Then poppy seed-and-cashew-breaded chital fish swam in dark raisin sauce, and duck meat was scented with cumin and black pepper topped by sweet and tender banana flowers, like tiny enoki mushrooms. Sour fish curry in coconut milk with tangy elephant apple cubes had a refreshing, palate-cleansing effect. Fried potato *pitika* balls, toasty on the outside and silky in the middle, were sweetened by onion and crunchy green chile. Fiddlehead ferns and bamboo shoots arrived, crunchy with soft potato, earthy curry, and bitter mustard greens; enhanced by the salty dried eel and Naga Jolokia chutney, the dish took on extraordinary heat, like ferns on fire.

Max fanned himself, trying to breathe through his open mouth, suffering happily. Every dish became topped with a different chutney, complementing its flavors and increasing the heat factor exponentially. Across the room, Lilah wiped her brow.

One by one, the footlong bamboo tubes stuffed with chicken were passed around the circle, each person sliding the steaming banana leaf cylinder from the top. Once unraveled on the platters, the minced contents filled the room with rich aromas of coriander and lemon, the meat white and tender. Scooping it onto a flat roti, Max topped it with the red ant chutney. Pickled bamboo shoots jumped out first, numbingly hot after a week with the Naga Jolokias in vinegar.

Across the room, Lilah said, "Whoa. Serious caliente," seemingly to herself. She could see the sheen of dampness building on Max as he scooped and grinned, cross-legged in worshipful culinary bliss. His ears glowed red. His nose ran. And as he wiped his face and grinned, she realized then that she loved him, fanatical sweat and all, a perfect balance of absurd and intense.

For a solid hour, the world was all about food. Jahnu, sitting next to Lilah, asked her what she thought of the meal. She placed her platter on the ground and thought for a moment. Though they did not understand much of what she said, everyone stopped to listen.

"Jahnu, Kriyo, Chudi, and Kaisa, this is the most extraordinary culinary experience I've had in my life," she said, looking mainly at Jahnu's mother. "Harvesting the ingredients from the valleys around your magical village has connected me directly to each dish. And being part of the preparation has given me a deep respect for your family's traditions. We will never forget this meal with your family and are at peace knowing we can now keep our heads, at least in this village." She bowed to each of them from her cross-legged position as Max gave her his two thumbs up with a mouth full of food, comical in his extraordinary bliss.

Jahnu's interpretation of her words caused many approving grunts and smiling nods, while Kaisa looked down humbly. The last statement elicited laughter, slapping of knees, and Chudi's childlike grin. A bottle of the potent clear *tengizu* liquor was produced, and everyone in the circle poured themselves a bamboo cupful for a toast led by Kriyo, the village headman. He spoke for a full minute, holding his cup toward his father and mother, his wife, brothers, sisters, and children, with Jahnu quietly interpreting for Lilah. Lastly, he addressed Lilah and Max in turn. Lilah thought she heard the words *Indiana Jones*.

"He says your respect, Lilah, for our culture and traditions is rare in these modernizing times and that you are as beautiful as Aishwarya Rai, the most famous Bollywood actress," said Jahnu.

Watching from across the room, Max saw Lilah blush, embodying but embarrassed by the compliment.

"And to Max Chota," continued Jahnu, "he sees in you a great warrior, like Indiana Jones, his favorite western movie character. He says you will keep your head in whatever conflicts are to come." Twenty bamboo cups were emptied in unison and then quickly refilled. Max stood, wiping the perspiration from his brow.

"Angami family of Khonoma, we are made richer by your hospitality, especially Jahnu, our guide in Nagaland. Your country is extraordinarily beautiful and bountiful. We came here seeking the hottest chiles on the planet, but we found much more than those. Food is discovery and culture. Food is family, food is history, and you have shared all with us today. I will strive to exhibit the strength of Kriyo, your headman, and the wisdom of your elder, Chudi. One day the Naga Jolokia will be among the most famous chiles in the world. Cheers!" He toasted the two men and then the family group, his interpreted words eliciting nods and chants of "Ho!" as cups were filled yet again.

Then a powerful voice filled the room. "Wait!" it said, as all turned to see Chudi standing on bowlegged legs at the edge of the circle. "*A puwe*, I speak. Max Chota, *themma hau viwe*. This man is good man.

One big sadhu chile hunter. *Itiye to moe khan sathi ase.* We are friends now. *A ungu niowe konhd.* I wish to see you one day again."

He walked over to Max, looking up at him, clasped him by the forearm, then raised their cups to drink, joined by all. Then he removed his traditional cotton sari and wrapped it around Max's waist, secured by a heavy pin. An uncle produced a simple, single-stringed instrument called a *libuh,* employed to accompany the litany of Nagaland folk songs that followed. Ceremonial dance came after, fueled by the beat of animal skin-covered drums. Rice beer and tengizu flowed as Lilah and Max took turns dancing with the extended family, and each other, with Max sporting the red, white, and black sarong over his jeans. Candles glowed, laughter filled the room, toasts were given, and it was midnight when people finally started to depart for their homes.

After many goodbyes, Jahnu suggested they grab their bags and led Max and Lilah across the family compound to a walkway secreted between two of the other family structures built against the hill's slope. He carried a thick candle, protecting its flame. A stone stairway cut into the hill behind the structures, leading to a small cabin on a promontory above and away from the other buildings. Like other homes in the village, it was constructed entirely of bamboo, with a thatched bamboo leaf roof and woven bamboo mats for walls. Jahnu opened the door to reveal a single room with two twin beds of bamboo. Candles were scattered around the room, and potted flowers sat on pedestals in the corners. Against one wall stood a washbasin and a long bamboo tube filled with water. Another door led to a rear patio.

"We keep this for our extended family who come to visit from the other villages," said Jahnu. "I hope you like it."

"This will be perfect, Jahnu," said Lilah. "We are profoundly grateful for your hospitality and your family's generosity. This has been an amazing day, right, Max?"

"Absolutely," Max fumbled. "And everything she said."

Jahnu smiled. "Good then. We are happy that you came, especially my grandfather, and hope you will return. And be sure to check out the view from the patio. Good night." He bowed and walked backward out the door.

They dropped their bags, too elated and exhausted to respond, and without speaking, opened the rear door to a polished flagstone patio ringed by a low fence. Two deep chairs were set, facing out over the valley which spread before them. Far below, moonlight glinted off the rice paddies, and stars peeked through puffy clouds backlit by the moon, swimming across the sky. Candles placed about the patio flickered in the light breeze. Two thick, dark logs hollowed out to act as tubs occupied the patio's center. Flower petals floated in the steaming water.

Without a word, Lilah began to undress, looking out over the moonlit valley, unbuttoning her gold kurta, and sliding it over her head. She peeled off her white blouse and slid white pants down over her ankles, revealing a white lace bra and panties, fluorescent in moonglow. These she dropped atop the other clothing. Now completely nude in the orange candlelight, Lilah was a glowing blend of curves and lines and shadowed places. Her gold amulet twinkled moonlight. As Max stood, staring, she looked over her shoulder.

"You're getting in, right?"

"Uh, well, yeah. Here I come."

Lilah slid into the warm water, parting the flower petals as Max struggled to get his clothes off, tossing his boots, shirt, and jeans across the deck. He almost tripped over the tub, struggling to get out of his underwear. Unencumbered, he lowered himself into his pool, submerging. Underwater, his ears rang, and a pounding heart made his entire body pulse. He worried his thumping chest would create ripples in the water as he rose to the surface and exhaled.

Three feet away, Lilah luxuriated in her log tub and the view, taking long breaths while Max attempted to control his. They sat in silence for five long minutes, staring out over the expanse, during which Max struggled mightily to regulate his breathing and heart rate. Finally, Lilah spoke.

"Alright, this is just too much," she said with a wave of her hand. "All of it. I was seduced after the meal and the headhunters and the dancing, and then this. You haven't done a thing, made a single move, but you've broken me down. I give in. I'm going to be a woman and change my mind. You absolutely must make love to me tonight."

The pounding heart and buzzing ears instantly overtook him, and an earthquake struck his pelvis and below. He struggled to speak, but his mouth had instantly dried, and his tongue turned to mush. He considered the logistics of the twin beds. Her glowing, naked body. Next to his.

"Maybe it's just India," was all he managed to say.

"Well, that's obvious," said Lilah. "But it's you, too."

Her statement reverberated to his core. "So much for mucking things up. But this is a muck I very much want to be in."

"Good," she said.

He reached across the space between them and gently grasped her hand. She squeezed back, exhaling with a drawn-out *mmmmmmm.* They floated, eyes closed, hearing only frogs and crickets and their own breathing. Max then listened to the splash of water as Lilah stood and got out of her tub. When he opened his eyes, she was standing at the foot of his tub, silhouetted by iridescent clouds, water dripping off of her. The form of her hips and soft curve of her breasts glowed in the candlelight. She had no tan lines. Lilah stepped to the side of the log basin and slipped in, next to and on top of Max. He made room for her as water sloshed out the sides, and she lay on him, her head on his chest, as her skin on his shot shockwaves throughout his sensory system. Nothing was said as they shared the rise and fall of each other's breathing. Max tried mightily to will his chest to stop pounding underneath Lilah's head, but the beat was so palpable that she placed her hand over his heart, aware of and tied to its force. She raised her head and looked into his eyes as she moved her mouth to his. He saw her understanding of him, his nature, and her desire. Their first kiss was slow and deep, and as she exhaled into him, Max felt Lilah release and give in completely, as vivid electricity coursed between them. For long minutes they explored each other. As the kisses grew in intensity, Max put his arms around her and picked her up as he stood, dripping. Bypassing the logistics of the single beds, she wrapped her legs around him, and they made love, standing, and wet in the moonlight.

Max awoke from a vivid series of dreams. He and Lilah made love on the patio. They made love in one twin bed, then the other. Then against the wall, Lilah supporting herself with both hands gripping the bamboo poles. As he came to full consciousness, he perceived that the dreams had been reality by the smell of sex in the air and the blissful soreness of his muscles. Turning over, he saw that he was alone in the room. And naked, partially covered by a sheet.

A minute later, Lilah came through the door, cheery and bright, toting two bamboo bongs of hot tea and doughy rotis drizzled with honey and cinnamon. Her hair was pulled back, she wore a shawl of red, white, and black woven cotton, the Angami colors, and around her neck hung a necklace of thick amber and orange beads, three strings wide.

"Hot black Assamese tea," she said. "Jahnu's mother says it's good after long nights. And the roti is delicious. I've been up for an hour, learning the art of Angami weaving. She gifted me the shawl and necklace. How do you like it?"

"You look positively Angami-esque," said Max. "What time is it?"

"Nine a.m. Khonoma time," she said. "When I got up, you were dreaming. With a smile on your face and a tent in your sheet."

He blushed, but only slightly. "My reality turned into dreams or vice versa. I can't figure out which, but they were all good. Fantastic, actually, life-changing. Come here and kiss me."

She placed the tea apparatus against the washstand, sat on the side of his bed, placed both hands on his cheeks, and kissed him sweetly.

"Now, have some tea and wash up," she said. "This place smells like an orgy happened in here."

Max chuckled. "From my recollection, it did. I've been savoring the moment. Or moments."

"So have I all morning. There will be more. Now get moving, Tarzan. Jahnu needs to be back on base this afternoon, so we leave in one hour."

She poured him tea from the bamboo bong, which he sipped on one elbow. It was robust, earthy, and rich with heady herbal steam. Then he reached for a towel hung from the washbasin and gave himself a full towel bath, spending extra time on his nether region. Sipping her tea, Lilah watched him. He moved lazily, pulling on clean socks and underwear, then a Jackson Browne T-shirt, jeans, and boots. She noted his body, its scars, and recalled how he had taken her in his arms and lifted her with ease. She wanted to run her hands through his sun-streaked hair. Once again, she found herself licking her lips, a response she didn't remember having before encountering the unique and colorful Max.

The trek to the airport in Assam carried strange emotions for Max, amplified by a steady tropical rain. The Naga Jolokia had been found, dissected, and experienced, and a dozen rode along with them in his duffle bag. He would ship them off to Chuck DeWindt in New Mexico priority status from Guwahati, where he hoped to find an internet connection and file his report. The reason for half his journey had elapsed, and the rest loomed uncertainly. He and Lilah had crossed a threshold, now partners in many delicious things, and he felt peace knowing they were together flying off into the unknown. She was a strong and capable woman, yet he felt a powerful desire to keep her from harm, now more than ever. He felt a responsibility to Delphine and Jones, to bring her back home. Max watched her in the back seat as she dozed, a soft smile evidence of her happy fatigue. Looking at her transported him to the night before, the intensity, the discovery, the acceptance, and he felt delicious, satisfying tiredness. The Seven Sisters rain fell in sheets, wrapping him in a grey blanket.

After a flight from Kathmandu, laid China and Kashgar at the Silk Road's end. Then, summiting the Tien Shan mountains to Kyrgyzstan and its mythical Fire of the Valley chile. If it actually existed, would he even find it? Max wondered about Gasanov, how he was faring, realizing that he strangely cared for the man and his plight. Or he was being manipulated, not seeing something obvious. He tried to picture his nemesis Ruslan Bakiyev in his imagination, unable to define the man, attempting to discern his motives and methods. How far would he go to get what he desired? He closed his eyes and saw the Kyrgyz gangster, faceless, standing in a black coat and hat between his two bodyguards, whose faces he knew well. They waited over the mountains. In his bones, he sensed the impending likelihood of another encounter.

While Lilah rested, he and Jahnu talked about life in Nagaland and Laguna Beach, with Jahnu resolved to visit California in the future. "I have seen pirated episodes of Baywatch on the base in Tezpur and would very much like to see where it is filmed and to imagine Pamela Anderson running on the beach in slow motion," he said shyly.

"Then we shall go, Jahnu," said Max.

Jahnu then paused before asking Max a question. "Do you think all the effort to keep this hottest chile in India for India is going to matter? All of General Chatterjee's secrecy and security seem so, well, pointless. It's a thing of nature. And nature has a way of choosing its own direction."

Max looked at the Angami man thoughtfully, seeing a bright and insightful young fellow.

"Though I honestly believe what I said to your family, that the Naga Jolokia will soon be famous across the world, it's only a matter of time before the seeds get out and people start cultivating their own, with local names. The dozen in my bag will be the start of that process, which is inevitable. Soon, chile-heads will be traveling here, searching the hills for wild specimens. And fanatics will hybridize them using selective characteristics to create ever stronger varieties with their own silly names. So yes, the general's efforts are pointless. China and Pakistan have other weapons in their arsenals, and I don't think an Indian hot pepper artillery cloud is going to make much of a difference except to control crowds of civilians."

While the chile's global spread would only be a matter of time, Max held secret his idea for a plan to join with the Angami people of Khonoma in developing a hot sauce derived from the original Naga Jolokia chiles, at their origin. Naga Warrior Assamese Chile Sauce would be an instant hit. He wanted the machinery in place before making promises and to keep inevitable competitors at bay.

Jahnu did not appear defeated, understanding nature, and people. "Oh, well. It has been an honor to be a part of its unveiling on the world stage. And to meet you both. You are most certainly the best candidate for this job, Max. A simple scientist could not have felt the uniqueness of our part of the world. Nor endured that chile firing squad in Tezpur."

He looked in the mirror at Lilah, still dozing dreamily. "Plus, you had an enchanting, smart scientist to back you up."

They wound down the canyons of Nagaland, skirting the frothing river Chathe, and five hours later arrived in the vast, flat, misty valley of the Brahmaputra and Guwahati. Jahnu knew of only two internet outlets in the city, and the Millennium Internet Café was fortunately near the airport. The internet was still relatively new in India, and dial-up access was expensive at a dollar a minute. Needing to get to Tezpur and check in at his military post, Jahnu deposited them at the café, where they could catch an airport taxi. Before they got out, he handed Max a small video card storage device and a videotape.

"Take these, Max. They may help support your thesis. The card has a low-resolution video from my phone when you encounter the Naga Jolokia in the wild and your theory of its evolution. Plus, your chile smoke baptism, which I imagine your Ring of Fire friends will appreciate. I certainly did. The videotape is the footage that was shot at the base in Tezpur. I made two copies, unknown to our esteemed generalissimo. And if you ever need a statement from someone who witnessed all of it, please do not hesitate to find me. Be well."

"And you be well, Jahnu, my friend," said Max. "You have been instrumental in our exploration. Of the Naga Jolokia, your country, and for us, of each other. We will see you again."

Lilah, still groggy, hugged Jahnu. "Thank you for showing us your India," she said. "It has changed us both."

Inside the Millennium Internet Café, young men sat before rows of iridescent square monitors while waiters served tea and snacks. Most played video games, giving the place the sound of an arcade. Max asked the attendant for an available machine with the best dial-up access and privacy and was led to a cluster of desks in the corner of the room. They ordered chai and fritters called *kordoi* to snack on while Max typed up a report for Chuck DeWindt in New Mexico. Avoiding the dollar-a-minute charge to type it into an email, he created a document first. Half an hour later, he finished and asked Lilah to look it over before logging on to send the report.

"It's a strong thesis, Max. It's smart you included that lab testing would be the ultimate qualifier, but I believe the science will support your theory. Well done. You really are an expert at this stuff, more than just a true believer. And good for Jahnu on the videos. Chuck will appreciate the sacrifice you made to gather the information."

Max absorbed her critique, internally emboldened by Lilah's honest praise, proud of what he'd accomplished. Sending the evidence out into the world would justify his unique way of doing things, and his passion for doing them. He logged on to AOL, his mail server, waiting for the familiar sounds of the 14.4-kilobyte modem connection and "You've got mail!" greeting. When he opened up the email account, he immediately thought something was wrong. Six hundred seventy-two emails, many with *Urgent!* tags stared back at him. The subject lines displayed an array of alarming and desperate pleas. *Call Immediately! Very Important! High Priority!* were the most popular. He also saw messages labeled *I'll Pay for Seeds! Let's Make A Deal! You're a Fraud! Totally Impossible!* and *Prove It!* Scrolling through the hundreds of messages, he found one from Chuck DeWindt and opened it.

Max, I hope you're doing well over there, and I look forward to your report. You sure know how to stir things up in the pepper world, my friend. It seems your esteemed General Chatterjee has released the video of your Naga Jolokia session all over the internet. He also videotaped your statement that it's the hottest chile you've ever tasted, along with their Scoville results. People are in an uproar, and my phone hasn't stopped ringing. Please get in touch as soon as you are able. Chuck.

Max sat back, stunned, while Lilah read through the communication.

"Looks like you're either a celebrity or a villain, Max. Get the report and specimens and video off to Chuck and let the scientists do their work. Probably a good idea that we go underground for a while and let this business work itself out. Heading to a desert oasis in western China seems like a good place to do that."

Of course, she was right, and Max replied to the email, attaching his report and informing Chuck that specimens and original video were on the way. He also uploaded the video from Jahnu's card to a private university server that only Chuck could access, which took half an hour. Max figured his field analysis and assumptions would give Chuck ammunition as the university worked on its own determinations, and he thought he'd appreciate the entertaining smoke bath.

He scrolled through the cascade of emails, looking for one in particular. He spotted it: a communication from Cesar Robledo, who ran the warehouse in Laguna and oversaw the shop in Max's absence.

Hola Max, just checking in. Hope it's going well over there. FYI, people are calling (the publisher of Chile Pepper Magazine called!), wondering where you are, and some are showing up at the shop wanting an interview about your super-hot India chiles. The business has picked up because of it. Can we get some to grow? Things are fine here, but I think

Gus misses you. He looks kinda sad. But then, he always does. Check in soon. Cesar.

Max sent off a quick response, letting Cesar know things were okay and that he still had more exploration to do. He also asked his partner to grill Gus a ribeye and let him enjoy it on the back deck. Before logging off, a single email caught his eye. The subject line read simply *Gasanov*. Max knew it would be cryptic as he asked Lilah to read over his shoulder.

Dear Max (and Lilah, your lovely accomplice), things are heating up, literally and figuratively, in Kyrgyzstan. While you were gallivanting across the Seven Sisters, Bakiyev tried to infiltrate the Buntun Lodge Guest House in Dostuk, however, his henchmen were run out of town by villagers carrying torches, very much like in Mary Shelley's "Frankenstein." Have you read it? Nonetheless, he found some specimens in the market in Osh and has sent them abroad for analysis. International inquiries have started to trickle in, it seems, though my ministry sources have diminished. The clock is ticking, and it is imperative that you somehow find your way here. Again, taking the overland route is recommended, and if you use Torugart Pass, make a side trip to Tash Rabat. An archaeologist is working there named Mishka Dubovya, who has done some excavations. Maybe she's found something of interest? As a captive, my sojourn continues, but I hold out hope that things will work out in my favor. I am counting on you for that, my friend. As you can see, I do have online access and have viewed your video from India, which has set the internet ablaze. Is it really that hot? You looked like you were experiencing some extreme sensations, though the three poor sods next to you clearly fared worse. I wonder what you thought of in those moments. The parallels with our situation here over the Tien Shan mountains, perhaps? Whatever the case, you are assuredly the current king of the Ring of Fire. I am proud of myself for choosing well and walking into your shop in Laguna that day. Don't make me wrong, do come soon. Destiny awaits. Gasanov.

They both digested the message, surrounded by the sounds of Donkey Kong and Final Fantasy gamers. Max expressed amazement at how much and how quickly Gasanov received information. "How does Gasanov do it? He knows everything we're doing. It feels like he, or someone else, is monitoring our movements. I don't like it."

"Then again, an appropriate time to go underground, and the Silk Road seems like a good place for that," said Lilah. Gasanov did not bother her a bit.

Max was more skeptical. "I don't know. Bakiyev has him, or so he says. What would Gasanov do to gain his freedom? Sell us out? Hand us to Bakiyev? Hell, maybe he was conspiring from the beginning. What if we're walking into a trap?"

Lilah placed a hand on his shoulder. "Well, I know you, and I know you wouldn't turn around if you were alone at this point. Now you have me, so realize that I'm an asset and not a liability. Plus, I like your company. Let's unravel the mystery. It's why you came."

She knew that he knew that she was right, which seemed to be always. "Okay, but if things get dicey we bail out. No questions," said Max.

"Deal," Lilah said. "Let's go catch a flight to Kathmandu."

KASHGAR

To follow the Silk Road is to follow a ghost.
It flows through the heart of Asia, but it has officially vanished
leaving behind the pattern of its restlessness: counterfeit borders,
unmapped peoples.
The road forks and wanders wherever you are.
It is not a single way, but many: a web of choices.
Colin Thubron – Shadow of the Silk Road

K ashgar is China's westernmost city, a central Asian oasis with a tumultuous history dating back over two thousand years. Perched at the far western end of the vast Tarim Basin and Taklamakan desert, its influences come from neighbors Mongolia, Tibet, Kazakhstan, Tajikistan, Afghanistan, Pakistan, and Kyrgyzstan, as much or more than China. It is the farthest major city from an ocean on earth. Though China today controls Xinjiang, the desert province home to Kashgar, Beijing is 2,500 miles to the east. Istanbul is the same distance, on the edge of Europe. It is surrounded by some of the highest mountains on earth. To the north lie the Tien Shan mountains, the west the Pamirs, the Hindu Kush to the south, and the east, the Taklamakan desert, which means "those going in never return." Chinese exiled by the emperor were dropped at the eastern edge and never seen again, though a few hardy souls made it to the western oases to find a thriving culture. Kashgar's strategic location made it a primary outpost on the Silk Road. Over the millennia, it belonged variously to the Tibetans, Mongols, Turks, Huns and Arabs, numerous warlords, and the Chinese. The legendary Jade Gate in Dunhuang marked the ancient western frontier of China, and Kashgar was still 1,200 miles to the west, almost all of it desert.

Starting in ancient Ch'ang-an, or present-day Xian, caravans were required to make a thousand-mile journey, skirting the Gobi Desert, just to reach Dunhuang and the Jade Gate. From there, northern and southern routes avoided the hostile Taklamakan desert, relying on strategic oases and caravanserai to replenish before reaching Kashgar, for centuries a major crossroads of the world. Following were the high passes of the Pamir and Tien Shan, China's only links to India, Persia, Arabia, and Europe. After the fall of China's Tang Dynasty in 907AD, the Mongols ultimately secured a continuous trading route from China to the Mediterranean, as they ruled much of the territory the trade passed through, the largest empire in history. In addition to Marco Polo, legendary Western explorers Sven Hedin, Jean Baptiste Tavernier, Benedict de Goes, Aurel Stein, Francis Younghusband, and

Nickolay Prezhalvsky had all recuperated in Kashgar after perilous desert and mountain crossings. The city represented a vital mix of cultures and history and a perennial outpost of Silk Road lore. For Max, it was an essential step on his journey to discover the global journey of chiles and the origin of the Fire of the Valley.

Max looked out the plane's window as they circled high above the Tarim Basin, beginning their descent into Kashgar. They had just flown over the Pamir range coming from Pakistan, where their flight from Kathmandu had connected in Karachi, and he could make out the long-pinnacled line of the Tien Shan range to the north. A pale purple haze was settling in over the Taklamakan desert in the fading light to the east. He felt the oasis city pulling him, destiny in its alleys and mountain passes beyond.

Max and Lilah spent much of the flight in silence, watching Bhutan, Nepal, Kashmir, and Pakistan pass below, their arms intertwined. They had flown along the rib of the Himalayas, and after breaking through the clouds, the pilot identified the sacred peaks of Nepal's Gauri Sankar and Kailash in Tibet. Three religions believed Kailash to be the birthplace of humanity and the center of the world. Hindus assert that Lord Shiva lives atop its peak, practicing yoga, making love to his consort Parvati, and smoking ganja.

When they reached their hotel, it was evening. The taxi driver had identified the Shenzen Guest House adjacent to the famous Id Kah Mosque as smaller, less touristy Kashgar accommodations, which they preferred. Too tired to seek out food in the late hour, they threw down their bags and collapsed on absurdly springy twin beds with polyester sheets.

Max regained consciousness late the next morning, taking a few moments to realize where he was. Lilah had gone, though her bag still sat beside the bed. A hot bath would bring him around, he thought. When he emerged resuscitated from the cramped, lukewarm shower, she was there again, with cups of tea and pastries that looked remarkably like bagels.

"They're called *girde naan,* and they're not bagels," she said, already an expert on the subject. "They're baked, not boiled, and the hole doesn't go all the way through. I bought them from a nice young fellow just down from the tea shop. And this is *kara chay*, black tea infused with saffron and cardamom, the preferred local style. I saw a table of old fellas in skullcaps dipping the naan into it."

They sipped and dipped, coming to the awareness that they were incredibly far away from literally everything. "It's like we've landed at the center of the earth," she said. "Isn't that amazing?"

Max smiled as he watched her speak, relishing her irrepressible good nature. "Yes. And I'm glad to be in this faraway place with you."

She jumped in his lap, and they kissed and giggled on the small, bouncy bed. He ran his hands through her hair and examined her green eyes with their gold flecks like stars. Max had never felt so enamored and at ease with a woman in his life.

Lilah sat up on an elbow, inquisitive. "So, what's the plan here, Max Chota? I know Kyrgyzstan is just over the mountains, but why Kashgar?"

He explained Kashgar's importance as a Silk Road outpost, then tied that into the migration of chiles and the unique fruit reported in Kyrgyzstan.

"Chiles most certainly came across the land passages until the Portuguese figured out the sea routes in the mid-1500s. *Capsicum chinense* went with the Portuguese by sea because they controlled the Amazon Basin where *chinense* came from, and why *chinense* varieties have historically been found in Eastern China. Sichuan and Hunan are much further west, known for employing *Capsicum frutescens*, the kind brought by Columbus and the Spanish from Mexico, and thus were historically connected to the overland routes, the Silk Road. Gasanov's description of the chiles he discovered in Osh was that they were round, like hen's eggs. That's either *Capsicum pubescens*, the round Rocoto, or a hybrid, possibly with *chinense,* or something else. Rocoto has never really migrated globally, so I want to see if there's evidence of either in the market here. Plus, remember what Bakiyev said in his poem about black seeds and white seeds. Only *Capsicum pubescens,* the Rocoto, has black seeds and all other varieties white, and I've never seen an example of both in a chile anywhere. So the trail starts here, at the eastern end of the Silk Road. First, we have to get our visas for Kyrgyzstan."

"Then let's go hunting," Lilah said.

They walked a block to the edge of the broad Id Kah Square surrounding the enormous, yellow-bricked mosque of the same name. Plain-clothed Chinese security men stood in small groups, monitoring the populace, resulting from numerous ethnic uprisings and historic distrust between the Muslim Uighur and Communist Han Chinese. The old town of Kashgar radiated outward from the 15th-century Islamic shrine, the largest in China, in a warren of ancient mud-brick houses and shops, where men in four-pointed Uighur caps still wore sheathed daggers and donkey carts transported all manner of goods through the narrow alleys. A hotel map directed them to Kyrgyzstan's small consular annex, which facilitated visas for border crossings. Torugart Pass was notorious as one of the most difficult border transits in all of Asia, with layers of security and bureaucracy adding to the physical challenge. Documents and transportation had to be prearranged before leaving China, with a connection on the Kyrgyz side. Numerous security checkpoints and document and baggage inspections lay ahead.

Waiting in line with a few dozen other travelers, none of whom were Westerners, the entire experience was surprisingly expedited in less than an hour. They left possessing transit visas inked in their passports for Monday, with contracts for drivers over both borders, all the way to Osh. The process appeared almost too easy, and the man who had waved them to his line seemed vaguely to expect them, smiling unnaturally. *Perhaps I'm being too wary*, thought Max. Permission to enter an isolated central Asian country he had never visited was a milestone, and he was excited as he stared at the ornate, official visa.

"It feels like it's calling me," he said without explanation as they exited the consular annex.

Lilah stopped. "What's calling you?"

"Kyrgyzstan. Discovery. The people of that small village. The many different directions the future might take. Starting from this moment." Worry clouded his face as he spoke.

"You've been headed in this direction for a long time, Max," she said as they continued walking. "Today, you got a stamp. In two days, we go over the pass. You were meant for this."

When he looked up at her, he smiled, but she noticed a more wizened person in his eyes than she had seen before. The weight of the task, laced with danger, tempered his demeanor.

On the other side of the old city lay Kashgar's bazaar, open every day of the year. It brought in sellers and buyers from all over the province, and bordering nations. Being Saturday, they had a day to explore and see what they could find before the world-famous and chaotic *Yekshembe* Sunday animal market and their Monday departure. Neither Max nor Lilah spoke Chinese, let alone Uighur, so they opted to let the city organically unfold before them without the pressure of a guide, and every corner brought new delights. The ancient allure of Kashgar was a delicious diversion far removed from the rest of the world.

Before they found the vast bazaar, alleys hosting specific vendors split off from the old city's main thoroughfares. Max found a woven Uighur cap in the alley of hats, called a *doppa*, worn by most non-Chinese men and representing ethnicity, not religion. Hat styles accompanied every ethnicity, such as the white Kyrgyz felt fedora with elongated top and elaborate embroidery, the Tajik cap made of yak fur, and the Uzbek fez of thick wool yarn. He picked a traditional Uighur one made of black and green wool, with a white felt band embroidered and laced with translucent white beads. With his week of beard, he looked quite at home in central Asia, thought Lilah, *a Silk Road nomad.*

For her, they found a multicolored Uighur version of embroidered flowers, made from silk thread woven over a wool base; it would facilitate interaction in a city where covering a female's head allowed greater access to ethnic businesses.

Heads suitably adorned, they wound through the alleys in what they believed to be the direction of the bazaar, encountering myriad offshoots, each with a unique offering of products. One hosted an array of items fashioned entirely from copper, tin, brass, and iron. Smiths hammered on pots over open flames, calling out as they labored. Simple one-burner stoves, sturdy wide woks, huge pots, kabob grills, and tinkling kitchen tools glimmered in the midmorning sun, and vendors held up the handmade woks as they passed, eager for a sale. Burka-clad women peered at them with piercing eyes from doorways, and children followed behind, singing "Allo Mister! Allo Lady!" posing for pictures with Lilah while Max clicked away.

Together they passed streets that for centuries had sold only Korans, each with elaborate scrolling on the covers and the alley of tea, redolent of flowering scents. They stepped aside for a moped stacked high with sixty long strands of garlic woven together, headed for the produce market, and a mule-drawn cart carrying melons and legendary Kashgari pomegranates, destined for hand-juicing. Barbers lined haircut alley, administering midday shaves with long razors to men sitting on crates, necks exposed. Many stopped their work as Lilah passed, their blades suspended centimeters from their clients' jugular veins. Signs standing out against facades of ochre mud were scrawled in Arabic, and Chinese and ethnic Uighur music played ethereally on radios, echoing down the narrow lanes.

Max watched Lilah as she almost skipped along beside him. Without warning, she darted into a shaded alley, pulling him with her. Ducking into a doorway, Lilah grabbed his shirt before he could react and pulled him to her, tilting her head sideways to kiss his face hungrily, one leg wrapped around him. She spoke in short gasps.

"I can't stop thinking about Khonoma. I feel like I'm in a dream, and you are my warrior guide. It's overpowering, and I need you to know that I'm absolutely mad about you and wild with desire. And lusting after the adventure with you. I don't care what happens or where it leads." They remained, pressed within the shaded doorway, for five eternally long minutes.

Then, Lilah pushed Max away. "I smell bread," she said, taking his hand and leading him, dumbfounded, back into the street.

They followed the smoky-sweet aroma down to its source. Vendors displayed table after table of Kashgar's famous delicacies made on round griddles and woodburning ovens of clay and stone.

Shining fat *ghizder*, poked with elaborate patterns from the quills of chicken feathers, sprinkled with sesame seeds. *Hemek nan*, giant thin rounds baked atop iron flat-tops, and doughy *Turpan nan* dusted with flakes of onion and black sesame seeds. The dough was mashed onto the sides of open circular ovens called *tonur* to bake, falling into the coals when ready. Max and Lilah shared one, steaming, tearing it apart after its seller dusted coal ash from its surface.

As they neared the enclosed bazaar, fresh-cut herbs perfumed the air, while mounds of onions and root vegetables, covered in the dirt they were pulled from, sat strategically stacked in geometric pyramids. Every farmer grew some version of peppers, with green and yellow bell peppers, long, thin cayenne and fat, stubby jalapeno-types the most ubiquitous. They identified dried Thai, tabasco, and bird peppers, with powders and spice mixes made from all of them. They inspected the product for three blocks, handling and smelling chiles and looking for anything unusual, like hybrids.

Max broke open and tasted several specimens, hoping to register unique flavors. In the process, he caught a glance of a shadowed figure down the lane, deliberate in the inspection of each stall. He ran his hands through chile powder bins and bit into whole chiles. *A total pro,* thought Max. Then, the man turned toward them.

"Holy shit," Max said, pulling Lilah between two stalls. "We've got company, and I can't tell if it's friend or foe today."

"Have they seen you?" said Lilah, startled. "Is it our boys from Kyrgyzstan?"

"No. Ed Garland of the International Spice Corporation based in Aruba, the largest spice buying company in the world. He's one of their four buyers working worldwide with unlimited connections and buying power. They have agents and sources in every market. It's not strange that he would be in Kashgar, or any place on earth, for that matter. But he's here now, inspecting chiles. Damn it. Do I tail him or confront him?"

Garland was a towering man, raptor-like, with a brown fedora and round spectacles, who stood out in any crowd. However, these faraway places' heat never bothered him, well above the masses and fixed on his objectives. He was pure business, representing the biggest spice conglomerate on earth with all its resources at his exceptionally long back. Max had encountered him at trade shows and on buying trips, where they had a few drinks together, talking shop, but they were never competitive. A chance encounter in Kyoto, Japan, in 1998 had caused Max to become wary of the agent, however.

Max had been touring Japan, intending to discover the country's relationship to chile peppers and spicy food in general. Chiles reached Japan at about the same time as China, peddled by Portuguese merchants and their Asian agents, but did not create nearly the impact as on the mainland. Only a few types of chiles were cultivated there, and he was interested in discovering why Japan was the Asian holdout. Only one variety in the nation, the *taka no tsume*, meaning "dragon's nails," was considered world-class spicy. In Kyoto, while visiting the famous Kiyomizudera temple built in 1633, he happened upon the Shichimiya Honpo spice shop in the city's ancient walking district. On a narrow alley at the top of the famous Ninenzaka steps, Shichimiya Honpo was one of the original purveyors of *shichimi togarashi*, or "seven-flavor spice," Japan's only piquant spice blend, and had been in the same location since 1655.

Max spent three hours in the shop after meeting the fabled business's ninth-generation proprietor, Akira Kawachiya, who possessed generations of spice knowledge. Over grassy green tea in the shop's rear salon sitting on tatami mats, he learned the story of chiles in Japan and the nearly three hundred fifty-year history of the Kawachiya family's company.

"Chiles in our island country were thought of mainly as exotic ornamental plants, too pungent for our nuanced cuisine," said Akira. "We treat food as an art, and chiles were like bright red paint on the subtle Japanese food palette. They became mainstream after Buddhist monks traveling from China introduced them as having spiritual and physical benefits. My industrious forefather took what he learned from the monks and developed a blend of dried red chiles, roasted orange peel, black and white sesame seeds, shiso leaf, hemp seeds, seaweed, and ground ginger, all with known health attributes. He used the blend to make a spiced tea for the monks who meditated under the Kiyomizudera temple's waterfall to warm their blood, and the local population followed suit. Now *togarashi* is an integral part of eating in Japan. Today, more varieties are cultivated for cooking, like the sweet *shishito* and *mangaji*, piquant *fushimi*, and very hot *taka no tsume*."

Max was enthralled by the long Kawachiya history and created a partnership with the family on the spot to develop a sauce from the seven-flavored blend, following strict guidelines. A purple sauce with the juice of red shishito leaf and a hint of seaweed with togarashi spice called Sauce of Seven Flavors sold well in Japan and Japanese markets in the U.S. Following shortly after, Dragon's Nails, dosed with wasabi, was a big hit in the Ring of Fire; a fire-breathing dragon on the label, drawn by a Japanese artist, had helped.

As Max pulled apart the curtain to return to the shop's main room, he saw Ed Garland on the other side of the counter, purchasing every item in the company's lineup, towering over the staff.

"Holy cow, Max, what are you doing in Kyoto?" Garland said.

"Learning about the Kawachiya company history, Ed. Looks like you're doing some spice shopping."

Thrown off guard, Ed spit out a weak lie. "Can't get enough of this stuff, the *togarashi*. I put it on everything, just like the Japanese." To divert attention from his presence in a random Kyoto spice store, he added quickly, "C'mon, let's go find a beer."

Three doors down was a Japanese gastropub, an *Izakaya*, where they took a table by the narrow walking street and ordered big Kirin beers. Ed parried first, warily. "What brings you to Japan, Max? You're not getting into the dried spice game, are you?"

"I've always wanted to come," Max said. "And always wondered why chiles hadn't taken hold here like the rest of Asia. Akira enlightened me, and we may do a sauce together. So what brings you here, shopping for spice blends in Japan's most venerable shop, Ed?"

It was obvious to Max that Ed and the International Spice Corporation sought ways to replicate the traditional Japanese *togarashi* spice and take it to the rest of the world.

"We're looking to expand our lineup of Asian spice offerings for the U.S. market, and this *togarashi* stuff has proven to be quite a hit back home. So I'm getting ideas. And why not from the oldest maker in the country? American chefs are asking for it, and we need to deliver before the competition. These artisanal startups are like flies buzzing around my ears."

International Spice Corporation's Japanese Seven Spice Blend hit the market nine months later, and Max developed a growing distrust for Garland and the corporate behemoth. He was one of the artisans.

Max related the story to Lilah as they watched Garland probe the chile vendors. Garland and International Spice Corporation did not historically compete with Max's business, but they had recently made a play in the sauce segment, acquiring several midlevel brands poised for growth. Max could be seen as an impediment or an asset in the global conglomerate's plans if they were after the Kyrgyz pepper. Either way, he had to play it cool. Before he could formulate a plan, Lilah walked off toward the man, calling back to Max.

"Let me go have a chat with him," said Lilah. "He looks nice enough."

She removed the Uighur cap, wrapped her head in a green scarf from her pocket, lowered her sunglasses, and sauntered off across the bazaar. When their paths crossed, she sidled up next to the spice buyer as he dug into a burlap sack of crushed chiles with his bare hands, leaning down to them from his perch. As he inhaled the aromas, she spoke in a heavy Cajun accent.

"Ahh been tryin' to tell one of these peppers from the other but am having no luck," she said. "The vendors look at me like I'm from Mars. My botany courses at Baton Rouge did not prepare me for China. And to think they believe chiles originated here. Why they have over forty different varieties they've cultivated that are unique to their own country. Did you know that?"

The man had not expected to run into an American woman in the Kashgar Bazaar, let alone one with a surprising knowledge of chiles.

"Why yes, actually, I did," he said, standing up, uncomfortably tall. "I'm Ed. I'm a spice buyer, by the way."

Without dusting off his hands, he extended one, then realized his faux pas. He wiped them on his khakis, creating red smears. "Almost spiced you there," he said, laughing nervously.

In her scarf and sunglasses, Lilah looked like a movie star attempting to be incognito.

"That's alright, it wouldn't be the first time. But it does explain why you're looking like you're ready to dive into that pile of chiles. I'm Ms. Khojakarta, in the middle of an exploration of the Silk Road. I'm writing a cookbook based on the old trading routes, and of course, I have to talk about peppers here in Asia. They are in just about everything." She took his peppered hand and shook it lightly with her fingers.

Facing her, he took in Lilah's long, wavy hair, golden skin, and height, which was always an issue for him.

"Chiles in China can be quite challenging," he said. "They've been cross-breeding and adapting them to conditions here since the early 1500s. The culture has adopted the notion that their nation must be the origin of chiles with so many varieties growing across the country."

He picked up a slick-red chile. "It helps to understand a few basics. The standard Chinese chile is *Tianjin*, or *Tian-tsin*, which refers to the northern port city where they first arrived with the Portuguese. 'Pointy' *Zhǐtiānjiāo* chiles, a *Capsicum frutescens* variety, are usually utilized green like a jalapeno. They call *Capsicum chinense* varieties like the habanero 'lantern chiles,' which gives away their shape. Then there's 'little rice' chiles, the bird's eye type, and 'wrinkled skin,' like Thai chiles that grow wild in the southwest, in Hunan. And *Shuan shuan*, which are found down near the border with Burma, so hot that the name likens eating them to dipping your tongue in boiling water. In Sichuan, they favor the 'double goldenness" chile, the long cayenne type. Native western Chinese chile cultivars are the 'facing heaven' chile—chao tian jiao, a short, slim, and cleanly hot *Capsicum annuum* chile that grows pointing upwards—and the 'seven-star chile' *Qi Xing Jiao*—a milder, very flavorful chile that grows in clusters of typically seven pods. You'll find *Niu Jiao Jiao* and *Yung Jiao Jiao*, which are 'bull's horn' and 'sheep's horn' peppers, used most often for making ground powder. And that's only the major players. So, there's a lot to learn about chiles in China." He concluded, quite satisfied with himself.

Lilah did her best to seem impressed. "Why you are certainly a font of information. I will jot down notes back at my hotel if I can remember all of them. What brings you to these far western reaches of the Middle Kingdom, Ed?"

"Well, in my job, I'm on the road three hundred days a year," he said, "and markets like this are where I find new and undiscovered products and better sources for our existing lineup. And check in with my regular suppliers. Right now, I'm looking for a special type of chile pepper, actually, something entirely new."

Lilah feigned surprise. "Three hundred? Holy Toledo! That's a lot of markets. But why here, in Kashgar? You must have seen everything they grow here before."

"I have a pretty wide network since I represent the largest spice packager in the world. Information finds its way to me. There has been talk of a possible new variety of chile, a hybrid perhaps, something unique to the Silk Road, and possibly from a centuries-old source. I have colleagues sniffing around the markets in Aleppo in Syria, Samarkand in Uzbekistan, Bishkek in Kyrgyzstan, and Ashgabat in Tajikistan. All were important stops on the ancient Silk Road. And Kashgar famously, the end of it. So, we're tracking down a lead to get ahead of the competition."

"But they're just chiles," said Lilah nonchalantly. "Why such an effort?"

"Imagine a chile emerging from the centuries-old spice route from Europe to Asia," he said. "In the spice world, it would be a phenomenon, the marketing value alone is inestimable, and we want it. First."

Lilah leaned in, speaking like an exaggerated spy. "Sounds clandestine. Where's the competition? Lurking about?"

"I doubt it. At this point, very little competition on this particular hunt. But there is one fellow, a maverick from California. He's a small operator, but he has a cagey reputation for discovering and creating unique new things ahead of most everyone else. We've heard he may be onto this information, and apparently, he's verified what looks to be the hottest pepper on the planet in India just last week. So we're putting all our resources into this tip, even if it's only a possibility. Can't have the 800-pound gorilla bested by a lone monkey, can we?"

"Certainly not," said Lilah, with extra Cajun flair. "International Spice Corporation has a reputation to maintain. And I use your brands in many of my recipes, so you better stay on top. May I send you a copy of my cookbook when it's finished?"

"Please do, Ms. Khojakarta," he said, handing her his card. "And if you use our brands exclusively, I can probably get you a sponsorship deal from our marketing people. We always like chefs talking about our products, you know."

"Why that would be magnificent," Lilah said, slipping the card very visibly into her bra. "And I'm Lilah. I'll send you the finished manuscript in a few months. Charmed to meet you, Ed." She turned and began to stroll in the other direction, pretending to shop.

Ed was not finished, having noticed her unencumbered ring finger. One didn't come across attractive American cookbook authors in far west China. "Uh, listen, I'm at the Radisson here, Lilah. Perhaps if you'd care to have a drink later...."

"Do they do Happy Hour in China?" she turned and asked, seeming interested.

Ed grinned. "Here, it translates to 'very happy for one hour.' The Radisson's *Very Happy Hour Times Two* runs from five to seven."

She lowered her glasses for effect. "Perhaps I'll see you there."

As he watched her walk away, it occurred to Ed Garland that he had not told the mysterious Khojakarta woman which company he worked for before he gave her his business card. The woman was a plant, a spicy spy, halfway around the world. His movements were being tracked, he realized, and though it was not the first time he'd been followed in his line of work, the American woman was a new twist. He determined something big was at play, and he returned to the hotel to fax an alert to the rest of his team, who were already plying the other markets of Central Asia.

"'Lone monkey'? That's what he said?" Max feigned indignance. "What a buzzard. The guy's got a team of people and an unlimited budget to buy millions of pounds of spices every year. It's no surprise that he's heard something. But I wonder just how much he knows. He didn't mention Osh's market, so maybe he's not that close, just hunting. Nothing about both white and black seeds. Bakiyev sending samples to a lab probably got people talking. We'll have to move fast, get over the pass to Kyrgyzstan on Monday. It would be a tragedy to see this get into the hands of a multinational corporation. If the mythical chile even exists."

Lilah could almost see gears grinding in his head. "Yes, over we go, to see what we can see. Perhaps we'll find nothing at all. But I have a sense that whatever is there will come to us if we disengage ourselves from all the possible outcomes. Let it find us, and we won't be let down trying too hard to find it. A little Buddhist dharma for your day, Max.

That'll be five bucks. And he invited me for a 'very happy times two' meeting if you recall."

He touched her face. "Lilah, you're right. Again. Another reason I need to beat this guy. Let's go find this hidden gem with open minds and prepared for possibility. I'm ready to eat. How about you?"

Choosing a route that took them away from the produce vendors and Ed Garland, they zigzagged, through the warren of alleys, following their olfactories to the location of the food district adjacent to the bazaar. Donkey cart drivers, loaded with goods, called out to pass them in the alleys. Women, some in burkas and others in colorful ethnic dress, shuffled past them in groups. Men clustered before televisions in cramped shops, smoking and drinking tea. Nearing the ancient souk, the smell of grilling meat found them.

Max and Lilah followed the thickening smoke, heavy with charcoal and spice, to the lane of the butchers. Each offered a grilling station in front of the indoor meat processing business behind, a living advertisement of their delicious wares. The grills represented an assortment of contraptions for roasting meat, and they chose the vendor with the shiniest apparatus and most evident grilling prowess. A foot wide and eight feet long, the grill at Charcoal Kebab House was abuzz with activity. The proprietor, who called himself Mehmut, hopped back and forth behind his prized iron workspace, a whirlwind of motion, spinning the metal skewers, fanning the coals, and calling out to passersby. To his left, a coal-fired oven produced flatbreads and embers for the grill, which Mehmut regularly refreshed. Goat and lamb were the preferred meats in Central Asia, and they bought fire-roasted kebabs called *kawap*, lamb sprinkled with cumin, salt, white pepper, and chile powder, the fat charred sweet and smoky. The still-sizzling kebabs were served on toasty flatbreads from the coal oven, *hemek nan*, seasoned with garlic, onion seeds, and oregano. They sat in an alcove, watching the street scene while they wrapped the meats in the flatbread, and juices dripped at their feet.

Crunching into the charred, well-seasoned lamb, Max hummed while Lilah held the food up for closer inspection. "Fantastic," she said. "It's like a meat lollipop in a blanket of doughy deliciousness. I could eat this all day."

"There's more to come," said Max, wiping his mouth. "Don't fill up."

They worked their way slowly through the food district, stopping to watch preparations and take in the scents. Steam from boiling water and smoke from grills and sizzling woks created a delicious haze. Men played pool at a table on sawhorses in a small square lined with vendors. Another group cheered on two men casually boxing, laughing, and placing bets. Seeing an opportunity, a noddle-wallah called across the plaza to Max and Lilah, beckoning them to his stall in a singing voice, promoting his family's product, Uighur *laghman* noodles. Wide woks sat atop yellow flames inside brick-built ovens fed by wood. They watched as wheat flour was blended with salt and water into heavy dough balls on a long table. The singing Uighur man, sporting two top and bottom teeth, took the doughy mass, stretched it across his chest at arm's length, and then spun it like a jump rope. Flour was tossed over the giant noodle to keep it from sticking to itself, clouding the air.

Once stretched, he raised both arms over his head and spun the doughy rope around itself vertically like a cowboy lariat to create a braided length of noodles, which he then slapped onto a massive wood table and doused with more flour, calling out as the dough hit the wood. The stretching and braiding were repeated twenty times before he extended his arms and displayed a network of exquisitely pulled noodles in giant loops around his hands, akin to a kid's string game, grinning with his four teeth. Holding the entire mass strung between his arms, he walked over to the wood table and slapped it onto the counter, chopping off the knotty ends he had held, then moved to an enormous wok, tossing the long noodles into steaming water. In other woks, three feet across, the individual ingredients were separately fried: green and red bell-type peppers, cubes of potato, tomato wedges, and roughly chopped onion with half cloves of garlic. Chunks of lamb on the bone with fresh herbs stewed in another, liberally doused with the Uighur spice blend of salt, pepper, and cumin. His son assembled each dish by ladling meat and bone and broth into a deep bowl filled with cut noodles a foot long and then topping it with the other ingredients, one at a time.

The last additions were a healthy dollop of neon orange *tien tsin* chile paste in sesame oil, which pooled with all the other ingredients, plus a handful of coriander leaves and a small bowl of green jalapeno-like *li jiao* chile wheels.

They dove into the steaming bowls while sitting atop wood crates, one set with a small round tabletop, oblivious to the desert heat. Adopting the local custom, they slurped the broth from porcelain spoons and plucked bits of meat and vegetables with chopsticks under the gaze of the noodle wallah, wiping stained hands. Heavy cumin flavoring was balanced perfectly by the sprigs of fresh coriander leaves, finished by a waft of pepper heat, and accompanied by malty Uighur black beers.

"*Lezzetlik*," said Lilah smiling, looking at the watchful wallah as she wiped her chin with a sleeve. Satisfied, the wallah returned to his noodle gyrations.

"Lezze-what?" said Max, surprised at her use of another language.

"It means delicious," she replied. "I picked it up at the bagel shop this morning."

They sipped their beers amid the operatic drama of noodle-making, content on their crates. Suddenly, the sun shining on their backs went dark, something substantial having blocked the light. They turned to see a tall figure in silhouette, its features darkened by the bright backdrop. And then it spoke.

"Max Little. I might have guessed. The charming accomplice threw me off. Hello Ms. DeVillier."

Shading their eyes, the hat and round glasses of looming Ed Garland, spice agent, became apparent.

"Well, hello, Ed," said Lilah cheerfully. "I guess I'm busted."

"Please," he said, showing that he had the upper hand. "You knew before we spoke that I worked for International Spice Corporation. And you have a small but recognizable part in Max's Naga Jolokia video from India, which the entire spice world has seen. A few calls allowed me to find out that you were traveling together and your identity. I have a large network and paid a local fellow to follow you here. How hot was it, Max?"

Max did not stand, continuing to sip the dark beer. He didn't want to acknowledge the man's overbearing height and tactical advantage.

"The hottest chile ever, by a longshot," he said, after a pause. "Sent me into another dimension. Lilah and the university lab will have to determine exactly how hot, but it is weapons-grade. I'm sure your people will find a way to package it for the global market in the near future. Nice to see you, Ed."

Ed stood still for a moment, making clear he wanted to choose his words wisely for impact. "If you hadn't employed your accomplice as a foil, I might have justified your being here to a spicy adventure on your way home from a fact-finding trip to India," he said. "But you're here for some other reason, one you wanted to keep me from finding out. Shall we cut to the chase?"

Max took a long draw from his beer, hoping to convey a casual attitude he did not feel. "With your vast resources and global network, I'm sure you've heard rumors of an undiscovered Silk Road chile, Ed. I know you and your team are searching for it, which is why you're here, an eight-hundred-pound spice gorilla blocking the Kashgar sun. In Kyoto, you made clear what you thought of the artisanal market, and I'm the embodiment of an artisan-inspired spicy foods business. I'm the fly buzzing around your billion-dollar company, a lone monkey with a track record of success. I'm going to beat you to this one, Ed, because it's my find. International Spice Corporation will be buying from me. When I find it."

The man's white teeth shone through a forced grin. "Not if I, and yes, my vast network, get there first. These fabled chiles are made into a spice blend I hear is extraordinary, so it fits my purview and my company's industry preeminence priorities. We're canvassing markets and villages across Central Asia as we speak, and sooner or later, we will uncover its origin. You haven't found it yet, so it's a wide-open playing field, Max."

Max remained seated, watching the noodle wallah and sipping beer. "We'll see, Ed. Looks like you'll be alone for Happy Hour Times Two today."

"Game on," said Garland, turning to leave. "Good day, Ms. Khojakarta."

The next day hosted the famous Yekshembe Bazari, the Sunday Kashgar animal market, and Max did not want to miss the centuries-old spectacle, tales of which he had heard and read about over the years. Despite the lingering inclemency of Ed Garland, they vowed to enjoy their night in Kashgar, acting nonchalantly like tourists. Their cover was blown, and spies were undoubtedly lurking, but they figured they might as well make the best of the ensuing thirty-six hours.

Plump with laghman and lamb kebabs, they set off to walk the alleys of the old city and see what they might encounter. The market had not yielded any pepper surprises except Ed Garland, and Max was confident that there were no discoveries to be made locally relative to his quest. So, they browsed and tasted, intimate explorers encountering the charm of the oasis city at each stall and alley. The low-lying sun sent angled shafts of light across the mud-red buildings as the day waned to dusk, and scents of tea and incense filled the air.

They strolled arm in arm, peeking into doorways and around corners. The thoroughfares were lined by narrow canals that fed shade trees and lush gardens secreted behind high walls. Men drank tea and played board games in the street while women labored at chores, mirroring ancient Kashgari life. Then, the haunting sounds of singing and stringed instruments echoed through the alleys ahead. Hands beat drums, giving a human rhythm to the wailing of a singer. They gravitated toward its source without speaking, winding through the old city and following the sound like a scent.

They stopped before a courtyard fronted by an eight-foot-high mud wall, an ancient double door as its entrance. Green-leaved mulberry limbs poked over the barrier, behind which they heard a group of musicians working in unison. The high-pitched voice carried above stringed instruments and drums, reflecting off the alley's walls.

Wordlessly, Max grabbed Lilah's hands and began twirling her in rhythmic circles, moving his feet to the beat, spinning himself. They drew together, then apart, looking in each other's eyes. Her silky pants billowed and flowed along with her hair beneath the beaded Uighur cap, and they danced alone in the sound-filled, shadowy space for what felt like an hour, far across the world.

Eventually, the music and song decreased in intensity, slowing, diminishing, and finally fading into silence. Max and Lilah stood facing each other, the only sound that of their excited breathing. They met eyes and bowed in unison, eliciting silent applause from unseen musicians as they bounded down the alley hand in hand, free of worry and carried along by passion.

After their Kashgar dance-off, they found the alleyways dark and muffled in silence. The only sounds were the far-off din of television sets and gurgling of water in the culverts along the thoroughfare. They made their way through the old city in the presumed direction of their room and the Id Kah Mosque, and watching for followers, stayed close to darkened walls and avoided streetlamps. Max was adamant that Ed Garland would go to any length to win and had the resources to do so. The hardest part would be getting across the expansive square and into their brightly lit hotel unseen.

Emerging from the shadows, they crossed the square, now empty in the moonlit night, save for a few plainclothes police monitoring the restive Uighurs. They giggled and flirted, assuming they were under surveillance and walked straight into the hotel's lobby. The combined energies of the musical experience and clandestine foray to the hotel got both their hearts racing. In the elevator, Max pressed Lilah against its wall, kissing her passionately. She wrapped a leg around him, pulling his advance in further, as their desire became a blur of locked lips and groping at clothes. Arriving at their shared room, they almost crashed through the door, realizing only briefly their twin bed predicament before falling onto hers. Clothes flew to different corners of the room before they made love on one bed, then the other, finishing in the space between the beds. The cold linoleum pleasantly counterbalanced the heat they had created as they lay panting on the floor.

"Is it just me, or does all this adventure and espionage make you horny?" said Lilah, already knowing the answer.

"You bet it does," Max replied. "It's like new hot sauce scorching my tongue or popping open a fresh chile in my hands. Quite erotic." They both broke into exhausted laughter at once.

Then, turning to face her, he said, "Watching you dance and holding your hand does things to my system I can't begin to explain, Lilah. You've got a magical hold on me, and I hope it doesn't end."

His words had the effect of stopping her breath before enveloping her entire body in warmth and a deep hum of emotional electricity, and Lilah rolled over to sit astride her lover. She placed her hands on his chest, feeling the rise and fall of his life force, and her eyes began to water.

"Max Chota, you are a creature unlike any on this earth," she said, as her tears dropped onto his chest. She wiped them away and looked into his eyes as her amulet swung between them. "You remember the ceremony at Delphine's house in Louisiana, right? I was very, uh, consumed by the whole thing. It affected me deeply, and we had only just met. Among the spirits called on your behalf that night was the Loa called Ezili. Ezili is the Loa of love and prosperity. Delphine felt our connection and directed me to call upon Ezili not only for your protection and benefit but for ours. She foresaw our connection, though it was then only beginning to grow in me. And magic has surrounded us ever since. So, it's good to know my spell is working."

Lilah slid off of him. "Now, let's rest, and tomorrow, please show me this ancient Sunday market everyone's so excited about."

The Yekshembe Bazaar of Kashgar, located at a pivotal junction on the Silk Road, took place regularly on Sundays for over two thousand years. Stretching for a mile on the outskirts of Kashgar and drawing more than a hundred thousand people each week, it remained among the largest markets of its kind in all Central Asia, rivaling even that of Osh in Kyrgyzstan. Traders made the long trek from across the vast Xinjiang province and Kyrgyzstan, Tajikistan, Kazakhstan, and Pakistan to peddle wares and engage in barter of all sorts. Furniture, musical instruments, produce, spices, dried foods, metalwork, animal skins, donkey carts, carpets, textiles, and hats of every imaginable configuration were among the vast array of items on offer. Bargaining was spirited and could consume hours, and it employed the traditional method of writing the desired price on one's palm while shaking hands. The animal traders were at the market's outer edges, with hundreds of camels, oxen, sheep, horses, goats, and donkeys vying for space and attention. Animals could change hands a dozen times before the trading finished, the prices always kept secret to ensure profitable margins. The market represented the sole source of family income for many, infusing commerce with lively, frantic energy. It was also the region's civic center, where friends and families gathered to trade news, hear traditional music, get a haircut, watch a boxing match, bet on outdoor billiards and grumble about the government.

And to eat. Hundreds of makeshift kitchens came to life every Sunday, filling the air with aromas and smoke. Vendors from several cultures shouted their offerings to the thronging crowds, seeking a savory meal or a sweet treat. For one day a week, it became the most enormous kitchen in all Central Asia.

Max and Lilah left the hotel, hand in hand, wearing their new hats, lighthearted. They chose to walk through the blocks to the city's outskirts and the market rather than a taxi. It was a given that Garland would have them tailed, so they went about their day as tourists, searching for nothing but memories. More and more people joined them as they ventured along, requiring no direction. Some led small packs of goats or sheep through the streets, driving them to the marketplace for sale. Emerging from the old city and crossing a bridge over the Kashgar river, a momentous sight greeted them. Hundreds of white canopies and ribbons of smoke lined the broad avenue, through which tens of thousands milled. Mopeds and donkey carts stacked with goods dodged a growing stream of humanity, beeping horns and ringing bells.

They merged into the flowing crowd, following sounds and scents, looking for nothing in particular. Rural farmers offered piles of Facing Heaven and Seven Star chiles, and they popped open fresh pods and bit into dried specimens, revealing no extraordinary discoveries. Edging their way into stalls, they watched metalsmiths hammer huge bowls and woodworkers spin lathes with their feet. Weavers put the finishing touches on multicolored spun wool coats. Max paid full price for a traditional red wool vest with brass buttons and embroidered white wool trim just completed by a woman from Uzbekistan, who seemed offended at the absence of a haggle. Lilah found an ethnic Kazakh metal necklace, an elaborate piece with rows of strung silver beads and tubes, handmade amulets, and turquoise that hung in layers to her navel. They came off as surprisingly native, except for their height.

A crowd gathered before a husband and wife and their makeshift oven, fueled by coals they fed into it from a nearby fire. The woman rolled and cut small dough circles, which she filled with minced spiced lamb, onion, and mint, then pinched them into half-moons before being placed into the oven by her husband. The pastries emerged from the fire, blistering and brown. Max and Lilah paid for four plump *samsas*, juggling their heat in wax paper before gingerly biting into one. Steam escaped from the first bite into the smoky, minty, meaty prize, which they washed down with cardamom-laced black tea.

Fifty yards on, another vendor sold *kawa mantis*, fried dumplings stuffed with pumpkin, and topped with thick yogurt and a blazingly hot red chile sauce ladled from a bucket, with a scent so potent it tickled the olfactories. A dozen expectant customers held up fingers to place their orders; Max and Lilah each had three, humming in unison. From a steaming cauldron, slow-cooked saffron lamb and yogurt stew called *shashlik* was ladled into bowls and served with toasty *girde naan* flatbread for scooping. Max requested a spoonful of dried chile flakes from a smiling Tajik woman to give the stew a kick and was sweating happily within minutes. This stop was followed by another fifty yards along by brazier-blackened kebabs of lamb and a cold vinegary chickpea and carrot salad called *nokot*.

Any thought of Garland and his operatives disappeared for the moment. For an hour, they wandered and ate and watched cooks and craftsmen ply their trades. Max vowed to take up baking and build a woodfired backyard oven.

"You'd like Laguna," he said absentmindedly to Lilah as they strolled. "You can hear the surf crashing on the sand from my apartment and smell salt in the air. Plus, I share my bed with an eighty-pound bulldog named Gus."

"Is that an invitation?" she asked.

"Well, uh, I suppose it is," he replied, kicking the ground, realizing that it most certainly was, though the thought had just found him. "There is something that will continue on the other side of this adventure, and I would very much like you in it. You make the adventure more adventurous."

They kissed in the middle of a thousand people, drawing whistles of admonishment from passersby. He pulled her into him, and they hugged, closing their eyes, enveloped in the sounds and smells, and each other.

An hour later, food and produce stalls began to dwindle as they neared the cloud of dust they had seen earlier. Lilah saw few women as they wove their way through a sea of bearded men in felt and wool caps. The fabled animal market lay just ahead, shrouded in haze, with the sounds and smells of livestock increasing in intensity.

Crossing an unseen border, they came upon a sea of animals stretching as far as they could see in the dense, dusty air. Trucks backed into the market's edge, disgorging flocks of woolly sheep. Lines of them stood tethered together, awaiting their fate. Goats arrived on mopeds and carts, piled together and restrained by thick nets as their owners sought a clearing to set them free. Groups of camels stood, looking above the crowd and snorting in indignation.

An adjacent clearing was bordered by hundreds of horses and their handlers. Prospective buyers were offered the opportunity to mount their selected ponies and ride them hard within the tight circle before an audience of hundreds. Donkeys brayed forlornly, passing from one owner to another, and long-horned cattle stood chewing on bits of hay. With raised voices and spirited debate over prices or quality, negotiations were frantic, utilizing the price-in-the-palm method, and no money visibly changed hands. Buyers inspected teeth and hooves, handling the animals like the commodities they were. A thousand piles of dung were trampled into the ground by humans and animals alike, and the air was thick with its pungency. Every man wore the hat that identified his ethnicity, and many passed bottles of clear spirits between them as they shopped.

"This would be an animal rights activist's nightmare," said Lilah, "Yet being here, it feels normal and alive and a part of these people's existence. Let's go see the ponies." She pulled her lover along toward the equestrian bazaar, like teens at an amusement park.

Horses from the steppes of Central Asia and its mountains were short and stout like those the Russian explorer Nickolai Prezhalvsky encountered, which now bear his name. Petroglyphs in the Tien Shan mountains four thousand years old depicted them running wild, and two millennia ago, the Chinese Emperor referred to them as *Tien Ma*, or heavenly beasts descended from dragons. Genghis Khan and Attila the Hun coveted them and waged wars to obtain the steeds for their invading armies, making Central Asian horses one of the Silk Road's primary economic drivers. They could travel far on little water without shoes as they pulled carts, plowed fields, provided transportation, and herded other animals.

They pressed their way through the throng of horses and humans, parties to an endless negotiation, and emerged onto the open expanse where horses and camels were taken for test drives. Lilah searched for the most forlorn-looking pony she could find, continuing to pull Max along. With days of beard, a new vest, and Kyrgyz cap, Max gave the appearance he might be in the market and was offered the reigns to dozens of ponies. Lilah stopped before a gray speckled specimen and stroked its mud-caked mane and scarred flanks. Looking past Lilah, its owner indicated with a wave that Max should take the pony for a spin.

"You like?" demanded the horse's owner, a particularly swarthy character in a tall Tajik hat. "Make try! Good horse you will like. Looks dumb but very smart this one."

He handed the rope reigns to Max, who passed them to Lilah. "Not for me, for her," he said. "She's the boss."

The man squinted in bewilderment as Lilah grabbed the horse's mane and flung her body over its bare back. The horse twitched and protested at the unfamiliar new load until Lilah leaned forward and whispered into its ear. The gray stiffened then relaxed as soft secret words were spoken that transformed its disposition. Holding the reigns loosely, Lilah surveyed the arena and its dynamics. With a click of the tongue and a gentle press of her thighs, the horse sprang into action, following the rider's direction to trot along the arena's border. After fifty yards, she spotted an opening in the horse testing melee and guided her mount through a brief gap, exhibiting a fluid mastery of riding. With another click of the tongue and pressure from her heels, the horse immediately changed course, emboldened with new purpose. She zigzagged randomly through the throng, dipping her torso along with the animal's turns, hair flowing, as the crowd recognized that a woman mastering a horse in public was a rare occurrence. The horse's owner, seeing his now valuable possession perform with skills he had not witnessed before, raised the price in his head by fifty percent.

"See, excellent riding horse. Genghis Khan chose these for conquering the world. Your woman is strong," the Tajik said to Max as he watched the spectacle.

"She is certainly that," responded Max, "though I doubt that we will be purchasing a horse today, my friend. It's a long way to America."

From across the arena, Max watched as Lilah spotted an opening and set the horse to an instant gallop, racing straight across the melee head down and directly toward them. At the last moment, she straightened and pulled the reins hard to navigate a skidding stop in a cloud of dust five feet from the two men. Claps and whistles went up from the crowd, and Lilah waved to them as she dismounted, handing the reigns back to the owner. The gray whinnied for more action, breathing hard and stomping a demanding hoof.

"That's a fine horse you have, sir," she said. "He has intuitive reactions and loves to race. I would like to buy him."

Before Max could state the issues with purchasing a horse at the Kashgar market, Lilah looked at him and winked, clearly conveying that she knew what she was doing. He put his hands in his pockets and watched how her decision would play out, incredulous but trusting her judgment. She reached out her hand to accept the seller's price, which he wrote on his palm. A dozen men in caps gathered to watch the negotiation, and the seller broke custom to write the inflated price on her upstretched palm as well. He wanted his competitors to witness a selling victory. Whistles went up among the bystanders. She imagined the price had gone up with her demonstration and countered with half, writing the number with a flourish for all to see. The Tajik man's eyes narrowed, and the negotiation began in earnest, though his confidence was shaken at haggling with a woman for a horse.

A back-and-forth game ensued, watched by a rapt audience, with the price edging up. When it reached a twenty-five percent increase from the original number, the man threw his hands up in fake disgust, as though he had been forced to make a concession, with grunting admiration from the crowd. Lilah peeled off the banknotes and shook the man's hand, who then presented her the reigns to her new possession. The horse whinnied and nudged his face into Lilah's ear, pleased with the result.

"I know what you're thinking," Lilah said to Max as they led the horse away, the crowd observing the Westerners with curiosity. "Just watch. I have a plan."

They moved to the outskirts of the trading area, where families with children watched the spectacle. Families with no sons were forced to watch from a distance. Spotting a small Uighur family she had caught a glimpse of during her ride, she approached a father, mother, and daughter. Most girls wore the standard colorful ethnic dresses, but the one she had noticed wore work clothes, most likely from a farm. While pointing at his daughter, Lilah gave the reigns to the father; he raised his hands to indicate he could not understand or accept the gift. Sensing the Western woman's intentions, the wife quickly grabbed the reigns and bowed to Lilah in gratitude. Lilah took the excited girl and put her atop the horse, then whispered words into the horse's ear, informing the gray of its new owner. His mane twitched, and he whinnied, turning around to see his new master, who pet his mane and cheeks, beaming with joy.

"*Kop rakhmat*," said the girl in gratitude, bowing from atop the horse.

Lilah took her hand. "*Izmingiz nime?*" she asked, wanting to know the girl's name.

The girl straightened, pointing to her chest. "*Mining ismin Mihrigul.* Like rose flower."

Pointing to her chest, she responded, "Lilah, Persian name like lilac tree."

The girl thought for a moment. Pointing to herself, then to Lilah, she said, "Flower and tree. Same!"

Lilah clapped, beaming at the likeness, saying, "Yes! Flower and tree. Pretty and strong, like us. Ride like the wind, Mihrigul!"

Lilah bowed to the family, hands clasped in thanks for accepting her gift. The women waved while the father stared blankly, unable to process the event. He became immediately besieged by prospective buyers, who had witnessed the horse's abilities. Receiving stern looks from both his wife and daughter, he grudgingly waved the offers off.

"Looks like you picked up some Uighur phrases. That was quick," Max said. "And I knew you were probably good on a horse, but that was something else. You gave those people quite a show."

"The moment called for a strong woman," Lilah said as they weaved through the onlookers. "Too many men in one place, making all the decisions, is never a good thing. And I could see in the girl's face she didn't like being on the sidelines. Maybe her father will treat her differently now. I think she'll make sure he will."

KYRGYZSTAN

M ax and Lilah awoke before dawn, packing quickly and hailing a taxi
to the Kashgar train station. They bought two tickets to Urumqi, a
twelve-hour journey to the province's far north, skirting the eastern
edge of the Tien Shan mountains near Mongolia. Certain that Ed
Garland had them followed, they boarded the train without bothering
to look for their pursuers, promoting their conspicuousness, then
shimmied out between the cars on the other side. Hopping over the
tracks to the next platform, they blended in with the crowd before any
rail officials were able to spot them, stooping low and making their way
to a rear exit. Max scanned the station for any sign they were being
watched, then, with Lilah, slipped out the door, confident of their
anonymity. They hailed a cab to take them back to town and the
gathering point for those crossing the Torugart Pass to Kyrgyzstan,
where they checked into the transit office to connect with their
prearranged driver and vehicle, standing next to a road-weary minivan.
Plainclothes Chinese police monitored the passengers, snapping
pictures.

"Anyone leaving from here must have prearranged their travel and
documents just like we did," said Max. "I doubt Ed Garland could have
pulled it together in time, even if he had figured out where we were
going. And if he does, we'll be a day or two ahead, and I think that
might make the difference. So, time for Kyrgyzstan."

"And pepper-head immortality," she said, looking into his eyes.

He kissed her deeply, holding her head in his hands. "I guess this
is a bit rogue-ish," he said. "I hope it's working for you."

Her green eyes glimmered. "Big-time turn on, your roguishness. I'd
follow you anywhere, Max Chota. So don't lose me."

Their Han Chinese driver, Wan, did his best to explain the country's
geography and topography as they made their way out of Kashgar
northwest toward the Tien Shan, looming in the hazy distance. Canals
called *karez* crisscrossed an otherwise arid landscape, ancient
engineering that sent snowmelt from the mountains to Kashgar and
the surrounding valleys. Poplar trees, sometimes three or four deep,
lined the roadway, their leaves fluttering in the breeze, windbreaks for
the canal-irrigated fields. In what would otherwise have been an
inhospitable desert landscape, orchards and vineyards bloomed, the
source of the region's famous fruit bounty. Beyond the reach of the
karez system, they entered a barren high-altitude desert with dunes
stretching before them to the foothills of the Tien Shan. Passing
through four separate frontier checkpoints, their documents and
baggage were inspected by armed guards, looking as though their

posting was a result of either misdeed or misfortune. They climbed the pass for hours as the snowcapped peaks came into view before reaching the final Chinese checkpoint, where they were x-rayed for contraband and their bags emptied twice.

After a mile of no man's land between the Chinese and Kyrgyz border posts, traversing a gray, treeless plain, a massive structure loomed before them: the fifty-foot-tall Kyrgyz/Chinese friendship arch, sitting in the middle of the bleak alpine wilderness at twelve thousand feet. Late in the day, they were deposited a mile farther along with other vehicles' passengers at the tiny Kyrgyz customs booth, now officially in Kyrgyzstan. After inspecting the group's documents, the customs official randomly chose to levy innocuous fines and fees, primarily directed at the tourists. Resisting was futile and would jeopardize entry into the country. Max and Lilah were at the end of the line and got off easy at $100 each. *I wonder if Bakiyev gets a piece of that action,* thought Max. Past border control, a cluster of vehicles awaited their passengers, pre-booked from Kashgar. Vans carried other travelers in big groups, while open-air trucks ferried locals and their belongings. Standing beside a faded and dented Toyota Landcruiser stood a frail man with more mustache than face holding a sign that read *DeVillier/Little,* and after confirming their identities, he ushered them into the back. Theirs was the last vehicle to leave the border post, which was closing for the day.

"You go to Osh, yes, DeVillier/Little?" he asked. "Seven hours. We go now."

Snow blanketed the peaks that surrounded them as they began the descent into Kyrgyzstan, buffeted by an icy wind. Compared to the graded and maintained Chinese part of the pass, the Kyrgyz section was like the surface of the moon, and they bounced along in the hard rear seat of the rickety Landcruiser over the deeply rutted track, deeper into the Tien Shan. The Kyrgyz driver dodged gaping potholes but proved entirely incapable of competing against the destroyed dirt track as the vehicle careened over the washboard highway. Max fought the tumult as best he could, bracing against the launches and landings. He could feel his kidneys jolting inside his body as he pulled hard on a lone strap for support to keep from bouncing off the side window. Lilah seemed to somehow find her groove, loosening her frame and working with the uncontrolled movements, a grinning, bouncing rag doll, laughing out loud at the absurdity and their helplessness. Few other vehicles attempted to ply the broken road, and for an hour, they passed only random transport trucks and a lone passenger van, overstuffed with travelers headed back to China and Kashgar.

As they rounded a sharp turn, the driver hit the brakes without warning, forcing Max's face into the headrest before him. The

Landcruiser skidded sideways, coming to an abrupt halt, consumed in a cloud of its own dust. As the breeze blew the air clear, their view of the descending road came into focus. A black Lincoln Continental sedan had parked sideways on the road, blocking passage in both directions, unafraid of any consequences. Max pegged the vehicle as early 1960s: it had heavy lines, suicide doors, and smoked windows, and it was entirely out of place on the rutted mountain crossing. Two men in dark glasses and black suits stood at either end of the Lincoln, arms crossed, facing their direction. One reached to open the front-facing rear door, allowing a stout, short man in a white suit, white hat, and camelhair coat to emerge. He used an ivory cane with a brilliant ruby handle to stand in the middle of the road, raising both his arms and beckoning the Landcruiser to come to him. Then he leaned against the Lincoln and waited, totally at ease.

"Turn around!" hissed Max to the driver, who sat motionless with his hands up, acting like he was being robbed.

"Shut up, no way," the driver hissed back. "We do what he says. Do you know who that is?"

"I can guess," said Max, his head spinning with his scenarios.

Bakiyev knew all along that they'd be using this route to enter Kyrgyzstan, he figured, and Gasanov had told them to employ this route numerous times. Guessing he was a chess piece in the middle of an increasingly odds-intensive game, Max muttered "checkmate" as he tried to formulate a plan.

"Well, there's our friend Bakiyev, here to welcome us to his country," said Lilah. "What do you think we should do, Max? Ask for a ride?"

He struggled to think. "Not a bad idea, actually, considering these rock-hard seats. But we need to get to Dostuk and connect with those villagers without his influence. He's a threat to our entire mission. I'm going to go see what he's thinking. Please stay in the car, no matter what happens," he said.

Handing a one-hundred-dollar bill to the terrified driver, he said, "Don't move, got it?"

Max got out of the car and stood next to the open door, surveying his predicament. They couldn't pass Bakiyev and company and couldn't turn around and return to China without the proper documents. They were stuck, and he would have to negotiate his way to a solution. Boris and Vlad sneered as he began the fifty-yard walk toward the Lincoln. A cold wind blew across the plateau, coursing down the Tien Shan's glaciers, creating dust devils.

Boris and Vlad closed around their employer as he approached the vintage car, holding their hands out for Max to stop. "Well, hello, Boris and Vlad," he said disarmingly. "You look much better than the last few times we've seen each other." The men's faces turned instantly icy. Vlad cracked his knuckles, readying eager fists.

It was Bakiyev who spoke. He had a jovial, round, laugh-lined face with prominent Mongol features and coal-black eyes. "Max, Max, Max. How nice of you to come. Their names are Josef and Antony, actually. People call them Joe and Tony. They're good boys, good employees, though you have managed to make them look foolish more than once, I will give you that. But now you are in my country, my turf, as you would say. I could command them to harm you if I wanted, but we will accomplish more if we simply talk."

"How did you know we would be here?" Max said.

Bakiyev grinned. "You do not know me yet and what I can manipulate, Max. You have been tracked since you departed Assam, flying through Kathmandu to Kashgar and over this mountain pass, the way I decided you would come. I have friends in many places, including the passport office of the Kyrgyz consulate in Kashgar. Now you are here. I have waited many weeks for this moment."

"And Gasanov," Max asked. "What has become of him?"

The question caused Bakiyev to smile warmly or wickedly; he couldn't tell. "Nickolai is in Osh, in good health. He likes you very much, which is one of the reasons I am being so nice."

Max played his only card, or so he thought. "Then let's get on with it. Take me and leave Lilah to go in peace. She doesn't need to be part of this. Whatever this is."

Bakiyev and his men began to laugh at once, shaking their heads. "How gallant," the mobster said. "However, you are not in a position to negotiate. This is our country. And you have misjudged the situation. We don't even want you to come with us today."

"Then what do you want?" Max said. "You're blocking the road."

"We are going to take your lovely accomplice, Miss DeVillier. I have set up a full laboratory with liquid chromatography testing equipment at my villa in Osh, where we hope she will do some work on our behalf. You, I believe, have another road to travel. You will go to Dostuk and work your pepper magic with the villagers there, and I hope you can achieve better results than we have. I recommend a stop at the ancient caravanserai of Tash Rabat along the way. It is the most vivid relic of the Silk Road anywhere in Asia. If you are successful, we will meet again in Osh. I am not difficult to locate."

Before Max could speak, he heard the sound of tires crunching on gravel behind him. The Landcruiser had released its brakes and rolled down the hill, now stopped just at his back. As he turned back to face Bakiyev, strong arms pinned his to the sides of his body while another set of hands began to wrap heavy tape around his arms, legs, and mouth. Once restrained, he was pushed to the ground, kneeling where the roadside ended, and a steep hill began. He breathed heavily past the thick tape, seething with anger. Boris stepped over Max, shoving his knee into the side of his head, and opened Lilah's door, saying, "Please, Mizz DeVillier, thizz vay. Mr. Bakiyev vishes you to travel in comfort with him to his villa in Osh. I will get your bag."

Lilah stood outside the car, weighing the situation and looking down at Max. Confusion and fear filled his eyes. She had rolled down her window and heard Bakiyev's words. It was clear that she was their prize and had no place to go but with the Kyrgyz men.

"Okay, I'll go with you," she said. "But if you hurt Max, it will be a cold day in hell before you get any help from me whatsoever. And if you hurt me, I know he will come to find you. All of you."

She turned and glared at Boris and Vlad. "And you oversized morons already know he's smarter than both of you. Put together."

Lilah allowed herself to be led by Boris. But while passing the Landcruiser's driver, who had opened his door to witness the proceedings, she delivered a hard kick to his shin, snatching back from him the hundred-dollar bill. "Loser!" she whispered, slamming the door shut on the same leg as he doubled over in pain. She then leaned down and held Max's face, looking into his eyes, now bloodshot as he struggled to talk to her.

"This seems like the only solution, my sweet intrepid Max. I have a strong feeling they won't hurt me. They need me. So do what you need to do and come find me in Osh. You're the only one capable of getting it done. I'll be waiting for you. I love you."

She walked toward the Lincoln and Bakiyev's jeeringly outstretched arms.

"Excellent decision, Miss DeVillier," the mobster said. "We mean you no harm."

"Then why the duct tape?" she asked icily.

He shrugged. "Your Max is very resourceful and seems to have gotten under the skin of my otherwise very skilled employees. They have determined not to take any more chances with him. The tape is their idea. He will not be harmed. And you will have a much more comfortable ride down the hill. Please come. We have a long journey ahead of us."

Lilah got into the back seat with Bakiyev, stealing a last look at Max as Vlad shut the doors and Boris tossed her bag into the trunk. She saw that he was already straining to escape from his binds. As Vlad and Boris climbed into the front seat, Vlad nodded to the Landcruiser driver. The Lincoln fired up and sped off. When the other vehicle was out of sight, the driver used his good leg to shove Max over the road's edge, and he rolled for a hundred feet down the steep embankment. He stopped in time to see the Landcruiser speed off toward Osh as his duffle bag was launched from the passenger side window, accompanied by a defiant middle finger. It rolled down the hill toward where he lay, bound and gagged. Alone at twelve thousand feet with night closing fast.

Max groaned as he strained against the duct tape around his limbs, thankful he hadn't struck any of the hillside's sizeable rocks above him on his way down the hill. Lilah's boot to the driver's leg certainly contributed to his absurd predicament, and he laughed beneath the duct tape, thinking about that moment. Rolling onto his belly, he slithered horizontally to a jagged boulder. He began moving his legs back and forth, bending at the knee to cut through the loops of tape on his ankles, struggling for oxygen in the thin air and his covered mouth. After a few minutes, he broke through and then set to work on the tape around his knees. Once his legs were free, the arms and wrists were an easier task. He took repeated, grateful inhales of the thin oxygen after freeing his mouth.

Sitting on the boulder atop the Torugart Pass, he took stock of his situation. His passport and wallet were still in his front pocket, and his duffle bag sat fifty feet back up the hill. No bones were broken, but his elbows were bloody, his jeans ripped, and he was caked with dirt. Lilah was gone, riding off to Osh with Bakiyev, farther away from him every minute. Ed Garland and his International Spice Corporation agents were off the radar now, though there was no way of knowing if they'd gotten to the market in Osh. As he thought it through, he reluctantly accepted that Bakiyev was right: he had to get to Dostuk and the Buntun Lodge Guest House. And to Tash Rabat, to unravel its mysteries. Two things Gasanov had told him he must do, as well, to find the Kyrgyz chile that evaded both of them.

Max considered that he was being double-crossed, caught in a Bakiyev-Gasanov conspiracy, and manipulated for their combined ends. A plot which had brought him to this point, to Kyrgyzstan on the Silk Road, and left him stranded without any means of help or support. Despite his anger, he had to trust that Bakiyev would not hurt Lilah so that he could focus on what he needed to do to get back to her. Bakiyev needed both of them to realize his goals, so Max, through his pain, resolved to carry on and uncover the Fire of the Valley mystery. Lilah's proclamation that she would follow him anywhere rang over and over in his head, as did her plea that he never lose her. He had failed in that.

Making his way to his duffle bag, Max was relieved to find the large bottle of water he always carried was still inside. He used it to clean up as best he could, then bandaged the scraped elbows. He used pieces of the duct tape to patch up the knee holes of his jeans from the inside, shook the dirt out of his hair, and changed into a clean Neil Young and Crazyhorse T-shirt. He then clawed his way up the embankment to the empty road. The glacial wind sweeping down from the peaks was a frigid reminder of his whereabouts, and a thick, worn Long Beach State hoodie from his duffle bag deflected the cold.

Max walked for an hour in the waning light, heading downhill and west into Kyrgyzstan, hurrying to lose as much elevation as possible. Even though it was late May, snowstorms and freezing temperatures at this elevation remained threats, and he didn't want to be caught in such conditions wearing only a sweatshirt. No vehicles came down the pass, while only a few lonely trucks passed going up the road, their drivers looking at him strangely, to wait out the night at the now-closed border station. Snow flurries began to fall, carried sideways by a swift mountain wind, as he pulled the hood of his sweatshirt closed in the enclosing dark. He scanned the hillsides for caves and overhangs as he trotted down the roadway, someplace to overnight away from the increasingly hostile elements, finding nothing. As his situation grew grimmer, so did his thoughts.

The ease with which he and Lilah had procured their travel visas to Kyrgyzstan in Kashgar was now obviously suspect. He reread Gasanov's letters from memory, looking for signs that he was being led into the trap in which he now found himself. Bakiyev's heavily accented English and charcoal eyes, and the mocking faces of Boris and Vlad echoed and flashed. He found himself wishing he had packed some kind of weatherproof coat. His head ached from the altitude, making thoughts painful and his mood increasingly dark.

Max pushed on. Getting out of the elements became the necessary focus for his energy. Finally, a slight overhang appeared, its rear to the freezing wind, and he was able to find modest shelter from the driving snow, piling on layers of clothes from his duffle bag.

Max stomped his feet and clapped his hands for warmth, thinking about a long night in this spot. There was howling in the distance. He thought about wolves, snow leopards, and the legendary Yeti, the Asian Bigfoot. For half an hour, he knelt, staring into the bleak landscape, his outlook even more dismal as the light disappeared. Sounds carried on the wind seemed like voices or predatory calls. A faint beam of light caught his eye, washing across the darkening landscape like a vehicle rounding a bend, then was gone. He strained to listen for some sign of human activity.

Sound began to drift in the gusts of wind, something vaguely familiar, distinctly guitar-like. And singing. Composed music was floating on the buffeting air, getting clearer. He then made out the distinctive organ and vocals of Jeff Lynne and the Electric Light Orchestra, singing their hit "Mister Blue Sky." *Mister blue sky please tell us why/You had to hide away for so long (so long)/Where did we go wrong?* At twelve thousand feet in Kyrgyzstan, weather declining, it had a distinct warming sensation. The sweep of light now appeared closer, rounding the turn just above and lighting the road before his scant shelter. He quickly rose, grabbed his duffle bag, and slid down to the road, feet planted in its center. He was an ELO fan to the core.

Max stood in the road, facing uphill, as the truck's headlights blazed around the corner. He shielded his eyes from the beams. A clear male voice sang along to the highly engineered composition of Lynne's lyrics. *Hey you with the pretty face/Welcome to the human race...*

The lights landed on Max just in time for the lorry, carrying a full load of Chinese refrigerators strapped to its bed, to skid to a halt five feet from where he stood. A swirl of dust and snow enveloped him as he covered his face with a sleeve.

The blaring music stopped, and a deep voice came from behind a fist thrust out the truck's window, speaking Kyrgyz. *"Ayak kakaya! Kotok Bash! Sen Jidi?"*

Max stepped to the side, out of the headlights, looking through the windshield. A thick, bearded man in Kyrgyz felt skullcap sat, glaring, with tattooed arms folded on the steering wheel. The man did not match the voice.

He yelled up to the truck's cab. "I'm afraid I don't speak Kyrgyz, but I am a huge ELO fan," was all that came to mind.

The driver's face brightened, incredulous at the sound of Max's English as he leaned out the window. "You like ELO? Are you English?"

"No, American," said Max. "Stuck in your country, and I could use a ride."

He craned his neck to take in the shocking realization. "An American! It is illegal to hitchhike on this highway, my friend, so hurry up and get in. The police will lock you up for a month. Fortunately for you, I got stuck at customs with a full inspection, or you would have been out here all night."

Max trotted to the truck's passenger side and climbed up into the cab, tossing his duffle bag behind the seat. The driver looked him over. "Did you fight your way into our country? You're bloody and dirty."

Max looked down at his torn jeans and bloodstained elbows. "Let's just say my driver reconsidered our contract," he said. "My name is Max."

"Aksim Azbekov," replied the man, extending a grimy hand.

"Thank you for stopping, Aksim. It would have been a cold night," said Max.

"If I had not stopped, you would have been flattened."

Max managed a chuckle. "What did you yell when you saw me in the road?"

"Holy shit. Dickhead. Are you crazy?" said Aksim with a laugh.

"Well, I probably deserved that," Max said. "But I was running out of options."

Aksim ground the truck into gear, causing it to lurch and bounce as it started down the road.

He had massive hands and forearms, sledgehammers at the end of tree trunks, which he placed over the wide steering wheel crossways to steer it. "Where are you going in Kyrgyzstan?" he asked.

Max thought for a few moments. "Ultimately, I'm going to Osh. I have to find someone there. But first, I need to visit Tash Rabat."

"Doing some sightseeing then," said Aksim. "But somehow, I don't think sightseeing is what you do. Are you CIA?"

The question surprised Max. "Well, if you mean the Culinary Institute of America, then maybe," he said, generating a confused look from the Kyrgyz man. "But no, I am not in the CIA or any other spy network. I'm a spice merchant, here to do some business and exploration."

He looked Max over carefully, weighing the truth of the American's words. "I believe you. Spice merchant is an interesting profession. And it would make an excellent cover for a spy. If you decided to be one. I am just saying."

Max shook his head. "Just a spice merchant. But things in the spice world have gotten a bit crazy of late, more espionage than commerce to tell the truth. I'm in a race with a huge multinational corporation to find a spice no one knows the origins or location of, somewhere here in your country."

Aksim looked over Max again. "You are not kidding, are you?"

"No, I am not. And I need to get to Tash Rabat. Somehow it plays into this story."

"There is not much at Tash Rabat except Tash Rabat," said Aksim. "And nothing has happened there for five hundred years."

"I'm interested in what happened there five hundred years ago," said Max.

"No one out there but sheepherders, who may let you stay in one of their yurts," said Aksim. "It is seventeen kilometers off the highway, so you will not get there tonight. And I cannot take you."

"I'm grateful for the ride, Aksim. I'll be alright," said Max, staring at the rutted road ahead. "Where did you pick up such good English?"

"I have driven trucks all over Central Asia, the old USSR, and Europe. English is the language of international commerce, so you must speak it if you want the big jobs. I once drove a load of semiconductors from Kashgar to London that had to get there in five days, across eleven borders. The load was too big for air freight and ocean shipping too slow. My cousin in London took me to see ELO at Wembley in 1986 before they broke up, and I felt like I went to another planet. I was changed forever."

They rode on without speaking, except for the Kyrgyz man's singalong to the entire *The Very Best of the Electric Light Orchestra* album. For a large man, Aksim imitated lead singer Jeff Lynne's falsetto exceptionally well as he navigated hairpin turns on the rutted highway. He had an additional shock absorption system installed below his seat, which cushioned the bumps and caused him to bounce in sync with the music. He occasionally raised one hand from the wheel to mock-conduct the elaborate compositions.

After another hour, Aksim pulled the truck to the side of the road. A small sign marked a dark, narrow track leading through the hills to the east.

"Tash Rabat is up that road to the right. I would walk it in the morning. Very few vehicles go up that way, except the occasional tourist van or load of sheep."

He reached behind his seat and pulled out a thick wool blanket, which he handed to Max. "Made from Pamir mountain goats in Uzbekistan. As warm as two blankets. You'll need it tonight. And here's a bag of dried fruit and nuts from Kashgar."

Max bowed in the truck's cab, pressing his palms together in thanks. "I am grateful and humbled by your hospitality, Aksim. And the ELO concert was just what I needed. Thank you."

"I am happy to have had the company," Aksim said. "Where will you go after Tash Rabat?"

"I will make my way to Dostuk, where I hope to connect with someone, then to Osh."

"Dostuk?" he said. "Stay at the local guest house. I've stayed there on journeys passing through the Naryn River Valley going to Kazakhstan. Best food for a hundred miles. The old lady is a bit rough, and the village menfolk suspicious of outsiders, but the food is more than worth it. Be well, Max. What is your last name, by the way?"

"Chota. Thank you again, Aksim."

Max jumped down from the cab, blanket and duffle bag in tow, as the Kyrgyz transport and its load of refrigerators pulled away. Once the glow of the truck's taillights faded, he found himself alone in the valley, enveloped by darkness. He fished out his mini flashlight and began making his way east up the gorge toward the ancient caravanserai of Tash Rabat.

Max swept the flashlight back and forth across the roadway. It had no lines and no shoulder on either side, flanked by a frothy stream on one and steep cliffs rising from the other. Glacial wind blew down the gorge, forcing him to lean into its gusts. He walked for half a mile, looking for anything that would suffice as a shelter, his light beam reflecting off of granite walls and rushing water, which drowned out all other sounds. He sensed that it would reach below freezing as a blanket of stars emerged in the strip of sky above the gorge.

The weight of Lilah's abduction bore down on him as he trudged onward. He marveled at her lack of fear at being forced to go with their adversaries. Now Bakiyev had her, using her for unknown ends, and had casually sent Max off on errands he deemed relevant. Tash Rabat was among the most remote places on earth, and Max had no idea what to look for once he got there.

Then he remembered the name Mishka Dubovya, the archaeologist Gasanov in his email had said might be working at Tash Rabat, doing excavations. The prospect of encountering her gave his immediate journey purpose, and what he might discover set his mental gears in motion, pushing the torturous image of Lilah pulling away in the Lincoln aside for the moment.

What's she digging for? he thought. *What has taken her to this faraway place, and what did she hope to find? Had she spoken to Gasanov? Was she compromised by influence from Bakiyev?*

Max walked in the dark for another ten minutes. Sweeping his light across the stream to his left, he made out a massive rockfall that had loosened from the cliff above, forcing the stream to flow between its tumbled boulders. One of the blocks, leaning against the cliff, loomed as big as a small house. Using smaller rocks to ford the stream, he made his way to the backside of the largest boulder, where it wedged against the cliff face. The wind blew only slightly behind the rocks, whistling through the spaces between them, and he found a flat spot, protected from the elements. Another traveler had built a fire ring in the small clearing, someone who had also walked this way seeking shelter. Scrub oaks and juniper grew in the cracks between the boulders, and he collected dead pieces for a fire, prying them from cracks in the house-sized monoliths. Soon, flames flickered off the rock walls, filling the small alcove with light as he cleared an area of grey gravel upon which to lay down. He wrapped himself in the Uzbek wool blanket, mummy-style, and drew his sweatshirt hood around his face, staring at a colossal display of stars as he drifted off to an exhausted sleep.

TASH RABAT

I ordered the ditches cleaned and maintained, bridges built over rivers, and the construction of caravanserai at distances of one day's travel across the lands. Each caravanserai had keepers and guards, whose responsibility it was to ensure the security of travelers and to guard against thieves.
-Amir Timur (Tamerlane), Ruler of the Timurid Empire, Tashkent 1336

"**I** *love you.*"
The words echoed across his psyche, creating a sensation of warmth that coursed through his body, finding its way to his limbs. It spread like light, slowly but wholly suffusing his consciousness even in sleep.

Lilah had found her way back to him in dreams. He saw her face, but she did not speak, her words careening off the walls of his trance. He watched her hand reach out to him to touch his face before she was snatched from his view in a burst of dust, gone. Her abrupt disappearance caused him to whimper out loud. Yet her absence did not bring darkness. She imbued his dream with the strong sense that he would be with her again, whole and happy. It was up to him to make it so.

Max returned to consciousness with the sensation of something cold and wet on his face. Attempting to swat the nuisance away, his hand became buried in deep fur. Realizing it was not his blanket, he froze. With a start, he rose to find a squadron of sheep had invaded his sanctuary, seeking patches of grass that sprouted between the boulders and along the creek. They scurried as he jumped up, tin bells clanging as they moved from the clearing. The warming fire of the night before had smoldered to ash, and the air was crisp and cloudless, cobalt blue sky filling jagged space between the rocks. The sun had not yet crested the cliff behind him, and he had no perception of actual time or how long he had slept. Quickly collecting his blanket and duffle bag, Max made his way out of the boulder maze to find a flock of animals gathered along the creek, eager for the sweet, late-spring grass that grew along its banks. Their handler walked along the creek with his back to the flock, a hundred yards up the road, singing as he strolled. He wore the typical Kyrgyz white felt hat with a high dome and turned-up fur brim.

Max tied the blanket around the duffle, which he slung over one shoulder, and gingerly crossed the boulders in the creek. Splashing his face with icy water and using his wet hands to slick back his unruly hair, he joined the procession. When the shepherd looked back, he merely waved at him, happy to have someone bringing up the rear. Max wore his Kyrgyz cap and had a week's worth of beard, so he must have looked somehow familiar to the man. The shepherd sang a folk song that the flock seemed to know as his voice echoed off the walls, following his verses through the gorge. After half a mile, the chasm's steep cliffs opened into a verdant, tranquil vale scoured by the creek. As the canyon relaxed, the herd of sheep spread out on both sides of the road seeking the thickest patches of grass. In an unspoken command, with his hand, the shepherd directed Max to stay with the group on the left while he went with the right, keeping them moving south up the valley toward Tash Rabat.

They moved at a leisurely pace for three hours, allowing the flock to forage, not speaking. Despite the cold spring air, a bright sun in a clear sky warmed them. Max had the nuts and dried fruit from Aksim, enough to sustain him on a long walk at high elevation, and used the time to absorb the scenery, clearing his cluttered mind. Lilah's face and voice reverberated through his consciousness, and he missed her balance and companionship. *She would love this place*, he thought. *I will find her and bring her back.* There was nothing he could do, he decided, except move forward, every step in the direction of discovery and resolution.

Finally, the shepherd signaled a stop to rest beside the creek, beckoning Max to join him on a rock. He wore the typical Kyrgyz embroidered wool vest and heavy, worn boots. His dark beard grew to a point, which he stroked with his hand, eyes golden-colored in a weathered face.

"*Salamatsyzby!*" he called as Max approached, with a raised hand. "*Siz kaydan keldingiz?*"

Max heard Gasanov use the same phrase in Jemez and figured it was a greeting.

"Good morning," he said, offering his hand. "I'm an American, going to Tash Rabat."

"Amedican?" said the man, surprised and shaking Max's hand. "Why walking? I was thinking you want work." He pointed to Max's cap. "You look Kyrgyz." Then pointing to Max's Long Beach State sweatshirt said, "Except for that."

"Just a traveler," replied Max. "But I am happy to help with your flock if it gets me to the caravanserai."

The man nodded. "Tash Rabat we go, to my camp. More grass down here, so I bring the animals this way." He reached into a shoulder bag and produced a puffy pastry. "You like samsa?"

"Yes, thank you," said Max, biting into the dumpling. The pastry was filled with fatty lamb, onions, potatoes, and carrots, excellent traveling food. "What is your name?"

"I am Dastan," the man said, smiling. "You?"

"Max, Max Chota. Chota means 'little.'"

"Hmph," said the shepherd. "Little Max. Don't understand. You are taller than me. Your father gave you this name?"

"Our family name," was all Max could say, with a shrug.

Dastan laughed at the irony. "A family of not little people. America is strange."

"It can be," said Max. "Your country is exceptionally beautiful. How much farther to Tash Rabat?"

The man looked up the valley. "Two hours, with animals. Many mountains in our country. Where will you stay at Tash Rabat? Most people come with a tour company. You are alone. You do not have a tent and no cars to the nearest town, two hours away."

"I don't know yet. I am looking for a scientist there. Perhaps she will have shelter."

"The Russian lady? She has only her yurt and not very friendly," said the shepherd. "You will stay with my family, Not Little Max."

They resumed their upward journey through the valley of Tash Rabat, leading the flock along the creek as they continued up into the Tien Shan. Max discovered that all he needed to do was clap his hands or call out a command to move the sheep along, and pleased with his job as a novice shepherd, the danger and chaos of the previous day melted away. The journey became a walking meditation, with the only sounds of the coursing stream, the animals' bells, and his occasional shouts of "Yo!" or "Ha!" to keep the flock moving. A crisp breeze blew down from the higher valleys, keeping them alert.

Rounding a bend in the road, around a sloping hill, they came to an intersection of three other valleys, snowmelt streams coming down each of them to feed the one they had been following. Treeless emerald hills flanked the entire tableau, climbing to far-off snowcapped escarpments. Built into the slope on the southeast side, a square stone structure with twenty-foot walls loomed. Nearly a hundred feet on either side, it appeared entirely out of place in such a remote location deep in the Kyrgyz mountain range. Circular towers guarded its corners, supporting a flat roof covered in grass, and in the center, a round dome rose another twenty feet. Marking the entrance was a massive, thirty-foot arched gate, outside of which a single gray car parked.

"Tash Rabat," said Dastan casually, as their two small flocks combined into one for the last leg of the journey. Sensing arrival at their temporary home, the sheep set out ahead toward a cluster of yurts beside the stream which ran in front of the caravanserai. Other small gatherings of yurts were set in two of the climbing green valleys, encampments of sheepherding families. Dogs barked, and smoke rose from metal stacks atop the round canvas dwellings as they approached.

Max stopped, letting Dastan and his flock make the last leg alone as he sat on a rock beside the icy creek. The ancient and remote feeling of the place was profound, a massive building in the middle of nowhere. While the location felt extraordinarily wild, it was not bleak, as Max pictured the life that once occurred in the high valley. *A crossroads of history*, he thought, and *a crossroads of this journey.*

He imagined the place as a traveler five hundred years ago might have seen it, rounding the same bend in the road, weary from weeks of travel. An oasis at nine thousand feet, offering shelter and food. Even now, the scent of food found its way to his senses, and he realized that he hadn't had a full meal in nearly two days. A well-tended garden across from the camp showed rows of melons and the leafy green tops of onions and potatoes. His stomach pointed him in the direction of Dastan's yurts rather than straight to the ancient structure which had brought him to this faraway place. Revelation, Max had found, was always better on a full stomach.

He walked the quarter-mile to the encampment slowly, taking in the magnificent setting. Impossibly green hills rose to become sheer granite spires and faces, their crevasses lined with spring snow. This valley was like a thousand others in the remote Tien Shan range, yet someone had decided to build a small fortress here centuries ago, the last Silk Road stop before Kashgar and the mysteries of China. He wished that he had arrived by camel to fully absorb the effect.

As he approached the yurts and sheep enclosure at Dastan's family camp, a pair of rosy-cheeked children peered out of one of the canvas doorways, pointing his way and calling to those inside. Their faces were a mix of Slavic and Tibetan, and given some inaudible command, the adolescents raced toward Max, followed by a pack of puppies tumbling over each other to get to where he stood. They tugged at his sweatshirt, pulling him toward the yurt that was their summer home while the puppies darted between his feet. Heavy wool felt pads draped the exterior walls and roof of the family yurt, protection from the cold. Aromas of meat and onion perfumed the air as he ducked inside.

The dwelling was about twenty feet across, and a fire burned in a pit at its center, the smoke exiting the ceiling. A pot suspended by chains from a metal tripod simmered over the heat, which a ponytailed Kyrgyz woman tended. Her windburned face welcomed Max warmly into her home, and she wore a patchwork coat made from faded blankets, it seemed, a pattern of stitched-together multicolored remnants. She pressed her palms in greeting, bowing from her place by the fire.

"*Salamatsyzby*," she said. Max returned the salutation.

"Welcome to our summer home, Max Chota," said Dastan, sitting against pillows from across the room. "This is my wife, Zamira, and the little ones tugging at your sleeves are Alik, my son, and my daughter, Aliya. They are twins but quite different. We have not had a guest since our family dropped us off in the high pasture weeks ago. Please join me."

The entire floor was covered with thick wool rugs in bright colors and intricate patterns, while other colorful fabrics covered the circular walls. Max removed his boots before crossing the room, customary in nomadic cultures and most of Asia, and sat on the floor against a stack of woven wool cushions. Puppies wrestled for a seat on his lap as Dastan offered him koumiss ladled from a tall ceramic pot. The sour, fermented horse milk warmed in his empty stomach, its added salt cutting the bitter flavor. Other than the fire, sun streaming through the smoke hole in the roof provided the only light, casting a bright circle on the floor. There was no furniture, apart from a chest holding blankets and bedding. Alongside one wall were stacked implements and equipment for handling animals, and on the other, a collection of pots, pans, and cooking utensils. Zamira sat on a small stool, chopping onions and chiles, tossing them into the pot.

The displayed weavings were hypnotic, an extreme contrast from the surrounding alpine landscape. Ram's horns and horses, koumiss bowls, heart shapes, geometric patterns, and elaborate scrollwork alternated along with vivid color palettes in the textiles' designs.

"Dastan, the blankets in your home are extraordinary," he said. "Can you tell me about them?"

"The blankets we use are called *shyrdaks*," Dastan said, waving his hand around the room. "They come from my wife's family, as part of her dowry, and made by her mother and aunts in their village of Ottuk, by Lake Issyk-Kul in the north. Cold air off the lake requires warmer blankets, so the kyrdaks from her village are thick and sought after. They use stronger camel wool fibers for the base and softer sheep's wool for the pile, which can last a hundred years. The designs are symbols important to Kyrgyz people, like the heart, which means hospitality, and the ram, which means prosperity."

Max lost himself in the various patterns, embracing the notion that he could easily live a nomadic life in a yurt of woven wool blankets. "How long do you stay up here in the high country?" he asked.

"We are here in this valley every year from May to October when the first grasses sprout to when the first snows fall," said Dastan. "Then we return to Naryn for winter, where we have a house and small farm, and I work part-time as an engineer. The high summer pastures in the mountains we call 'jailoo,' when the sweet grass sprouts after snows have melted. Families from Naryn valley have been bringing herds to these mountain pastures for generations. When my father got too old, the herd became my responsibility, and it is mine until my son takes over."

Max envisioned summers herding in the high country, living in a yurt with colorful rugs. And a great sound system. "The Kyrgyz seem to be a proud people," he said, "and the nomadic culture seems alive, even today."

"For two thousand years, we have roamed the mountains and plains of Central Asia," said Dastan. "These mountains are sacred to us. We fought off the Chinese and the Mongol horde to defend our lands, hiding in the high valleys and raiding their armies, which were greater than ours. Kyrgyzstan means 'the place of forty tribes,' represented in the sun's forty rays on our flag. Nature is our guide, and our lives are defined by the seasons and our history. Come, let us eat."

Zamira brought the men heaping bowls of Kyrgyz paloo, rice, and mutton with potato, carrots, onions, chopped chiles in a rich meaty broth. The chiles were dried, tabasco or cayenne-type, and moderately hot. She next served the children, then herself, and they sat in a circle, staring at Max, who grasped that they were waiting for him to begin.

"Does it not look appetizing, Max?" asked Dastan.

"I haven't eaten hot food in two days," said Max. "This meal prepared in your home is heaven to me, and I am grateful."

"Then eat!" said Dastan, adding, "Would you like more spice?"

He spoke to his wife, who brought to Max a small ceramic jar, the handle of a small wood scoop peeking from its lid. "Try this," he said, "It is a blend of spices made by the people of this region. We call it *Ot Boyanca Oroon.*"

Max wondered where he had heard the term before. He opened the lid and looked down into a colorful mix of dried spices, red, orange, green, yellow, white, purple, and black flecks. He brought up the jar to his face, inhaling as his nose went all the way in, while trained olfactories immediately went to work. The presence of chiles, though dried, was unmistakable, and he noted sweet and smoky scents. There were no seeds in the blend to define chiles' inclusion, but their presence was undeniable. *So, dried and roasted or smoked chiles,* he thought, and not just the skins. There were tiny, black, non-chile seeds and floral notes, like daffodil. Strands of saffron. Nutty tones. Also citrus, maybe orange peel. Salt. Dried onion flakes. Earthiness, like rich clay soil. He spooned several of the small scoops over his paloo and watched the multicolored mix spread across the broth's surface before stirring it into the other ingredients, changing the dish's color.

"It comes from the people of the At-Bashy River Valley, which flows into the Naryn at Dostuk," said Dastan. "Nomads and shepherds of the Tien Shan make frequent use of it to season our stews, as we have for many years. It is only found in this area, in the foothills and mountain valleys."

The description caused Max to freeze before even taking a bite of his meal, despite gnawing hunger. He put his spoon down. "What does *Ot Boyanca Oroon* mean, Dastan?" he asked.

"Let me see, in English, *fire from valley.*"

"And it comes from near Dostuk?"

"Only."

A wave of revelation overtook Max as he stared down into the bowl before him. He was close to the source, and his ears began to tingle, his unfaltering harbinger of discovery. He recalled Hedin's description of the same condiment consumed in these same valleys as Max was transported back to Delhi and Rudra's archives. Tash Rabat was now a vortex on his journey, a focal point of the mystery and the springboard into the rest of the story.

He thoughtfully composed bites from the dish, ensuring every ingredient found its way onto the wide spoon and then slurping every drop. Dastan and his family followed suit. Only the sounds of eating and the crackling of the fire were heard.

Without Max asking, his bowl filled again. And once more, he doused the paloo with the Fire of the Valley blend. It was not immediately hot; its heat grew slowly, evenly, building as it suffused in the stew's broth. Herbaceous and earth notes emerged at the forefront. The range of colors suggested a variety of different chiles, or the same one, harvested and dried at varying levels of ripeness. Though he never saw one exhibiting so many colors. The purple, like eggplant skin, was the most mysterious. Floral and citrus hints became layered into the savory fats of mutton and the richness of fire-roasted vegetables. The black seeds, probably poppy, popped with a fresh nutty crunch. He took some of the mix and dropped it into his hand for closer inspection, then touched his tongue to the dried mass, registering more up-front heat, citrus, and earth. Salt, indeed, then garlic, and smoke. Subtle saffron. It was a nuanced blend of flavors and balanced heat that he found thoroughly unique as it danced on his palate, causing him to hum inwardly and outwardly and awakening his spirit. Every spoonful spread starbursts of flavor and waves of satisfaction.

Catching himself, he looked up to see the entire family watching him. "Do you always make such noises when you eat?" asked Dastan, smiling. "I almost thought you were humming a song."

"I didn't know I was," Max said. "Perhaps only when I have found food that truly makes me happy, as this does, Dastan. Zamira, I am very thankful for this hearty meal in your home. Some meals are not only life-affirming but life-changing, and here in your yurt, that has happened. I feel nourished and rejuvenated and must find some of these spices for myself in Dostuk."

Zamira acknowledged his pressed-together palms, not understanding the words but knowing what he felt. They sat in collective contentment for another fifteen minutes, saying nothing, bonding over food.

"Max Chota, koumiss is called for," said Dastan, summoning Max to his side. They reclined on fat pillows while Zamira delivered mugs of koumiss and bowls of dates. The children retreated to a corner, playing a small board game. Aware of the customs of Central Asia, Max decided to try and reinterpret them.

"Dastan, I would like to make a request of you. I would very much enjoy it if your wife and children could sit and join us. I want to hear more about their lives if that's alright with you."

Dastan's eyes rose at the request. He scratched his beard as he looked at his family. Then he spoke to them in Kyrgyz. Max watched while their faces changed upon hearing the patriarch's words as he summoned them to the best cushions where usually only men held court. It was a simple request that broke with an ancient, but not entirely fair, tradition.

With Dastan's tacit consent, Max asked Zamira about her and her family, the weavers from the high plains near Lake Issyk-Kul. Through Dastan, he heard about the generations that had scratched out a life on the alpine steppes, luckily avoiding, for the most part, the reach of the Soviets. How her uncle had known Dastan's uncle in the military and her shyness at their first arranged meeting, and how she became enthralled at his education and drawn to his desire to retain a connection to his nomadic lineage. On the day of their engagement, Dastan's entire clan had traveled from the Naryn Valley to their village, Kyzyl-Suu, to present him to her family, arriving in a green felt coat and white Kyrgyz cap astride a stout mountain pony. Dastan's father had presented her father with a very respectable *kalym*, or bride price, of twenty fat sheep, one of which became the engagement dinner.

Zamira looked at her husband as she told Max how she wanted to marry him and live life with him from their first meeting, and Max watched Dastan's eyes swell with affection and pride. Alik and Aliya watched, wide-eyed, as they heard the story of their parents' coming together explained in detail to them for the first time, sensing on a fundamental level that it was what created them and their being in the world.

Aliya, giggling, asked when they first had kissed. Zamira responded by clicking her tongue at the cheeky girl, noting that it was obviously on their wedding day. They peppered Max with many questions about his life, Dastan interpreting, and he did his best to describe America and summarize his many adventures as the family listened raptly. Stories and laughter continued well into the evening after the children had fallen asleep curled next to Max. As the koumiss crept into them, Max noticed Zamira had inched closer to her husband, who softened with the hours and allowed her to hold his hand.

When Max awoke the next morning, buried in a pile of pillows, the yurt was empty. The morning's cooking fire smoldered, warming a pot of steaming tea. A plate of fresh figs, onion-laced flatbread called *katama,* and a cup for the tea had been placed nearby. He poured from the brass pot a milky black brew that tasted subtly like chai but saltier, then tore some flatbread and bit into a fig. No outside sounds penetrated the yurt, and the blanketed space was calmly silent as he enjoyed the light breakfast and played back images of the previous night's warmth. Finishing the meal, Max pulled on his boots and ducked the yurt's doorway to find a vivid arena of blue sky and emerald-green mountainsides cascading from stone promontories. Zamira and Aliya knelt at work in the vegetable garden, pulling up potatoes and onions. Dastan, Alik, and the herd of sheep were nowhere in sight. As he approached the tiny but fertile garden, fenced with sticks to keep out the sheep, Zamira made a motion of eating. He nodded that yes, he had, pressing his hands together in thanks. Then she motioned to a point far up the valley, in a high meadow beneath the steep rocky escarpments. Two tiny dark shapes, Dastan and Alik, strode behind the fluffy white dots that identified their herd, looking for fresh grass. Then she pointed to Tash Rabat, five hundred yards across the valley, monolithic and gray.

"Dastan says go there, zee Russian voman," she said.

Approaching Tash Rabat, Max noticed the sturdy gate spanning the arched entrance, which had been left ajar. Thinking he should call out but mesmerized by the eerie silence, he decided not to signal to whoever might be wandering the halls so early in the morning. Icy wind descending from the mountaintops whistled through openings in the massive structure. Gray, rough-cut stone had been bleached white over millennia, and it was ancient to the touch as he ran his hand along the stacked layers. When he stepped through the gateway and into the shadows, the air felt thick with history.

Eyes adjusting to the dim light, he passed through three feet of wall and into what seemed a greeting salon, topped by a small dome. A beam of light spilled through its top opening, angling to the floor, revealing specks of dust in the lightly moving air. Laid with flat stones, the foundation floors had been burnished smooth over the centuries. A wide hallway ran into the middle of the structure, darkened doorways on either side. He could see a more brightly lit and larger room ahead. Looking left and right, Max made out halls following the exterior wall line to each of the building's corners, the external turrets marked by rounded walls. Nothing moved anywhere his senses could reach except gasps of air.

Max chose the left passageway, built to a rounded dome, with tiny skylights providing visibility without a headlamp. Entrances to interior rooms were fronted by openings so small they required kneeling on the floor to pass. He ducked into the second one, a small chamber with a tiny skylight, packed dirt floor, and a single stone bench suitable for sleeping built into the left wall. There was enough room for one person and their belongings, maybe a few sheep. *A thousand years of travelers*, he thought, *all craving a meal.*

A continuous long bench was built into the outside wall along the side and rear hallways, a stone platform that could have held a hundred men, end to end. Venturing into yet another room, he found a square hole in the center, falling into an underground chamber below. A barred grate covered its opening, identifying a prison cell. As Max reached the rear hallway's center, the main chamber opened through an arch before him.

The central room measured about thirty feet on each side, with hallways radiating from four points. Arched alcoves six feet deep punctuated the spaces between the hallway openings. A dozen glassless windows and skylights dotted the massive stone dome some forty feet above, providing illumination and casting shadows. The expansive room was empty of any altar or formal ceremonial structure to suggest it was once a temple. Max craned his neck to follow the arc of the ancient dome, rays of light descending through its openings and splashing onto the stone floor. Wind breathed through the hallways, sounding like faraway voices. He closed his eyes to imagine the caravans' long lines, happening upon the stone sanctuary a thousand years before, and the refuge it promised.

"It feels like both a temple and a fortress," said a Russian-accented female voice, startling Max out of his daydream. "We haven't figured out which, so the easy answer is both."

Max turned to face the woman, who was standing in an archway. She had black hair cut to a straight line of bangs and wore camouflage fatigues, dusty work boots, a red hammer and sickle T-shirt; she was, in fact, very Russian and all business.

"The children told me that an American had arrived," she said. "You look like one. I am Mishka Dubovya, doing research here for the Minsk Institute of Archaeology in Belarus."

"And I am Max Little, representing New Mexico State University." *Almost the truth*, he thought.

"Are you here in a research capacity? I would have imagined some advance communication if that were the case," she said, planting her hand on her hips.

"Yes, I'm on a rather long and extensive research trip," he said, "and had no idea when I would arrive. Tash Rabat was an important stop."

"And now, here you are. What did you hope to find?" she asked.

"My interest is in the foods of the Silk Road," Max said.

"Interesting," she said thoughtfully. "A caravanserai would be an excellent site to explore this. The ancient Greek Herodotus wrote that the Achaemenid emperors built one hundred and eleven of them between Persia and Central Asia, and this is among the best examples. We estimate that thousands of travelers would have passed through this place. Yet the interior has yielded little, only some bits of pottery. We have just begun a series of excavations along the outer edge of the structure that may prove interesting to you, Mr. Little." She approached and extended her hand. "Welcome to Tash Rabat. History resonates very deeply here, does it not?"

They shook hands, and Max could feel her sense of purpose.

"It's in the air," he said. "In every footstep and stack of stone. I was imagining the caravans happening upon this welcome outpost after long journeys, removed from civilization."

"And looking for a good meal, no?" she said.

"The evidence of which I'm hoping to uncover," said Max.

She looked at him with more depth. "So, what is your field, Mr. Little? History? Botany? Archaeology?"

"Paleoethnobotany. A bit of all of them, I guess," he said. "Food connects us to history's humanity. My interest is in the migration of certain New World foods worldwide and their influence on the various societies they reached and impacted. One in particular."

The archaeologist led Max from the ancient chamber through the darkened main hallway and the arched opening. The chill air outside found its way to his bones, and he shuddered, instantly overcome with the thought of Lilah hitting him like the cold blast. How he wished she was there to experience this moment and to share warmth.

Rounding the corner of the structure's west turret, Max saw a series of square pits cordoned off with rope in a checkerboard pattern through the grassy fields outside the caravanserai. Some had been covered by canvas awnings framed to protect the research pits, which looked freshly unearthed.

"A month ago, we received funding from a Kyrgyz individual to expand our work from simply repairing and maintaining the structure. So, your arrival is timely, Mr. Little."

Max stopped. "A Kyrgyz? And not the government? I can't imagine many individuals in this country could underwrite an archaeological research project. But I guess it's fitting given the renewed national pride of Silk Road countries."

"You are correct," replied Dubovya, "a Kyrgyz philanthropist has provided the resources specifically to excavate the exterior areas of the site. No structure or repair work is funded. It seems he has an interest in the things left behind by the caravans."

Bright lightning flashed in Max's mind. "Who is this person?"

"His name is Bakiyev, a wealthy businessman from Osh," she said. "He sees himself as a Silk Road enthusiast."

The blood drained from Max's head at the utterance of the name. Lightheaded, he stopped to sit on a rock. He looked up to the high peaks of the Tien Shan. "Has he been here?" he asked in a weak voice.

"No, not himself. But his two representatives were here last month to check on my progress."

"Boris and Vlad," Max said lightly, mostly to himself.

"Come to think of it, they never said their names. They merely took pictures of the excavations and my findings for their employer, our benefactor. It seems you know this man."

"Only by reputation," said Max. "And did you provide proof of any significant discoveries?"

The woman thought for a moment and said, "Not really. They showed up too soon, and I had not covered enough ground. Without email communication out here, sending updates is difficult. But the weeks since have yielded some promising results. Come see for yourself."

They followed a route among the excavation pits to a rectangular tent, set up to clean and examine the findings. On tables set throughout the canvas room sat piles of items, pulled from the pits to be sifted and sorted. Dubovya led Max to the first table.

"Here are potsherds and ceramic pieces. Over there, bigger pieces that made up large kettles for cooking. As you can see, they are all blackened from use around or in fire. The pits we've chosen were all heavy with ash, clearly from cooking, and it is there we have had the most success."

Max examined the pieces, many laid out in puzzle patterns in an attempt at reconstruction. "What about organic materials?"

"Evidence of human consumption consists of both plant and animal remains, and some fossilized feces, both animal and human," Dubovya said. "Nothing can be accurately dated here in the field as we lack the proper radiocarbon technology, but materials often change as we progress through to the deeper, older layers. Look here."

Another table held an array of bones, from thick, femur-type specimens down to tiny, bird-like bits. Curved ribs eight inches long sat in a row beside sets of vertebrae.

"We have identified sheep, goats, pigs, rabbits, pheasant, and chickens. All blackened from roasting over a fire."

"What about seeds?" asked Max, edging closer to the thing that had brought him to this place and this moment.

"Unless it has been tempered by fire," said the archaeologist, "most organic material decomposes, especially over hundreds of years, though we have found some. Over here."

On three attached tables sat piles of dirt in various phases of analysis, each sifted and the findings identified. Across from them were more tables housing the separated specimens.

"The oldest layers yielded seeds from foods most commonly identified with this region and Central Asia before European arrival. Barley, flax, wheat, sesame, and rye. Chickpeas, peas, and lentils. Mustard seed, a few almonds. And these are only the things that might have found themselves in the fire. Fruits and greens we find no evidence of. Later come okra, gourds, and eggplant, with the arrival of India. Rice and buckwheat from the Chinese. But the layers closest to the top reveal a wider bounty. Beets, broccoli, caraway, fennel, and hops from Europe. Last, potatoes, beans, squash, tomatoes, and quinoa from the New World. Oh, and peppers. Lots of them. It seems that chile pepper seeds are some of the best-preserved specimens we've encountered."

Max passed over the sorted piles of blackened seeds until he came upon the familiar flat, round seeds indicative of most peppers. They were ashen, mostly blackened, and primarily from the annuum and frutescens families in their distinctive circular shape. No odd-shaped *pubescens*. His mind immediately registered defeat. He was looking for something else that would have stood out in a pile.

"There are some seeds which we've been unable to identify over here," said Dubovya, beckoning him to another table.

He moved with a teenage eagerness to look over the findings, zeroing in on the shapes. Max's heart pounded as he made out the unique random seed outlines of the *Capsicum pubescens* variety, the round rocoto. And among the always black rocoto seeds were evidence of light-grey examples sharing the same undefined shape. They could easily have been white before their journey through the caravanserai's cooking fires. Or could they? They had seared in smoke and fire and could have turned gray as they began to ash. He reached down and took a few in his hand, rolling them around in his fingers and trying to puncture one with a fingernail. He wanted to see if the interior was white or black. But they proved ancient and brittle, near fossilized. He envisioned the high elevations in the Andes that the rocoto emerged from eons ago. *Rocoto grows in temperate mountainous regions of the central Andes between six and ten thousand feet*, he remembered from botany journals.

The archaeologist watched Max curiously, witnessing his mind work. The man was either very eccentric or very skilled.

"Do you recognize these? We have never seen them."

"Yes. The seeds are also from the pepper family but are an exceedingly rare variety. What is the elevation here?" he asked.

"Almost three thousand meters."

Nearly nine thousand feet, he thought.

Dubovya read Max's mind. "Much too high for growing most fruit and vegetables, I would think, except briefly in summer. And we have yet to find evidence of farming or gardening."

Max thought for a moment. "Too high for most chile peppers, you are correct. I would assume that gardening would have occurred further from the traffic of the caravanserai. Probably in those flats at the foot of the hills. But the seeds here are also pepper variety, and from a unique species that grows up to ten thousand feet only in the Andes mountains of South America called *pubescens*. These were either grown here or brought by traders, then possibly cultivated. By chance or design. That they are here at all is incredibly significant, particularly during the late Silk Road period before the trade routes left for the sea."

Max immediately awoke to the distinct possibility that the Valley of the Fire chile was genuine. His palms began to perspire. He wrang his hands together, pondering.

"There may perhaps be some DNA material left in the seeds," said Dubovya. "You will want to take some and have them analyzed at your laboratory in New Mexico."

Max poured some of the seeds into the amulet bag around his neck. "I'm indebted to you, Mishka. These are what I have traveled extremely far to find. And doing so leads me further on my quest, to the Naryn valley," he said. The village of Dostuk and its knives awaited him, and the hidden valleys beyond, the most significant question mark of all.

"I see you have no vehicle, and it would be two days' walk if you didn't have a ride," she said.

Her statement hung in the air. Max visualized the long, lonely journey yet was determined to move forward, to Dostuk and then Osh. "Then walk I shall. I've had good luck thus far hitchhiking."

She considered his words for a moment, and he sensed her demeanor change. She addressed him matter-of-factly. "Or I could give you a ride. Tomorrow. My yurt is warm and has not had a man in it for months. And you are a unique specimen." She was a scientist to the core.

Though Max was surprised by the suggestion, he did not show it. She looked mysterious, almost dangerous, with her black hair and eyes, as if no one would ever see through to the vaulted interior. In another time, he might have hopped into the yurt for an off-grid tussle and a ride the following day, but he was laser-focused on his destination. And Lilah.

"A gracious offer," he said with a smile. "But science calls, and I must move on with haste. More answers lie in the village of Dostuk, and I must go there, today. Other forces are at work that requires all my focus. I am grateful for the warm invitation and the generosity of your time and knowledge, Mishka. You have helped me more than you know, and I am in your debt."

She looked him over. "Then perhaps if you ever return, feel free to knock on my yurt's door. It will always be open. To you, Max Little, for repayment of the debt. Good luck with the peppers. Perhaps tell me the story sometime about what you are really up to."

He bowed in thanks, perhaps too deeply, for effect. As if to say, *possibly*. Leaving Mishka standing in the tent, Max made his way to Dastan's family yurt compound to collect his duffle bag and begin walking the five miles to the Naryn-Kashgar highway. The family had returned for the midday meal, and sad to learn that he was departing, begged him to stay for food. Max eagerly dove into a deep bowl of paloo with mutton and peppers, liberally enhanced with Dastan's dried spice blend. The mood was light despite the children's pleas for Max to remain. Yet, he was keen to move ahead. Evidence was unfolding, and answers, if they existed, lay down the valley.

"Your encounter with the Russian woman was rewarding, I take it," Dastan said. "It seems you found what you seek here in the Mountains of Heaven, Max Chota. And the next journey shows in your face. If I had a vehicle, I would take you myself."

Max smiled. "I believe you, Dastan. You are a good man. And I would do the same for you and any of your family. Yes, adventure lies ahead, and my love even further. I will return."

Max trundled down the road from Tash Rabat with a new, richly patterned Kyrgyz blanket among his gear, a gift from Zamira. Every step, he knew, took him closer to Lilah. He planned to camp in the same protected spot he had found two dark nights before along the road, wrapped in the new tapestry and sustained by nuts and dried figs from Dastan's larder. It was near the highway, where he would walk until a ride found him for the leg to Dostuk, to the west along the Naryn River.

The walk back down the valley plagued Max with questions, assertions, riddles, and possibilities. The *pubescens* rocoto was clearly present in the region centuries ago. That the rare, remote chile had traveled so far buttressed the assertion that it could have taken hold naturally or been cultivated by locals. But were the seeds he had seen a possible hybrid, naturally occurring, or created by an ancient farming accident? Unable to ascertain the presence of both black and white seeds, he had no way to project the potential of a unique hybridized chile. He had witnessed what nature could do in a closed environment with the Naga Jolokia only ten days prior and sensed that he was far closer to understanding the Kyrgyz chile myth. He knew that he would have to see the unique variety growing in the wild, or less plausible, propagated by the local populace, and Gasanov's story of Dostuk's villagers echoed in his mind.

He walked for two hours, skirting the creek on a cloudless, breezy day, spinning scenarios in his head. The names of Adilet and Nazaat Buntun of Dostuk had become etched in his mind, keys to the Fire of the Valley. How to break through to them and navigate the latent distrust of a remote mountain village? The magical, mystical spice blend, *Ot Boyanca Oroon,* had keened his senses and brought on waves of satisfaction, like sprinkled starlight. Inescapable was that Bakiyev or his accomplices had been to Dostuk and Tash Rabat before him. He figured they were somewhere in the city of Osh, waiting for him to unearth the hidden fruit and knowing he would come to them to reach Lilah. Then, he assumed they would somehow coerce Lilah to verify the variety's uniqueness to capitalize on the find.

The sun arced across the sky as he pressed on, conjuring possibilities until the Tien Shan's southern peaks cast lengthening shadows across his path. The canyon narrowed as he neared the location of his previous bivouac among the boulders, and it would be a cold and lonely evening, though without the sheep as an alarm clock.

Max imagined the Swedish explorer, Sven Hedin, and his entourage, clothed in furs as they attempted a December crossing of these mountains almost a hundred years before. How they were fortified by a meal, much as the one he just had in Dastan's yurt. Alone on the dimming road, Max was encouraged by the day's discovery and ensuing revelations, despite the unanswered questions. *Sleeping under the same stars as Hedin, fortified by the same paloo, I am on my path,* he thought. *Seeking a different prize than the better-equipped Swede. Though a camel would be an advantage right now.*

Reaching the point where he was to cross the creek and dip into the boulders to make camp, Max heard a clanking sputter from the valley behind him. A grey sedan careened down the road, gunning its engine as it dodged divots and rocks. He waited by the side, becoming aware that the only car at Tash Rabat belonged to Mishka Dubovya. It skidded to a stop at the point where he stood, and the passenger window rolled down, revealing the black bangs of the Russian.

"Get in," was all she said.

Max briefly considered his options. Decline the offer and sleep in the rocks, then try his luck on a ride in the morning or hop in the sedan and reach Dostuk by dark. He opened the back door and threw in the duffle, then climbed in the cramped passenger seat.

Mishka accelerated and resumed the ditch-dodging and boulder-swerving dust storm that was her driving. Like a rally car in the Sahara, she gunned the old East German Lada to an unseen finish line, saying nothing. At the end of the canyon and the Tash Rabat road, she slid into a right turn onto the Kashgar-to-Naryn highway, a two-lane dirt track with fewer boulders.

"I decided I needed some supplies in Naryn, and Dostuk is on the way. No need to sleep on the ground tonight. Though my yurt would have been more...comfortable," she said as an explanation for her arrival. "Plus, I need to report to my new benefactor."

"To tell him about me? And the new seed discovery?" asked Max.

He instantly understood that Bakiyev would assume he had gone to Tash Rabat and interacted with the archaeologist.

"Well, certainly, I will tell him. I need his money," Mishka said without guilt. "I am required to report once weekly, and tomorrow is the last day for me to do so. I could have left in the morning, but I thought of you sleeping in the dirt. This works out well for everyone."

"And the pubescens seeds, the Rocoto?"

She considered the question. "At this stage in the excavation, it is evident that there are numerous instances of food remnants, including peppers, but the seeds you tentatively identified have not been corroborated. Thus, they will not become included in my report. These seeds seem to be of importance to you, no?" she asked, looking straight ahead.

Max looked at her, trying to get a read. Why would she help him in this way after his rebuff of her advances? "They're the reason I have traveled this far. And why Bakiyev has had me followed across two continents. It is a significant discovery in my particular field."

She pondered his words. "Yet whatever his interest in these tiny seeds, it looks to me that he needs your expertise, whatever that is exactly. And why he funded my dig so that you would find them. My work is meant to aid yours, it would seem."

She was right. Whatever Bakiyev hoped to achieve, Max and Lilah were crucial to its success. And Bakiyev seemed to be paving the way. It was the strongarm tactics that had Max baffled.

"Let's just say that buying me some time would be beneficial, Mishka. There are pertinent discoveries I have yet to make. So, the omission would be much appreciated. My confrontation with your benefactor Bakiyev lies ahead, in Osh."

She nodded her understanding. "Then that is twice that you owe me, Max the paleoethnobotanist. Or whatever you are. You are a mystery."

They sped down the dirt highway, crossing the At Bashy River in its gorge through the receding Tien Shan mountains, and eventually, the canyon widened, revealing the broad valley of the Naryn River. The dirt road met the paved Osh-Naryn highway, where they headed west, skirting the mountain foothills and the river, which cut a deep gorge into the plain. Shafts of late afternoon light spilled from the valleys and filled the golden expanse of the plain.

"The Kyrgyz tribes escaped into these canyons to hide from the Huns, the Mongols, and eventually, the Russians," explained Mishka. "That they were never entirely conquered speaks to their considerable national pride. They have been caught in the middle of many regional conflicts and been able to retain their culture."

Max watched the shadows crawl across the valley and the darkening river gorge. "And here they remain, wedged between Russia, China, Persia, and half a dozen other 'stans,'" he said. "Still pawns in the Great Game. Part of my effort is to help them regain more pride."

Dubovya regarded the American anew. "You mean that you are here to help the Kyrgyz? I wouldn't have guessed that about you. An American in jeans and carrying a duffle bag looking for pepper seeds. You look more like a hippie cowboy chasing adventure."

"You're perhaps not far off," he said. "Though the goal of my work is to benefit the people it impacts. It's why I do it. And why Bakiyev must be held in check. Oh, and I love food and the community and equality it inevitably creates. Food is the thread that connects all of human history."

She regarded the scruffy American. "So that's who you are. It sounds like we should share a meal sometime."

The sky glowed purple as they approached the hamlet of Dostuk, veering off the highway onto its dirt road. He asked her to deposit him at The Buntun Lodge Guest House, marked by a hand-painted sign worn by time. As he reached for the door's handle, Mishka pulled him towards her and kissed him deeply on the mouth.

"One debt repaid, Max Little," she said. "The other shall be a sumptuous meal somewhere in time. I wish you well on your journey."

Max smiled appreciatively. "Somewhere in time," he said, exiting the sedan. "I am gratefully in your debt." He offered a warm wave as she drove off.

Many miles away, Lilah stood on a balcony overlooking the Ak-Buura River valley. A high, protective wall bordered the surrounding grounds. The sun had set, and the purple twilight reflected off the river's course. Lights began to twinkle across the city of Osh, its teeming center not far to the south. Slouching somewhat in a wrinkled white laboratory coat, her eyes were tired, her hands chafed. Lilah loosened the ponytail she had been forced to wear in the laboratory, allowing her wavy locks to fall over her shoulders, and slowly exhaled the day.

Her thoughts were on Max and where he might be, somewhere to the darkening east.

She had become acutely connected to him, tethered to his lifeforce, and was anguished by their separation. The image of him, scruffy and slinging his worn duffle bag, filled her mind. She felt sure that he was out there, somewhere in the Tien Shan or along the Naryn River, working his way to her. Knowing Max's resolve and uncanny good luck caused her to smile. He was without a doubt the right man for the job fate had tasked him with.

Sharp knocking on the door just inside startled her.

"What do you want?" she called, not turning from the view.

"I have brought you dinner," said a muffled voice.

"Leave it outside," she demanded. She wished only to interact with her thoughts and the emerging stars.

The Buntun Lodge Guest House inhabited Max's imagination almost mystically, fueled by Gasanov's tale of an elaborate and transcendent food experience. It was the repository of the secrets halfway around the world that would lead him to the Fire of the Valley.

And the home to the two main obstacles to its discovery: Adilet and Nazaat Buntun.

He arrived after dark, his duffle bag on one shoulder and Zamira's colorful tribal blanket on the other. A week's worth of beard and a green and white Kyrgyz cap made him appear like any other traveler in the country, but he was taller than most, and a furry Patagonia sweater concealed the Led Zeppelin T-shirt. Opening the front door's heavy latch, he ducked under the low frame and into a faraway diorama.

The lodge had no front desk, and Max stood square in the main room's front, holding his belongings. Heavy wood tables and benches filled every square foot of the space, jammed with families or groups of felt-capped men. In one corner, a wood stove cast a smoldering glow, and shadows danced across the room. Candles flickered from recesses in the block walls, and worn planks made up the floor, polished by ten thousand boots. People looked up at the newcomer and, sensing some commonality, dove back into their bowls.

From the rear of the canteen, a short, round woman approached. She wore a long black skirt under a stained yellow apron, head covered in a mismatched scarf. A scattering of white hair poked out of a wrinkled chin. After an up-and-down look, she addressed Max.

"*Baaraky ne Tamak?*" she demanded in Kyrgyz.

He held out his hands to indicate that he couldn't understand. Russian and German attempts registered no response from him either. "English?" he asked.

Her eyes widened and then narrowed. In her thick accent, she barked out, "Room or food?"

Relieved that he would be able to communicate, Max replied, "Both, please. I have come a long way."

"Travelers usually do," she replied, unimpressed. "It is late. You must eat first and then I will show you your room. Leave your bag. Sit over there." She pointed to the same corner table that had hosted Gasanov. "Koumiss?" she then asked.

"Koumiss, yes. And may I wash before dining?" Max asked.

"Down the hall past the kitchen," she replied, gesturing.

While the woman set off to fetch the drink, Max sought out the washroom. The single hallway led to the lodge's six rooms, with the shared bath at its end. An open doorway revealed the tiny kitchen, where another scarved woman chopped meat into cubes atop a well-worn section of a halved log, her massive cleaver glinting at it rose and fell. He walked straight into a wall of scents that stopped him at the kitchen's threshold. Charcoal glowed in a combination stove and grill inside the room, atop which oiled meats sputtered, pots steamed, and peppers blistered. Small ceramic bowls held an array of aromatic ground spices that the woman used to season, tossing pinches liberally in pots. Balls of dough were dropped into a wok of sizzling oil, adding sweet smoke to the mix of aromas wafting from the small workplace. He made out bowls of chopped vegetables and greens on a dented metal table, where garlic cloves and whole ginger root sat in piles awaiting the knife. A wide-brimmed basket held stacks of dried pods on long stems, which appeared to be poppies. Handfuls of seeds from the pods were transported to the mouth of a hand-cranked press, the coaxed oil slow-dripping into jars. In the corner was a sizeable wooden platter bursting with a rainbow of chopped peppers, green, yellow, red, orange, purple, and black. He looked around the room for the diced chiles' parents, seeking the rocoto's distinct round shape. Before he could poke his head in any further, the whiskered woman's voice shooed him from behind.

"The lavatory is at the end of the hall," it said. "Don't bother us while we cook. Your koumiss is on the table. Now go."

He made his way down the dimly lit hall, passing the few guest rooms. On one wall, a faded, yellowed picture hung. It showed a spectacled man in furs sitting beside a Bactrian camel before a yurt on a grassy plain. It was the quintessential Kyrgyz setting. Max washed and splashed his face in the lavatory, which held a small shower, toilet, and single sink. Looking in the mirror, he saw a ragged traveler, tufts of hair straggling from beneath the Kyrgyz cap. Looking into his eyes, he thought: *This is it, the apex of your journey. It's here that the mission succeeds or fails, Max Chota.*

Max returned to his corner table and found a pint-portioned ceramic cup filled with the frothy mare's milk brew. Mildly chilled, it registered tart and salty on the palate, exhibiting only a slight heat of alcohol going down. He scanned the room, taking long drafts of the beverage, hearing the clanks and grunts of hearty degustation. While some muttered to themselves as they ate, few people talked, no one paying attention to his stares. Out of the kitchen shuffled his host, a round tray spread with dishes and bowls on her shoulder, some steaming. She rested the tray on the edge of the table and then distributed the items.

First, she presented a plate of steamy dumplings partnered with a clear, golden sauce for dipping. Wheels of sliced, Thai-type chiles swam in the liquid alongside green leaves of coriander. Next came a large bowl of amber-hued broth with onions, carrots, cabbage, potato, ginger, and herbs, with the diced multicolored peppers floating atop. A bowl appeared, offering three different shades of rice blended and wilted greens breathing garlic. A wood platter appeared to be the star of the show, with oiled and grilled mutton and smaller pieces, probably goat, dusted heavily with spices and charred from the fire. Finally, she offered a small earthenware jar topped with a lid, a tiny ladle poking out, and a small bowl of blended spices.

The woman watched as Max examined every item, smelling each and using his hands to fan the aromas. Her sudden command of the language he understood startled him.

"Since you are a foreigner, I will tell you how to best enjoy our food. The dumplings are called mantis, with minced onion and mushrooms from our cellar. Dip them in the vinegar sauce. Then the main dish. While other places combine the ingredients to make a paloo, we separate them *kuurdak*-style so you can add the amounts you want into the meat and mushroom broth. In older times, it was called a besh barmak because it is so rich that it can be eaten by hand. And we season and grill the meats instead of boiling them, which is much more savory. In the basket is *borsook*, traditional fried bread good for soaking up the broth. The smoke from its frying, we say, carries messages up to the dead. Over there are wet and dry spiced condiments for extra flavor. And some warmth."

Besh Barmak, thought Max. The same dish savored by Sven Hedin a century ago. He was getting closer, an epicurean Sherlock Holmes peeling away a mystery.

"Looks delicious," said Max casually, though his insides were rumbling like a freight train and his palms damp with anticipation. "Tell me, what do you call this condiment?" he asked, lifting the lid.

The woman snorted. "We call it a condiment. Why should it need a name? It enhances the food, a local concoction. Now eat."

He spooned white, black, and red rice and the garlicky greens into the broth concoction, then pieces of crispy-charred mutton and goat. He set the steaming bowl to the side to let the flavors marry and picked up one of the doughy manti dumplings, biting off a corner. It was rich with mushroom and caramelized onion, revealing a hint of ginger and mint. He soaked it in the clear sauce, allowing the tart vinegar and fresh hot chile to permeate the dough and balance the savory filling. Four of them disappeared in as many minutes, Max humming happily as faint beads of moisture appeared on his brow.

Max gulped the brewed koumiss before pulling the steaming broth bowl in front of him. He leaned forward to let the scented vapor cloud his face, inhaling the aromas. Then, holding the small ceramic jar in one hand, he lifted its lid with the other. The sauce inside was predominantly orange, slightly oily, and flecked with a mélange of other colors and textures. Putting the top down, he held the jar in both hands as he raised it to his face. Lowering his head, Max breathed in reverentially.

Familiar notes presented themselves. Vinegar certainly, though he could not discern which kind, sweet, and a shade of malt. Mildly garlic.

Onion, sweet and not overpowering. A blast of smoke and fire. Grassy hints, probably parsley. Citrus, though the understated kind derived from chiles. Possibly some orange peel. And the faintest hint of saffron. He lowered the jar, ecstatic in his corner of a rustic dining room, the only foreigner and thousands of miles from home.

Max dipped the tiny wooden spoon into the mixture and raised it from the jar for a visual inspection. There appeared to be a pureed base, orange in hue. Pools of yellow oil. Flecks of black from something roasted. Multicolored bits of finely chopped chiles, no seeds. White nuggets of onion. Strands of saffron, and tiny black poppy seeds. Green bits of herb and granules of dry spices. He tipped the ladle and let the condiment spill into his soup in a long falling drip, illuminated by firelight. It spread as it hit the surface, sinking purposefully while it infused into the broth. The complex aroma of the combined scents became intoxicating.

Before diving into the bowl, he scooped another ladle of sauce, placed it in his mouth, and let the flavors unleash their mystery on his palate. *Sweet citrusy peppers, roasted and pureed for the base*, he guessed. Caramelized onion. Grassy parsley. Salt. *Sweet vinegar, probably from sugar cane, maybe a little malt vinegar, too.* Oil, thick on the tongue, perhaps the poppyseed. Pungent earth and minerals. Then, biting down, meaty bright bits of fresh chiles. *Not like habanero, the chinense, it's thicker skinned.* He identified many actors at play in the ensemble of flavors he was auditioning.

The heat arrived last, subtly, merely a compliment to the other ingredients, though it increased like a rising sun. This was no Scoville heat monster but a sublime balance to its ingredient partners, a lightly flaming collaborator. It registered inside his cheeks and tickled his tongue, finding a home just inside his forehead like a third eye, where it would stay for hours. A heat accompanied by an identifiable endorphin release, without the pain.

Uncharacteristically, he did not perspire, except in anticipation. The heat was more reserved than frontal, encompassing yet not overpowering, splashing in waves across his palate. It infused his entire body in an internal warmth that was at once relaxing and invigorating, requiring no wash of koumiss to douse its flame. Max felt something extraordinary occurring but was unable to define precisely what. So, he had more. Two spoonsful more faced his satisfying evaluation, humming at a characteristic frequency.

Morsels of crunchy fat and meats crisped in the grill fire punctuated each mouthful of the kuurdak-style paloo. Rice soaked up the liquid, expanding and taking on the other flavors. Carrots, sweet cabbage, and diced potatoes added body and texture. Leafy greens crunched, and chiles popped in his bite, with the broth now infused by its elegant condiment accompaniment. Cinnamon notes registered as he dissected the bits of chiles, a precursor to a building heat. Tearing open the fried borsook breads, Max watched the puff of sweet fryer steam rise to the ceiling, sending prayers to the dead. Saturated with broth and spice, they became savory, soggy pillows. His head buzzed at a low pitch at the same time he found his toes curling, telltale signs of pepper-head revelation. Over and over, he added ingredients from the side dishes into the large bowl, ladles of sauce doused over them, dipping borsook, humming along.

Dustings of the dry spice mix were generously added, introducing a higher level of heat. Flavors jumped out: dried chiles, granulated onion, garlic, salt, black pepper, and poppy seeds, followed by dried orange peel and saffron. Flavors danced through Max's senses, swimming to his belly, trailing a warm curtain of pleasure. Forty-five minutes later, he pushed the bowl away and sat back, happily exhausted, heat coursing through his body. He put his hands behind his head, awash in a dizzying sense of gustatory satisfaction, and suddenly aware of the entire room watching him.

Shyly, he gave the room a weak wave before downing the last of the koumiss. The ensuing belch he proved unable to resist, finding its way from deep within his soul, lingering, then allowing the room to continue its collective ritual, satisfied.

The host shuffled to his table to clear the empty dishes, not bothering to ask if Max had enjoyed the meal. So, he spoke first.

"That was extremely satisfying," he said, hands still crossed behind his head. "Tell me, is there a roasted pepper puree in the sauce along with fresh peppers? I'm trying to figure it out. It was superb."

"Perhaps," she said. "The recipe changes based on what we get that is fresh. And how busy we are." She was giving up nothing.

"And the peppers you use, the meat is thick and sweet. What kind are they?"

"Local peppers. What else would we use?"

Max figured that she would be a challenge to crack. *A viable Ring of Fire candidate*, he thought. *All business and no secrets.* "And what is your name, if I may ask?"

"In Kyrgyzstan, men don't ask women's names," she said, stacking dishes onto her tray.

A crude segue, as he had already guessed who she was. "My apologies. My name is Max Little. I assume you are the owner?"

"There is a name over the front door. And I didn't ask your name."

"How many years have you been making such memorable food in this place?"

"Questions. Always so many questions from foreigners! Questions are suspect. Silence is trustworthy. Look at these people eating. No questions. They eat and take nourishment. They are happy and come back. Three months ago, a man from Osh came asking too many questions. He was a fake! We sent him away. Then last week, two Russians, again asking questions. They acted tough and were run out of town. Now you."

It was time for the hook. Max assumed an air of slight indignance. "My apologies then. I shall ask no more questions as it appears contrary to the local custom. While the food transfixes me, I have other motives. I am following the Swedish explorer Sven Hedin's footsteps, who journeyed through this area a hundred years ago. In his memoir, he recounts traveling through the Naryn valley in 1893 to the Torugart Pass and Kashgar. I am retracing that journey and have been to Kashgar, over the Torugart Pass, and Tash Rabat, the ancient caravanserai. In the book, he writes of being fed by the Kyrgyz people of the Tien Shan mountains, sustained by a meal much like this. He wrote of a unique spice that enriched his food, like the one I have so enjoyed on your table. At Tash Rabat, I was served a spice blend similar to this and heard from my shepherd host that it came from Dostuk. And that is why I ask. It is part of the history I am following. If I have offended you, then I shall leave and find lodging elsewhere."

She snorted. "There is no other lodging."

But her eyes narrowed, and she looked at him more closely. Max froze under her gaze, aware that his entire mission hung in the balance.

Her stern face softened, but only a little. "Sven Hedin, you say? And Tash Rabat? It seems you are an explorer of some type. We know of this man. You may find some answers in our village, maybe not. Enjoy your night, historian, and I will bring more koumiss." Walking away, she said over her shoulder, "And you are right about the peppers. Roasted and pureed, as well as whole and diced."

Closer. Max drank from his cup, replenished by the pitcher of koumiss left by his host. He watched the inn's guests relishing their meals amid splashes of the fermented mare's milk brew. A collective air of bonhomie had spread through the canteen, with laughter punctuating the conversations. Someone launched into song, a proud ethnic number with a chorus echoed by the entire room. Max could not help but chime in as he picked up phrases, and for an hour, he raised his glass many times to others across the firelit canteen. The full realization that these chiles were capable of providing a portal between the mundane act of eating and a magical, transformative experience shared with others would be etched in his memory.

When he finally shuffled to his domicile, exhausted and entirely happy, he felt in his bones that he had reached Shangri-La. The small room glowed with a warm fire in a corner stove as he fell into a futon bed made pillowy by layers of Kyrgyz blankets.

He didn't know if he dreamt, but something found a door into Max's deep sleep. Into his slumber intruded a sound akin to screeching brakes or fingernails struggling to find a purchase on a metal roof. Opening weary eyes, he became aware that the heating stove's glow silhouetted a large form. A man was sitting on a low stool, barely three feet from Max's head. Gigantic hands like anvils deftly wielded a blade, making slow, grinding passes over a sharpening stone. The knife had a handle of walnut wood and bone attached to an eight-inch edge, slightly curved and entirely menacing.

Startled, Max rose to one elbow. In no position to resist the man, he chose to determine the intruder's motives. "Do you always enter your guests' rooms to sharpen your blade in this manner?" he said.

The blade continued its eerie scrape across the stone. It held the oversized man's gaze as he spoke, calmly confident.

"I am a knifemaker. I was trained in metallurgy by the Russians but didn't enjoy building their tanks. When we gained our independence, I returned to my village to make tools for my people. Now I am the head of our clan, the *Adygine*, the people of the south." The sharpening halted. "My wife has told me about you. She likes very few people but has decided that you are somehow worthy of my time. I am Nazaat. What have you come to discover besides the fact that a Swedish explorer came through this area?"

Max played the eager historian, sitting fully upright. "Then it's true? Hedin came through here? Is there proof?"

The knife resumed its sharpening for three long minutes. Finally, the Kyrgyz spoke, somehow resigned to sharing information with the American.

"He was most definitely here. We lived happily as nomads until the Russians came in the late 1800s and began forcing us into villages. They wanted us to settle so they could control us, then they blocked the mountain valleys and our pastures and created conflicts between the tribes to divide us and keep us weak. The Russian explorer Prezhalvsky came to map the area for the army, so we did not trust him, like all Russians. Boundaries are controls, and he got little assistance from our people. But Hedin was different. He didn't see us as subjects like the Russian. My great-great Uncle, Khoat-Bi, was head of Sufi-Kurgan's encampment when the Swede and his party arrived, nearly starving. Our clans' people fed the wretched group and sheltered them before they went over the passes to China, and our people thought that was the end of it. We felt certain they would perish. In 1926, a copy of his book arrived here, translated into Russian, and our people were immensely proud to be mentioned in such a great tale of adventure and exploration. The story has been passed down through our generations, and since then, our clan has welcomed travelers. My great-grandparents opened the inn where you now rest in 1931, in the spirit of Sven Hedin. A picture of him hangs in the hall outside, taken here in Kyrgyzstan a hundred years ago. Do you require more evidence than this?"

Max had no other option but to engage the man and somehow win his trust. "I require little. However, the reason that Hedin holds my interest is in the food he ate. I am tracing the journey of foods along the Silk Road. I am a historian, drawing the map of food as it migrated across the world, particularly chile peppers from the New World. At Tash Rabat, I saw fossilized evidence of an exceedingly rare chile from the Andes Mountains in Peru. That it was here is quite significant. If it is *still* here, even more so."

The blade stopped. "And why is such a thing of significance? They are only peppers. Many people cultivate them."

Silence consumed the room as the man waited for Max's answer, which emerged slowly.

"I have traveled the world discovering new and unique varieties of chile peppers, Nazaat. I am what you might call a chile fanatic. Word has emerged of a possibly unique variety of these coming from the Tien Shan Mountains of Kyrgyzstan. I am here to discover the truth to these rumors, and I believe you may hold the answers."

The man inspected his shiny, now razor-sharp blade. "And what would you hope to gain from such a discovery, Mr. Little from America?"

Max did not feel an imminent threat from the burly knifemaker. He sensed, instead, the wariness of a clan leader protecting his people. "If I have received this information, and come this far to ascertain its veracity, then there will certainly be others, some of whom I believe you have already encountered," he said. "My goal is discovery, yes, and to help your people protect a resource that could have inestimable value. I see a pepper-rich future for the people of Dostuk."

Nazaat's deeply set eyes narrowed to slits of menace. "You refer to the fake knife seller from Osh and the bumbling Russian thugs? All went away with no answers. We are quite able to protect ourselves. Yet I feel that you may know these people, am I correct?"

Max sighed, fatigued by his pursuers, the recent past looming like a dangerous farce. Somewhere in Kyrgyzstan, a gangster and his henchmen held his paramour captive.

"Yes, I know them. People in my passionate line of work tend to encounter each other, particularly in discovering new varieties. What you don't know is that they are all under the control of Ruslan Bakiyev, among your country's most prolific, uh, businessmen. If he is not outplayed, Bakiyev will exert pressure, then force, to control this resource. I believe I can help."

Buntun pondered the information. "And why should I trust you?"

"Because I'm very good at what I do," Max said. "I can help you turn this into an enriching opportunity for your people. I've done it before. I am a skilled professional in the field of chiles and the products they make. And because Bakiyev is holding my girlfriend captive, somewhere in Osh."

The clan chief looked at Max thoughtfully for a long, disconcerting stretch.

"How do I know that he will not use your woman as leverage to achieve his ends?" he asked. "Or that he is not already using you because of your desire to set her free?"

Max rubbed his temples in anguish. The image of Lilah held against her will was crushing, yet he held out hope that he could change the course of events.

"I believe we are smarter than he is. She most of all. And you remain in possession of the secret to the entire affair. Plus, our intentions are clear. Let us help you and your people realize this groundbreaking discovery's potential and share it with the world before it is taken from you. Behind Bakiyev are others, circling like vultures, though you cannot see it yet."

Buntun considered this weight of this information, gazing into the dull sheen of his knife. Then, looking at Max, he said, "And how do you propose to rescue your woman?"

The strained look on Max's face was unmistakable. "I don't exactly know. But I believe that if we are partners and create a plan, I can force his hand. He wants this very badly."

"You say that we need you to protect us from these outside forces," Buntun said carefully. "But it seems you need us as well."

Max looked into the man's eyes, dark brown and flecked with gold. Grey peppered a mountain of beard. He looked rough but showed concealed empathy beneath layers of a leader's responsibility. "Yes," he said.

Nazaat turned to stare into the fire. He sat quietly for a full minute, with Max aware that his quest hung in the balance. Both of them recognized that freeing Lilah depended on the people of Dostuk. Nazaat rose to leave, hulking yet not fearsome in yellow firelight, and ducked under the ceiling beams.

"I will speak with my wife, Max Little," he said at the door. "You appear honest, yet I must think about the people of my clan and how this will affect them," he said at the door. "Change is suspect in our culture. Sleep well if you can."

Max slept fitfully, unable to release the thought machine that ground within his skull. Buntun's scraping knife had been imprinted on his memory, repeating over the hours, its rhythm maddening. The massive frame of the man, outlined by fire. Bakiyev's gold smile. Lilah looking over her shoulder, hair waving in the wind, ankles shackled. Tangents shot out like spiderwebs, intersecting repeatedly as possibilities or calamities. He struggled to piece together what he knew and identify what he did not, arriving at very few definitives. Once the light of dawn crept through the small window of his room, he knew there would be no rest and headed for the shower, groggily saluting the image of fur-bedecked Swede Sven Hedin in the hall.

It was you that got me here, old man.

The lukewarm spray of water helped only a little, and as he shuffled back down the hall, he saw a tray placed outside his room's door: borsook breads with honey, a pot of steaming tea, and a mug. He reached down to retrieve the tray and, upon standing, came face to face with Buntun's handcrafted blade, stuck into the door. Black from the forging fire and etched with swirling tribal symbols, it pierced a handwritten note.

Meet me at the intersection of the village road where it meets the road to Osh, behind the houses. Dress warmly and bring your belongings. Nazaat

The implication of the communication leaped out at him. He would either be escorted out of town or entrusted with the clan's great secret. Knowing that he had no power to change the outcome, he sat on his bed and drank the spicy black tea, its steam wafting around his head, clearing the mind just a little. *I will either turn west, toward Osh with no answers, or south, into the mists of the Tien Shan*, he thought. *To where the fire lives.*

He dressed warmly, readying himself for an extended day in the outdoors, one way or another, and packed all his belongings tightly in his worn duffle. He wore the Tajik vest over his thick hooded sweatshirt and Kyrgyz cap from Kashgar. Passing the kitchen, he saw Adilet and her assistant busied with culinary pursuits of peeling, slicing, dicing, and boiling. Despite a lack of sleep, he felt replenished in the presence of food. The kitchen scents sparked his appreciation, recalling the previous evening's extraordinary experience, and he called out to the Kyrgyz woman.

"Adilet, thank you again for guiding me through such an extraordinary meal. I feel the passion and legacy when I eat here. It's extraordinary. And revelatory. I met your husband late in the evening, and now I am off to wherever the winds take me."

Her sharp paring knife continued its task of potato peeling. "The winds are blowing up the valleys today, American. I sense that you will blow with them," she said, unsmiling. "But I did not tell you my name. Yet, you seem to know it, and about us. It would appear you have been planning to be at this place for a while, traveler. I believe time will tell if it is good you have come. *Kostosuu*. Farewell."

The Fire of the Valley

Max dipped under the low front door and stepped out into a crystal-blue Tien Shan mountain day. He ducked between two houses across the main street and looked across an open pasture, following a route that met the southern road, snaking along the At Bashy River. Late spring snow still clung to the highest peaks, their slopes emerald with new grass. As he set out across the pastures, Max looked back towards the town, and on the roofs of every home sat wide baskets of multicolored chiles, drying in the sun. The mythical peppers had been hiding in plain sight.

A half-mile along the track, Max made out a familiar massive shape standing beside two horses, grazing at the intersection with the Osh highway. He felt the cold steel of Nazaat's curved blade stuck into the rear of his jeans, wondering what he was supposed to do with it, and as he approached, the man turned and called out to him.

"Max Little, it is a fine Kyrgyz morning. Today we go into the mountains of heaven, the Tien Shan. I assume that you are comfortable on a horse?"

Relief that he wouldn't be forced out of the village washed over Max. "It is a fine day, and yes, I am good on a horse," he said.

The idea that he was riding toward the Fire of the Valley chile made his ears tingle and his belly twitch as his body registered an impending discovery. He would not be going to Osh empty-handed. He then pulled the hand-forged blade from his jeans to return it to its owner.

"I believe this is yours," he said.

Nazaat Buntun produced a goatskin-covered scabbard with a leather loop that snapped over one's belt. "I meant it for you. It will live nicely in this on your hip, and I hope it will serve you well. We will ride most of the day to reach our destination. The others are already there."

Others? Max thought, trying to picture what lay ahead. He swung a leg over the sturdy mare, a reliable trail horse, stroking its neck. Once again employing Lilah's horse whisperer approach, Max leaned forward and spoke in the mare's ear.

"Please allow me to be a burden atop your back on my journey, madam," he said. "I will find apples for you upon our return."

The mare whinnied and scratched the earth with her hooves. Nazaat turned his own broad-backed mare to the south, following a two-track road that skirted the tumultuous, glacier-fed river. Farmhouses dotted the valley, and Buntun waved at the workers in their fields and pastures. As they pierced deeper into the river valley, the mountains began to close in, surrounding them on three sides. They rode in silence for nearly an hour, though it strained Max not to pepper his guide with questions. Then the Kyrgyz spoke.

"I know nothing of the world of chiles that you speak of. Or peppers. Whatever they should be called. Tell me what makes them so special around the world."

Max took a few minutes to formulate the right answer as he swayed to the horse's gait. He needed to establish his authority on chiles to the Kyrgyz. He canvassed his memories for examples that would illuminate the Tien Shan mountains situation and resonate with the man, and he required a quick and compelling narrative.

"Chiles and peppers are the same things. I use both words interchangeably. Chile is an ancient Aztec native word, and pepper comes from the Sanskrit language of prehistory India. History dates the use and cultivation of chile peppers back at least six thousand years in the Americas, and evidence exists of people consuming them dating back ten thousand or more. They became an important part of central and south American cultures, used in rituals, and ever-present in foods over thousands of years. For five centuries, they have spread across the globe and become entwined with every culture."

Buntun looked up at the peaks as Max spoke, thinking how generations of his people had cultivated chiles in their own way. "So, our experience is not unique," he said.

"On the contrary," said Max, "I believe what has occurred here in these valleys may be perfectly, magically unique. There are five species of chiles and over four thousand varieties now around the world. Twenty-eight more are entirely wild varieties, and a very few naturally occurring hybrids, like the one I recently unearthed in India. And I sense the possibility that the Fire of the Valley is a unique variety in all the world. Every type is special to the people who grow and harvest them and the millions more that consume chiles worldwide."

Max dug into memory for an analogy that would bring the story into focus for the Kyrgyz.

"In the southernmost part of America, in the desert state of Arizona, there is a diminutive pepper called the *chiltepin,* which flourishes only in the wild, growing under the shade of specific host plants and trees. This tiny chile spread from South America solely through a journey in birds' stomachs and only produces its bold flavor and intense heat after germinating in the birds' droppings. The domesticated varieties are nowhere near as flavorful, making the wild variety incredibly valuable. Every fall, thousands of foragers trek through an unforgiving desert searching for the tiny red pods, which can command a thousand dollars for ten pounds, and American chefs fight over them at the farmers' markets. They are the only native variety found in the United States, and there is a growing effort to designate the valleys where they grow an agricultural preserve, which would be the first of its kind, anywhere. I have been there and backpacked for five days, searching for the chiles, where I witnessed hills turned red as the bushes ripened. They packed an amazing piquant punch after roasting in our campfire and cooked with fried pork and pinto beans. One of the most extraordinary meals I've ever had, out in the middle of nowhere, at the source of a species."

Buntun considered the information. "So, a very rare and special chile could command a high price on the international market?" he asked.

"Yes, without a doubt," said Max. "There are places around the world that have birthed entirely unique and valuable varieties. In Mexico, in the province of Oaxaca, there is an exceedingly rare variety called the *Chile de Agua*, the 'water chile.' It has long been cultivated in isolation by the village people of Hidalgo Jaltepec and is extremely hard to find, selling for three times that of other chiles. I rode a bus there and spent a week learning about this unique fruit and the villagers' centuries-old farming method that makes it so special. The climate is very arid, and the chiles grow only in years when there is enough rain, increasing demand. They plant in long mounds of mud topped with the tiny cutter ant's manure, extraordinarily high in nutrients. After the first rain, the wet manure is covered again in mud, sealing in the moisture for months since there may be only one rain in some years. These extreme conditions and careful methods give the chile a unique flavor, and they are highly prized, sold only in bags of twelve due to their scarcity. A sauce made from the fire-roasted chiles was powerfully smoky when spooned over grilled strips of beef seasoned with salt and the dried *chile de agua* powder. I will never forget it, and the villagers have become like family."

He stopped there to let the specifically curated stories settle in Nazaat's mind as they rode up the valley. Fifteen minutes later, Buntun spoke.

"These tales are much like our experience here in the Tien Shan mountains. They give me hope. And you are right in assuming we have been cultivating chiles in these canyons in secret. The farmers you saw below are members of our clan, so no person climbs this valley I am not aware of. You are about to witness something special that we have been able to keep hidden for generations. You will be the first outsider to see, and I think the right one," he said, swaying atop his horse. "You live and breathe these peppers, Max Little. You understand."

Finally, thought Max. *At the source. On a horse, riding up a canyon into the mountains of heaven to the valley of fire.* A sustained buzzing coursed through him. He was on the cusp of possibly a second groundbreaking revelation in the Ring of Fire in two weeks.

"It's true that my life is pepper culture, Nazaat. And this is how I got here."

Nazaat nodded his understanding with something suggesting a smile and then looked southward. Mist gathered in the vale ahead. "I think you will find new meaning to your quest in this place," he said.

The sun rose to its midday apex in the sky. In time, a road had diminished into a single horse track skirting the river, bordered by steep faces as they climbed in elevation. Inevitably, Max's thoughts turned to Lilah as he rocked back and forth on his horse. *She should be here,* he thought, *taking part in this discovery. I could use her knowledge and skills. And her company. How is she more valuable held prisoner in Bakiyev's villa?*

For four hours they rode, speaking little. As the canyon continued to narrow, large boulders released from the cliffs above choked the river valley. Charging through the massive stones caused the At Bashy river to cloud and mist, dimming the view ahead. Late afternoon sunlight created mountain-sized shadows as swallows and swifts hunted insect dinners. Eventually, the path stopped where the river issued from an impassable rockfall, clearly the end of the line. Max's Kyrgyz guide hopped down from his horse, and taking the reins, began to climb the steep grade to the left of the boulder pile. A barely perceptible animal track led up and around the barrier, and both horses and men strained up the incline as mist clung to their clothes. Once beyond the impediment, Max stopped, stunned.

Behind the rockfall, a lush, fertile, but narrow valley opened. Sediment had collected, built up behind the water's thwarted cascade, and filled the valley in a small, flat plain cut by the river. Through the mist shone diffused patches of color, which spread across the valley and climbed the hills. *Poppies,* realized Max. *Everywhere.* The flowers and their bulbous pods covered the terrain. Opium poppies, *papaver somniferum,* in a display reminiscent of the sleep-inducing fields in The Wizard of Oz, blanketing the landscape.

The poppies became enmeshed with green bushes at the valley's base, wild entanglements eight feet tall in a flat field, some sixty yards square. The river bisected the orchard before it cascaded through the boulders, the current throwing off steamy gasps. Among the bushes moved a group of men carrying baskets, inspecting branches, and plucking round fruit. The fruits they harvested varied widely in hue: green, yellow, orange, red, purple, and black. *Capsicum pubescens, the round Incan rocoto of the Andes, here in Kyrgyzstan. Incredible,* he thought. With revelation arriving in a cascade, he said quietly to himself, "Ot Boyanca Oroon. The Fire of the Valley. This valley."

Nazaat watched as Max surveyed the scene before him, sweeping his head left and right and processing information.

"What is the elevation here, Nazaat?" Max asked.

The Kyrgyz stroked his beard. "Let me see, about fifteen hundred meters."

Five thousand feet. Max's analytic mind cataloged data, weaving strands of information together. "How much snow falls here?"

"Very little, actually," said Nazaat. "The peaks capture most of the snow, and in the canyon's bottom exists a unique, uh, situation."

"A microclimate is what you mean, I think." *And what creates the microclimate? It has to be the water.*

Max's eyes traced the river's path from where it cascaded through the rocks, gurgling and dancing through the pepper and poppy forest, and back up the valley to the glacier fields that birthed it. Finally, he spied a point along its journey where the mist stopped altogether. At that precise point, red water flowed into the At Bashy from the east, bursting into steam, then diluting in the frothy tumult. From his vantage point, Max followed the red ribbon of water across the valley floor and up the steep south hillside. Halfway up the near-vertical grade, a steaming, circular stone pool captured the red water. A hundred yards higher, the colored water spilled out of a fissure in the mountain, cascading over rocks and boiling on its journey to the rock pool below. At its base, a large yurt contrasted the green grass along the river, horses hobbled outside.

Max blurted his thoughts almost faster than he could form them. "Magma heated water is flowing down that hill into the At Bashy, expanding into mist and warming the colder river as it flows through your fields above the rocks. Warm, moist air keeps the temperature consistent. This end of the narrow valley is climatologically unique because of this phenomenon and allows peppers to grow year-round. And if I am correct in assuming that this pepper plant is *Capsicum pubescens* or some linked hybrid, then the plants favor a mountain environment like the temperate lower Andes mountains where they originated. They are among the only naturally occurring perennial chile plants, providing year-round growth. Hence the plants' immense size. They like sandy soil, and the river valley provides that. But how do they get enough sun? The poppies I have to figure out."

Nazaat was impressed, knowing that he was accompanied by a hound that had picked up a scent. "Let us go down and meet the plants," he said.

They led the horses to a clearing below the boulders and tied them to a stout sapling. They followed a path through thick underbrush, emerging into the pepper and poppy field along the river. Max found himself facing the grandest and wildest pepper plant he had ever seen, about nine feet tall and six feet wide. Its woody stalk resembled a young tree, and long branches spread from its center, falling outward and to the ground. Purple and white flowers hid between the leaves and multicolored fruit the telltale shape of hen's eggs hung heavily from green stems.

The discovery, for Max, was like seeing a fully dressed Christmas tree birthed from the earth, a gift to open excitedly. He greeted the plant, spreading his arms in recognition as if it was a familiar work of art or a long-lost friend. He reached in and gently handled the flowers, counting the petals, fascinated that a plant could spawn both white and purple buds. Along with the black and white seeds, they presented another revelation. *Pubescens purple and annuum white*, Max remembered, possible evidence of hybridization. Then, he overturned the leaves, finding them predictably fuzzy beneath.

Finally, he began to handle the fruit, squeezing them, examining their stems and shape. He recognized that the entire journey had led to this singular moment, his reason for living, and breathed deeply while regarding the mythological pods. They were more pear oblong than apple round like a traditional rocoto, and the orbs hung in an array of colors representing various stages of maturation. Green, most underdeveloped, progressing through yellow, orange, red, purple, and finally, fully ripened black. Some possessed slight ridges, like those of an heirloom tomato. He plucked a purplish-black candidate from its stem and bit the whole pepper in half. Before chewing the pepper's meat in his mouth, Max examined the internal structure. Hiding in the recesses between the piquant membranes were soldierly rows of seeds, alternating between yellow/white and grey/black. *In a thousand chiles, I have never seen this before*, he thought. *Extraordinary*. Then he bit down into the freshly plucked chile.

The flesh popped as he bit through it, releasing a burst of alkaloids and oils that jumped from the fruit. *Thick walls, plump skin. Citrus. And tree fruit, like apple, pears, or quince, with a suggestion of effervescence.*

Factoids blipped into his mind. The rocoto is called Manzano, or apple fruit in Mexico, not just for its shape but also its flavor. Hints of spices like clove and cinnamon emerged in his mouth, more pear-like than apple. Then a powerful smoky note, and earthiness. Rocotos are fruity and slightly acidic. Yet it exhibited a smokiness that was reminiscent of something more like a poblano chile. Poblanos were the large, medium heat chiles used to make rellenos in Mexico, prized for their balance, resilient skin, and earthy quality. They thrived in fire by being smoky in nature and taste, and they traveled well.

He again examined the chile's exterior. It had pale ridges, more akin to an *annuum* chile like a poblano than a *pubescens* like rocoto. As he inspected the fruit, a progression of heat took over Max's mouth. Not like an eruption but a wave. A slow tsunami progressed from the front of his head to the rear. It was hot, almost as a habanero but balanced by fruit, smoke, and earth. Heat perfectly balanced by flavor. Complex but not overpowering, a beautiful marriage of attributes. He strove to understand where it came from. Birds? Human trade?

And poppies. Everywhere, growing in the patches of light between the oversized chile bushes. Many still existed as their telltale latex-filled pods atop straight stems, while others had burst open with purple, white, red, and blue flowers. They scented the moist air in a minty sweet perfume with hints of vanilla and cocoa detectable in the breeze.

The Kyrgyz man's deep voice disrupted Max's mental workings. "I know you have many questions. Come, let us take a drink."

Ducking between the oversize chile bushes, they encountered random men carrying deep baskets, tossing handfuls of their contents from side to side as they wove between and around the plants. The ground felt thick with compost underfoot. Max signaled that he wanted to see inside one of the baskets and, reaching in, pulled out a handful of tiny black seeds. Closer inspection revealed a smattering of larger grains, both white and black, in the mix. Given his surroundings, it was easy to infer that the seeds were a mix of poppy and chile, apparently the black and white, oddly shaped hybrid rocoto. Or, in this case, the Fire of the Valley.

"It takes one thousand poppy seeds to produce just ten plants," Nazaat said. "The rest decomposes into the soil and leaves trace elements of their magic. Nearly all the pepper seeds germinate, so they participate in smaller amounts."

Following the sounds of the river, they eventually arrived on the far side of the orchard. In a clearing before the giant yurt, a half dozen Kyrgyz men of varying ages and stature were seated on stones in a circle. Each had on the traditional cap and sported a full beard. Some were missing teeth, but all were smiling, and a large jar of koumiss was being passed.

Nazaat introduced Max to the men, in Kyrgyz, including scattered words of improvised English.

Eyes both widened and narrowed looked Max up and down, gauging his mettle. That he was clothed in traditional garb and sporting a custom Buntun Kyrgyz blade on his belt seemed to bolster the men's opinion of the American. He was offered a seat and presented with the koumiss jar, from which he took a long draft and left the mare's milk dripping from his scraggly beard. More jars appeared to celebrate a day's work done, and the Kyrgyz conversation increased in animation. Nazaat, perched on his rock next to Max, translated bits and pieces.

The eldest man present pointed to Max while asking Buntun a direct question. "He wants to know how it is that you have come here and how you found out about what grows in this hidden valley," said Nazaat.

All eyes were fixed upon him as he spun the tale of his journey from Laguna Beach, pausing to let it translate into Kyrgyz. Koumiss passed, and the men seemed particularly interested in his experience in Assam and the Naga Jolokia, how the chile had remained hidden for so long. The name Gasanov elicited laughter at the memory of his strapped donkey ride out of town. However, Bakiyev's name produced cautionary whistles and low mumblings from the men, while Tash Rabat generated knowing nods of understanding.

Half an hour later, his story complete, Max sensed a level of acceptance from the men of Dostuk. The effort and distance of his journey and broad knowledge of chiles worldwide elicited increasing respect. However, he had some burning questions to ask.

In a gesture of respect, Max addressed the eldest villager, seated across the circle. "How did these peppers come to this place, and how long have they been here?"

Nazaat translated, then waited for the man's response. The elder stroked his beard and cleared his throat before embarking on the explanation, speaking for a full five minutes. Details central to Max's quest spilled forth, requiring all his will not to stop and ask for interpretation. Finally, the man's tale ended, and Nazaat began to speak.

"Many generations in the past, our people were nomads, living off the land. Dostuk was not a village yet. After the Mongols conquered all the known world, we began to see the caravans stretching in long lines across the river valley, heading to the east. We heard of the gatherings of men and commerce at Tash Rabat and began to take our sheep and mountain horses there to sell. The Westerners and Chinese were always looking for horses that were fit for the high passes and rough terrain of the Tien Shan. Some of our clan moved to Tash Rabat to engage in trade and sell our foods to foreigners. Our people began to encounter foods at the caravanserai they had never seen and heard stories of far-off lands, bringing both back to our people. They planted gardens using the seeds of new foods from both west and east and used these new things in the paloos, kuurdaks, beshbarmaks, samsas, and mantis they made for the travelers. One of the last things to arrive was chiles, strange-looking and full of fire. They added spice to our bland mountain foods and were easier to obtain than peppercorn. Different types began to arrive, and all were planted in the gardens of Tash Rabat. The various fruits were new to our people so telling the seeds apart was not often possible. They planted different types to see which ones would flourish in the mountain climate and cultivated the hardier varieties. Eventually, one type stood out for its ability to thrive in the mountains and year-round under the right conditions. Circular and thick-skinned, it was brought back to the Naryn valley, where our people started cultivating fruits and vegetables to feed the nomadic clans. But it was here in this valley of the At Bashy that something phenomenal happened. The steam from the hot mineral water created the ability to grow plants throughout the year and produce multiple crops, surviving even winter. Poppies have always grown in these hills, scattered on the winds. My great-great-great-grandfather planted seeds of the peppers in this plot, sensing the unique conditions, where they flourished alongside the flowers, even in cold weather. The fruits that grew were stronger, sweeter, and produced many colors and different flavors in each. And they made people happy and at peace simply by eating them. When travelers ate foods prepared using only this fruit, they were mesmerized and wanted to know our secret. Word spread of the spices used by the people of the Tien Shan. When the Norwegian and his party came through this place one hundred years ago, they were nourished by our clan people. When accolades of our food became published to the world in his book, we knew we had to protect our prized possession, which came to be known as *Ot Boyanca Oroon*, the Fire of the Valley. My grandfather opened an inn in the new village of Dostuk in 1931, and now it belongs to my son, Nazaat."

Max was dumbstruck as he sat on the rock by the At Bashy river, learning the tale of the magical, rare chile. Yet questions filled his mind as the sun hid behind the peaks, and a fire was lit to warm the circle of men.

"Have the seeds always been both black and white?" he asked.

Nazaat and the men conferred, and he presented their conclusion. "The seeds and fruit that came from Tash Rabat to us were both, yes."

So, the hybridization occurred at the caravanserai, where different chiles were planted in the same soil, Max decided. *And by chance. Or maybe not.* "How do they get enough sun with all this mist?"

Nazaat spoke as one possessing the knowledge of generations. "The steam clouds form in the coldest parts of the day before the sun crests the mountains. When the sun warms the earth, it burns away, letting in the sunlight. In winter, it is foggy, which protects the plants that go dormant. We get flowering and fruit three times a year, in spring, summer, and fall, and the plants will grow for fifteen years."

Fifteen-year-old plants and three crops a year? Extraordinary, Max thought. *And rarely heard of.* "And what imparts the euphoric feeling from ingesting these chiles?" he followed, though the answer already germinated in his mind.

Another group discussion in Kyrgyz commenced, with Nazaat delivering the hypothesis.

"The poppies have always grown here, as long as anyone can remember. They grew and died in this place alongside the chiles and decomposed in the sandy soil, adding nutrients. But it also imparted its dreamlike quality through the seeds and pods. Believing this, we began to plant poppies everywhere and used the seeds in our cooking and seasonings, which carry trace amounts of the opiate. The dried pods lack the potent latex that makes pure opium, and we make compost of the stalks and pods we have extracted the seeds from. Their attributes are mixed into the soil and enhance the pepper plants through their roots. We call these poppies the 'seeds of peace,' for they sow a peaceful nature in people. We have never made concentrate from them, to protect our secret from outsiders looking for a source of opium. Yet now our secret is out. The time has come to decide what is to be done about it, and this is our village council assembled to discuss our future. Your arrival has come at a meaningful time, Max Little. But first, let us bathe and take in the spell of this place."

Responding to some unheard command, the men rose as a group. Nazaat led the silent party across the valley floor, skirting the steaming ribbon of red water that had flowed for eons from the hillside. Outside the bank of fog, hundreds of cut poppy pods lay drying in the sun, their hypnotic latex evaporating to dust to return to the soil. The village women would arrive to extract their seeds, Nazaat informed Max.

They crossed the valley, wading through poppies until a thin trail zigzagged up the steep grade toward the rock pool he had seen earlier. The older man took Max's elbow as they walked, and he assisted the elder over and around rocks in the trail. His walk proved unsteady, but his grip firm. "I am Damir," he said.

It was clear to Max that Nazaat's father played a significant role in the community, and he escorted him in deferent silence. Once off the valley floor, the mist cleared, and warming shafts of late-day sun washed across the hill from a gap in the peaks to the west, shining a golden glow on the ascending path. Birds sang happily in the sun, and prairie dogs scattered as they passed.

A pool about fifteen feet wide had been constructed of boulders to dam the scalding mineral waters issuing from the fissure above. Red mineral deposits carpeted its bottom and stained the watercourse crimson as the waters tumbled down the hill. On its far side, the water continued its path downward to the At Bashy River, where it met the colder body of water with a gust of steam. Without a word, the men began to undress.

"Islam says that we should not show our naked bodies," Nazaat said as he lowered his hirsute frame into the water. "But our mountain traditions are older than Islam, and our clan has used this pool for hundreds of years. Our village women come here to bathe by themselves without fear and participate in the harvest and seeding. The water cools just enough from boiling out of the rocks above, and our forefathers constructed a pool on this spot where it becomes the perfect temperature. It is rich in iron, good for health, and a source of strong minerals in the soil, which spawns the chiles below."

Max waded into the red pool, opting not to wear his traditional cap like the rest of the Kyrgyz. *I guess that makes them not entirely naked*, he thought. *Obeying a small piece of their faith.* More koumiss was produced and partnered with the heat, suffusing the men with cheer. They inquired about the beaded Ethiopian necklace around his neck, and he told them the story of his time with the Amhara ethnic group, eliciting grunts of approval. A burlap bag appeared, from which Damir withdrew a strange headpiece. Small round balls of muted colors had been stitched together with animal ligament into a round skullcap, which the man placed atop his crown. After a healthy gulp of koumiss, he raised his hands to the sky and the four directions, then launched into a poem. He presented a tale in Kyrgyz comprising dozens of verses. Numerous grasps of the strange cap on his head punctuated the story, which Max felt but could not understand.

The headdress was passed, along with the mare's milk, as poetry and song rose from each man. Nazaat went last, his voice full and passionate, and a tear formed in his eye as he addressed his father in rhyming verse. Upon finishing, he held out the hat to Max.

"This was made by my father's grandfather. I think you can see from what it is constructed. These poems and songs are the stories of our forefathers. The discoveries at Tash Rabat and Sven Hedin's tale, the secret valley of our magical chiles. Poetry is important to remember our people's history, so please add something you feel is fitting."

Max examined the unique headdress, turning it over in his hands. It was composed entirely of partially dried Fire of the Valley chiles, lacquered to maintain their rainbow colors and protect them from time and the elements. It flexed and gave, adjusting to the different poets' various head sizes. He pressed the hat onto his head as it slid down to his eyebrows, cool with its shiny finish. *A head of peppers*, he thought. *Indeed, a pepper-head moment. This is what Nazaat referred to.*

He breathed the mineral steam deeply, taking in the profound moment. Then he scoured his mind for something timely to add to the collective story. A favorite Johnny Cash song he deemed appropriate for the ceremony, and following another gulp of koumiss, he sang its many verses, loud enough for all to hear.

Love is a burning thing, And it makes a fiery ring
Bound by wild desire, I fell into a ring of fire...

The final phrases of the song echoed across the canyon. Though not understanding Max's English, his new companions could follow the piece's rhyme and melody and applaud in response to the musical contribution. A heavy hand clapped his back, causing him to spray koumiss as Nazaat looked at him fondly.

"An excellent choice, Max Little," he said, sporting a broad grin. "Is this man a prophet in your culture?"

"No, but many would say he tells people's stories better than most," said Max. "He speaks to all, especially the working folk. And he loves chiles. A true pepper-head like all of us here."

"Yes, pepper-heads," agreed Nazaat, looking around the pool and fully respecting the colloquial term.

His explanation of the word to the gathering brought cheers of approval. Max floated in the surreal moment, absorbing the experience in a remote misty valley surrounded by generations of Kyrgyz pepper-heads. He sat back, gazing out over the aboriginal scene, surrounded by tribal voices, and understood he was near the end of his quest. Being at the source always imparted a sublime emotion upon Max, connecting to the earth and time and people far and wide. He had reached the pinnacle of his life's purpose.

After an hour in the rejuvenating ritual pool, Nazaat signaled it was time to adjourn to the yurt below. Stars began to flicker in a cloudless sky as the men threaded their way back down the hill, damp in their clothes, to the warm confines of a colossal yurt, which was erected for use by the villagers who made the trek to harvest poppies and peppers and manage the soils. Piles of thick, colorful Kyrgyz blankets and cushions made from them awaited, forming a circle around a fire lit for tea. Max felt an immediate and powerful kinship with these people along with a growing responsibility to promote and protect their future. Once reclined and warmed by strong spiced black tea, Nazaat initiated the next phase of their interaction. His gigantic ears were half as big as Max's face, biceps big as thighs, yet his voice was as soft as it was deep.

"So now you know about these peppers, Max Little, and about us. What do you think we should do?"

Max looked into the fire, sifting through ideas that he had been percolating for weeks and that he found he already possessed. He closed his eyes to picture the activity around the caravanserai and the specimens he had seen pulled out of the earth from four centuries before. He envisioned the same seeds, arriving in pouches and fresh produce itself, traded in whispers. Gardens spread in the plain around the trading post, and chiles grew, the spice-laden new fruit from the West.

"It seems quite probable to me that your seeds originated at Tash Rabat," he said, as Nazaat translated. "There will need to be genetic testing to determine if they are a unique hybrid, a cross between two distinct varieties. I believe this occurred in the merchant gardens around the caravanserai, and I will need to return there to gather more specimens. The unique conditions in this valley have certainly contributed to its development, and the opiated poppies add a mystic aura to the story. I believe the poppies and their byproducts in the soil and spice blends contribute a noticeable euphoria. Testing on the soil and the chiles will be done to determine the opiate content levels. Too high, and the products will not be marketable internationally; however, I believe what you have is one of the most truly fascinating and special chiles on the planet, with considerable potential value to your people."

Beards were scratched as the men pondered the assessment. Finally, Nazaat looked at Max and spoke. "You have said that there are others who have an interest in what we do here and that they want what we own. How do you propose we should deal with them?"

This question signaled significantly more risk, and the solution formed in Max's mind as he spoke. "Bakiyev wants to capitalize on these peppers. He knows that they are rare and that the people of Dostuk produce them. He has sent his associates here to discover the secret and has obtained samples from Osh's market. He is already trying to cultivate them, even in America, on the farm of a grower named Jones, my friend. But you possess a great advantage in the conditions at this location, what the French call *terroir*, the place's identity. This is indelibly part of the chiles. Once he realizes that only the chiles from this valley possess the most marketable attributes, he will try harder to acquire them. Eventually, he would find this place, and it would be ruined. Imagine trucks driving up this valley. So, our solution is more important every day. He knows I am here and believes I'll reveal your secret to see my companion again. She is being held against her will in his villa in Osh, and outsmarting him is the best way for me to get her back."

Max paused, running hands through his hair in thought. He could not imagine how Lilah was faring in Osh and desperately needed to see her again.

"It would be difficult to recreate the conditions which make your chile unique, particularly how the poppies become integrated into the seeding and cultivation of the Fire of the Valley and the hot mineral spring. Bakiyev, I'm afraid, has many resources, and he will be relentless in his pursuit. The only way to keep him away is to make him your partner."

The men responded by cursing in Kyrgyz and spitting on the ground in disgust. One threw an angry knife into a tentpole while Nazaat showed signs of visceral confusion.

"Partners with our country's most well-known criminal?" he sputtered. "How can you ask this of us?"

"Let me finish," implored Max. "He will not expect our proposal, and we will convince Bakiyev to pay for a factory in Dostuk to produce wet and dried products. You will be able to protect your methods, and it will create jobs for your people. I will compel him to see that this is the only way to access what you so passionately protect."

Nazaat held his head in his hands, defeated. "And how will we manage Bakiyev?" he asked. "How will we be able to guarantee he will do what is agreed?"

"Because I too will be your partner," said Max. "I will set up the businesses and write the contracts and monitor Bakiyev. I will handle selling the products in Europe, India, and the Americas, and Bakiyev will oversee Asia, Persia, Africa, and the Middle East. His interest will be vested in a successful business operation with reliable partners. Any other result will be a failure for all."

Nazaat remained skeptical. "People will still come here. Dostuk will be ruined, and this valley."

"I have already given thought to this," said Max. "Bakiyev has the Minister of Agriculture of Kyrgyzstan in his employ, the superior of the man Gasanov. With his role and Bakiyev's influence, I believe that this valley could be designated as a heritage preserve, a protected place. Once the story becomes known of these chiles and their link to Silk Road history, your country will maneuver to preserve it for national pride. Perhaps even the United Nations will designate it as a world heritage site. I will assist you in crafting the story and will lend my reputation to the effort. We can protect this place, and I will make Bakiyev's participation contingent upon it."

Silence filled the yurt. The men stared at the crackling fire, contemplating the information that would surely change the lives of their people. Tea was poured, and quiet debates ensued. Finally, after fifteen minutes, Nazaat rose and spoke to each of them in soft tones. Lastly, he spoke to his father, who had remained silent throughout the exchanges. Then he stood before Max.

"My father has let the men each decide on their own. It would seem your fate is attached to ours, Max Little. All are in favor, with reservations. We will do these things only with your participation and guarantees. And you must agree to come here often to ensure Bakiyev's honesty. Our people do not engage in contracts because so many were broken in the past with outsiders. We will only be satisfied with your regular presence. This part has come from my father to make you return here and prove your trustworthiness. So you are now an ally of our people, and there is trust. A new path for the avlod Adygine, our clan, is to be forged, and you have brought the future to our door. Pass the koumiss!"

Max felt a rush of adrenaline, then a wave of calm. Relief that his proposal had been accepted balanced the excitement of a new Kyrgyz partnership. One that would benefit its people and consume the Ring of Fire. Yet Max understood that essential steps and significant luck would be required to execute the plan, with Bakiyev being a gaping unknown. Moreover, he still needed help to get it done at all.

"I require something of you, Nazaat, to achieve the results we desire," he said. "You must take me to Osh and help me locate Bakiyev. A donkey from your village will take too long, and I haven't the time."

Without hesitation, Nazaat said, "I will do this, for you and our people. And to rescue your woman."

A long evening of oaths and toasting followed, with sustenance provided by a kettle of mutton and Ot Boyanca Oroon *shorpo*, a fatty and supremely peppered stew. The combined warmth and seductive magic of the mare's milk and opiated shorpo generated a firelit, lightly hallucinogenic camaraderie. A single drum initiated a whirl of dancing and song as the men locked elbows and spun on the carpets, kicking high to the claps of the Kyrgyz. Max whirled and dipped, performing to the whoops and hollers of his new associates until the fire subsided to amber, dusty coals late in the night.

Max awoke tangled in wool blankets. A hirsute foot hung dangerously close to his face, its toes twitching, and he heard several snores of different pitches at once. He raised to one elbow to observe a room spread with sleeping men. The scent of smoke hung in the air while old Damir knelt by a morning kettle, preparing tea. Wrapped in his colored blanket, he motioned for Max to join him at the fire, patting the cushion to his left.

They sat in silence, sipping the potent brew and staring into the fire for long minutes. Then, Max felt a tap on his knee. He turned to the clan's white-haired elder, who looked back at him with piercing, slate-blue eyes, watery with age. Damir touched his heart then waved his hand over the men in the room. Then he pointed to Max, signaling that he should do the same. Max touched his chest then moved it across the room in a wide arc, making sure not to miss a single sleeping tribesman.

"My people," said Damir. "Your people."

Then he took both of Max's hands in his and, closing his eyes, began a quiet, rhythmic chant. Max sat transfixed, watching the elder deliver the prayer. A wave of mutual commitment flowed through the two men, bonding with a shared purpose in the firelight. He knew at that moment that he would do anything in his power to protect the man and his people.

The serene setting became immediately beset by chaos. A new Kyrgyz, fully clothed for the day, burst through the canvas door of the yurt.

"Where is Nazaat?" he asked frantically.

Snores were the only response.

"Nazaat!" he yelled, "Father!" The hairy-toed man asleep where Max's head had been sat up. The rest of the group shot up as well, alarmed by the intrusion.

"Tagaev, what do you think you're doing, boy?" Nazaat demanded.

"There are men below the rockfall. I followed them from the village yesterday because none of the farmers knew who they were. They appear dressed as Kyrgyz, but they have binoculars. I took the trail over the high ridge to reach you before they did."

Nazaat's brow wrinkled, more fierce than afraid. "Thank you, my son. You have done well." He thought for a moment, formulating a plan. "Sultanov, you and Dagaev gather the horses. Make sure they are ready."

He turned to the remaining men of the council, issuing fast orders. Then, addressing Max, he said, "We will surround these intruders at the rockfall by the river and find out who they are. They will prove no match for us, and men are already circling behind them. Shall we go and see what the day will bring?"

Max strapped the Kyrgyz dagger to his belt and washed down the black tea. "I have a feeling I know who these men are. We have met on several occasions. It's not hard to imagine why they're here, and I suggest you inform your men that they have Spetznaz combat training. However, I would prefer if you allowed me to confront them, Nazaat. They took my girlfriend."

The Kyrgyz nodded in understanding. "We will duck among the pepper bushes and surround them as they enter the clearing below the rocks."

He called out commands to his compatriots. They fanned out through the foliage, bent low and avoiding twigs that would betray their presence, and at the edge of the pepper border, they waited.

Two hissing voices echoed over the rockfall as Max and the Kyrgyz men watched from the bushes. The immense boulders required drops from one to another to navigate, and the men cursed in Russian painfully as they descended, rolling in the dirt and gasping at their final landing. Through the vividly hued forest of dangling of Fire of the Valley pods, Max recognized Boris and Vlad - outfitted in ill-fitting Kyrgyz garb, short beards, and high-powered binoculars. He interpreted from their hand gestures that they planned to split up to surveil the scene.

Bakiyev will get nothing, Max determined. He rose from his crouched and concealed position and strode out into the clearing.

Startled, the two Russians assumed defensive postures at the sight of their nemesis, more Kyrgyz in appearance than they, a curved blade on his hip.

"Hello, boys," said Max. "Yet another excellent costume choice. Once again, today is not your day."

Thrusting his hands out karate style, Vlad snarled. "Max Leetle, we are here to...."

Ten Kyrgyz wielding blades in each hand burst from the undergrowth as two more appeared on the rocks behind the interloping Russians, aware now of imminent capture.

Boris and Vlad were bound and gagged as the men secured them atop two extra Kyrgyz mountain horses. The camp was broken, and the return journey to Dostuk began. Max slowed to ride alongside the hobbled men, who could only curse him with their enraged bloodshot eyes.

Nazaat pulled next to Max, looking over their captives. "I do not understand why they would come. They were driven away once already, these two. Not very smart."

Vlad glared at Max and the Kyrgyz while Boris attempted to scream some message through his tightly gagged mouth, struggling against the taught bonds. He looked ahead as he spoke to them, to Bakiyev.

"So, you were sent to spy on me again? Or to reconnaissance the environment where the chiles are grown? You should have trusted me to do what I do and leave the smart work to me. Now you have an uncomfortable couple of days ahead of you. And you're going to be my entry into Bakiyev's compound. This is the last time we'll be meeting like this, fellas."

The ride back to Dostuk took four hours. Baskets laden with multicolored peppers and poppy pods rocked on the ten horses' haunches. Max and Nazaat rode side by side, sharing ideas for their joint venture.

"The plan calls for a factory in Dostuk, so we will need to produce a higher quantity of raw product to meet the demand, no?" asked Nazaat. "How will we be able to do this with the very exact growing conditions and limited space in the valley? A smart person would say we should erect greenhouses closer to town."

Max had been pondering this question from the first moment he had climbed the rocks and looked into the verdant valley. An entrepreneur to his core, he had already begun to juggle and optimize the factors that created and sustained the extraordinary fruit and develop the story elements that would amplify demand for them in the marketplace.

"Greenhouses in town is not a bad idea, perhaps as a stage two plan," he said. "However, I see expanding the growing area by erecting hoop houses, more temporary greenhouses, up in the valley."

Nazaat considered this. "But what about the mineral water and its impact on the microclimate?"

"I've thought about that," said Max. "What if the mineral spring could be diverted and redirected to run through a network of hoop houses before flowing into the river itself? The microclimate could be recreated over and over. And seed and treat the soil with the poppies in the same way. Growing could be expanded across the entire valley floor. Transporting by trail for hours would remain a challenge but imagine the marketing bonus created by lines of donkeys carrying baskets of chiles from the magical place in the mountains. People will love it. They will come from all over the world to see this place and stay in the new Buntun Guest Lodge Hotel."

The Kyrgyz clan chief shook his head, chuckling. "I see how your mind works, Max Little. You have already worked it out, and it is a good plan."

Lilah stood before a computer screen in a basement laboratory in Osh, watching results appear from liquid chromatography testing. The workspace to which she had been remanded by Bakiyev was too-brightly lit, and her eyes ached as she rubbed fatigue from them. The testing she had done at her captor's command revealed that the Kyrgyz chile contained a level of capsaicin higher than an *annum* chile and lower than that of a *chinense,* and at 110,000 units, it fell right in line with *Capsicum pubescens*, the rocoto. The lab was also equipped with gas chromatography-ion trap mass spectrometry, which allowed her to measure opioid levels after extraction with methanol. She discovered minute traces of opioid alkaloids present in the Kyrgyz chiles, though at levels far below what would cause alarm. A scientific source of the reputed euphoria, she surmised. Yet questions loomed.

The sound of the latch on the lab door alerted her to someone entering. Vlad appeared sheepishly in the doorway. She looked at him with irritation.

"Mr. Bakiyev is interested in your progress," he said, shuffling his feet.

"Tell him the chile is moderately spicy and that it has trace amounts of opiate," she said. "If he had consulted with me before setting up this laboratory, I would have recommended that he include equipment for genetic testing. Unfortunately, there's no way to ascertain what type of chile this is or if it is a hybrid. A lot of money spent not to get a definitive result."

Vlad winced. "Very well, I will tell him. He would like to know if you would join him for dinner."

"I still have more tests to run," said Lilah impatiently, peering into the monitor. "I'll take my dinner in my room. Again." She rubbed her arms, exhaling with something more than frustration.

The small caravan pulled into Dostuk late in the day, and individual riders fanned out through the village to deliver the crop at family homesteads. Max and Nazaat headed for the Buntun Lodge, the two Russians in tow. Boris and Vlad were escorted to the haybarn in the Buntun's small pasture behind the lodge, where they were given water and shackled to the wall. Their bunkmates would be a small herd of goats and a resounding warning that Nazaat was an expert knife thrower and light sleeper. Plus, the entire village knew who would be sleeping with the goats this evening. Escape was futile.

Inside the lodge, Max and Nazaat carried baskets of chiles and poppy pods to the inn's kitchen. Adilet and her assistant greeted them with feigned indignance.

"You're late," said Nazaat's wife. She tossed a look at Max. "And I see that you are still here." Then, the slightest appearance of a smile showed on her face. "Go wash up, and I will feed you supper."

Nazaat set off to do as instructed, and before leaving, Max turned to speak to Adilet directly. "Adilet, may I ask you a question?"

Her hands went to her hips in customary impatience. "Yes, but make it quick. You can see that we are busy."

Max spoke thoughtfully. "These peppers have been a secret for generations, and yet you sold them in the market in Osh. For how long did you sell them there?"

A steely set of eyes looked back at him, understanding Max knew more than she believed. She was exposed.

"I went to sell in the market for one week during our slow season last winter. We needed money. No one bought our peppers because they had never seen them before. Only one man bought a kilo. The rest

I brought back to dry for powder, so they were not wasted. How did you know, and why do you ask?"

"Because that man was Nickolai Gasanov, the man who compelled me to come here," Max said. "The man who posed as a knife seller to learn your secrets. He sent the seeds to America."

Adilet wiped her hands in her apron and sighed. Then, motioning for Max to follow her, she sat at a table in the empty dining room, folding her hands atop the worn planks.

"We have kept this secret hidden for so long, and no one remembers why," she told Max, sighing. "I felt the world closing in, and someday, someone would find out. If the wrong people discovered our secret in the hills, there would be no benefit. I felt there had to be someone, away from this village and out in the wide world, that could help us figure out what to do. I took the peppers to market so that they might be discovered, hopefully by the right people. One man bought them, and he found you in America. And here you are. I made the right decision." She held both of Max's hands in hers, looking into his eyes with the hint of a smile. He could not tell if the water in her eyes was from age or emotion, though he grasped her hands and smiled back warmly.

"It is a testament to you and the magic of these chiles that I have come around the world to understand them both," Max said. "I give you my word that I will do all in my power to protect your village and share its secret wisely. The fact that your people have hidden it for so long is an incredible tale. Now I am off to finish the story, and one more of your meals will fortify me for the journey that still lies ahead."

They got up from the table, fully aware of the understanding that existed between them, partners in what had become a global odyssey. They would be forever linked by their actions and decisions that would change the world in a small way and their own lives indelibly.

Max turned toward the hall and felt a soft slap on his backside. "Go and wash, and I will feed you, Max Little," said Adilet. "You have earned it."

An hour later, the lodge's dining room was filled with expectant villagers summoned for an important announcement and a complimentary meal. Nazaat and Max assisted in ferrying the many trays of food set before entire Dostuk families, and the air was rife with excited conversation. Many wondered at the foreigner who served them, as often the only face they saw was that of Adilet Buntun. And they had never eaten for free.

Before the service ended, Max requested a tray of food, which he took out to the haybarn's overnight guests. To their amazement, he ungagged Boris and Vlad and freed only their hands as he set the tray before them. Then, before they could speak, he raised his hand.

"Now, you'll get to taste for yourselves the reason I traveled to this place and why your employer has forced you to harass me for so long. Do not be afraid of the spice, as I feel you have gotten used to it by dealing with me. See you in the morning, and remember the entire village is carrying knives."

He gave them a wink, relocked the haybarn door, and returned to the dining room, where koumiss flowed for all. Nazaat Buntun signaled a speech by banging the handle of his blade on a table corner. The clan's leader stood by the fire and told of Max's journey, eliciting looks of incredulity from around the room, and outlined the plan that would change their lives forever. Astonishment gave way to cheers, with many toasts exchanged. Even women and children stayed until late in the evening at the Buntun Guest House Lodge's first-ever party. More would undoubtedly follow, though, on this night, the unanswered question of Bakiyev loomed ahead.

The next morning, Max was roused by a knock on his door, opening it to find the familiar tray of tea and honeyed borsook. Nazaat soon arrived to get Max's help in unshackling their uncannily happy prisoners, and they used the van which had brought Bakiyev's men to the village as their transport to Osh. Rather than asking for directions, they opted to prevent Boris and Vlad from talking by gagging them again. The bound commandos bounced around contentedly in the back, cushioned by sacks of Fire of the Valley peppers on the daylong ride to the city.

"Bakiyev's house should not be hard to find," said Nazaat. "Everybody knows this man, and I have friends in Osh."

Late in the afternoon, they arrived at the city's outskirts, and after a stop at the Osh Metalworks in the industrial district, they had directions to Bakiyev's villa provided by a connection of Nazaat's.

"It sits alone on a large, fenced property fronting the Ak Buura River," they were told by a welder. "A garish white fortress with statues and columns off Lenin Avenue."

By sunset, they had located Bakiyev's three-story compound. Surrounded by a spiked metal fence, the property hosted acres of hedges and gardens that hugged a fifteen-foot wall surrounding the villa itself, brazenly secure. They parked outside the villa's view.

Nazaat quickly worked the padlock on the front gate using bolt cutters he found behind the van's passenger seat. Then, with the help of Max, he pulled the men from the vehicle and forced them to walk before him in the dimming light. As they neared the villa wall, Max heard alarming cries coming from the other side.

The shouts of anguish were punctuated by strikes of something hard. A woman's voice, Lilah's, carried through the air, registering pain. It was followed by a man's voice tinged with sadistic pleasure and glee.

Immediately frantic, Max tried the handle on a double door to no avail. He quickly examined a rain gutter pipe extending the height of the wall about ten feet away from the door.

"Nazaat, I'll have to shimmy up that pipe and over the wall," Max said, breathing hard. " I will open the doors for you if I can. If not, try and think of another way in. I have to go help Lilah."

Adrenaline overtook Max as he grabbed onto the pipe and pulled himself up the wall. Whatever awaited him on the other side, he was ready to confront at all costs. Reaching the top, he vaulted over and dropped into the unknown.

He landed hard on concrete, rolling to break the fall, and used the momentum to propel himself upright, curved Kyrgyz blade held out before him. Not twenty feet away stood Bakiyev, dressed in white shorts and a polo shirt with an upturned collar. He was holding a tennis racket, which he raised to his face in self-defense. Max quickly scanned the space for danger, crouched for confrontation. On the far side of the expansive courtyard stood Lilah, dressed in a short white skirt and sporting pigtails on the opposite side of a stretched net. A small, fuzzy yellow ball rolled past her.

Tennis. *They're playing tennis*, realized Max. Courtside, Gasanov sat at a table mixing martinis.

"Max, what in the hell are you doing?" yelled Lilah.

Suddenly self-conscious with the blade in his hand, Max shrugged and said, "I thought he was hurting you."

At that moment, the double doors crashed open, destroyed by Nazaat Buntun's massive shoulder. Behind him, he dragged Bakiyev's unlucky henchmen. Dropping Boris and Vlad to the ground, their hands still bound, he opened his vest to reveal a dozen glimmering throwing knives, prepared to unleash them upon any assailants. Bakiyev ran and hid, crouching behind Gasanov.

"Max, my long-lost friend!" proclaimed Gasanov, calmly stirring his drink with a finger. "You have completed your quest! And what an entrance! Come, let us celebrate, and you can tell me all about it. Though your lovely associate Lilah has told me much already. She is a passionate and compelling advocate, not only for you but for the chiles themselves, I must say."

Max stood speechless, confused by the scene. Lilah, unharmed, cavorting at her captor's villa. Gasanov, comfortably encamped courtside as Bakiyev's guest, playing bartender. Nothing was adding up. The hero looked absurd, dressed as a mountain tribesman, sporting a month's worth of beard and an oversized knife in hand. He sheathed his blade, and Nazaat slowly closed his weaponized vest.

Bakiyev stepped from behind Gasanov. "I see you have bested my boys yet again, Max Little," he said. "However, I sent them to give you a ride knowing you had no transportation. I had predicted that you would complete your tasks and wished to assist you in returning to your charming counterpart. We have had a lovely time."

Max was confused. "Then why track me and slink around with binoculars?"

At that moment, Boris and Vlad began to struggle mightily in their restraints. Sensing no imminent threat, Nazaat freed them from their bonds with a whisk of his blade and pushed them towards their employer. They rubbed their chafed wrists.

"Our directive was to locate you," said Boris in his heavy Russian dialect. "To offer a ride. When we saw you go up the valley, we followed. That is all. We wanted to tell you, but you imprisoned us with your surly tribesmen. Thank you for the wonderful food, though. Best meal ever."

Lilah watched the unfolding drama, leaning on her racquet. Max looked at her and shrugged, embarrassed by his over-the-top actions. She was safe all along. Then, she jumped over the net and ran to him, clamping him in a full-body wraparound hug.

"My hero," she said as she kissed his face over and over, applying an over-the-top Southern accent. "You came to rescue me. Don't ever lose me again."

The encompass of Lilah's body combined with her sweet voice and kisses brought Max undefinable relief, her warmth a most welcome light at the end of a dark tunnel. She was safe and unharmed and gladdened at his return. Bakiyev appeared not to pose an immediate threat, and the tennis and martinis he would have to figure out.

"I think we could all use a drink and a meal," said Bakiyev. "Let us meet in the dining hall in two hours. Max, I feel you will want to get reacquainted with your eminently capable and enchanting partner." Then, turning to Nazaat, he said, "You must be the infamous Buntun. My people have told me about you. There is much we need to discuss. Please, come."

After retrieving their belongings and two bags of Fire of the Valley chiles from the van, Lilah led Max through the palatial villa to her suite.

They ascended a sweeping staircase to the second floor, finding a pair of doors at the end of a long hall. Garish art hung everywhere, depicting scenes of past Kyrgyz greatness. Lilah threw open the doors to reveal an expansive space punctuated with too many ornate columns and more Kyrgyz myths illustrated in oversized oil paintings. She led him to a wide balcony overlooking the Ak Buura river, with expansive views in every direction. Unusual for Max, words escaped him.

He leaned on the railing, looking out over the river valley and mountains beyond. Images of his journey from the moment Lilah climbed into the black Lincoln flooded his mind. There was much to tell but finding where to start proved challenging. He had worried so much.

Lilah took his hand and spoke, looking into Max's eyes.

"I can only imagine what you must have gone through since we were separated. It was killing me that you didn't know I was safe. As soon as I got in his car, Bakiyev assured me that he had only our best interests at heart. Knowing what he did of you, he had to motivate you to find the answers and figured that you worked best alone. I've been busy in the lab almost the entire time. I know he regrets taking me the way he did and has made it up to me in good behavior ever since. Boris and Vlad have been complete gentlemen, and Nickolai is a most charming conversationalist. He admits to coercion and manipulation to get you here but knows no one on earth was better equipped to complete the journey. Now please, tell me about everything. Including the Russian archaeologist, Mishka."

The last statement startled Max. "You know about her?"

Lilah laughed. "Well, she now works for Bakiyev, and her reputation preceded her. I can only imagine what encountering the pepper world's Indiana Jones would have done to a lonely woman stuck in the wilds of the Tien Shan mountains. Tell me your story while we take a bath. I'll bet you could use one."

Max followed her into a bathing lounge larger than his entire apartment, marbled from floor to ceiling. Under a bay window in the corner sat an absurdly wide and deep clawfoot tub. Lilah twisted a spigot into a torrent of steaming water that filled the vessel in minutes. Hunger built between them as they both stole glances at each other while getting undressed, though he was certainly dustier. They locked eyes as they lowered their bodies into the water at the same time, and for an hour, they soaked and kissed and talked as Max told his fantastic tale. He admitted to the archaeologist's unexpected kiss and that he owed her a debt of gratitude for her part in his discovery.

"Then we'll have to go back," said Lilah, "for you to repay the debt. And I hope you brought some of the damn seeds for testing because you'll flip at the lab Bakiyev built in the basement. Almost better than the university. With a few strategic upgrades, I could do lots of work here. Kiss me."

They pressed their lips together hard and long and made love in the steaming tub. The bath salon hosted its own small balcony, and they took their blissful intercourse outside as the stars began to shimmer. Once back indoors, they played naked slip-and-slide in the water that had splashed from the tub, giggling across the salon. After days of rugged travel and worry, the juxtaposition for Max was striking, cavorting nude in a marble palace with Lilah. He had found his love and never would lose her again.

When they finally emerged from the spa-sized bath, they discovered that somebody had laid out bright clothes for them during their balcony romp. Lilah dressed in a sky-blue shining silk gown with long, broad sleeves past her wrists; the body of the garment flowed down to the floor at her feet, which she slid into beaded slippers. A translucent embroidered silk vest covered the gown, and a wide cotton belt with floral designs adorned her waist. She placed a cap that matched the vest on her head, with a white fur band around the brow. Freshly shaved, Max put on a white silk shirt and trousers, which he tucked into calf-high gold felt boots. Awaiting his frame was a long jacket just his size patterned out of thin, soft felt, featuring long gold and white lines with a single button, and embroidered ethnic patterns followed the edges from waist to back. He capped it all off with a *kippa* hat, a black felt four-sided dome stitched with shining gold thread in swirls and waves. After giving each other sartorial approval, Max and Lilah exited the suite and descended the grand stairs hand in hand.

Bakiyev's dining hall was covered in blue velvet. Even the marble floor had been tinted blue. A blue granite table that could hold twenty had been set for seven, and the other guests were also in elaborate costumery. Bakiyev wore satiny gold from head to toe, his headpiece more a crown than a hat. Gasanov sported the long gown of a vizier, purple and stitched with stars. Nazaat's garb was more understated, in deference to his nature, while Boris and Vlad wore garish military uniforms of Czarist Russia, fake medals and all. French wine flowed before Bakiyev commenced a speech from the table's head, arms spread expansively, and his voice echoing across the chamber.

"For three thousand years, the city of Osh has been a center of Kyrgyz culture. It was known as the Silk Road's exact center a thousand years ago, a halfway marker between Europe and Asia and a crossroads of cultures. Arabs, Mongols, Persians, Turks, and Russians have battled over it for its strategic importance here in the Fergana Valley. It is the repository of our national pride, and I see myself as a protector and promoter of an ancient and proud Kyrgyz culture.

"I came from nothing, and became a bigshot learning to cheat the behemoth Soviet bureaucratic machine. Yes, I have diverse interests, not all of them seen as legal by the government. But they are themselves corrupt, are they not, Nickolai? Do I pay for information and bribe government officials to get what I want? Yes. Have I been ruthless in business? Yes. But I am first and foremost a Kyrgyz.

"As you can see, my operation is a small one despite its reputation, which has been good for business. My security detail consists of only two men, and their skills have certainly been tested by you, Max Little. I use subcontractors much of the time. But they are good boys, Josef and Antony, and have served me well. They are like my sons, and their families are looked after. But times are changing, and so must I. Diversification is now the order of the day. My psychotherapist recently helped me realize that if I am not evolving, I am dying. Our friend Nickolai, too, has influenced me, opening my eyes to the lives of our people, who have struggled to preserve their national identity. So, I am cultivating more sedentary pursuits, making investments in businesses rather than forcing my will upon them to make the world a better place. Plus, I was lonely, and this venture will bring some fascinating new people into my life."

As Bakiyev spoke, Max's gaze fell upon a gleaming silver tray in the center of the blue marble table. It held a dozen or so bottles of varying shapes and sizes, and as he reached out to inspect them was struck by the realization that they represented an entire collection of the sauces he had created for Little's House of Fire. He inspected the familiar labels one by one. There was his first creation, Mocha Lava, created with the Costa Ricans. Bere Bere Hot Sauce and the Ethiopian sweat lodge memory; Biblical Fire, resurrected in Israel; the Chinese Golden Emperor, Calabrian Devil's Kiss, and the Hoppin Hot Hopi Fire sauce. As he handled each bottle, the stories and adventures that had led to their creation flashed before Max's eyes, realizing that his particularly offbeat journey had brought him to a palace in Kyrgyzstan and the surreal crossroads he found himself. Bakiyev had not missed the moment, either.

"Yes, Max, those are your creations and represent your uncanny ability to find compelling stories and craft delicious concoctions from your discoveries. They are each unique and tell the story of who you are, and why you are here. I confess to being a rather ardent chile-head, as is all of Central Asia. When Nickolai's superior told me of his discovery, he came to me with the information, expecting a payoff. Instead, he ruined Nickolai's career in the hope of getting rich. His former boss has now advantageously retired, with my influence. Perhaps Nickolai will take his place if he wants. It was then I decided that I must possess and own these chiles. When Nickolai went to

America to locate you, Max, I sent my boys to follow him as I intended to steal whatever he discovered. Unfortunately, they misunderstood my directive and captured him instead. Under questioning, he divulged that both you, Max, and Lilah were the best candidates to achieve our goals. So, you were then followed, as I desired to first co-opt, then underwrite your mission. My apologies for the problems that were caused. The boys attempted to be thorough, perhaps too much. Ultimately, I hoped to deliver a message to you that I had an interest in your pursuits, not to thwart them. Joe and Tony have offered to pay for repairs to your business from their salaries, though it is officially my responsibility.

"When I got to know him, I learned that Nickolai operates only with our people's best interests at heart. His early attempts to locate and develop the mythical fruit hidden for centuries in the Tien Shan mountains had been failures. Nazaat, you and your people were unbreakable, worthy owners of a hidden legacy. Nickolai ultimately convinced me to lead you here, Max, to uncover the mystery and connect us to the people of Dostuk, and you, Lilah, have been a most fortunate and irreplaceable complement to the package. It is fitting that this adventure has brought you both together. However, I bear responsibility for forcibly separating you from your 'partner in crime,' as she calls herself. I like that description, though I apologize. It was meant as motivation. Only you could have unearthed what remained hidden for centuries, Max, in the valley of the At Bashy river, and I have been proven right.

"Now here we are, at the conclusion of this adventure, deciding the path forward. Nazaat has made clear the will of his people and put forth the plan he and Max have developed, which I have come to fully support. He is very persuasive. I will agree to finance the facilities and undertake sales and marketing in this part of the world. I wanted fifty percent but have been convinced by my new partner Nazaat that my twenty-five is a fair bargain. The people of Dostuk will enjoy the majority ownership of fifty percent, and you, Max and Lilah, and Nickolai will share the remaining twenty-five percent. Nickolai will become president of this company, and I will sit on the company board with Max, Nazaat, Lilah, and him. Max will help us develop the products and markets with his connections, and Lilah will oversee testing and compliance, utilizing the laboratory I have constructed below. Josef and Antony will have new careers in distribution. Everyone desires that you and Lilah should return here regularly, Max, to ensure the operation's efficiency and success, and your suite will be waiting. Are these circumstances agreeable to all?"

Max tightened his grip on Lilah's hand under the table. Hearing Bakiyev's words forced him to admit he had long misjudged the man.

That his entire adventure had been dogged by doubt simply due to a misunderstanding was an unforeseen conclusion. No crimes other than a shattered storefront had been committed, an event that had brought him to this surreal moment. Though smiling, he slowly shook his head in disbelief. He looked at Lilah, who shrugged a nonchalant "why not?" Then, he raised his eyes to Bakiyev and nodded yes to the man. The attendees looked around the table at one another before nodding affirmatively, and Ruslan Bakiyev raised his etched crystal glass.

"Then let us toast to the Fire of the Valley, Kyrgyzstan's magical fruit. Kyrgyz Fire of the Valley Hypnotic hot sauce will proudly sit atop tables everywhere, enchanting meals worldwide. I saw that you brought some of the delectable pods, and my staff has been preparing Kyrgyz foods with their influence. And do try Max's delectable creations. Let us eat, friends."

There ensued a culinary extravaganza that none outside of Bakiyev's villa had ever experienced, every course creatively infused with the peppers from Dostuk. Platters arrived, stacked high with doughy mantis and samsas fresh from a wood oven, their insides stuffed with meat, garlic, mint, onion, and peppers dipped in tangy vinegar sauce or sweet chile paste. Golden, steaming, richly seasoned shorpo broth in crystal bowls were set before them, with leafy greens, floating multicolor chiles, and a course of crisp cold soup, *ashlyann-fu*, a peppery sour broth with noodles and poached fish from Issyk-Kul Lake. Glistening beshbarmak appeared, slick with fatty lamb and wide noodles in scorching garlic pepper sauce. Silent servers brought Laghman stew with radishes, carrots, onions, and fat wheels of the egg-shaped Oy Boyanca Oroon chile, followed by fire-grilled shashlik kebabs of lamb dusted with hypnotic purple Kyrgyz chile powder and cumin. They ate and laughed with joy and new purpose for hours, and afterward, Max hugged both Boris and Vlad, who cried and apologized.

Well after midnight, with the Milky Way arching across the sky, they gathered outdoors next to an enormous firepit lined by deep couches, sipping a velvety Chateau Petrus from Bordeaux. Max swirled the wine in front of him, watching as it caught and amplified the fire. The merlot-dominant blend's cassis evolved with layers of spice in the glass, with an incandescent ruby hue highlighted by the flames.

Max turned from savoring the wine and spoke to Gasanov. "It feels a lifetime ago when you walked into my shop, Nickolai. What an adventure you have led me on. In the end, I am grateful."

Gasanov stared into the roaring fire. "I could not imagine we would be sitting here sipping wine after that day in Laguna, my friend, though I have always believed you would be the one to usher this story into reality. I knew from the moment we met. Our generous and entirely unpredictable benefactor has been a surprise, and I truly believe he likes food even more than money. Chiles are your life and breath, and you care about the little people, as evidenced by your success in this quite interesting venture with the Kyrgyz. My apologies for leading you on with my communications though I always had our mutual interests at heart. I needed you here; it was the only way. I was only briefly sequestered at the Ministry, having carelessly locked myself in my office for an entire weekend until others arrived on Monday. It gave me time to spin a tale and draft the series of communications that were sent at strategic intervals to grease the wheels of your progress. In retrospect, I might have explained the entire situation; however, it was still unfolding. Ruslan Bakiyev has been a revelation to me as well. This experience has changed him. Now, I look forward to our adventures here in Kyrgyzstan and in America, Max, and of course with you, Lilah. By the way, I would check your email. The internet and your Ring of Fire friends have gone berserk, trying to guess where you are. You will soon have another great unveiling to bait them with. Oh, and the President of the International Spice Corporation has been calling."

They raised glasses and toasted the future many times. As he held Lilah's hand, sipping wine and watching the stars, Max felt another chile-fueled adventure coming to its end. He breathed out slowly, playing out the events in his mind. The journey had closed in upon itself and birthed a future alive with delicious possibility. The lone monkey had bested the corporate gorilla. Enemies had become friends, and he had love by his side. From across the fire, Nazaat Buntun put his enormous hands together and whispered, "Thank you."

They spent a week relaxing in the luxury of Bakiyev's villa, seldom leaving except to explore the vast Osh market. There were meetings held, details sorted, plans made. A new company was formed to house their venture, called Adilet Foods Kyrgyzstan. Max had proposed the name, keeping close the secret that she had caused the wheels of the entire escapade to turn.

With their departure scheduled for a week later and the business formalities concluded, Max and Lilah accompanied Nazaat on his return to Dostuk. Bakiyev had given him the van to begin building his operation, and they spent a long firelit evening under the spell of Adilet Buntun's cooking. She hugged Lilah the moment she walked through the door and joined in the koumiss and laughter, a surprising repository of bawdy jokes. The next morning, Max and Lilah drove up into the emerald mountains to Tash Rabat, where they were met gleefully by Dastan, Zamira, and the children. They rode horses and hiked the green peaks of the Tien Shan, feeling Kyrgyz.

In the twilight, Max walked over to the small yurt belonging to Mishka Dubovya, knocking on the door's frame. Light glowed faintly from the inside as he heard the shuffling of feet. Opening the canvas door, the only emotion she revealed was a raised eyebrow. "So you've returned," she said.

"Yes, I have," said Max.

"And are you a success or a failure, Max Little?"

"We have succeeded, and much thanks goes to you for revealing the special seeds that prove the origin of the Fire of the Valley chile, Mishka. Come, I have someone for you to meet."

Lilah and Mishka Dubovya bonded over science as they all gathered in Dastan's yurt for a night of food and storytelling. Max led Lilah among the archaeologist's pits in the morning, examining seeds and layers of history. Then, he took her hand, passing through the ancient caravanserai's gates on a breezy mountain day. They wandered silently through the halls, listening to the whispering wind, envisioning the life that occurred therein, and running their hands over the stacked rocks until they entered the domed central chamber. Light washed over them as they drank in the powerful atmosphere of the structure, the gathering of history along the Silk Road.

As she followed the ray of light toward the ancient floor she found it had landed squarely on Max. His eyes were closed as he bathed in its warmth and the silent power of the caravanserai as he spoke.

"I wanted you to see this place and share its magic with me. This journey began here, five hundred years ago, and here it ends. My journeys ahead will not have the same meaning without you in them. And it would certainly be less interesting without your voodoo spells. We should be partners," and let the statement climb the ray of light.

"We already are partners. In the culmination of this adventure, and Adilet Foods Kyrgyzstan," she said, watching his serenely calm, illuminated face.

Max breathed in deeply, settling into whatever thoughts the Tash Rabat sun was bringing to the surface.

"I mean we should have a farm. Grow things."

Lilah cocked her head to the side, trying to grasp the full meaning of Max's statement.

"Partners," she said, letting the word float around the room. "Does that include in other things like homemaking, paint selections, global adventures, and making babies?"

A wide smile crossed Max's face as he looked into his lover's eyes. "Yeah, all that kind of stuff too."

She held his face in her hands, and through flowing tears, said, "You are a crash course in love, Max Little. So yes, of course. But I refuse to change my name to Little."

For three days, they walked the verdant valleys, sifted through archaeology pits, and made love in a guest yurt provided by Dastan and Zamira. With Mishka Dubovya, they spent hours around the cooking fire in Dastan's yurt discussing Silk Road history and the events that might have brought two random chiles together in the alluvial soils of Tash Rabat. The relief of a successful outcome to their quest blessed the hours with mirth and ease, the future promising.

"The fact that in the world only these chiles possess both white and black seeds is extraordinary," said Lilah, her head on Max's chest. "And flowers of two types, purple and white. As far as I know, that's never happened before, something totally unique, and only in this faraway place. How do you think it came about?" Eventually, after some more time spent in Bakiyev's laboratory, she knew she would publish a paper in botanical journals on the scientific processes that birthed the Fire of the Valley.

Max stared into the fire, stroking Lilah's hair. He thought of lines of pack animals five hundred years before, converging on the very place where they lay. Chiles from Mexico and the Andes, both dried and fresh, traveled from saddlebags and into meals along with their seeds, which finally found a home in the Kyrgyz earth. Conical poblano annuums, pencil-thin tabascos, and round, fleshy rocotos, each adding their character. He pictured men stoking a fire after weeks atop their animals, contemplating a passage over the roof of the world, weary and thankful for a cooked meal made savory by the aromatic spice from the New World, which could be grown for free. Leftovers fed to animals or scraped into pits, seeds spread around the caravanserai, transported by birds, and fertilized by composted food or animal dung. Cultivated by enterprising merchants who realized the unique pods' potential in the arid alpine climate. A hardy mountain-friendly hybrid sent from the slopes of the Andes and jungles of the Yucatan, which flourished along the Silk Road at Tash Rabat in the Mountains of Heaven, the Tien Shan of Kyrgyzstan. The earthy magic dance of the opium poppies and the capsicum to create a culinary euphoria unlike any other. He imagined seeds of *annum* and *pubescens* varieties buried together by chance, brought to life by moisture, their fates intertwined, fighting to reach the sun. How proximity and fate caused them to become allies, joining forces and DNA to survive, deliciously altering the course of natural history. And Max's own life.

The chiles, their myth, and their possibility had set Max on a path of discovery that would change the chile pepper world, bringing Gasanov, Bakiyev, the Buntuns, and the people of Kyrgyzstan into the Ring of Fire, widening it in the process. Chile heads in backyards and cantinas would tell the tale of Max Little, Lilah DeVillier, and their extraordinary quest to unearth both the Naga Jolokia and the Fire of the Valley, warming and enriching the world as a result.

"Total fluke," said Max over the crackle and sputter of the flames. "Random, uncontrollable, just the way nature likes things. Is anyone hungry?"

The taxi bounced down a dusty country road outside Brousville, Louisiana, stopping finally before a weathered but well-kept white clapboard house. Two passengers got out slowly, taking in the setting, a green leafy sea bordered by flowering trees. The early summer air showed a growing humidity, and salt floated on the breeze, carried up from the Gulf, the fluttering of leaves the only sound Max and Lilah heard.

At that moment, the front door of the house creaked open. Out of the house bounded a pair of beagles, braying like the hounds they remembered. The dogs leaped on Max as he knelt to greet them, taking him down in a raw display of canine fondness while they rolled as one slobber-covered mass in the dirt.

"We was just taking a nap, us four," said a voice from the porch. Jesus Jones stood in the doorway, hands in his overalls, nodding with approval.

Delphine beamed at his side. "It seems your journey has concluded," she said. "Max, you look like you could use a bath, like always. Come, let's have a lemonade, and you tell us all about it."

Over three hours, they told their story as Jones took mental notes. "So was the Kyrgyz chile a hybrid or not?" he asked.

"It turns out it was," said Lilah. "A totally unique hybrid of Rocoto and Poblano, *Capsicum pubescens,* and *Capsicum annuum.* Whether naturally occurring or manipulated, we can't yet determine. But, it must've happened long ago, in the isolated valleys of the Tien Shan at Tash Rabat."

Though their adventure had lasted only five weeks, Lilah and Max were concerned as they looked at Jones. He walked with a cane, his posture slightly more bent. "Twisted my hip jumping down off the darn tractor," he confessed, "and it's taking too much time to heal. Delphine has been kind enough to help, and her potions are working their magic." He looked out over the fields of peppers ripening in the warm air and sighed.

"I've been thinking. I'd like to get some golf lessons in Palm Springs. Perhaps five years' worth, learn the game. Go to Belize and see if I have family there. And spend more time with Delphine on the bayou while I still have the time. Time, the great equalizer," he mused.

"It's time you two took over the farm," Jones continued. "It was given to me, and now it's time to pass it on. I hadn't thought of it before now but seeing that you're going to be Mr. and Mrs. Little, it's the best plan. The beagles will be fine with it, I can tell. And I know you'll take care of the place. Maybe just send some dividends once in a while."

"We are not going to be Mr. and Mrs. Little," said Lilah defiantly, drawing a confused look from Jones and a stifled chuckle from Delphine.

"But we are going to get married someday," interjected Max with a laugh, "and you both have been a large part of that coming about. Delphine, I know there have been spells cast, and I've felt it, the magic. I thank you for seeing what I could not. And we would be honored to continue your legacy, Jesus, in this magical place. With fifty percent of the profits sent to you every month, of course."

Jones smiled. "Just Jones'll do."

THE END

Morgan Miles Craft has been a journalist, magazine publisher, restaurateur, winemaker, tour guide, and itinerant epicure. He's lived in twelve US states and Japan chasing adventure and compelling stories, or cultivating extraordinary food and wine, and grew up by the beach in Pacific Palisades, California. His vibrant Mexican restaurant in Miami Beach, Moe's Cantina, was a South Beach legend in the 1990s, and where he cultivated a passion for fiery foods. Morgan lives today in the red rock southwestern desert of Sedona, Arizona, with his wife, Nanaiya, and hairless black terrier Bruce Wayne. His next epicurean adventures take place in the southern Barbeque Belt and a wine country caper in the Napa Valley, where he worked in the farm-to-table culinary and boutique wine industries.

Please stay in touch, and I welcome questions and a conversation about The Ring of Fire.

Ringoffirenovel.com

Made in the USA
Middletown, DE
09 January 2023